FIRE ON THE HILL
FRANK ROCKLAND

Editor: Allister Thompson
www.altereditorialservices.com

Designer: Jonathan Relph

Cover image: J.B. Reid, Library and Archives Canada, C-010776

Library and Archives Canada Cataloguing in Publication

Rockland, Frank, 1956-
        Fire on the hill / Frank Rockland.

Issued also in electronic format.
ISBN 978-0-9917050-0-9

        I. Title.

PS8635.O33F57 2013   C813'.6   C2012-907985-5

AUTHOR'S NOTE

Fire on the Hill is a work of fiction. All incidents, dialogue, and characters, with exception of historical and public figures, are products of the author's imagination and are not to be construed as real.

Where real-life historical or public figures appear, the situations, incidents, and dialogue concerning the person are fictional.

In all aspects, any resemblance to the living or the dead is entirely coincidental.

PREFACE

When Canada entered the First World War, there were fears that German sympathizers in Canada and in the United States would try to cripple Canada's war effort through acts of subversion and sabotage.

When a fire destroyed the Centre Block of the Canadian Parliament Buildings on the night of February 3, 1916, German saboteurs were suspected. The Royal Commission appointed to investigate the origin of the fire concluded:

The fire started in a file of papers on a shelf on one of the reading tables near the House of Commons. The first person to see the fire was Francis Glass, ESQ., M.P., who stated that the fire originated while he was in the reading room; that he had been in the reading-room a short time when he felt a wave of heat passing up alongside of him from a hot-air register, and he turned around and almost immediately smelled the burning of paper; stooped down and saw smoke coming out.

* * *

As to the question whether the fire was deliberately set the commissioners made the following conclusions:

Your commissioners are of the opinion that there are many circumstances connected with this fire that lead to a strong suspicion of incendiarism, especially in view of the fact that the evidence is clear that no one was smoking in the reading-room for some time previous to the outbreak of fire, and also to the fact that the fire could not have occurred from defective electric wiring. But while your commissioners are of such opinion, there is nothing in the evidence to justify your commissioners in finding the fire was maliciously set.

* * *

Your commissioners feel very strongly that it might be possible at a later date to obtain evidence (which they cannot reach at the present time) which might establish beyond question whether this fire was incendiary or accidental, and with the approval of Your Royal Highness, your commissioners would humbly suggest that this report be treated not as a final report but as an interim report, and that the commission be

CHAPTER I

He held the long wooden match to the fire hissing in the room's gas fireplace. When the sulphur flared, he raised the matchstick to the tip of the Cuban cigar clamped between his teeth then drew on the cigar slowly and carefully. He savoured the smooth, sweet chocolate flavour. It had been several months since he had a good supply of Havanas, and he was planning to enjoy them while they lasted.

The Cuban soured slightly when Count Jaggi's gaze fell on the Queen Anne-style writing desk set against the far wall. Waiting on the desk were several sheets of writing paper, a few postcards, and a decanter of cognac alongside two tumblers. A blue cloth button was sitting at the bottom of the one of glasses, slowly staining the liquid yellowish. He had been avoiding the task of preparing his messages all morning, but he couldn't avoid it any longer.

He sighed and lowered himself onto the red, floral-patterned upholstery seat of the chair before the desk. He lifted the bottle and half-filled the empty tumbler. Then he removed his cigar from his mouth and placed it carefully in the brass ashtray stand beside the desk before lifting the cognac to his mouth. It was not the best quality, but smooth enough, he thought as it slid over his tongue. He knew he was beginning to depend too much on the alcohol, but the need to stay constantly alert was draining. He rubbed his neck to relieve the knot developing there.

He retrieved his cigar and took another pull. The smoke now had a bitter taste. He had sufficient material now, but transcribing it was tedious and time-consuming. He took another taste of the cognac. He stared at the respectable European landscape painting above the desk and wished he were home enjoying a cold beer. He gave another tired puff and placed the cigar back on the ashtray stand.

He picked up a black, gold-accented pen, unscrewed the barrel, dipped the nib into the now deep amber-coloured liquid, and then squeezed the rubber bladder. He withdrew the nib when the sac was full. Gently squeezed the latex, returning a couple of drops, then dried off excess ink from the tines with a piece of tissue.

He began to write, pausing from time to time to take another sip of or puff on his cigar, allowing time for the ink to dry. When he left open, and in the event of your commissioners be able to get further evidence at a later date that they be permitted to do so.

a
t
st
an
sig

dipp
sque
He ge
the ex
He
cognac

heard the squeaking of the hotel's elevator approach his floor, he turned towards the noise then relaxed when it didn't stop to open its doors into the hallway outside his room. He reluctantly returned his focus back to the letter he was composing. The Count grunted in satisfaction as the sentences he had just written slowly faded then disappeared.

He had not been working long when someone rattled the doorknob to the hotel room. His eyes shot to the moving brass handle. How the hell did they get to his door without his hearing it? He moved to cover the incriminating evidence on his desk. When he heard the door rattle again, he quietly eased open the right-hand drawer of the desk and rested his hand on the butt of a Webley .455 revolver.

"Shit, the key won't open the door! Why won't the door open?" A man, slurring and loud.

"Silly," answered a woman's voice with a girlish giggle, "you have the wrong room."

The man laughed uproariously. "Hey, Mister. Sorry! Let's go, dearie."

Count Jaggi moved his hand away from the Webley and closed the drawer. He wiped the cold sweat from his brow. He could hear his heart pounding. He refilled the tumbler with a shaking hand and downed the cognac in one gulp. He rose sharply up from his chair and began pacing back and forth to burn off the adrenaline pumping through his system.

Eventually he returned to his task. He had no choice but to finish. He rubbed his neck again to loosen the tightening knot.

When he finished half an hour later, some of the tension had left his body. He stuffed the letters into envelopes that he had already stamped and put them and the postcards into a black leather briefcase resting beside the desk.

He glanced out the room's window and shuddered. It was cold out there. He didn't want to leave the warmth of the fire, but he had an appointment that he must attend. He opened the armoire and reached in for an overcoat. There was already a dark blue woollen one thrown on the bed, but it was missing a button. He didn't have time to sew it back on now. He took a thin, herringbone-patterned coat off a hanger and pulled it on then picked up the briefcase. He thought of the Webley but decided it was too risky to carry it.

The letters and postcards were dangerous enough.

Before leaving, he scanned the scene from the doorway, trying to memorize where everything was, in case the room was searched while he was out. Then he walked out, locking the door behind him.

When the Count stepped out of the Château Laurier's entrance, he immediately regretted not wearing the overcoat. It was warmer and thicker, which would have cut the edge of the bitterly cold wind that knifed through him better than the one he was wearing.

"Would you like a cab, sir?" asked the doorman brightly. He seemed unaffected by the temperature, but then he was dressed in the winter livery of a Grand Trunk Pacific hotel doorman: fur-lined winter boots, dark-coloured wool pants, a double-breasted knee-length heavy cloth coat, buttoned to the neck, with matching brass buttons on the sleeves and epaulets on the shoulder, and topped off with a Russian-style fur hat.

The Count was tempted to take the doorman up on his offer, but he was going to be here for a while, and he would have to adapt to the cold. He waved the man away with a gloved hand. "*Merci*, I prefer to walk. It will do my constitution good," he replied. He drew in a deep breath and released it in a puff that steamed in the air, to emphasize his point.

"As you wish, sir," replied the doorman. He returned to his post, conveniently sheltered from the wind. The doorman's response was polite, but the Count sensed the amusement at his determination to walk.

He nodded to the doorman, touching his hat, then strolled towards the dark sandstone Parliament buildings looming to his right. The snow crunched under his booted feet. He passed two men heaving shovelfuls of snow into a horse-drawn wagon. Between grunts, they were swearing about the cold. His lips parted in a smile when he saw the "Donate to Belgian Relief" banner on the wagon.

At the sound of the train whistle, he turned towards the Grand Trunk Railway station across from the Château. A plume of smoke rose into the turquoise sky from the stack of a train slowing to a stop. His eyes moved from the soot-stained white station to his task of scanning Sapper's Bridge for surveillance.

A crowded tram with frost-covered windows blocked his view for a moment, but everything appeared normal — or what passed as normal in Ottawa. He crossed the bridge, and when the harsh wind howling down Sparks Street hit him, he realized why he really should have used a cab. He took the right fork on the bridge leading to the post office on the corner of Sparks and Elgin and understood why the doorman had been amused. The wind sliced through his thin overcoat. Shivering, he spotted two blue-uniformed Dominion Police officers on the corner chatting with an attractive brunette. The police officers didn't worry him. Anyone searching for him wouldn't be in uniform.

He dropped the letters and the postcards into the red Royal Mail box in front of the post office. Out of the corner of his vision, he noticed the brunette walking towards him. She was in her early thirties, he thought, and dressed in a sombre charcoal grey, with her hands tucked warmly into a beaver muff. In his mind he unwrapped her heavy coat and pictured what lay beneath, and he was pleased by the image.

He tipped his hat and smiled gallantly. It had been a while since he was with a woman. It took him a moment to realize that she was not reciprocating. But she wasn't averting her gaze either. Before he could form his next thought, he heard her say, "I know what you are."

The words stopped him. How, he thought, how could she know? He watched helplessly as she slowly pulled her hand from the muff.

"For you," she said and pressed something into his gloved hand. He glanced it: a white ostrich feather. He looked up sharply to reprimand her, but she had already moved briskly away and was disappearing down Sparks Street. The Count extended his hand then turned it over, letting the feather fall onto the slushy sidewalk. He then headed up the Hill for his appointment.

CHAPTER 2

"No!"

"But Sir Robert..." Inspector MacNutt protested.

"No," Sir Borden interjected, "I respect your feelings on this and I admire that you are willing to volunteer. However, I will not allow you to resign so that you can join the Canadian Corps. You are much too valuable where you are."

MacNutt's hands trembled slightly on the chair's armrests as he refrained from throwing them in the air. It would not have been wise in front of the prime minister. Since the war's beginning he had been begging the prime minister to accept his resignation so that he could join the Canadian Corps in France. And every time Borden denied him his request, and for the same reason. As the head of the Dominion Police's Secret Service, he was too valuable a man to be wasted as a simple foot soldier in the muddy fields of Flanders.

He figured that if he kept asking, Borden would eventually tire and grant his request. What he hadn't included in his calculation was that Borden was the leader of the Conservative Party of Canada. Anyone who could survive the leadership trials and tribulations of such a volatile and fractious party could easily handle the cajoling of a frustrated civil servant.

Borden had never sought the leadership of the Conservatives. Until Premier Fielding foolishly attempted to take Borden's native province, Nova Scotia, out of Confederation, he had been a Liberal. His cousin, Sir Frederick Borden, was once Laurier's minister of militia. Furious at Fielding's stupidity, Borden decided to run as a Conservative, and he won easily. He would have remained a simple Member of Parliament if Sir Charles Tupper had not decided to retire as the leader of the Conservatives after losing his seat in the 1900 election. The party caucus pressured Borden to take the position as acting leader, for a year, while they searched for a new leader. He had reluctantly agreed. Borden would have gladly resigned after the year, though they still couldn't agree on a replacement, if it hadn't been for his wounded pride. What must have greatly offended him were the cabals and intrigues that swirled in the Conservative party. After two electoral defeats it seemed to his enemies, both in and out of the party, that Borden was finally on his way out. His stunning electoral victory in 1911 changed all that. While he gave no gloating speeches upon hearing the election results, the magnitude of the victory must have given Borden enormous satisfaction.

With Borden's firm no, MacNutt finally realized his leader was not about to acquiesce. MacNutt had made the mistake of becoming indispensable.

Borden chose not to notice MacNutt's stiffness by lifting a newspaper from his desk. "Did you read yesterday's *Ottawa Journal*?"

"I'm afraid so," replied MacNutt as he folded his arms. He had the sinking feeling he knew where Sir Robert was heading.

"The Mayor of Pembroke claims that his city is a centre through which news of the Canadian military reaches the enemy and that there are a thousand paid agents in Canada," read the prime minister. Borden peered expectantly at MacNutt over his glasses. "Is this true?"

"Of course, Prime Minister," MacNutt replied, keeping a straight face. "You know as well as I the critical role that Pembroke plays. Without Pembroke the war would be lost!"

Borden stared at him then chuckled as he put down the paper. "Just give him a call and give him some reassurance from me, please."

"Yes, Prime Minister. If you'll give me an increase in my budget, I'll try to find those thousand agents for you," responded MacNutt with a crooked grin.

At the mention of money Borden gave MacNutt a disapproving frown. Though he was a wealthy man and didn't like being teased about it, he was notorious for his penny pinching. In the summer, he rode his bike to work instead of paying a nickel for the tram. "I think that extra one hundred thousand dollars we gave you in the last budget should be sufficient for now. Unless there is more going on that I don't know about?"

When MacNutt crossed his legs and relaxed his hands on the armrest, Borden knew there was some new information. "What?"

"The Americans are about to declare Captains von Papen and Boy-Ed as *personae non gratae*," replied MacNutt. Captain Franz von Papen was the German military attaché in Washington, D.C., while Captain Karl Boy-Ed was von Papen's naval counterpart.

"That is good news. When were you informed?"

"I received word this morning. I thought you would like to know right away," answered MacNutt.

"Excellent. Excellent. It's about time. So Lansing is beginning to lose his patience with their shenanigans, then," beamed Borden, referring to the American secretary of state. Lansing was appointed to the position in June 1915, a bare five months ago.

"I guess so. Considering all the Hun provocation," replied MacNutt.

"At least he is taking our concerns more seriously than Secretary of State Bryan did," Borden said with a hint of satisfaction. "I can appreciate the fact the States want to maintain their neutrality. But claiming that they could not post guards at their end of the international bridges because it was unconstitutional was ridiculous." It was Bryan's contention that since a bridge was inside a state, each state was therefore responsible for law and order within its boundaries. Washington could only become involved if the state couldn't handle the situation and called on Washington for help. "And this was after that German what's his name...?"

"Werner von Horn."

"That's him. Even after he tried to blow up the CPR bridge at Vanceboro," said Borden.

"I know," agreed MacNutt. "Bryan was determined that not only should the letter of the neutrality laws be maintained but also the spirit of the law. The consequences be damned."

Borden's gaze lost focus for a moment. He gently stroked his bushy moustache with two fingers of his right hand. When he refocused he said, "A thought just struck me, Andrew. Will the Americans' new attitude apply only to the Germans, or will it apply to our activities as well?"

MacNutt bowed his head slightly and stared at the desk's front panel. "You have a point. I never thought about it. One of the reasons we have people in the States is that the Americans were not taking our concerns seriously."

"Which they are now."

"Which they are now," said MacNutt. "Our agents have all been instructed to avoid doing or saying anything that could cause complications. We also use the Pinkerton and Thiel detective agencies for many of our investigations. Any information they obtain that may be of interest or concern is passed on to the United States government. The only fly in the ointment is the British Secret Service. We never know what they are up to."

"I know the feeling," Borden said. His brow wrinkled with unease.

"So far we have managed to be discreet and keep a fairly low profile," MacNutt reassured in an attempt to calm the prime minister's concerns.

"Good. That's what I like to hear," Borden said as the lines on his forehead slackened.

"It also helped that the Americans were able to get a hold of Dr. Albert's papers." Dr. Heinrich Albert was the German embassy's commercial attaché based in New York.

"It was careless of him to leave his portfolio on that elevated train in New York," said an amused Borden.

"Yes, it was." MacNutt smiled too. "You do know what they call him behind his back in Washington?"

"No."

"Minister without portfolio."

Borden groaned. "That's an awful pun. But it was also useful that his papers were published in the New York dailies. I'm sure that put a lot of pressure on Lansing to do something about the German embassy in Washington and their consulate in New York." The papers found in the Dr. Albert's portfolio provided ample evidence that he was the paymaster for German sabotage activity in Canada and the United States.

"I'm sure it did."

"When is he going to declare them *personae non gratae*?" Borden asked.

"I heard either the third or fourth of December. Monday, the fifth, at the latest."

"Does anyone else know?"

MacNutt shrugged. "The papers will be reporting it soon enough. I wouldn't be surprised if the G-G already knows."

"Yes, it would get to him first, wouldn't it." Borden couldn't keep the irritation out of his voice.

MacNutt knew the prime minister felt that the U.S. government didn't take his government's concerns seriously. By custom, as well as constitutionally, Britain handled nearly all Canada's external affairs because Canada was still considered a colony. While there were a number of consuls general from foreign countries in Canada, only four lived in Ottawa. The most senior was Colonel J.G. Foster of the United States. The other consuls general represented China, Belgium, and Japan. The consuls of Germany, France, Holland, and Argentina resided in

Montreal. Canada didn't recognize them as diplomatic representatives, even though they occasionally played that role.

What this meant was that his government didn't communicate directly with the Americans at the diplomatic level. If Borden had a concern, he would have to ask the governor general to express it to the British embassy in Washington. The embassy would then forward his government's concerns to the State Department. The State Department would respond to the British ambassador, who would usually forward the reply to the governor general. Rarely would they send the reply back directly to Borden.

The quality of the Foreign Office staff assigned to Canadian matters was at best questionable. MacNutt doubted that being assigned to the Canadian desk was regarded as a good career move. This, he knew, was what frustrated Borden. The prime minister felt that Canada was getting short shrift.

There had been a number of instances where Canadian interests conflicted with British interests; it was inevitably Canada that got the short end of the stick. What made a difficult situation worse was the bad blood between Borden and the governor general. Borden was always searching for ways to bypass Whitehall and take control of Canada's foreign affairs.

"You know Bennett will make sure of that," MacNutt added.

"God help us. How he ever became a consul general I'll never know. We had enough trouble with the rumours he spreads about a possible invasion of Canada by German reservists," said an exasperated Borden as he ran a hand through his white hair.

"I know," agreed MacNutt with a raised palm. "We've wasted a considerable amount of time and money trying to confirm his reports." The prime minister winced at his reference to the waste of money. "Not to mention the effect that has on the morale of our people. Our people in the States are not too happy with us forcing them to investigate his reports. Pinkerton has told us a number of times that they consider them a waste of time. The only reason they investigate them is that we are paying them. And it doesn't help our credibility with the Americans."

"I know. I know. By the way, how many men do they have assigned for our work?" Borden asked.

"They've informed me that they have a half-dozen or so," replied MacNutt.

"Their best men?"

MacNutt rubbed his chin. "They have other clients. When things get busy for them, they always have to take care of their biggest clients first."

"They haven't found anything so far?"

"So far, no, Prime Minister. But as to the rumours of an imminent invasion by the Germans, you know a lot of people remember the Fenians. That is the only reason people listen to the rumours. If it could happen fifty years ago, it could happen again. And you know as well as I do that was the reason the Service was created in the first place, to deal with the Fenian threat from the States."

Although the Fenian raids took place nearly fifty years earlier, they were still fresh in peoples' minds. It caused MacNutt no end of trouble. Every Canadian knew that when the American Civil War ended, both Upper and Lower Canada were terrified that the Union Army, the largest, most modern, and battle-hardened in the world, would turn its sights on conquering Canada. It was one of the reasons that the Confederation was formed. It was fortunate for Canada that the Americans, war-weary and anxious to go home, had little appetite for another war. However, the disbanded Irish battalions had different ideas. Fresh from helping the Union Army defeat the South, they felt that they could easily capture Canada and hold it for ransom, guaranteeing Irish freedom. From 1866 to 1870 the Fenians mounted a number of raids from the States into Canada, and they all failed.

"You don't think the Germans will try something similar?" Borden asked.

"No, Prime Minister, there is no evidence to support the rumours. There is no unusual activity in the possible staging areas in New York State. The RNWMP reports the same along the 49th parallel." The Royal North-West Mounted Police patrolled the U.S. and Canadian border east of Ontario.

"I hope you're right," said Borden as he lifted his face from his hand.

"I'm not saying there isn't a hothead or two out there or that the German Secret Service will not try some kind of mischief. Just that a full-blown invasion is not in the cards. If they try, we would have plenty of warning — and the Americans would definitely not put up with it. They'd be upset if anyone but them invaded us."

Borden rubbed his temples. "Prepare your report on the von Papen and Boy-Ed situation. But, it is very good news. Very good news, indeed. Now, I have one more thing to discuss." Before he could continue, the door to his office opened and his private secretary, Jocelyn Boyce, entered.

"Excuse me, Prime Minister. You requested that I inform you when the Belgian Relief people arrived," he announced with a raised eyebrow.

"Thank you, Joe. I'll be done in a moment," said Borden with a slight nod.

"Yes, Prime Minister. I also would like to let you know that the Australian cadets are scheduled to visit the Privy Council chamber right after the Belgian Relief people," Boyce added.

"Very well, Boyce. I'll be done in a moment," repeated Borden.

Boyce's visage told MacNutt that the PM had more important things to do than gab with MacNutt. He acknowledged the man with a respectful nod. Boyce was not an ordinary private secretary. He was formally a clerk in the Privy Council Office. In 1913, Borden had appointed the man as one of his private secretaries. He also acted as a liaison with the External Affairs department, which was located on the same floor of the East Block as the prime minister's office.

"I'd forgotten about the relief people," Borden groused. "Is Katherine still helping out?"

"She seems to enjoy making her contribution to the war effort," MacNutt replied. He really didn't want to discuss Katherine, though Lady Borden and Katherine were good friends. To change the subject he inquired, "You said you had another thing to discuss?"

"Oh yes." Borden paused, choosing his words carefully. "I'm afraid it's about Mrs. Ramsey."

MacNutt groaned. "Not her again."

"I'm afraid so."

"Isn't there any way we can get rid of her?"

"Someone suggested sending her to France. They said it would guarantee the war would be over by Christmas." Borden was trying hard not to laugh.

"But who would have won? Us or them?" asked MacNutt with both palms held open.

"I know," said Borden. "It's highly doubtful that she has any useful information, but she's driving me and my staff to distraction."

"We could introduce her to Hughes."

Borden regarded MacNutt with horror. "Oh my God! I can only deal with one war at a time. No, I'm afraid I have to give the matter to you."

MacNutt sighed. "As you wish. I'll get my sergeant to interview her next week."

Borden frowned then commanded, "I'm afraid that it will have to be you. Some time in the next week or two."

MacNutt lowered his eyes then replied in a resigned tone. "As you wish, Prime Minister. I'll arrange an interview as soon as possible."

"Good." A buzzer above Sir Robert's desk sounded. "Yes. Yes. I'm coming," Borden muttered as he rose slowly from his chair. The inspector had already risen and held open the door for Borden.

"Thank you, Andrew," Borden said as they left his office. Standing in Borden's outer office was the Belgian consul general, Goor, and four other Belgian Relief officials. MacNutt was familiar with the consul general, since Katherine did a lot for Belgian relief work. One of the men he did not recognize. He gave the men a friendly nod as he walked out of the office and past them.

Borden had put on his best face before greeting his quests. "Count Jaggi, it is indeed an honour and a pleasure to meet you. Please come into my office." With a welcoming motion, the prime minister ushered the men into his office.

CHAPTER 3

MacNutt's feet echoed on the blue Ohio stone as he made his way to the staircase located just past the governor general's office. He took the carpeted stairs down to the ground floor. Halfway down the staircase, he returned the absent-minded salute of a uniformed officer who was passing him on the stairs on the way up. MacNutt noticed a blemish on the uniform that made him stop. "Constable Edwards," he snapped.

The constable froze then came to stiff attention. "Yes, sir."

"Can you explain this, Constable?" MacNutt approached the young man and flicked his unbuttoned collar. The man's cheeks blushed a faint pink.

"Sir, I was in the lounge, sir. Well, the sergeant said he needed these papers delivered to the Mounties, sir. Right away, sir," he replied nervously. If MacNutt hadn't known the young man's history, he would have almost felt sorry for him. Because his department was responsible for vetting new personnel for the Force, he knew a great deal about young Constable Edwards.

The man believed that the army had rejected him because of his poor eyesight. He had a certificate attesting to that fact. What was not in any written report was that his mother, distraught at the thought of losing her baby, had used her family's connections to *ensure* her son was rejected from the army. The boy's father was furious when he learned how his wife had interfered, but there was very little he could do once the deed was done.

Still wanting to be in uniform, the young man applied to join the Dominion Police Force. Normally, the Dominion Police would have rejected him as well. He didn't really have the characteristics the Force favoured. Most of the uniformed officers were a rough and ready lot, chosen mainly for their brawn and their ability to follow orders. Edwards was a slight man of medium height and relatively well educated. He also had a softness about him that would be a definite liability on the street. When his father came to the inspector and asked if there was a capacity in which the boy could serve, MacNutt reluctantly agreed. The lad reminded him very much of Jamie. He justified his decision by reasoning that with the war the Force needed men and couldn't be too choosy. He did warn the boy's father not to expect any special consideration for his son. Young Edwards would be treated in the same manner as any other officer.

"It was such an urgent matter that you were unable to take a moment to button your collar?" asked MacNutt.

"No, sir ... Yes, sir ... I mean, sir," Edwards stammered as he avoided looking directly at the inspector.

"Please take the snow out of your ears and button your collar," MacNutt ordered.

"Yes, sir." Edwards raised his hands, but he seemed confused about what to do with the papers he held. One moment it appeared he would tuck them under his arm, the next it seemed he would drop them on the stairs.

MacNutt finally put out a hand. "Give them to me." Edwards handed the papers to the inspector and quickly buttoned his collar. "I won't put you on report this time, Constable, but if I catch you not adhering to the proper dress regulations, you will be fined. Even in wartime one must maintain standards. Do I make myself clear?"

"Yes, sir. Thank you, sir," replied the constable with such relief that it almost brought a smile to MacNutt's lips. He stifled it quickly. It wouldn't have inspired confidence in the young constable.

"Be on your way now, son," MacNutt ordered. Edwards gave the inspector a snappy salute and marched rapidly up the ornately carved wood-panelled staircase.

As he watched Edwards disappear around a corner, sadness flickered across MacNutt's face. Since the beginning of the war, the Dominion Police had changed more than he liked to admit. He once knew every one of the one hundred and forty members of the Force. Now the Force had expanded to one hundred and ninety. Some of the officers were replacements for those who had volunteered for the Corps in France.

He knew he shouldn't resent Edwards, because MacNutt himself owed his position due to his father's connections. He had just mustered out of the Lord Strathcona's Horse when the Boer War ended. Serving with the Horse in peacetime didn't appeal to him. He had hoped to get a position with British intelligence, but his contacts informed him there wasn't one available for a colonial at the present time. It was their polite way of saying that they were unlikely to engage *any* colonial, no matter how promising his talents. He was at a loss as to how he would support his young wife and son when he received a note from Sir Percy Sherwood. The note stated that Sir Percy was in Toronto and requested that MacNutt dine with him. Curious as to why the chief commissioner of the Dominion Police would want to sup with him, he had accepted.

They had met for dinner at the Queen's Hotel. It wasn't until they were having a cigar and a glass of port that Sir Percy got to the point.

"So, young man, what are you planning to do now that the war is over?" he asked as he studied MacNutt between slips of port.

"I have a few prospects," MacNutt replied cautiously. "I haven't made any decisions yet."

"I see." Sir Percy rolled his cigar in his hand. "I also understand that during the war you were seconded to military intelligence."

"I was," MacNutt replied, eyeing Sir Percy. "I did the usual. Interrogate prisoners and prepare estimates of the Boer forces and their intentions."

"Did you have dealings with Lord Kitchener?"

"No. I've met him briefly but I didn't have any dealings with him. May I ask why you are asking?"

"Quite," Sir Percy said. "My boy, I have need of an experienced intelligence officer, and you were recommended to me."

"You have need of an intelligence officer?" MacNutt blinked in surprise.

"What do you know about the Dominion Police Force?"

"Very little, sir," he replied honestly.

"I'm not surprised." Sir Percy continued, taking a taste of his port. "Along with the RNWMP, we enforce the federal laws for the Dominion. The RNWMP polices west of the Manitoba and Ontario border. We police east of that border. We enforce some specific federal laws against counterfeiting and the white slave traffic. We are responsible for paroled prisoners, and we also protect the government buildings in Ottawa and the naval shipyards at Halifax and Esquimalt."

"That is all quite interesting, sir. But I don't think that I'm interested in police work," MacNutt replied.

Sherwood eyed him in amusement. "We also run and maintain a Secret Service."

MacNutt remembered turning red with embarrassment and the feeling that he had made a poor impression. "I am sorry, Commissioner. I didn't know..."

Sherwood waved away the apology. "What is the point of having a

Secret Service if everyone knows about it? And I hope that I can depend on your discretion?"

"Of course you can, Commissioner Sherwood," MacNutt replied.

Sherwood leaned closer and lowered his voice a notch so the diners at the table beside them couldn't overhear. "One of my inspectors is retiring from the Dominion Police shortly, and I am searching for a replacement. Someone with some secret service experience."

"And you think that I would be suitable for the position?" MacNutt asked as he mirrored Sherwood's posture.

"Yes," Sir Percy replied as he moved back into his chair, "you came highly recommended. I spoke with your colonel and with the Imperial War Office. They spoke well of you. If you are interested, we will bring you in as a chief inspector, and you will be paid at that pay scale. So what do you say?"

"I was not expecting this, Mr. Sherwood," MacNutt replied honestly. "I'm definitely interested. I must discuss it with my wife, of course, but I am definitely interested."

"Good," Sherwood declared with a pleased expression. "By all means discuss it with your wife and let me know by Monday."

"Yes, sir." MacNutt paused then with a raised eyebrow said, "I was just curious, sir — who recommended me?"

When MacNutt reached the bottom of the staircase, he turned right just in time to escape the brunt of the cold air that rushed in from the opening of the main door. The edge still caught him, sending a shiver up his spine as he walked briskly towards his office. He glanced at the five men sitting in chairs in the corridor with a constable keeping a guard on them. The men were either Germans or Austrians on parole. They had come to the attention of the Dominion Police for one reason or another. Some were on parole because they'd been overheard making a casual remark supporting the German Fatherland during this time of war; others had committed petty crimes. Since they were on parole, they were required to check in with the Dominion Police regularly. If they didn't, they would be sent to an internment camp.

The Dominion Police occupied offices 120 to 135 of the East Block's first floor. MacNutt opened the door numbered 135. Staff Sergeant Pierre Lacelle was sitting as usual at his desk. A pile of papers was in the in-box on the far corner of the desk. His back was slightly rolled forward. Lacelle's hand was supporting the weight of his head as his elbows rested on the desktop. He was scanning a report and frowned when he saw MacNutt's expression. "He said no?"

MacNutt sighed. "*Tiens, sergent, vous me connaissez trop biens.*"

The right corner of Lacelle's lips rose a couple degrees in sympathy. When MacNutt first met Lacelle, he wasn't very impressed with the man and also got off on the wrong foot with him. MacNutt couldn't decide whether to be insulted when the commissioner assigned Lacelle to teach him the ropes. He felt that he had learned everything he needed to know in South Africa. What could he learn from a sergeant, a French-Canadian Catholic to boot? It hadn't taken long for MacNutt to learn that he was wrong. He really did have a lot to learn, not least of which was the need to get over some of his Protestant prejudice. Lacelle, he found, was as sharp as a whip, and greatly devoted to his wife and four children. MacNutt also realized the French Canadian's perspective was invaluable in the assessment and analysis of the information their investigations gathered. He had also stumbled across the fact that Lacelle liked it when MacNutt attempted to converse in fractured French. He was one of the few English who at least tried.

"Sorry, Andrew, how did the rest of the meeting go?" Lacelle asked, switching to English.

"Borden was happy to hear about von Papen and Boy-Ed."

Lacelle's lips widened into a smile. "It's a bit of good news, and he needs it. But I do have some mixed feelings about them getting kicked out."

MacNutt matched Lacelle's smile, then it thinned. "I know. Sometimes it is better to have the devil you know than the devil you don't."

Lacelle gestured in agreement. "The Bosche will send people to replace them. They will not be as incompetent as those two. And if I were them, I would try to keep the new people away as much as possible from the embassy in Washington or from consulates, especially the one in New York. They could cause all sorts of trouble before we get a handle on them."

"So what do you suggest we do?" MacNutt asked, rubbing his chin.

"We will have to keep surveillance on those two for the next few weeks. The Bosche will send a replacement and he will need to be briefed before they get on the ship to take them home. We have to follow and identify anyone they met," answered Lacelle.

MacNutt stopped rubbing his chin. "I had the same thought. Let's do it."

"Who do you want to do the job, the Pinks or one of our own agents?"

MacNutt thought for a moment. "Let the Pinks do the initial surveillance. If they report anything of interest, we can send someone down there to supervise. I don't want a parade. I'm certain that the American Secret Service will have them under surveillance as well. The Pinks are already familiar with the Secret Service people. I don't want any complications."

"*Comme vous souhaitez*, Andrew," replied Lacelle.

"Oh. I almost forgot — Mrs. Ramsey's name came up." Lacelle's eyes rolled to the ceiling. "It gets worse. We're going to have to interview her."

"But Inspector, you know what she's like. She's a waste of time," Lacelle protested.

"I know, I know," replied MacNutt with a calming gesture, "but we don't have much of a choice. Prime minister's orders."

Disgust flickered across Lacelle's countenance. MacNutt knew that Lacelle, like all cops, didn't like politicians. It seemed that half their work was done just to keep one political hack or another happy. Lacelle lifted a coffee-coloured ledger from under several red-striped files on his desk and began to flip pages. "Let's see who we have. We are very busy at the moment. I can give it to Sergeant Carroll."

"I'm afraid I'm to take care of it." He would have liked to delegate the task. It was a waste of his valuable time, but he had an order that he couldn't ignore. When Lacelle gave him a questioning look, MacNutt responded, "Borden said I have to take care of it. This week. Give her a call and arrange a suitable time."

"*Oui*, Inspector," replied Lacelle as he wrote a note in the ledger.

"Anything pressing in the morning reports?"

Lacelle glanced unenthusiastically at the pile on his desk. Then he gave them a disdainful wave. "The usual. I put some intercepted mail on your desk. Those reports you wanted from Naval Intelligence are there as well. There are some telegrams from London that need to be deciphered. And we've got a cartload of 'white feather' sightings of suspected German agents. I really wish that the Russell Theatre wouldn't put on *The White Feather*. Every time they put on that play they call us. How anyone could think that there would be a German agent in Carlsbad Springs, of all places, I have no idea. I barely know where it is, let alone the Germans."

MacNutt laughed. "I told Borden the same thing about Pembroke."

Lacelle's eyebrows rose in surprise. "He asked about the *Ottawa Journal* story?"

MacNutt acknowledged with a shrug. "How's the planning for the governor general's trip going?"

"I got an update first thing. He'll be leaving for Toronto tonight, and he will give a speech at the 50,000 Club in Toronto tomorrow night. He is expected to visit a munitions factory in Hamilton the day after. It should go smoothly."

"Did you arrange security with the Toronto and Hamilton police?"

"All taken care of," Lacelle confirmed.

"Good..." MacNutt was about to say something else when the outer door opened and William Lyon Mackenzie King entered.

"Good morning, gentlemen," he greeted in his monotone.

"Good morning, Mr. King. This is unexpected. How's New York?" asked MacNutt, taking charge. He was pleased that he and Lacelle controlled their surprise. He knew whatever had brought the former Liberal minister of labour to his office was not good news.

"Do you have a moment to talk with me?" King asked with a polite smile. MacNutt knew it would not be a wise decision to refuse him. One never knew; he could become the next prime minister.

"Of course, Mr. King. Right this way," he said, opening the door to his office.

MacNutt, just before he closed the door, gave Lacelle a *when it rains it pours* expression. As King seated himself in the red leather wing chair in front of MacNutt's regulation government oak desk, the inspector made his way behind his desk. He glanced out the window and saw the troop of thirty-five Australian cadets get into parade order. The cadets, ranging from ages twelve to nineteen, were on a year-long goodwill and educational tour to various countries. During stops in Canada, the young boys raised money for the Red Cross by giving musical concerts. Borden would be meeting them in the Privy Council office on the second floor in the southwest corner of the East Block. He turned to King and asked, "May I offer you a drink? Coffee? Tea?"

"No, I'm quite all right," replied King.

"So, how are you enjoying working for the Rockefellers?" MacNutt asked, making polite small talk. He knew that since 1914, King has been working for the Rockefeller Foundation in New York. He was helping the Rockefellers deal with the fallout from the labour strikes and the Ludlow massacre at the mines they owned in Colorado.

"Actually, I enjoy it. It's quite interesting and challenging work. It also allows me to travel a great deal in the U.S. I'm learning a lot about our American cousins."

"What is your sense about their attitude to the war?"

King folded his hands on his stomach and pursed his lips as he considered MacNutt's question. "They are sympathetic to Britain, but they are trying hard not to get involved if they can help it."

"Do you anticipate them eventually coming into the war?"

King tilted his head back and forth. "It is possible, unless the Germans are very careful in how they handle the Americans and do not provoke them any more than they have."

"They have been provoking them a great deal of late." MacNutt leaned back in his chair, his hands steepled.

"True. But, how long the Americans' patience will last is a different matter."

"You're right," said MacNutt.

"And how was your meeting with the PM?"

"News travels fast," MacNutt said.

"Ottawa's a small town."

"So how can I help you?" MacNutt asked, switching the topic. When he saw the twinkle in King's eyes, he knew that he was in trouble. King loved nothing more than to set the fox loose in the henhouse and watch the feathers fly.

"Sir Wilfrid has been hearing some disturbing rumours," King finally declared with an airy wave of his forefinger. "Rumours concerning a personage that was in town last week."

MacNutt simply shrugged. The best tack was not to commit himself until he knew where King was heading.

"I hear a lot of gossip about a number of people. Anyone in particular?" he asked King cautiously.

"I believe you know who I'm talking about."

"Ah," replied MacNutt in kind. *How the hell did Laurier find out?* he thought.

"Are you playing games with me, Andrew?" King gave MacNutt a hard stare.

"Mr. King, you know I never play games," MacNutt replied blandly.

"Are you watching him?" King asked bluntly, observing MacNutt's reaction.

MacNutt's clasped hands tightened somewhat. He was treading on delicate ground here. He reported to the present government in power, and he really could not discuss anything of importance with a member of the loyal opposition. However, MacNutt recognized that King had helped the Service in the past. It was on King's recommendation that William Hopkinson, a British agent from India, was hired. In Vancouver, the Secret Service had waged an intense campaign against the Indian nationalists for nearly the past decade. Hopkinson uncovered nationalist attempts in the Sikh community to buy arms, raise money and infiltrate Sikh groups in the United States. Hopkinson did much good work until his cover was blown after the *Komagata Maru* incident. In 1914, the *Komagata Maru*, a Japanese steamship, was not allowed by Canadian authorities to disembark the 376 passengers from the Punjab in Vancouver. The ship was forced to return to India. Shortly after the incident Hopkinson was shot and killed in a courtroom in British Columbia by a Sikh extremist.

"I'm afraid that I can't tell you that," said MacNutt politely.

"You are aware that this is extremely dangerous. If this ever gets out, it will tear the country apart." King's voice rose a hair.

MacNutt couldn't keep the annoyance out of his own voice. "Hell, Mr. King, half the country wants to hang the man, the other half wants to make him a saint. Why doesn't Laurier tell him to stop giving speeches?"

"I too wish he would be more circumspect. But Sir Wilfrid insists that he be left alone. That's still no excuse to spy on him." King then squinted at MacNutt. "What the devil do you know that I don't?"

MacNutt cursed silently. He knew better than to fence with King. "I've said too much already," he said as he crossed his arms.

"Don't give me that, Andrew. You wouldn't have mentioned it if it weren't important," King retorted.

MacNutt turned and stared out his office window at the wide, snow-covered expanse of the Hill's central lawn. He had a decision to make, and he was trying to think out the ramifications. He decided on the lesser of the two evils. "We have information from several sources that the Germans may have an interest in our friend Henri Bourassa." MacNutt hid his pleasure in King's stunned expression. It wasn't often that one got the better of King.

"What are you saying! Who told you this?" King finally demanded with flared nostrils.

"I'm afraid that I cannot say," replied MacNutt.

King glared. "What do you mean you can't say?"

"I have sources to protect," protested MacNutt. It was a weak defence, but it was the truth.

"Andrew, he would never be involved with the Huns."

MacNutt lifted his hands to calm King. "I agree. But my job is to ensure that he doesn't get used by the Huns or that they don't harm him."

King reluctantly nodded. "If von Papen is any indication to go by, I don't think we have anything to worry about."

MacNutt couldn't argue with King's reasoning. It was difficult to conduct secret operations if they kept getting reported in the American papers. It would be comforting if what King said were true, but the Germans were not noted for making the same mistake twice. "I would not underestimate them. They have to replace him, and I doubt that the replacement will be as incompetent as he was. The States are becoming more and more important to the war effort. We want them in on our side and the Germans do not. If they can use the French Canadians against us, it would be an added bonus," explained MacNutt.

King snorted. "I wouldn't worry about it. We are doing more damage to ourselves than the Germans ever can."

"True. But, my job is to ensure that nothing happens to him..."

"As you wish. I'll inform Sir Wilfrid. Can you keep me informed?"

MacNutt winced. "I will, if I can."

"That's all that I ask." King took a pocket watch out of his vest. He then rose to his feet. "I'm sorry, but I have to go. I am running late, and I have a train to catch to New York tonight."

MacNutt got up as well to escort King out of the office. "When will you be coming back to Ottawa?"

"I was planning to come up for the Liberal caucus on the twentieth and then spend Christmas with my family in Toronto," replied King.

"I'll see you then."

King smiled knowingly. "Yes. I'm sure you will."

When he was sure that King was out of earshot, Lacelle peered up at MacNutt expectantly.

MacNutt shrugged. "He knows about Bourassa."

Lacelle chin dropped a fraction in surprise. "*Merde*! How did he know that?"

"He wouldn't say. But it would be nice to find out," said MacNutt as he scratched his scalp.

"Yes, sir," replied Lacelle thoughtfully.

MACNUTT RESIDENCE, LAURIER AVENUE WEST, OTTAWA
9:30 P.M., WEDNESDAY, DECEMBER 1, 1915

MacNutt's legs felt heavy as he walked up his front stoop stairs and opened his front door. The warm hallway was a relief. It had been a very long day, and he was feeling the effects. He had just come from Rideau Hall, where the Royal Highnesses, the Duke and Duchess of Connaught, had officially met the young Australian naval cadets. The young, innocent faces of the boys and their enthusiasm made him a smile for a brief moment. One of the boys was asked by one of the governor general's military attachés, he forgot which one, how old he was. The boy replied that he was thirteen. The officer then remarked that by the time the boy came of age, the war would be over.

The boy, fighting back the tears, his voice quivering, said "Please, sir, can I join up now? Please, sir. I don't want the war to be over before I get a chance to fight." Everyone grinned.

MacNutt felt a sense of sadness recalling the boy's words. It took him a moment to realize why. For the boy to get into the war, it would have to go on for three more years. Three more years of war. It was a sobering thought. And now that he was at home, he didn't want to be sober. He needed a couple of shots of rye. He wrapped his scarf around his hat and stuffed them into one of the overcoat's arms that he then hung on the coat rack.

He flicked through the letters and cards on the brass plate on the gleaming hallway table. Nothing of interest. He then spotted the black-and-brown beaver muff lying under the table. He bent down and picked it up. A couple of white ostrich feathers fluttered to the floor. He stared at them for a moment, then his lips tightened as he clenched his teeth.

"Kathy. Kathy!"

"I'm here in the salon," answered a female voice.

MacNutt walked down the corridor and entered the salon. Only a small fire flickering in the fireplace lit the room. His hand reached for the light switch. "What are you doing in the dark?"

"Nothing," replied Katherine. She was sitting on their black leather couch. She turned towards MacNutt. Her figure hadn't changed much in the twenty years that he had known her. She was still trim with strong, shapely arms and legs. Her features seemed to have softened as she aged, making her even more attractive. The first day he saw her running wild down the street, in front of her father's farm equipment store, her loose chestnut hair fluttering above a wide grin, there was no one else but her. Part of him wanted to reach out and stroke her soft hair. However, he stopped when her pupils took on a steel colour as she stared at him. It was as if she had put a knife through his heart. His anger flared to shield him from the piercing shaft of that gaze. They were at war, and sometimes there was no room for sentiment.

"Can you explain this?" He held out one of the white feathers. She turned away from him and stared into the fireplace. "You don't have anything to say?"

"I'm tired, Andy. I just don't feel like arguing with you tonight."

"Well, I do. This business of the white feathers has got to stop." MacNutt cursed the day that Alfred Mason's novel, *The Four Feathers,* was published.

"I know, but I just can't, Andy. I just can't. Every time I go out there are young men walking without a care in the world. I know it isn't their fault that Jamie's dead, but when I see them I think that if they were there, Jamie would still be alive."

MacNutt gazed on his wife, not quite sure what to say. He had never seen her like this before. The quiet confidence and the warm personality that had attracted him to her were gone. He didn't really know the woman who was seated before him. He wanted the old Katherine, and he simply didn't know how he could bring her back.

"You're shaming honest men. Men who want to fight but can't," he said, trying to make her see reason.

Katherine snapped her gaze towards Andrew and searched his face. "You asked Borden again? Didn't you?"

MacNutt didn't say anything.

"How could you, Andrew? How could you? Losing Jamie isn't enough. Do I have to lose you too?"

MacNutt couldn't answer her questions. All he could do was attack. "I expect you to put the white feathers back to where you got them and I expect you to stop handing them out. I will not have it. Do I make myself clear?"

Katherine kept silent as she watched the flames.

MacNutt took Katherine's silence as compliance. He had lost his need for a drink. "Let's go to bed. I need some sleep. Tomorrow's going to be a long day."

"Go ahead. I want to sit here a while longer."

"As you wish." MacNutt placed the white feathers on the parlour table under the light switch and took the stairs up to the master bedroom.

In the salon, Katherine rose from the settee and stepped over to the fireplace. She caressed the onyx-framed picture of a young man dressed in military uniform, next to a framed silver star on the mantel.

CHAPTER 4

MacNutt was having breakfast at a greasy spoon on Sparks Street a few doors down and across from the *Ottawa Citizen* building. Through the window he could see people stop on their way to work to read the early edition of the newspaper set in a glass case beside the front door. From the corner of his eye, he saw a stout woman with bread-basket breasts weave her way around several tables where half a dozen Dominion Police officers were eating their meals. A few were eating breakfast while the others were eating supper. Gertude's was a regular haunt of the Dominion Police. On occasion an Ottawa Police officer would stumble in, but they and the RNWMP had their own haunts. The woman placed the large platter of fried eggs, sausage, and potatoes in front of him and refilled his cup of coffee.

"Thank you, Gertrude," he said.

"You're welcome, Nutty," she replied with a smile. She was one of the few he allowed to call him that. Allowed maybe was not the right word. Whenever he tried to correct her, she would laugh loudly and slap him on the back. "So Nutty, how's the wife?"

"She's fine," he replied stiffly. A flash of anger at the wife caused him to sharply pull the coffee cup towards him, spilling some into its saucer.

She gave him a piercing glance. "That bad, huh?"

MacNutt stared back then shrugged by way of apology.

"Well, she'll come around. You'll see. If she don't, I'll take you," she said with a wink. She then barrelled off to the kitchen to get another order.

MacNutt couldn't help but smile as he dug into his breakfast. Gertrude would never change. She treated her customers as family, for better or worse. There were things he liked to keep private, like his disagreement with Katherine's handing out of white feathers, but somehow Gertrude managed to learn about it. He had taken several bites when Sergeant Lacelle entered the restaurant. He scanned the room, then spotted MacNutt and headed for his table.

"Good morning, Lacelle."

"Good morning, sir. How are you doing this morning?"

"I'm fine. Have a seat. Did you have breakfast yet?" MacNutt swept the room, trying to locate Gertrude.

"I'll just have a coffee," Lacelle said.

Gertrude emerged from the kitchen and MacNutt caught her attention, then inclined his head toward Lacelle and raised his cup. He turned back to Lacelle. "I hope everything is fine in the office."

"Thank you, Gertrude." Lacelle grinned at her as she placed a heavy white mug in front of him and poured a cup of steaming coffee.

"How's Marie and the kids?" she asked with a concerned frown.

"They're fine," Lacelle replied in a resigned tone.

"They're still going to that Guigues school, ain't they?"

"Yes, they are."

"What a shame," Gertrude said as she gently patted Lacelle's shoulder "Sometimes it's best to let things alone. And it's always the little ones that suffer. Tell Marie that I said so. I wish the little ones the best." Gertrude then bustled off to greet a customer hovering at the door.

"Things are pretty rough with the kids?" MacNutt asked.

"What can one say. *Les Oranges* want to assimilate us. And we will not let them." MacNutt listened with a sympathetic ear. The Ontario government had recently passed Regulation 17, which demanded that all French-language schools teach two hours of English a day. The French Canadians from Ontario and Quebec were up in arms about it. In Ottawa, two sisters who taught at the Guigues school, Béatrice and Diane Desloges, refused to comply with the regulation and there appeared to be a showdown looming.

"Did you have a chance to get to the office this morning?"

"I'm afraid so," the sergeant answered as he focused his attention on stirring the sugar in the coffee.

MacNutt caught Lacelle's tone. "Let me have it."

Lacelle sighed, stopped stirring, and then gave MacNutt a lopsided grin. "You will not like it."

"Of course not," retorted MacNutt with a slight edge to his voice.

"There was a problem in Hamilton."

MacNutt's pupils widened. "What happened? Is the governor general okay?"

"He's fine." Lacelle made a calming gesture.

"What then?" demanded MacNutt. His knife and fork, held tightly, were pointing upright.

"Do you remember that German that escaped from the Kingston internment camp?"

MacNutt put down his cutlery at the mention of the internment camps. When the war started, the public and the governments were in a panic. The fear was rampant that the thousands of German and Austrian-Hungarian immigrants in Canada would commit acts of terrorism and sabotage to support their mother countries. The Secret Service always operated on the premise that any threats to the Dominion of Canada would come from either the U.S. government or the Clan na Gael, the secret Irish nationalist organization, in New York. The Service had kept a watch on both for any indication that they might be planning to invade Canada.

Of course, the Service ran operations against the Sikhs in B.C., who were plotting mischief against the British Empire in India. Those operations were run at the behest of the British government. It was small comfort to MacNutt that no one else in Canada ever contemplated such a threat from a European country. If they had, Sifton would not have spent so much time and money recruiting farm workers from Europe for the prairies. MacNutt had no sources in the German or the Austro-Hungarian community in Canada or the U.S.

When Cabinet issued the Order-in-Council in August 1914 that ordered the internment of any alien of military age attempting to leave the country and of any alien who posed a security threat, the police and militia rounded up the local suspects and sent them to the internment camps. About 8,500 men, 80 women, and 160 children had been interned in twenty-four camps across the country. The women and children were allowed to accompany their husbands, since their husbands were their only means of support. There were two camps in Ontario, one at Fort Henry and the other in Northern Ontario at Kapuskasing. MacNutt didn't have much of a problem with those trying to leave the country; what offended him professionally were those who did not pose a security threat. However, many had been detained for reasons of jealousy, personal animosity, and war paranoia. In one case, the man had been hauled in simply because he was the only German in town. Even though, in early 1915, Colonel Otter and the responsibility for the camps had been transferred from the Department of Militia and Defence to the Department of Justice, it always fell to the Dominion Police to track and return detainees who escaped from the camps.

MacNutt raised his eyes from his plate. "Yes. We never did locate him. Why?"

"The Hamilton police found him," Lacelle replied remorsefully.

"Good for them. Why is that a problem?" MacNutt asked with a puzzled frown.

"It is where they arrested him that is the problem."

MacNutt was still puzzled, then his jaw dropped. "No!"

"*Oui.*" Lacelle nodded slowly. "He was working in the munitions plant that the governor general was going to visit."

"Aw, hell!" MacNutt exclaimed, slapping the table and causing the dishes to rattle. "Hell! Don't tell me that he was planning to blow up the plant with the governor general in it?"

"It doesn't appear so," Lacelle said. "He needed a job, and he applied for one at the plant."

"Didn't they vet the man?" MacNutt demanded.

Lacelle shrugged. "The manager said he seemed like an honest man to him. He had orders to fill, and he needed workers. According to the manager, he was one of his best workers."

"Next you are going to tell me that the manager wants him back," snorted MacNutt.

"How did you guess?"

MacNutt rolled his eyes. "I really shouldn't have gotten out of bed this morning. Okay — let's finish breakfast." He seized his knife and fork, sliced into the sausage on his plate, and then stabbed it with his fork. "When we get back, I want you to pull the file we have on him. I want to ensure that our asses are covered when I submit a report concerning this to the justice minister and the PM. This meal is the only peace and quiet I'm going to have today."

"Yes, sir," acknowledged Lacelle with a brisk nod.

"Better finish your coffee," commanded MacNutt, "it's going to be a long day."

PRESBYTERIAN CHURCH, SLATER AND KENT STREETS, OTTAWA
11:00 A.M., THURSDAY, DECEMBER 2, 1915

Katherine's heart was pounding as she picked her way carefully across the slick, snow-covered street to get to the Presbyterian church on the corner of Slater and Kent. Her hands clutched the white feathers in her beaver muff. There were several fewer than there had been when she left home earlier this afternoon. She didn't want to think about one young man's reaction. His weary, dispirited visage kept intruding in her thoughts.

Damn it, why do they have to look at me that way? Her feet slipped slightly on the thin glaze of ice that had frozen on top of the path that led to the church's entrance, causing her heart to jump into her throat. She barely glanced at the sixty-year-old stone walls as she concentrated on getting to the entrance upright.

It was with relief that she reached the door. It opened grudgingly and with a great deal of groaning at Katherine's tugging. *They really should oil the door*, she thought when she finally got inside. The small foyer was not any warmer than the outside. Her feet echoed on the wood steps as she took the stairs to the basement. At the foot of the stairs, she handed her coat to an excited young girl, who took it into the cloakroom.

Katherine turned and entered the brightly lit basement. The room was already crowded with women ranging from sixteen to sixty. They were dressed predominately in dark colours. She nodded with approval at the large "Give to Belgian Relief" banner hanging at the north end of the room above the small stage where religious plays were usually staged. Under the banner were two crossed flags, the Union Jack and the Red Ensign. In front of the flags was a small wooden table with four chairs. Offstage to the left, there were a variety of sweets and two large urns of coffee and tea on a long table. Two waitresses dressed in black with plain white aprons stood guard. Talking with one of the waitresses was Mrs. Jenkins.

As Katherine made her way to the table, she smiled at several acquaintances. Anna, a young brunette dressed in an ultramarine frock, intercepted her. She put a hand on her ample bosom as she caught her breath then asked, "Has he arrived yet?"

"He will be along shortly, Anna. Never fear," replied Katherine reassuringly.

"Have you met him? What is he like?" Anna said in a burst. Her breasts quivered as she bounced lightly.

"No, I haven't met him yet. But I'm sure that he is quite nice," replied Katherine.

"You think so? I really would like to talk with him. Do you think he would mind?" Anna glanced constantly towards the door.

"I'm sure he wouldn't. I'm sorry — I must speak with Mrs. Jenkins. Have fun, Anna," Katherine said as she slowly disentangled herself.

What have I done to deserve this? she thought as she approached Mrs. Jenkins at the sweets table.

"Hi, Nicole, is everything going well?" asked Katherine. When Mrs. Nicole Jenkins turned towards Katherine, she stroked her hair in worry. Katherine had always admired that Nicole kept a figure that still turned men's heads.

"Hi, Katherine. I don't know how we can do. We only have one platter of sweetmeats out. What are people going to think? Only one platter of sweetmeats."

Katherine smiled confidently and touched her arm. "There is another platter of them in the kitchen. I made sure of it last night. When this platter is empty, one of the girls will bring it out."

"You're a lifesaver, Katherine. How would we ever do without you?" Nicole was visibility relieved.

"Oh, you would have managed much better, I'm sure," Katherine teased. She expected Nicole to reciprocate, but her friend's visage turned serious.

"Did you hear about Elizabeth?" Nicole asked.

"No, why?"

"She lost her husband two weeks ago."

"Oh, God. How is she doing?" Katherine's smile was replaced by a thin line of pain and sorrow.

"As well as can be expected," Nicole replied with a matching grimace. "She found out yesterday."

Katherine sighed. "I'll drop by her house later today and see if she needs anything."

"She'll like that," Nicole said as some movement behind Katherine caught her attention. Katherine turned in the direction of Nicole's gaze. She noticed that the rest of the women had turned their attention to the doorway as well.

Standing at the threshold was Mrs. Ramsey. Her plump face beamed with pleasure and self-satisfaction. Katherine knew why. When she shifted her attention to the tall, distinguished man beside Mrs. Ramsey, she gasped.

"Something wrong?" Nicole asked as she leaned slightly forward to view Katherine's right cheek. Katherine eyes were open wide and her mouth gaped a little.

"It's nothing," she replied quickly. How could she explain to Nicole that she had given a white feather to Count Jaggi, the Belgian Relief representative from London? She wanted to crawl under the table and hide, but she couldn't. All she could do was hope that she wouldn't be recognized.

Katherine watched as Mrs. Ramsey, the Count, and the Belgian consul general Maurice Goor, whom she hadn't noticed in her shock, walked royal procession-like across the hardwood floor to the stage. They were followed by Kelly Sanderson, the organization's secretary, and Kim Crane, the treasurer. As they made their way, Katherine edged slowly to the back of the room, keeping the women in front of her as a screen against the Count's view. She eyed the door that beckoned, but she couldn't leave without being noticed. As the group settled into their seats on the stage, Katherine lowered herself into a chair at the back of the hall.

Mrs. Ramsey rose and stepped to the podium. To get the crowd's attention she cried out, "Ladies! Ladies!" The buzzing slowly died. A few had to be hushed.

"Thank you. Here we are," she continued as she surveyed the room. "When the Women's Canadian Club of Ottawa first started its patriotic work, we expected the war would last for a few months. As you are all aware, our Soldiers' Comforts committee has been greatly expanded. Our wool and knitting committee has sent nearly 2,400 socks and 2,000 scarves to soldiers at the front. The sewing committee has sewn utility bags, 2,000 towels, and face cloths, handkerchiefs, pillows, and hammocks. Nearly 1,200 magazines were sent to France and 20,000 were sent to the Atlantic fleet by the magazine committee. With Christmas near, the packing committee is currently preparing nearly 900 Christmas parcels to be sent to our troops overseas..." She was interrupted by the audience's applause. Mrs. Ramsey waited until it subsided then continued.

"Each parcel costs $1.50. We are still fundraising so that that we can send as many as possible before Christmas. The City Battalion committee has provided appetizing lunches with fruit for the members of the 77th Battalion. We also received a testimonial to the value of the three motor ambulances we have donated. We had raised nearly $6,500 to buy the ambulances. One donation covered the cost of an entire ambulance. Mrs. Whitney, can you stand and take a bow, please?"

Mrs. Whitney, who was sitting in the front row, rose and bowed. She blushed when she was greeted with applause.

"Our correspondence committee has sent 900 letters of sympathy and best wishes to wounded soldiers in the past year. The club has also agreed to furnish and maintain 14 beds for the Sir Sandford Fleming Convalescent home for wounded soldiers that will be opened in January. We have opened a register in our club offices where women who are willing to do men's work until the war is over may enter their names. The number of women who have signed has exceeded our expectations.

"In addition, the club has been raising funds for Belgian Relief. Many of you have seen the letters of appreciation we have received. For me, the one that stands out is the gracious letter of gratitude sent to us from the Lady Lugard Hospitality Committee after Lady Perley had given them our cheque for £61 in London, England."

Mrs. Ramsey turned her shoulders and gave the man sitting beside her a broad smile before going on. "We have also donated thousands of dollars and clothes for the poor Belgians. It is, therefore, with great pleasure that I present to you, the women who made this organization such a great success, the man we have heard so much about over the past year. Who has given us so much encouragement when times are darkest and whom we have never met until today. Ladies! Count Jaggi!"

The women clapped enthusiastically as Count Jaggi rose gracefully to his feet. He took Mrs. Ramsey's hand and kissed it gallantly. He turned to the crowd and tried to calm the women's applause with his hands. It took a few moments before the room became quiet again.

Count Jaggi began to speak in a strong voice that carried to the back of the room. "Thank you, mademoiselle, for the wonderful introduction. I admit that I am a grateful man today. As I meet for the first time the flower of Canadian womanhood, the women who worked so generously and unselfishly to help my people who have suffered at the hands of the despicable Huns, I cannot say in words the feeling that I would like to express. I hope that you will accept this token of my deep appreciation."

From the briefcase he pulled out a plaque and handed it to Mrs. Ramsey. She took it in both hands and displayed it to the women. Katherine's curiosity was piqued when the Count leaned towards Mrs. Ramsey and whispered in her ear. Mrs. Ramsey's lips first creased open in surprise then smiled in agreement. She stepped to the podium to speak.

"Ladies!" Excitement could be heard in her voice. "I have an announcement to make. The Count has graciously agreed to give a special speech and slideshow to help in our fundraising. It will show the horror of the German occupation of Belgium. It is a great honour to organize this meeting. A date has not yet been set, but it will be early in the new year. Ladies, please enjoy the tea. I will now be accepting volunteers, and you all may take the opportunity to have a word with the Count."

The crowd jumped to its feet and burst into applause. The Count escorted Mrs. Ramsey to the sweets table and was handed a cup of tea. As the ladies lined up, Katherine lagged behind trying to keep out of the Count and Mrs. Ramsey's line of sight. She studied the door then the crowd, trying to gauge when it was acceptable for her to leave.

"Isn't he wonderful," gushed Anna, who had rushed over when she finally spotted Katherine in the back. "And handsome," she added as she gazed at the Count with adoring eyes.

"Yes," replied Katherine. She couldn't keep her eyes off the man either. "Why don't you go speak to him?"

"I couldn't. I really couldn't," Anna replied quickly, then, after a moment: "Do you really think I should?" Her chest quivered with excitement.

"Didn't you tell me you really wanted to meet him when I first came in?"

"Yes. Yes, I did," replied Anna.

"Well, there he is." Katherine indicated the Count still standing near the sweets table. "Why don't you go over to speak with him then?"

"Ow, I'm so nervous. Why don't you come with me, Katherine? You're not shy."

Taken momentarily aback by Anna's request, Katherine couldn't help stepping back a bit. She thought frantically for a moment then latched onto the perfect excuse. "I'm sorry, Anna, I can't right now. I promised Mrs. Jenkins that I would make sure that an extra platter of sweetmeats is served."

"Please, Katherine! For me, please," Anna begged, grabbing Katherine's arm.

Katherine stood firm as she gently retrieved her arm. "Go along, dear. I'm sure that he won't bite. Go along."

"If you say so," Anna said nervously as Katherine pushed her towards the Count. Anna gazed at him longingly, her back straightened, emphasizing her chest as she screwed up her courage and then headed towards him.

Katherine watched as the woman wove her way through the crowd. The Count just happened to be looking in Katherine's direction when they locked gazes. She quickly averted her eyes. She hoped that he did not recognize her.

Katherine floated to another group of women. As they chatted, she felt her eyes return to the Count. She had to admit that he was a fine figure of a man. She guessed, based on his silvery grey hair, that he was in his early forties. She liked that his smile seemed to come from his eyes rather than just his mouth. *Stop that*, she scolded herself. But still, her gaze was drawn to the man.

As she watched the Count with her peripheral vision, he leaned over and whispered in Mrs. Ramsey's ear then pointed in Katherine's general direction. Mrs. Ramsey followed the finger and squinted. She broke into a grin when she recognized who it was. Consternation crossed the Count's gaze when she beckoned to Katherine.

Katherine pretended not to see her. She kept nodding as if she was engrossed in the group's conversation. Mrs. Ramsey waved at her more insistently. Katherine had no choice but to acknowledge her when one of the women in the group touched her shoulder and pointed to Mrs. Ramsey. Katherine extricated herself from the group and reluctantly made her way over.

"Mrs. Ramsey," she said in a slightly defensive tone.

"Katherine, I would like to introduce you to the Count. Count Jaggi. Katherine MacNutt." Katherine missed the start that the Count gave when he heard her name. Katherine offered her hand half-heartedly to the Count, though she tried to avoid his stare.

"I had the pleasure of already having a rendezvous. But we were not properly introduced," the Count disclosed as he took her hand and gave a slight bow. Katherine felt her cheeks turn pink.

"You have! That's wonderful." Mrs. Ramsey peered at them expectantly.

"Yes. We did meet, didn't we?" Katherine gave the Count a pleading glance. She was hoping that he would not say anything about the white feather. She was embarrassed enough.

"When did you meet?" Mrs. Ramsey asked. Before either of them could reply, a waitress touched her sleeve to get her attention. As the waitress whispered in her ear, Mrs. Ramsey's forehead wrinkled in annoyance. "Excuse me — I must take care of a problem in the kitchen."

"Can I help?" Katherine asked a touch eagerly. Her expression brightened with the thought of escape.

Mrs. Ramsey nodded. "Please take care of the Count for me. I will be right back." She rushed away with the waitress in tow, leaving Katherine standing awkwardly with the Count.

Katherine turned to the Count and spoke first. "If I had realized who you were, Count Jaggi, I wouldn't have given you the feather."

She slightly recoiled at the glare he gave her and the cold tone in his voice when he spoke. "I do not approve of the giving of white feathers."

"It is necessary to ensure that shirkers do not escape their duty," she replied defensively. She wondered why she was trying to explain her actions to this man.

Count Jaggi cocked his head slightly. "There was a young man of a good family I knew in London who died of your little white feathers. They are light, but they bend a man's shoulders and break his heart."

"Unfortunate that he did not have the courage to die in uniform," she retorted.

"Courage!" replied the Count contemptuously. "You English have a strange idea of courage. He was wounded defending Antwerp. Lost a lung. Tried to soldier on but the army did not want another wounded young man. A young man with great pride and honour. He was found suspended from his chandelier with a dozen white feathers at his feet."

"Oh my God," replied a shocked Katherine.

"Once you've seen the face of war, Madame, it is sometimes difficult to believe in God."

"I ... I..." Katherine stammered, not knowing what to say. She was saved by the reappearance of Mrs. Ramsey. She glanced from one to the other, gauging their chemistry with a crooked grin.

"Well. How are you two getting along?" she asked.

Katherine replied first. "We're getting along fine."

"Splendid! Splendid! By the way, Katherine, I spoke with Andrew. We will be meeting next week to discuss this spy, Denon."

Katherine gave Mrs. Ramsey a thin smile. "That's nice. Don't let him bully you. I'm sure he will like to know your views."

Count Jaggi interrupted. "An agent provocateur? Here in Canada!"

Mrs. Ramsey fixed her watery gaze on the Count. "Oh yes. The country is full of them. Why, even here in Ottawa we have spies, and the authorities are doing nothing. Nothing at all."

Katherine knew that if she didn't get Mrs. Ramsey off the topic, she would bore the poor Count to death. She interjected, "Mrs. Ramsey, have you decided who will organize January's fundraiser?"

"The meeting is at two o'clock tomorrow," she replied.

"What meeting?" replied a perplexed Katherine.

Mrs. Ramsey with smug satisfaction said, "I have given you the honour of helping Count Jaggi in organizing his presentation. There you are. I knew you would be pleased." She took the Count's arm and started to lead him away. All Katherine could do was stare helplessly as Mrs. Ramsey and the Count walked away. The last thing she heard was Mrs. Ramsey say, "Now I will tell you all about this spy. Denon..."

BAR, CHÂTEAU LAURIER, RIDEAU STREET, OTTAWA
10:00 P.M., THURSDAY, DECEMBER 2, 1915

Count Jaggi stepped out of the McLaughlin motorcar and acknowledged the doorman who opened the car's door. By the time the doorman had slammed it shut, Jaggi was enveloped by the lobby's warm air.

He headed straight for the front desk where he checked for his mail. He wasn't really expecting any. He was, however, leaving on the four o'clock train to New York the next day, and he didn't want to leave anything behind.

The Count then made his way to the bar. He needed a drink after the evening's long, tedious affair. When he entered the smoke-filled bar, he paused and scanned the room looking for familiar faces. He didn't see any, but he noticed that there weren't any women. As was to be expected, since the Château's bar was restricted to gentlemen only. He found a spot at the bar where he had a good view of the door and most of the room.

He caught the bartender's eye and ordered a cognac. A moment later the bartender placed a glass in front of him and poured the cognac from a half-empty bottle. The Count picked up the glass and swirled the drink to warm it.

From his vantage point he was the first to notice the two women enter the bar. When the other patrons spotted them, they turned and stared. One young woman stared back at them with defiance in her coffee-coloured eyes. The Count recognized that look: the same expression he had seen on Katherine MacNutt's face when she gave him the white feather. One of the waiters hurried over to the pair. Before he could get to them, the young woman spoke in a voice loud enough to carry over the din.

"Gentlemen! Gentlemen! Please hear me."

More of the patrons turned in the women's direction, some hostilely.

"I implore you not to imbibe the demon drink. Think of your wives and your families. For the sake of your immortal souls, do not drink the demon drink. You will be condemned to the fires of hell." She was quite earnest.

"Well, lady, if I have to go to hell, I might as well go drunk!" a patron shouted.

"If not for your souls, think of the soldiers that are fighting and dying in France. With every drink you are prolonging the war in Europe." The patrons booed and hissed in reply. The waiters finally reached her and her companion. They politely, but firmly, held them by the elbows as they showed them to the door.

The Count downed the cognac and motioned the bartender for another. When he came over with a new glass the Count asked, "What was that all about?"

The bartender raised an eyebrow in surprise. "Temperance supporters. They maintain that all libations are the devil's work and should be abolished," he explained.

The Count stared at him in disbelief. "They have a large following?"

"I'm afraid so. I might be out of a job soon," the bartender said as he rolled his eyes. He then went to fill another patron's request.

The Count stared at his drink, lost in thought. He pictured Katherine; he knew that she was available. It was something he couldn't explain, but he generally knew who was available and who wasn't. He also, however, sensed that she was very inexperienced and that she wasn't ready to accept that she was available. All that was needed was the key to unlock her gates. What was more enticing was the fact that she was the wife of the local security chief. If he could turn her, she would make an invaluable asset.

A shiver ran down his spine. A premonition that if he got involved with her it might bring disaster. But to learn the opposition's plan would be well worth the risk. Yes, it would be worth it, and besides, he didn't believe that the locals were sophisticated enough to detect his plans.

The Count took another sip of his drink with a satisfied sigh and took out his pocket watch. It was late, and tomorrow would be a long day. He wasn't looking forward to getting on the night train for New York.

He was thinking of that when he was jostled from behind and spilled his drink. He cursed, remembering to do it in French, and then glowered at the man.

"Sorry," the man said. He weaved slightly. His plump cheeks were red from too much rye. He was dressed in a cheap suit that pulled tightly across the expanse of his stomach.

"*Il est rien*," Count Jaggi murmured. The drunken man scowled when he heard the French.

"You're a Frenchie, eh?" he slurred.

The Count shook his head. "I'm Belgian."

"Well, Frenchie," the drunk repeated, ignoring the Count's words, "I gotta ask. This Bourassa fellow, can you explain that son of a bitch to me?"

"I don't know who you are speaking of," replied the Count in a cold tone. He had heard the name before, an article in the local paper, but he didn't really have a clue what the man was about. He made a mental note to delve into the matter. He hoped that when he got to New York he would be better briefed.

"Hey — Mark!" the drunk shouted to a man sitting at a table near the door. "This Frenchie doesn't know who Bourassa is." His friend grimaced, embarrassed.

"Henri Bourassa, that goddamn Hun-loving bastard," the drunk sneered as he poked the Count with his finger. "You know, he's in league with the Hun. Yep. I've got it on good authority that he wants us English lads to die in France while these French yellow bastards stay at home and make babies."

"Come, Sean. Give it up," begged his friend when he saw the Count turn stone cold.

"Mark — you know it's true!" he scoffed loudly. By now the other men in the bar were watching them. Count Jaggi cursed silently. He didn't need the attention.

"Give it rest, Sean," Mark said tiredly as he came over from the table. He had heard it all before. "I'm sorry, sir. He's two sheets to the wind."

"No harm done," replied the Count stiffly.

"Hell no — I'm not done yet! Let's have one more for the road. What do you say?" the drunk argued.

"It's late, and there is the devil to pay with the missus. Come, Sean. I'll take you home," Mark said as he put his arm around his friend and steered him to the door.

The Count watched the two leave, then turned to his drink. Mark and Sean had made the decision for him. Maybe there *was* a way to exploit the situation in Canada.

CHAPTER 5

The conductor's voice announcing that the train's next stop was New York's Central Station finally roused the Count out of his sleep. He sat up in the sleeper's bunk bed and turned on the light. He fished his watch out of his pants pocket; it said ten after six. It was a godawful hour, but unfortunately the Grand Trunk train had left on schedule from Ottawa at 4:45 p.m., and it wouldn't get to New York until its scheduled arrival time of 7:26 a.m. The Count took a moment to try to clear the fogginess. He never got a good night's sleep on a train, even when he booked a sleeper car. He finally got out of the bunk bed and slipped on his trousers. From his valise he took his shaving kit and entered the washroom. In the mirror, he ran his hand over the light stubble. He glanced at the straight razor, but with the train's motion he decided it would be prudent to wait till he got to New York. There was no point in getting his throat cut, even accidentally, until he found out the situation in New York.

He wasn't particularly happy when he had received orders on November 3 from Berlin that he was to leave London for New York. London had been very good for him. The women were easygoing with their charms. That he was able to charm more than their undergarments off had kept Major Nicholi of Abteilung 3B quite happy. Actually, he hadn't charmed the undergarments off as many as he would have liked. Just enough to satisfy himself regularly. He found that lending a sympathetic ear paid more dividends in the long run than a quick tumble. The orders also said he would be contacted for a detailed briefing before he left for New York.

He had met his contact a few days later in a pub in London's East End. He would have preferred to meet in a safe house away from the crowds so they could talk more freely, but his contact wouldn't have it. The contact was worried about being betrayed to British intelligence, which seemed to be particularly effective of late. The only reason he had agreed to meet with the Count was that Berlin had informed him that the Count had the necessary papers and money that he needed to get out of England.

When he entered the pub, he spotted his contact sitting tensely at a back table with a glass of beer and reading a newspaper with a torn front page, which was the agreed-upon recognition signal. He headed to the bar to order a beer before he approached his contact. As he waited for the bartender to pour the beer he scanned the room searching for someone who didn't belong. He could feel the contact studying him. When the bartender finished pouring the beer, he took the lukewarm pint to the man's table.

"So how are you doing, Kurt? It has been a while."

"As well as can be expected," the man replied sharply as he snapped the paper closed and slapped it on the table.

The Count sat at the table in the chair directly across from him. Uncomfortable with his back to the door, he moved his chair to improve his line of sight.

"I understand you have something for me," said his contact.

"It depends," replied the Count.

Kurt leaned forward and hissed, "Do you have my papers and my money?"

The Count, taken aback, leaned away. He gave a quick glance at the pub entrance, but he doubted he could leave without a scene.

"Well, do you or don't you?" Kurt demanded as he stabbed the table with his forefinger.

The Count took another sip of his beer and said calmly, "Tell me about New York."

Kurt glared at him. "So it's going to be that way, is it?" The Count gave him an unapologetic grin. "What do you want to know?"

"Everything," replied the Count. He wanted to get a feel for the situation before he actually committed himself to the mission.

Kurt laughed. After he took a large gulp from the mug, it landed on the table with a thump, sloshing the beer. "Is that all?" The Count simply nodded.

"I guess I don't have much of a choice," Kurt said bitterly. "Things are not well in England. I need to get back to the Fatherland."

"What has happened?"

"The British picked up one of my agents two days ago," replied Kurt. "It's only a matter of time before he talks, if he hasn't already. I don't dare go back to my flat. They could be waiting for me, and I don't want to join Rintelen in the Tower."

"It's unfortunate, but in our line of business these things happen," replied the Count.

"Do you know how he ended up in the Tower?" asked Kurt.

The Count gestured to indicate he didn't.

"Rintelen blames von Papen," said Kurt.

"He does, does he?" The Count couldn't hide his unease. So far he had been very careful about with whom he dealt. He avoided most face-to-face meetings because he did not trust the reliability of his contacts.

"Yes, he does," returned Kurt.

"Does he have any proof?"

Kurt fiddled with the handle of his mug. "Just suspicions."

"I see. So why was Rintelen in New York in the first place?"

"His father's fault. He was a banker. Rintelen joined the Imperial Navy in 1903 and when war broke out he was attached to the Kaiser's High Command. They decided they needed a naval officer who understood ships and how to sabotage them."

"And so they sent him?"

"I'm afraid so. He had the necessary skills. He spoke fluent English, and he lived in America. His father's banking interests there provided a perfect cover."

"And when he arrived in the United States?" the Count asked.

"He and von Papen, unfortunately, did not get along."

"Does anyone know what happened?"

"I'm not entirely sure," answered Kurt, leaning back in his chair. "It seems that Rintelen offended von Papen. He had informed von Papen that he was in charge of undercover operations in America."

"Was this true?"

"No. Rintelen had been sent to devise schemes to sabotage Allied shipping from New York. How he got the impression that he had a free hand to do as he liked is a mystery to Berlin."

"Sounds as if this Rintelen did not have the temperament for the work," remarked the Count. "So who do we have there now?"

Kurt took a slurp of his half-empty glass of beer. "Count von Bernstorff, the German ambassador; the army attaché, Captain von Papen; the naval attaché, Captain Boy-Ed; and Dr. Heinrich Albert, the commercial attaché." All of them were attached to the German embassy. The Count wondered if the embassy was compromised.

"What exactly am I supposed to do there?"

"First, you're to cripple the Allied shipping out of New York. We need to starve England into submission," said Kurt. "Second, you must do as much damage as you can to British interests in America and in Canada. Third, you have to keep the Americans out of the war."

"Understood," said the Count thoughtfully. "To whom will I report?"

"The ambassador, von Bernstorff."

"Monies?"

"Dr. Albert will make arrangements for you," replied Kurt.

"I understand." The Count finished his beer then asked, "How are you planning to get out of England?"

The contact became expressionless. He said pointedly, "Leave that to me. I just need money and papers. Do you have them?"

"Of course." The Count grimaced as he pulled an envelope from his right pocket and handed it to Kurt under the table. Kurt took a quick gander at the contents, gave the Count a sharp nod, and left the table. The Count would never see the man again after he left the bar.

* * *

After he finished his morning's ablutions, Count Jaggi went to his sleeper and changed his clothes before heading to the dining car for breakfast. He was seated at an empty table, for which he was grateful. The waiter gave him the menu in the form of an order slip and a pencil.

The waiter filled the china cup with coffee as the Count ticked the items he wanted to order. When the waiter finished pouring the coffee he took the Count's menu and headed for the galley. As Count Jaggi drank the coffee, he scanned the dining car. He spotted a man a couple of tables over who was giving the breakfast crowd a professional check-over. He glanced away when he noticed the Count examining him. A few moments later the man got up, and when he reached into his coat to get his wallet, the Count glimpsed the butt of a gun sticking out of his waist pocket. The man picked through the change in his hand and placed a couple of coins on the table. He caught the eye of the waiter, who gave him a quick nod. The man put on a battered fedora and left the restaurant car.

The coffee cup in the Count's hand trembled slightly as he placed in on the table. It happened when he felt tired and his paranoia was getting the best of him. But no one in Canada or America knew who he was, at least not yet. He suspected from the exchange that the man with the gun was a regular on the train, probably a railway detective investigating petty thieves. All the same, he had taken the time to memorize the man's features. One never knew.

MacNutt was shown into the meeting room by an RNWMP constable. The walls were covered with lithographs showing the Mounties in heroic poses as they rode across the prairies. A few moments later, Inspector Hewitt, who was chairing today's meeting, entered the meeting room. They tried, when possible, to rotate the meeting locations. Today was the RNWMP's turn. Hewitt's weather-beaten face cracked a thin smile when he saw MacNutt. MacNutt returned the smile. While MacNutt liked the gruff inspector, he needed to tread carefully. He did not want to further complicate an already complicated situation.

There was no love lost between the commissioner of the RNWMP and the commissioner of the Dominion Police. The ambition of the commissioner of the Dominion Police was to have a single Dominion-wide force with him as its head. The RNWMP stood in his way. What did not help matters was the Dominion Police's belief that the RNWMP were nothing but dilettantes and publicity hounds. The RNWMP was initially set up as a military organization to prevent the Americans from annexing the Canadian prairies. Unfortunately for the Dominion Police, the Canadian public had become enamoured with the romantic image of the red-coated Mounties. The Dominion Police's mundane duty of guarding the government buildings and naval bases could never match the aura surrounding the Mounties. The addition of the Royal prefix in 1904 made the disbanding of the RNWMP politically impossible.

MacNutt knew that what rankled the Mounties was that they were required to make regular security reports to the Secret Service and render assistance when required. MacNutt's quandary was that sooner or later the commissioner would retire. When that time came, the Mounties would surely move in and take over the Dominion Police. Would the Mounties remember that it wasn't anything personal? That he was simply trying to do his job and that he was obeying orders? He doubted it.

With Hewitt entered Robert Atwell from the Department of External Affairs. Atwell grinned at MacNutt. His smile got bigger when Mac-

Nutt simply acknowledged him with a curt nod. MacNutt despised the man. The man was an imperialist, a rabid Anglophile who believed that England could do no wrong, and he made no effort to hide his contempt for Americans. Ever since he was appointed to the committee, MacNutt had been trying to get rid of him. Unfortunately, the man sitting across him was well connected with both the Liberal and the Conservative parties, so he was not so easy to remove.

Commander Stephens, from Canadian Naval Intelligence Branch, and Colonel Denny, from the Army's Intelligence, entered together. Commander Stephens was Admiral Kingsmill's chief of staff and was responsible for any intelligence that would help in protecting Canadian coasts and shipping lanes.

As for the army, each of Canada's twelve military districts had a District Intelligence Office who reported regularly on suspected German activities in their district.

Hewitt said, "Let's get started then. I guess Mike is going to be a bit late. When he arrives, we will bring him up to date." Mike O'Neal was the Customs Intelligence Unit's representative to the committee. "Do we have questions on the minutes from last week's meeting?"

Hewitt took the silence as agreement. "Now to business."

"Okay," MacNutt said as he removed a file folder of mimeographed pages from his portfolio and handed everyone a copy. "Now, I've reviewed all of your reports. Can you take a peek at this list and determine if I missed any?"

Hewitt grinned as he took his. "Rather dangerous carrying this around, old boy."

"Oh, I think they are quite safe. I'm no doctor," said MacNutt, making a subtle reference to Dr. Albert's lost portfolio in New York.

It took a moment for the reference to sink in, and then Hewitt chuckled. "You're right, Andrew, you are no doctor." After he studied the list he said, "The list looks fine to me."

"Hmmm," Atwell murmured as he read his copy.

"Is there a problem?" asked MacNutt with a touch of pique.

"It's embarrassing, but the list is not complete," said Atwell, folding his hands on the table.

"What do you mean, it's 'not complete'?" MacNutt's voice rose a notch. For the last several months, he had been trying to get the various government departments that dealt with Canadian intelligence matters to coordinate their activities, and it had been an uphill battle. It seemed that every time he thought he had everything under control, something came at him from left field.

"I just found out last week when we received a request for monies for secret service work from a man in Seattle," replied Atwell with a calm that grated on MacNutt. "It seems that he was engaged by us since January of 1915. He was to keep track of German activities in Seattle. We spoke with the officer who hired him, and he said he thought he had informed us and that we were handling him."

"You got to be kidding. Didn't he send any reports?" asked MacNutt, holding up his palms.

"He said he sent them to the British consulate in Seattle. The consul general there said they forwarded the reports to us, but we don't have any record of receiving his reports."

"So he now wants to be paid for his services that he rendered for the government?" MacNutt demanded.

"Yes. One hundred and fifty dollars," replied Atwell with a sly smile. "The Secret Service has the budget for this kind of work."

MacNutt, his lips pursed, struggled to keep from losing his temper. "I have to pay a hundred and fifty dollars to an agent from whom, you say, we never received any reports. I don't think so."

"Well, I'm afraid that someone will have to," Atwell said simply. It was obvious to everyone that he was enjoying himself.

"Why?" asked Denny.

Atwell broke eye contact with MacNutt and turned his attention to Denny. "He feels that he has been hard done by. He says that he put himself at considerable risk for little reward. And if there were complications, he would have to extradite himself from them without any help from us. If he doesn't get his money, he will go to the newspapers."

MacNutt couldn't believe it. What he had feared most was happening. Any exposure of the Canadian government's operations in the United States would be politically embarrassing. Other than himself, everyone in this room was new at the game, and there were bound to be problems because of inexperience and lack of training. So far the problems had been of slight consequence.

The most serious was when Naval Intelligence nearly gave a Slater code book to a German agent in Tacoma, Washington. The Slater code was the telegraphic code in use by most telegraphic offices in Canada. The code was first published around 1870 in England, when the telegraph system throughout the United Kingdom came under control of the British government. The code consisted of a 25,000-word vocabulary, with each word assigned a five-digit number from 00001 to 25,000. By adding a special key number to each of the five-digit numbers being transmitted, telegrams could be sent in relative security from prying eyes. The Slater code had been the standard for the Canadian Militia and Defence for years, until it was replaced by the Playfair code, and was indeed still being used by the Canadian government for low-level confidential traffic. For secure communications, the government used the latest in the alphabet series of cypher codes, the most recent being Cypher F. For sensitive economic communication, the Economic Telegraphic Codes were used. In Tacoma, the intelligence officer hadn't bothered to check the man's reliability. When Naval Intelligence mentioned the man's name to MacNutt, it rang alarm bells. When MacNutt investigated, it turned out the man was in the Dominion Police files as a known German sympathizer. When he informed the Navy, they sent urgent telegrams ordering that the code book not be given to the man — or if it had been given to him, to get it back right away. Naval Intelligence claimed that they had received the telegram before handing over the book. MacNutt had his doubts, though, and recommended that a new code be introduced. He was overruled.

MacNutt unclenched his jaw. His teeth were starting to grind in frustration. "For God's sake, if you engage special agents I need to be informed. I know that you are all very busy. If you can ask your staff to verify so that we don't have any more unaccounted special agents out there, I would appreciate it." He hoped that this message would finally sink in. Everyone except Atwell agreed.

"You have heard that Captain von Papen and Boy-Ed have been declared *personae non gratae*," Hewitt said, moving on to the next item on the agenda.

"It is about time," said Stephens, grateful that they had moved on to another subject.

"Very," agreed Atwell.

"However, it is not over yet. I'm certain that the Huns will be sending somebody to replace them soon," said MacNutt.

"You mean another military attaché?" asked Stephens.

"I doubt it. I mean, if you were the Secretary of State, would you accredit another military attaché? No — what I suspect is that they will be sending someone else who is not directly connected to the German embassy," replied MacNutt, wagging a forefinger.

"So what do you want us to do?" asked Denny.

"Ask your people to keep an eye out for any activity out of the norm and to wire us if they find information of interest," said MacNutt.

"Maybe we should offer them a reward for any information?" suggested Denny.

MacNutt grimaced and then said, "I prefer not to offer money now."

"Okay. Maybe we should take another look at the Hamburg-American Line. Four officials there were just charged for sending coal and other supplies to German cruisers in the South Atlantic," said Stephens. It was a major concern of the Canadian and Royal navies. With a large number of German immigrants on both the east and west coasts of the United States, the fear was that they would be keeping German Imperial Navy surface ships and subs supplied with fuel, food, and ammunition. He continued, "And don't forget about the German Counsel-General in San Francisco. The papers claim that he received $400,000 for work in connection with the destruction of wharves, ships, and munitions plants there."

"Well, if we believed everything that the papers said we'd be out of a job," snorted Hewitt.

"Hmm, Mike didn't make it? That's unusual. He always attends these meetings. Something must have come up. Does anyone have anything else to add? Andrew?"

"The governor general has been in Toronto for the last few days. He should be back by Monday. We've begun preliminary planning for the security for the levee," replied MacNutt.

"Let's hope it's better security than the sloppy work that was done in Hamilton," said Atwell sarcastically. MacNutt had hoped the subject of the escaped detainee would not be brought up.

He was grateful when Hewitt interjected. "He's still going ahead with that, is he?"

"I'm afraid so. It's political. He needs to reassure the public that all is going well with the war effort. There shouldn't be a problem unless the Germans invade us," said MacNutt.

"Anything besides von Papen and Boy-Ed from the States?" asked Hewitt, peering at MacNutt.

MacNutt shook his head. "There have been several incidents but it's too early to tell if they are accidents or German sabotage."

"What are we are using down there? Pinkertons?" asked Stephens.

"Yes," replied MacNutt.

"They're a good outfit," said Stephens.

"As I have said before, we shouldn't be using the Americans. We really should determine if we can put our people down there," snapped Atwell.

In this MacNutt was in agreement with Atwell. The Pinkertons were supposed to be just a stop-gap until he got his network in place. It seemed it could be more permanent than that. "The PM has indicated that if the Americans got wind of our spying on U.S. citizens, the use of Pinkertons would not be as upsetting as the use of our own officers."

"But have the Pinks been proven to be reliable?" argued Atwell. "Even after that letter they sent?"

Seeing Stephens and Denny's confusion, MacNutt explained. "Robert and William Pinkerton wrote personally to us assure is that while the war is on, they will not accept work from the German government." It was not the first time that Atwell had brought up the rumours that the Pinkerton Detective Agency had been hired by the German government to do some work for them. Robert and William Pinkerton, who had taken over the agency after their father, Allen Pinkerton, passed away, had indeed sent a letter to the Canadian government, assuring them that they were not doing any work for the Germans.

"What would be the American government's reaction if they found out if we were using the Pinkertons?" asked Stephens, turning his gaze back to MacNutt.

"Invade!" barked Atwell.

"If they decide to invade, there won't be anything really to stop them," intervened Denny. "We have *plans* in place to stop an American invasion, but with all our troops in Europe, in actuality there wouldn't be much we could do to keep them from it."

"The more important question is: What are the Germans doing in the U.S.? They want to make sure that the Americans stay out of the war," said Hewitt, sitting back in his chair.

"We also have the additional problem of the Shell Committee," said MacNutt. General Hughes had created the Shell Committee in September 1914 to arrange and place contracts for artillery shells for the British government. However, the British government was not impressed by the committee's performance. Out of 170 million dollars worth of contracts, only 5 million dollars were delivered to England by the summer of 1915. The shortage of shells contributed to the fall of the Liberal British government in May, forcing Prime Minister Asquith to form a coalition government. Lloyd George was appointed the Minister of Munitions. Last November Hughes' Shell Committee, at the insistence of the British government, was replaced by the newly formed Imperial Munitions Board, the job of which was to reorganize production in Canada.

"Ah hell, you're stuck with that mess," said Hewitt with sympathy.

"It's come up a couple of times. We've been asked to investigate," said MacNutt, "and I may need to go to New York."

"Hughes?" said Hewitt.

"Hughes," replied MacNutt sourly. He was well aware of the reports suggesting that some of Hughes' appointees had profited handsomely during their time on the Shell Committee.

Denny grimaced. "I respect the man for what he has done, but he is a real loose cannon." MacNutt knew that Denny was being politic. He, like most permanent members of the Canadian military, despised Hughes. Their entire mobilization plan, which they had spent years working on, was scrapped by Hughes and replaced with one of his own. What infuriated the Canadian military the most was Hughes' annoying habit of promoting people on the spot without due regard to normal protocols and procedures.

"Do tell," said Atwell icily. He was a fan of the general.

"So what are we to do?" asked Stephens.

Hewitt shrugged. "There isn't much we can do at the moment. Does anyone have more to add? I think we covered everything in this week's agenda." Everyone shook their heads. Hewitt glanced at his watch. "It's lunch. I'm going to the Parliamentary Restaurant for a bite to eat. Anyone want to join me?"

MACNUTT RESIDENCE, LAURIER AVENUE WEST, OTTAWA
1:00 P.M., SATURDAY, DECEMBER 4, 1915

Katherine picked up the three newspapers on the front porch, took them into the kitchen, and placed them on the kitchen table beside a steaming cup of tea. Andrew insisted on receiving both the *Citizen* and the *Journal* to confuse the neighbours as to his true political affiliations. Everyone knew that if you were a *Journal* reader, you were a Grit, and if you were a *Citizen* reader, you were a Tory. To confuse them even more, he had a copy of *Le Droit* delivered too.

She sat at the table, placed *Le Droit* aside for the moment, and began reading the *Ottawa Journal*. She turned the pages, searching for the casualty list. When she found the list of dead and wounded, she ran her finger down the list carefully, reading the names. She was halfway down when there was a knock at the back door. She rose from her chair and peeked through the lace curtains. It was Nicole. She opened the door with a mile-wide grin. "Come in out of the cold!"

"Love to," Nicole replied cheerfully as she stepped into the warm kitchen and took off her coat.

"Isabelle not in today?" Nicole asked, referring to Katherine's part-time maid. Isabelle came in every second Saturday to clean the house, do laundry and, when needed, for dinner parties, to help prepare and serve meals.

"Yes, she needed to do some shopping," Katherine replied as she took Nicole's fur down the hallway. She called over her shoulder. "I just made some tea — help yourself."

Nicole found a rose-patterned china cup and poured out the tea. As she sat down at the table with it, Katherine joined her. Nicole gestured at the open page lying on the table as she flicked a lock of hair from in front of her eye. "Anyone we know?" she asked, slightly apprehensive.

"Not so far. Do you want to take a look?" Katherine asked.

"Anything else of interest?" Nicole asked as she slid the paper towards her for a closer peek.

"The usual," replied Katherine. "Henry Ford's peace ship finally set sail for Europe last Saturday."

"It's about time," said Nicole firmly.

Katherine snorted in disapproval. "Do you think he and his group will be able to stop the war?"

"It can't hurt," argued Nicole. "Just think of the lives they would be able to save if they could convince the Germans to end the war."

"I guess. I just don't trust the Huns," said Katherine emphatically. "What will stop the Huns from holding them prisoners?"

"I don't think so, Katherine. The Americans wouldn't stand for it."

"I guess you're right. So, what did you think of the meeting with the Count?"

"I think it went well, don't you?" Nicole replied.

"I guess."

"Ah," Nicole said knowingly.

"What?" said Katherine, irritated.

"You like the man, don't you," Nicole teased, amused.

"He seemed a decent enough sort," Katherine replied defensively.

"If you say so."

"Well, I say so. I'm no hussy, unlike Émilie," Katherine countered, making reference to Laurier's mistress.

"Katherine, that was most unkind," Nicole protested. "Not all of the rumours are true. She is a lovely lady." There had been much speculation about the relationship between Sir Wilfrid Laurier and Émilie Lavergne, much of it to do with her son's remarkable resemblance to Sir Wilfrid.

Nicole leaned forward conspiratorially. "But do you know who *is* having an affair? Clara!"

"Clara! You've got to be joking!" said Katherine.

"You wouldn't believe with who!" Nicole paused dramatically. "The butcher at Messier Butcher."

"No," Katherine said, putting a hand to her mouth.

"Well, yes," Nicole assured her, "there were always rumours concerning the shop and horses. We always thought it was about the meat."

Katherine giggled.

They were interrupted when a knock sounded at the front door. "Who could that be?" asked Nicole.

"It's Mrs. Ramsey," answered Katherine with a sigh. "She said she would be dropping by today." She rose to answer the door.

"Good morning, Katherine. How are you doing today?" asked Mrs. Ramsey. Her sable coat made her appear even rounder than she already was.

"Good morning, Mrs. Ramsey. I'm fine, and how are you?" returned Katherine as she closed the door.

"Fair to middling. Fair to middling. Who's that?" Mrs. Ramsey asked when she noticed someone in Katherine's kitchen.

"It's me," replied Nicole, coming into the hall.

"Ah, Mrs. Jenkins. I didn't expect you here today," said Mrs. Ramsey with a slight frown.

"I was in the neighbourhood and decided to drop in on Katherine," replied Nicole.

"Hmm…" replied Mrs. Ramsey stiffly. No one ever dropped in on Mrs. Ramsey. It just wasn't done. "I have to tell you, Katherine, that your husband can be an infuriating man," she said in an accusatory tone.

"What did he do now?" asked Katherine with a worried frown.

"It's what he hasn't done," Mrs. Ramsey said indignantly. "I was informed by the PM's office that he would come visit me at my convenience."

"And he hasn't as yet," said Katherine with a raised eyebrow.

"No, he hasn't. I have valuable information of an urgent nature." said Mrs. Ramsey.

"Really?" asked Nicole. "What kind of information?"

"It's very important information of a serious nature," reiterated Mrs. Ramsey.

"Ah," said Nicole. She winked at Katherine behind Mrs. Ramsey's back. "Then you must talk with him as soon as possible."

"That is what I've been trying to do," snapped Mrs. Ramsey. After a moment she recovered her composure. "I'm sorry," she said to Nicole, "but it's very trying."

"Of course. I'll let him know and make sure that he arranges a meeting with you as soon as he can," said Katherine. "Come into the kitchen. I have some tea that will refresh you."

"Ah yes, that would be pleasant," said Mrs. Ramsey and she sailed after Katherine and Nicole into the kitchen.

CHAPTER 6

Mrs. Ramsey was sitting royally on her flowered sofa. She glanced at the grandfather clock in the corner. It read five after two. She glanced at the tea table upon which were set a sugar bowl, two cups and saucers, a creamer, and a once-steaming teapot that was getting cold. She frowned. Beside the teapot was a pile of letters neatly tied in red ribbon.

She impatiently muttered, "Tsk, Tsk." A moment later she heard her doorbell ring. She heard the feet of her maid, Suzanne, trudging past the salon to answer the door. A moment later she led Inspector MacNutt into the salon. Mrs. Ramsey smiled to cover her irritation.

"Inspector MacNutt, madame," the maid announced.

"Thank you. Please ask if Myrtle needs any help in the kitchen," Mrs. Ramsey said as she dismissed her with a wave of her hand. Suzanne curtsied and left the room. Mrs. Ramsey turned her attention to the inspector. Coolly she pointed to a chair. "Please have a seat, Inspector."

MacNutt took a seat in the wing chair directly opposite her. "Thank you. I apologize for my tardiness. I was in a meeting with the PM."

Mrs. Ramsey was mollified. To be kept waiting by the PM was a piece of gossip to mention to the girls. "I see. Would you like some tea, my dear Inspector?"

"Yes, please," he replied. Mrs. Ramsey picked up the teapot and poured some tea in his cup, then filled her own.

She dropped a sugar cube into her tea, poured in some cream, then gave the cup a quick stir. "So here we are. Afternoon tea is one of the pleasures in life. One of the ties that bind us to the empire. Do you not agree?"

She took a sip as she waited for his reply.

"Yes, madame," he replied stiffly. He knew full well that Mrs. Ramsey had never set foot in England. She was born in Chelsea on the other side of the Ottawa River. She was, it was true, born of English gentry. Her father was the third or fourth son of some earl in England. Like most of the sons of gentry, who would not inherit lands, money, or titles, her father had emigrated to Canada to make his fortune. Made it he did by marrying the daughter of a rich lumber baron. Because of her English heritage she was more imperial than the Orange Lodge.

"And it makes discussing disagreeable things so much more pleasant." She paused, letting the silence build. It was a trick she had learned long ago: people ended up saying things they wouldn't normally to break an uncomfortable lull in conversation. She was vexed when MacNutt didn't comply. He simply took another sip.

The tension was nearly unbearable when at last he spoke. "Sir Borden mentioned you may have some information for me?"

"Yes, I do," she said with some relief. She pointed at the stack of letters on the tea table. "These are letters from my sister in Edmonton concerning German spies in that city."

MacNutt gave the pile of letters a quick glance but didn't make a move to pick them up. "I get regular reports from the RNWMP in the West, and I assure you, madame, that there are no German spies in Edmonton."

"My sister says otherwise," Mrs. Ramsey replied, patting the pile of letters, "and from what I've seen on the streets of Ottawa I believe her."

"I assure you everything is in hand," MacNutt restated.

"Mayor Morris of Pembroke says otherwise," Mrs. Ramsey said pointedly. "I just read in the *Ottawa Journal*. The mayor says that the Germans have over a thousand paid spies in Canada. Over a thousand. Why, if he hadn't taken personal action, they would have gotten the entire enlistment list for Pembroke. I understand that he has a difficult time with all the Teutonic population in Pembroke. And I know that we have the same problem here. Why is Denon still walking the streets? Everyone knows that he is a German spy. Why isn't he in the Kingston internment camp?"

MacNutt clenched his jaw. "Mrs. Ramsey, Denon is not a German spy. He does not pose a threat to Canada, and therefore, he is free to go about his business."

"We will see about that," she retorted. Once the words were out of her mouth, she realized she had made a mistake.

MacNutt pounced. "*We*? Who is we?"

"How dare you question me, Inspector," Mrs. Ramsey said indignantly. "If you were doing your job, I would not have brought this matter to the prime minister." She tried to cow him with her stare, as she had intimidated most of local Ottawa's society ladies. However, MacNutt wasn't cowed.

"Mrs. Ramsey. I keep the prime minister fully informed. I would suggest that you leave Denon be. These matters are best left to those who know best."

"I see," she said simply. She couldn't help the disgust she felt appear on her face.

"Very well then. I'll convey the information you have given to the PM." He placed his cup of tea on the table and rose from his seat, signalling the end of the interview.

"You've forgotten my sister's letters," she remarked.

MacNutt gave her a wry smile as he picked up the letters and stuffed them into his jacket pocket. "I'll have my men look at them. We will return them when we are done."

"Thank you. Suzanne will show you to the door." She picked up the silver bell and rang it. It took but a moment for Suzanne to appear at the salon's entrance.

"Yes, ma'am."

"Please take the inspector to the front door," she ordered.

"Yes, ma'am." Suzanne escorted the inspector from the salon. A few moments later she returned with a tall man dressed in a khaki military uniform. His shoulder boards indicated that he held the rank of major. He walked with a slight limp. He took the seat that MacNutt had vacated just a few minutes earlier with a bit of relief since the cold bothered his wound.

"So you see what I mean, Major?" Mrs. Ramsey said to Major Simms. The major had been out of sight in the neighbouring room, where he could overhear her conversation.

"I agree. He is not doing enough to allay my concerns for the governor general's safety," he replied sourly.

"We have to do something," exclaimed Mrs. Ramsey.

The major gave her a conspiratorial smile. "We are, madame. We are. We will be taking care of him in one form or another."

Mrs. Ramsey returned the smile as she picked up her teacup to take a satisfying sip.

TIMES SQUARE, MANHATTAN, NEW YORK CITY
3:30 P.M., SUNDAY, DECEMBER 5, 1915

Count Jaggi stood in Times Herald Square listening to a stump speaker. It appeared to the Count that the Americans had imported the British tradition of Speaker's Corner in Hyde Park. The woman standing pontificating on the stump was middle-aged, with features so stern that it would have intimated a crack Prussian regiment. It took several minutes for the Count to determine that her speech, a long, rambling affair, was a demand that women be given the right to vote. The men in the crowd hooted and howled derisively. Some shouted that she should go home and take care of her husband. Others jibed that with a face like hers it was unlikely there was a husband to go home to. Several women gave their husbands stern looks, telegraphing that if they said a word there would be hell to pay.

When she finished her piece, her place on the stump was taken by a young man. Once the man began speaking, the Count realized that he was a German patriot. He was slow and deliberate in his manner of speech. His main argument, with which the Count wholeheartedly agreed, was that Germany hadn't started the war — the British imperialists were responsible. It wasn't enough that they dominated half the globe. They wanted the rest. It was right and proper that the Americans stay out of the war, since it wasn't their dispute.

There were hisses and boos from the pro-English crowd. A few shouted that he should go back to Germany. Others shouted, "*Lusitania! Lusitania!*" recalling the British liner sunk by a German submarine on May 15, 1915, killing 1,198 passengers. Among the dead were 128 Americans.

The speaker retorted angrily with a raised fist, "Lies! British lies!"

Several men in the crowd responded with their own fists. The Count noticed that several groups of young men wearing cold stares had positioned themselves near the stage. He recognized trouble when he saw it.

"He's going to be fine," said a voice softly behind him in German.

"Will he?" the Count replied calmly in English. It was wise not to speak German in the crowd. He tried, without turning, to catch a glimpse of the speaker from the corner of his eye.

"You'll see," said the voice just outside his view.

The Count watched as another group of men appeared and arranged themselves in a protective screen around the man when he finished his speech and got off the stump. At that moment several burly police officers appeared with their billy clubs at the ready.

The largest approached the two groups of men and addressed them in an Irish brogue. "We don't want any trouble, do we, boyos?" The billy club slapped his left hand a couple of times. Both sides glared at each other and without a word exchanged agreed that another time, another place they would pick up their "discussion."

"See what I mean?" the man said as he stepped forward to stand beside the Count. He wore a white carnation, and a white silk handkerchief, folded into two points, was visible in his outside breast pocket. The signals they'd arranged. "We can't talk here. Meet me at Papa Joe's on 10th Street in an hour. You can't miss it."

Not waiting for the Count's acknowledgement, the man stepped forward and then blended into the crowd. The Count headed in the opposite direction in a leisurely stroll around the park. He paused from time to time, seeming to listen to other speakers, as he watched for the telltale signs of surveillance. A few in the crowd seemed like plainclothes police to him, but none gave him more than a cursory examination; they were scanning the crowd for troublemakers. He eventually made his way out of the square and headed towards what he believed to be the Hudson River. He wanted to ensure that he was clear of any tails before he met his contact.

PAPA JOE'S RESTAURANT, 10TH STREET,
MANHATTAN, NEW YORK CITY
4:30 P.M., SUNDAY, DECEMBER 5, 1915

As his contact had indicated, it wasn't too difficult for the Count to find Papa Joe's Italian restaurant on 10th Street. When he entered, he gave the room a quick scan but didn't spot his contact. Several patrons gave him a glance before they returned to their pasta.

A waiter initially showed him to a table near the window. When he asked for a more discreet table, the waiter's face brightened as he jumped to the wrong conclusion. The waiter led him to a small table in the back and then left for the beer the Count had ordered.

"Good afternoon, my friend. Sorry I'm late. Have you ordered already?" said the same voice that had spoken at Times Square. The Count peered above the menu at the plump man dressed in a pewter-coloured business suit.

"Just a beer. Nothing else yet," the Count answered as his contact took the chair across from him. "Would you like one?"

"*Ja*. A beer would be fine," he replied with a hint of a smile.

The Count signalled to the waiter for a second glass of beer. The waiter craned his neck to get a view of who was now sitting at the table.

When he saw a bald, middle-aged man sitting opposite the Count, he shrugged.

"So, how have you been enjoying New York?" asked the man, clasping his hands on the table.

Count Jaggi had spent the last day and a half visiting the tourist sites. That was the easiest way to quickly become familiar with the city in which he was to operate. He had done the same in Ottawa, but it had taken only half a day to get his bearings there. What gave him some excitement was dodging the local reporters who wanted an interview. He would have to deal with them sooner or later, and hoped it would be later. He also called on the Belgian consul in New York to introduce himself. There would have been undue speculation if he had not. For now his cover suited him, but he was already thinking about developing a new one.

"So what is good to eat here?" asked the Count as he read the menu.

"I'm afraid this is the first time I've been here. I thought it might be wise to meet you in some place other than those that I regularly attend," replied the man blandly.

The Count glanced up from the menu approvingly. "I'm glad that I'm working with someone reliable."

"Thank you," replied the man, pleased by the compliment, "but I'm rather new at this. Herr ... What do I call you?"

"Count Jaggi will do for now," replied the Count with a wry smile.

His contact offered his hand and the Count shook it. "And I'm Hans Müller."

"Pleasure to finally meet you, Herr Müller," replied the Count. The waiter approached the table with the beers.

"Have you been doing this for long?" asked the Count.

Müller lowered his eyes to his menu before he replied. "I work in the commercial section at the German consulate at 45 Broadway here in New York."

"For someone who is new at this game, you seem to know what you are doing," the Count remarked.

Müller blushed a pale pink. "From time to time I've had to negotiate certain delicate commercial contracts that require a degree of discretion," he explained. "I simply approached this in the same manner. It seems quite logical that way."

"I understand," the Count said. "You work for Dr. Albert then?"

"Yes," Müller answered, still focused on the menu.

"Ah. It was most unfortunate what happened to the doctor," the Count said in a sympathetic tone, observing Müller's reactions.

"What can one say?" Müller replied stoically.

"If you don't mind me asking, how did the unfortunate incident happen?" The Count kept his tone sympathetic. He wanted to know if Dr. Albert was a fool or just unlucky.

Müller sighed tiredly, as if he had told the same story so many times that it was becoming a chore to repeat it. He met the Count's gaze. "Dr. Albert takes the elevated train from his home to his office at the Hamburg-American building every day. He always carries the most sensitive papers with him. He likes to work at home, and he does not trust the security at the Hamburg-American building. He was always worried about British intelligence breaking into the office and stealing his papers. On that particular day, at his regular stop, he got off the train but left his briefcase behind. It was just a moment before he missed it. He hurried back on board and to his seat, but the British swine had already stolen his portfolio. He was beside himself."

"Are you sure it was the British?" the Count asked.

Müller shrugged. "Who else would it be? If it were the Americans, would they have embarrassed us by publishing the story in the *New York World*? No, it was the British who stole the papers and gave them to the press. The English swine."

"What can one say? It's an unfortunate state of affairs."

"*Ja*. But I regret there is more bad news," said Müller, eyeing his glass of beer.

The Count squinted. "Well, let's have it."

"The Americans have declared Captains von Papen and Boy-Ed *personae non gratae*." It was the most diplomatic display of censure that a country could apply to a foreign diplomat.

"It's not totally unexpected. When do they have to leave?"

Müller snapped the menu closed. "The Americans are determined that von Papen and Boy-Ed be sent home as soon as possible. We have only a couple of weeks at most. I wouldn't be surprised if they are gone by the new year."

"That soon!"

"*Ja*. I'm afraid so." Müller leaned towards the Count and whispered, "We have to get you up to speed with our U.S. operations quickly. We have three problems to deal with: the economic problem of supplying Germany and checking supplies to the Allies, the diplomatic problem of keeping America's friendship, and the military problem in Canada and Mexico. I'm arranging meetings with the appropriate people. I have one scheduled for tomorrow afternoon with Captain von Papen to discuss the military problem. Will you be available?"

"I'm not scheduled to return to Ottawa until next week."

"Why are you returning to *Kanada*?" asked Müller, perplexed.

"My orders are to conduct sabotage in Canada and in the U.S. Is that not so?" challenged the Count.

"*Ja*. But, the U.S. takes priority over Canada. We don't want you to waste time if it is of very little of importance or interest," Müller pointed out.

"Of course. But from time to time I will need to make excursions to Canada," said the Count.

"There isn't a woman involved, is there?" asked Müller, peering at him suspiciously. "I have heard of your reputation."

The Count met his eyes then smile thinly. "I have to maintain my cover. I promised that I would attend a couple of Belgian relief functions in Ottawa. In that capacity I will have access to quite a number of people who may be of interest to us."

"Makes sense," Müller said.

"There are several things I need to be clear about. The first is, who do I report to?"

"You will report to Ambassador von Bernstorff," replied Müller. "Through me."

"I see," said the Count with frown. He wasn't happy about that. He would have preferred to report directly to the ambassador.

Müller saw that the Count was not pleased by the news. "Count von Bernstorff does not want to meet with you nor does he want you anywhere near our embassies or consulates. It's nothing personal, Count. Our embassies and consulates are all under constant surveillance. Your being seen with the German ambassador would raise questions."

"I understand. So you are arranging briefings then?"

"*Ja*. The ambassador has been trying to slow down the Americans' attempts to declare von Papen and Boy-Ed *personae non gratae* for that reason. I'm trying to arrange meetings with the captains to brief you on the status of their operations. I'll let you know as soon as I find out their official date of departure."

"So we do not have much time."

"I'm afraid not," said Müller. "As I just have said, I'm trying to arrange a meeting for tomorrow afternoon. Where can I contact you?"

"I'm staying temporarily at the Waldorf Astoria until I can locate suitable lodgings. You can send me a note or telegram there," replied the Count.

"The usual code?"

"Yes."

"I can help you find lodgings," said Müller.

The Count gave Müller's offer some thought. It would save him some time, but then Müller would know where he was staying. The fewer who knew, the better. "I would prefer to seek my own lodgings. It will help me to become familiar with the city. But thank you for the offer."

"As you wish. Please, let me know if you need anything. I have contacts that can help," said Müller.

"I just need one thing for now," said the Count, grinning crookedly.

"What?"

"Would you like to order?"

Müller smiled for the first time as he picked up the menu. "Why not."

CHAPTER 7

MRS. MILLER'S FLAT,
GREEN STREET, LONDON, ENGLAND
1:45 P.M., TUESDAY, DECEMBER 7, 1915

"Go away or I'll be calling the police. Be disturbing decent folks in the wee hours," said an elderly voice through the green door. Sergeant Connell marvelled at the woman's audacity. He rapped on the door again.

"Madam. We're from Scotland Yard, Special Branch," he said, loudly enough to ensure his voice would penetrate the door.

There was a moment of silence before the voice said, "Oh dear. One moment while I get decent."

Connell turned to his superior, Inspector Owens, who gave Constable Donny Watson a questioning gaze.

"There are no other exits," the constable stated.

Good lad, thought Connell, *he'll go far if he manages to survive the inspector.* He gave a glance at the Matron Evelyn Hamstone, who stood behind Watson. Her long brown hair was pulled into a bun and was covered by a brimmed hat with a Women's Police Service badge displayed prominently on the headband. The woman was there to provide assistance with any female prisoners.

At the sound of a latch being unbolted, he returned his attention to the door. A grey-haired woman poked her head out and took in the scene. Her right hand clutched the top of her flower-patterned robe.

"Mrs. Emily Miller, you are being detained under the War Measures Act for sedition and treason," the inspector formally announced.

"Will you come in for tea?" she said cheerfully as she tightened her robe's belt.

When Connell arched an eyebrow, Owens shrugged and followed Mrs. Miller into her flat. Connell allowed Watson through before entering himself.

The saloon was furnished comfortably, with a sofa upholstered in a sturdy gold fabric, several slip-covered chairs, and other bric-a-brac collected over a lifetime. A large roll-top desk was set against the far wall. The lid was closed. The walls were covered with photos of family members and of the Royals. The doorway leading to a small kitchen was covered by a beaded curtain.

"You are aware that these are serious charges," Owens informed her brusquely.

Mrs. Miller surprised them again. "Oh yes. I've been expecting you."

"You were? But how? Who?" Owens sputtered. Connell felt a smile creep to the corner of his mouth. It wasn't often that the inspector lost his composure.

"It was terribly exciting while it lasted. Pity — but all good things have to come to an end, do they not?" The whistle of a kettle could be heard from the kitchen. "Please take a seat — I'll get the tea," she said as she turned towards the kitchen.

"Madam!" Owens said. "The matron will take care of it." Connell noticed that Hamstone's lips thinned slightly at Owens's command.

"Oh no," Mrs. Miller said. "I couldn't do that — you're my guests. Besides, it won't take but a minute."

Owens cocked an eyebrow at Hamstone, telling her to follow. It was not a good idea to let suspects wander about unattended.

"I'll be glad to give you a hand, mum," she said with a curt nod.

"If you insist," Mrs. Miller said. The two women left the two men standing in the saloon.

After a few moments Mrs. Miller emerged carrying a tray. On it were a brown Betty teapot, five cups, a creamer, and a small precious bowl of sugar. She set the tray on the tea table, perched on the edge of the settee, and poured some tea into each cup.

"Madam!" Owens interjected, barely containing his impatience.

"A moment, sir. Here's your tea," she said as she handed him a cup. "One lump or two?"

Owens licked his lips. Connell was aware of the inspector's sweet tooth. With the war on, sugar was becoming hard to come by, nearly as precious as gold.

"Two," the inspector said, sighing in resignation.

She turned to Connell with a questioning look. "I'm fine," he said, covering the cup with his hand.

"Madam, about our business," Owens said, trying to regain control of the situation.

"Oh dear, yes. As to why you are here," she said with pout. "They said it wasn't illegal. All I had to do was receive letters from strange places and post them to the new addresses. It was a bit strange, but they tossed a few bob into the bargain."

It matched the information they had on file. She was what was called in the trade a postbox. Enemy agents couldn't send their information directly back to Berlin, so they would send it to a post-box like Mrs. Miller, who would readdress them and forward them to a new address, in this case Sweden. It was a lucky break that they discovered Mrs. Miller. A clerk in the Mail Censor office noted the increase in mail to her and was curious. He lived in her neighbourhood and knew she didn't have very many relatives or friends. They quickly discovered that for a woman who never travelled, she received an unusual number of letters from abroad.

"Where are these letters now?" Connell asked.

Mrs. Miller gave Connell an enigmatic smile.

"I'm afraid, madam, that you will have to come with us," Owens said as he placed his cup on the tea table. He turned to Hamstone. "Matron, please ensure that she gets properly dressed."

"Yes, Inspector," replied the matron.

"I would like to finish my tea if I may?"

Connell glanced at Owens and said sadly, "I'm sorry. We'll have some Earl Grey for you at our office."

The matron led a disappointed Mrs. Miller into the bedroom and closed the door.

"Well, let's get started," Owens said, rising to his feet.

Connell and Owens started to search the small flat. Owens was of the slash-and-smash school of searching. He started with the desk, and as he opened the drawers he dumped the contents onto the floor. He shuffled through the papers to see if there was anything among them. Connell felt some sympathy for the tidy Mrs. Miller.

Connell continued his search of the rest of the flat until Owens motioned him over to the roll-top desk. Connell placed a vase back on the mantel and went over to the inspector, who was staring at the desk, perplexed.

"Do you note anything wrong with this desk?" he asked.

"Sir?" asked Owens. At first glance, it appeared to be an ordinary desk

"It's a big desk that could hold considerably more" — he indicated the papers on the floor— "yet it doesn't."

Connell examined the desk more attentively. He took a drawer and measured it against the side of the desk. The drawer was two inches short.

Owens raised an eyebrow. Connell tapped the wood panels. The sound was hollow. Connell examined the intricate cornice carvings of the panel. He pressed some of the raised carvings until one moved and a panel fell away. A large bundle of letters fell to the floor.

"Well, well," Owens said with a satisfied smile.

"Oh! It didn't take long, and I thought it was a nice hiding place," Mrs. Miller said, disappointed. She was standing in the doorway in a serge dress.

"It was the nicest hiding place I have ever seen," Connell said.

Mrs. Miller gave Connell a pleased smile. "You really think so?"

"I do," answered Connell with a brief grin.

Mrs. Miller lectured Owens sternly. "Now, my good man, I expect this mess you created to be tidied up. This is a respectable place."

Owens was so taken aback that he actually nodded. Connell bent forward slightly to hide his grin. Matron Hamstone took Mrs. Miller's arm and led her out of the room.

Connell then turned his attention back to the letters. "This is interesting."

"What?" Owens asked

Connell showed Owens a letter with a red one-cent stamp in the corner. The stamp said "Canada."

"Well, well," Owens said, "Evert will be interested in this. Just put it in the pile and someone will take a read it later."

Connell put the letter with the rest of the correspondence and they continued their search of the flat.

CHAPTER 8

For some reason that Katherine couldn't fathom, thoughts of Count Jaggi kept intruding at the most inconvenient times. She knew he was in New York and would be back soon, exactly when she was not sure. But something about the man irritated her greatly and intrigued her as well. The butcher had to call her name several times before he finally caught her attention. She inspected the roast that he had cut and placed on the scale. The needle pointed to five pounds. A pound or two more than she needed, but she could always use the leftovers for sandwiches. Katherine nodded and said, "That will be fine." The butcher smiled, picked up the roast, wrapped it in a heavy, waxed kraft paper, and tied it with twine. On the wrapper he wrote $1.65.

"Will that be all?" he inquired as he handed her the package.

"Yes," answered Katherine.

"It is a fine roast, ma'am, your husband will like this very much," he stated amiably.

"I'm sure that he will," she replied, trying to keep her eyes fixed on the man's face. She could feel them drifting downward, her curiosity getting the better of her. The counter blocked her view. Katherine's nose twitched in annoyance; she would have to have a word with Nicole. Why did Nicole have to tell her that Clara was having an affair with the butcher?

"I'm afraid that we will not be seeing many more of these," said the butcher with regret.

Katherine peered at him, hoping that she wasn't blushing. "Why?"

"It's the war, madame. It's getting harder and harder to get good sides of beef. They are being set aside for our lads overseas."

"We all have to make sacrifices," Katherine stated bluntly.

"Yes, madame. I don't mind making the sacrifices," he said, flushing. He was well aware that she had lost her son in France. He leaned forward and whispered, "But between you and me, there are some people who complain all the same."

As she placed the parcel in her green-and-pink-flowered grocery sack, Katherine said tartly, "I really don't understand some of those people's attitudes. Don't they understand that there is a war on?"

"What can one say, madame." The butcher shrugged helplessly. "You have a good day now."

"You as well," replied Katherine as she left the shop.

She paused to cross out the roast from her list with a pencil stub. She ran a finger down the list and sighed. She understood but did not care for the complaints. What did people expect during the middle of a war? Yes, it was true that it was harder and harder to get the simple little things that one had always taken for granted. And, yes, Christmas was fast approaching, and it was even more difficult than usual to get supplies for the festivities. They should make do, as she did, with what they could get, with as few complaints as possible. She dropped the list into her bag then pulled on the plum-coloured woollen mitts that didn't exactly match the purple shade of her winter coat. She pulled her toque down further to protect her ears from the cold. She was heading towards Eaton's when she recognized the elegant form of Beth Winslow walking toward her.

Beth broke into a wide grin when she saw Katherine. Beth was a friend and a former neighbour. She and her husband had lived a couple of doors down from the MacNutts before they decided to move their family into a new house in the Billings Bridge area. They needed the extra room for the four kids and Beth's mother. It was a bit remote, but they seemed to like it. It meant that Katherine couldn't drop in as frequently for a chat with Beth as she used to.

"Katherine!" Beth called, waving at her with a hand gloved in black leather.

Katherine waved back. "Hi, Beth."

"So how are you doing?" Beth asked cheerfully.

"I'm fine. What about you? I haven't seen you for a while?"

"Busy with the kids and my mother." Beth rolled her green eyes. "And with my volunteer work. What about you? I saw you give that note a serious going over. A love note from a secret admirer perhaps?"

Katherine laughed. "I wish. It's just my shopping list," she replied, patting her bag.

Beth laughed as well. "It can't be that bad, though the stores are a bit bare this year."

"I'm not going to complain about it," replied Katherine, suppressing the complaint on the tip of her tongue.

"So have you gotten all your Christmas shopping done?" asked Beth.

"I'm working on it. It's not easy," Katherine grumbled.

Beth pursed her lips. "It's the war," she said. Beth understood about sacrifices; she had two brothers in the army. One was a training officer at Val Cartier and the other was with the Army Corps HQ in London, England.

"So you are here shopping today?" Katherine asked.

Beth shook her head. "I'm just coming back from a meeting concerning the official opening in January." Katherine knew that she was referring to the official opening of the Sir Sandford Fleming Convalescent Home on Chapel Street. It was the first convalescent home to be opened in Ottawa for wounded Canadian soldiers.

"So how is that coming?" asked Katherine with a raised eyebrow. "I've heard that some of the wounded have already been moved in."

Beth's feather hat bobbed up and down briskly. "Just this week. We should be full by January. The official opening will not be until January 26. I know that you are busy helping the Canadian Club with recruiting for the 77th Battalion, and you are on the machine gun fundraising committee as well. But we really do need your help."

Katherine glanced away as she considered the request. "Okay, I'll help. I don't know where I will find the time. But I have one condition."

"Anything, I really need your help," Beth said.

Katherine grinned wickedly. "Come Christmas shopping with me."

Beth laughed. "Of course I'll come Christmas shopping with you." She hooked her arm through Katherine's. "So where you do want to start?"

"Eaton's."

"Eaton's it is," Beth said as they headed towards the department store.

HENDERSON TAILORS, SUSSEX STREET,
BYWARD MARKET, OTTAWA
2:35 P.M., FRIDAY, DECEMBER 10, 1915

Normally, MacNutt would have lingered in the Market to enjoy the warm weather that the clear skies had brought. The sunlight and the mild temperature were a welcome relief from the bitter cold and grey skies that had kept him indoors for the last few weeks. The only time he ventured out was to get a sandwich to eat at his desk from the Parliamentary Restaurant. He would have enjoyed a good bowl of good French onion soup, and he knew just the place in the Market where the broth was laden with onions and the cheese was extra thick. It seemed that a great number of Ottawans felt the same way, to the delight of the local merchants. The bitter cold had kept their customers close to hearth and home, and Christmas sales had been slow this year. But the day's crowd seemed to make up for their recent losses.

The bright smiles and enthusiasm of the crowds were infectious and seemed to lighten MacNutt's spirit. It lasted for at least several blocks, until he arrived at Henderson Tailor Shop. He was about to cross the street, but a tiny voice at the back of his mind said that something was out of place. He scanned the street, trying to identify what was bothering him. His eyes narrowed when he finally saw it. It was the group of boys hanging about on the corner. On such a pleasant day, they wouldn't be hanging around on this street. They would, to the amusement of the streetwalkers, be down on Murray Street, trying vainly to pick one of them up.

He was about to go up to the boys to have a quiet word when he was distracted by the man who exited the store with an iron shovel and began clearing some of the slush forming on the sidewalk in front.

Denon wielded the shovel with compact, precise strokes. He was a short, thin man who would always have a boyish look whatever his age. MacNutt knew that as a young man Denon had apprenticed as a tailor in a small village just outside Bern, Switzerland, barely earning a living for his young wife, Karla, and his daughter, Liesel. He had seen Sifton's ads promoting the bracing air and wide-open spaces of the Canadian prairies. But the ads alone would not have been enough to sway him to make the move. Then a recruiter passed through his village. Like most of the villagers, he had gone to the recruiter and heard him proclaim the virtues of a promised land where the streets were lined with gold and where there was land available for everyone. He didn't believe the streets of gold part, but if it were true that land was there for the taking, it might be worth the risk. He heard that a cousin, thrice removed on his mother's side, had emigrated to Canada, so he wrote his cousin a letter asking whether what the recruiter had said was true. When his cousin wrote back glowing accounts, he was convinced to take a chance. When he arrived in Canada, he did spend the first two years farming in the Pembroke area. Times were hard, but there was food on the table — until the depression of 1900 hit, wiping him out and costing him his farm. He moved his family to Ottawa, where he found his skills as a tailor in demand. When the owner of Henderson's decided to sell the shop, Denon had saved enough money to buy it. He decided to keep the original name, since most of his customers were English.

Denon had cleared several shovels of slush when he spotted Mac-Nutt peering at him. He gave MacNutt a glare then went back into his shop. MacNutt crossed the street and followed Denon in. The door chime tinkled above MacNutt as the door closed behind him. It was several months since he had been in the shop, though he had it under sporadic surveillance. There had been changes, he noted. The suit rack along the wall was not as full as it once was. Several shirt shelves were empty. The shop once prided itself on its selection of hats, but the collection had become rather mundane. Anti-German sentiment ran strongly in Ottawa.

Denon stood behind a highly polished oak counter, on which lay a brown-checked jacket. "So, Inspector," Denon said in strongly accented English, "searching for spies in my shop today. They are in the back if you want to arrest them."

"Please don't even joke about it," MacNutt replied sternly.

Denon sighed tiredly as he placed the jacket on a hanger and hung it on the brass and wood coat rack beside the counter. "It is true. There isn't much to joke about these days. So what would you like today?"

Before MacNutt could reply, he heard the sound of breaking glass and a thud on the floor behind him. He turned and gaped at a brown brick lying on the floor amid a heap of broken glass as more shards tinkled to the ground. He followed the glass to identify where the brick had come from and saw the broken window where the curtain now flapped in the breeze. Through the broken pane, he saw the group of young boys he had noticed earlier running away with scornful shouts of derision.

"*Gott in Himmel!*" Denon bellowed. MacNutt's instincts asserted themselves and he rushed out of the store and around the corner, but the kids were already out of sight. When he returned to the shop, Denon was staring forlornly at the mess. He gave MacNutt another frosty glare then went to the back of the shop. He was back in a moment with a straw broom. He began to sweep the glass into a pile.

"I'm sorry," MacNutt heard himself say.

Denon stared at him and yelled angrily, "You did not arrest anyone."

"I know who they are. I'll speak with their parents."

"Hmmph," Denon snorted in disgust. "The parents are the ones who probably gave those ruffians the bricks. And if you arrest them, they will not go to jail. Only Germans are the ones who go to jail today."

"We are at war," stated MacNutt stiffly.

"Yes, we are at war," retorted Denon. He stopped sweeping. "So why are you here?"

MacNutt glared at Denon. What he liked about the man was how he got directly to the point. "I'm investigating a complaint."

"What makes this complaint different from all the others?"

MacNutt simply shrugged. Denon examined the glass shards for a moment, then up at MacNutt again. "Mrs. Ramsey?"

MacNutt didn't say a word.

"I understand. She has been a nuisance of late," he continued as he went back to his sweeping. When he had made a neat pile, he went off for a dustpan. MacNutt glanced outside and saw that a small crowd of curiosity-seekers had gathered.

"Move it along, there is nothing to see," he ordered.

"*Ja*," Denon snarled when he returned from the back.

"Dirty Hun," yelled someone from the crowd. A moment later an Ottawa police constable arrived. He recognized MacNutt. When MacNutt indicated the crowd with a toss of his head, the constable acknowledged and began to disperse the onlookers. MacNutt studied Denon briefly. He was not pleased by what he saw but there was little he could do. He turned, left the shop, and headed to his office.

TENEMENT BUILDING, RIVINGTON STREET, LOWER EAST SIDE,
MANHATTAN, NEW YORK CITY
8:30 P.M., FRIDAY, DECEMBER 10, 1915

The Count arrived in the general vicinity of their meeting place about an hour earlier than the time indicated in the telegram Müller had sent him. They had made arrangements that any messages should be sent care of general delivery at the Western Union office a few blocks down from the Waldorf Astoria.

He had used most of the hour before the meeting wandering around the various side streets to get a feel for the neighbourhood. It was a busy one, the streets crowded with pedestrians, and a strong smell of German cooking permeated the air. He identified the familiar smells of Christmas cooking: baked fruit loaves, *bratwurst*, roasted nuts, *lebkuchen*, gingerbread, and *glühwein*. In snatches of conversation in a variety of German accents and dialects, he overheard neighbours discussing where they could get a decent *tannenbaum*.

When he arrived at the address, he saw a row of dilapidated brown brick tenements. There was very little traffic on the narrow street but a number of children were playing on it, laughing and shouting. No one paid him any attention as he went up the concrete steps into the building. Inside, he climbed a creaking flight of stairs to the second floor. He knocked at 2D.

"*Ja!*" asked the man who opened the door.

"Captain von Papen?" asked the Count quietly. The man matched the description Müller had given of the German military attaché. The captain was of medium height with a thin frame. He was wearing an expensive three-piece suit.

"Do come in," the captain said curtly, and he stepped aside.

The apartment he entered had two rooms. The main room contained a small kitchenette furnished with a battered pine table and four chairs. On the table were a bottle and two glasses. Also, on one of the kitchen chairs was a worn leather satchel. Across from the table were a plain tan sofa and two mismatched armchairs.

"Take a seat," von Papen said, pointing to one of the table's chairs. "So, you were able to find the place without much difficulty?"

"No problem at all," replied the Count. He took off his overcoat and placed it on the tan sofa. He took a seat at the pine table. The chair creaked in protest under his weight.

"Would you like a drink?" asked the captain as he joined the Count at the table.

"No, I'm fine." The Count preferred to keep a clear mind this evening.

"I have need of one," said von Papen in a tired voice. He filled one of the glasses.

"A convenient place you have here," said the Count.

The captain's nose wrinkled slightly with disgust. "It is convenient. It belongs to one of Paul Koenig's men."

"Good. I'm anxious to meet him. What's he like?"

"Like me, he is a Westphalian. He's a superintendent of police for the Hamburg-American line. He's brutish, but he has his uses," replied the captain. The Count nodded in approval. It was an asset having someone who worked with the German transatlantic passenger liners because it meant that he was familiar with New York's docks. And having someone who was willing to do the unpleasant work was always useful.

"So you've been sent to replace me," said the captain sourly.

"I regret that those are my orders," replied the Count in a falsely sympathetic tone. The briefing had not painted a flattering picture of

78

the man. Captain von Papen had risen quickly enough up the ranks. As the son of a wealthy aristocrat, he had been sent off to a military school. When he graduated in 1907, he was given a commission in the Kaiser's army. He had served on the German general staff for six years before his first diplomatic assignment as a military attaché at the German embassy in Mexico City in 1913. Then he was sent to New York at the outbreak of the war as the German military attaché to the United States.

"Ah yes, orders," von Papen said, staring at his drink.

"Is it definite that you will be ordered out of the country?" asked the Count.

The captain glanced at him with a pained expression. "It appears that way. Count von Bernstorff is trying to convince the Americans not to declare me *persona non grata*, but he is only delaying the inevitable. I'll probably be back in Germany by the new year."

"So we don't have much time then."

"I'm afraid not," replied the captain gloomily.

"So where do you want to start?" asked the Count in a crisp, businesslike tone.

The captain sighed sourly as he downed his drink. "Let's begin with our American and Canadian operations." He picked up the leather satchel, reached in, took out a map, and laid it on the table. He unfolded the map carefully, anchoring it on the table with the bottle and glasses. The Count moved to von Papen's side to get a closer view. The map was a standard one of North America.

"As you may know, shortly after the war began, Berlin ordered us to disrupt the Canadian railways to prevent supplies and troops arriving in Europe," explained the captain. "Especially after Japan entered the war and seized our Shantung peninsula in China. Berlin was afraid that Japan would start shipping troops through Canada to reinforce the Allies in France."

The Count nodded agreeably. "That should be easy enough."

"Not as easy as you think," von Papen said. "There are five railway companies in Canada: the Canadian Pacific Railway, the Canadian Northern, the Grand Trunk, the National Transcontinental, and the Intercontinental."

"All of them run from coast to coast?"

"Only the CPR, the Canadian Northern, and the Grand Trunk railways."

"So you need to disrupt all three train tracks, otherwise they will shift the trains from one track to another," said the Count thoughtfully. "Unless there is a critical point where you can strike at all three in a single blow."

Von Papen traced a line on the map with his finger. "There is. The CPR railway begins here at Point Moody in British Columbia and has to cross the Rocky Mountains to get to the prairies. To cross, the trains have to go through the passes starting at the town of Kamloops. The trains then emerge clear of the Rockies at Banff into Alberta."

"Tunnels or bridges?"

"There are a series of bridges and tunnels through three critical passes: the Eagle Pass, Rogers Pass, and Kicking Horse Pass. Setting explosives at any of the passes would disrupt train service for several months, maybe even as long as six months."

"Hmm. Sounds good. Have you put a plan in motion?" the Count asked.

The captain tightened his lips. "We have made an attempt. Von Brincken, one of our agents in San Francisco, had recruited Van Koolbergen to do the job for us. Von Brincken found out that Van Koolbergen had papers to enter Canada. He was going up for several weeks. He offered Van Koolbergen one thousand dollars for the use of his passport, and he refused."

"But one thousand dollars is a generous amount for a passport, is it not?" asked the Count.

The captain nodded sharply. "We acquire passports regularly in the Bowery. We pay about twenty dollars for a very good one. Instead he told von Brincken that he would be willing to take any mission, even blowing up bridges, if there was money in it."

"So he really wanted the money for the job," remarked the Count dryly. He could guess where the story was going.

"Yes. We negotiated a three-thousand-dollar fee as a down payment. We provided him a map of the CPR, told him where to buy the dynamite, where to plant it to produce the greatest damage, and gave him the schedule of the train."

The Count gazed at the map doubtfully. They had probably offered the man half of that and kept the rest. "Was he successful?"

"*Ja,*" said the captain with a thin smile. "Van Koolbergen told von Brincken to check the Vancouver newspapers for a story that a tunnel had caved in in the Selkirk Mountains."

"And did von Brincken verify his story?" asked the Count, picking up von Papen's tone.

"There was a story, but it didn't mention sabotage, only that one of the passes was closed temporarily," conceded the Captain.

"Could the Canadians have censored the story?"

"Possible," said von Papen with a shrug. "However, Bopp didn't trust Van Koolbergen. When Van Koolbergen didn't provide more proof, he refused to pay the man."

The Count regarded the captain expressionlessly, trying to keep his feelings to himself. He suspected that the Hollander had been in league with the British. If this episode was typical of the captain's methods, then no wonder the entire American operation was in a shambles. Now they had to deal with an unhappy agent who could seriously embarrass the German name in America. It was messy.

"Did you make another attempt?" asked the Count after a pause.

The captain shook his head. "The problem is finding someone reliable, familiar with the area, with explosives, and who speaks perfect English. We also have to get him out once he completes his mission. The Canadians have become quite paranoid about security. They've been arresting and interning anyone with a hint of a German accent."

The Count frowned. "Did you explore recruiting Sikh and Irish militants for these missions?" The Count was referring to two terrorist groups, the Society for the Advancement of India and the Clan na Gael. The Society for the Advancement of India was established in 1907 in New York. Its cover was to provide scholarships for promising Indian students. But it was really promoting sentiment against the British rule of India. It mostly thrived on the Pacific Coast and in British Columbia. The Clan na Gael was the terrorist organization dedicated to freeing Ireland from British rule.

"Our agents in San Francisco are currently recruiting Sikh sympathizers, but we do use the Irish to sabotage Allied shipping leaving New York harbour. I do not believe that they are very reliable, since most of them are well known to British intelligence," replied the captain.

"You said that the Canadians have increased security. Why?"

Von Papen crossed his arms and answered stiffly. "I decided that if we can't attack the CPR on the West Coast, we should attack the CPR on the East Coast." With his forefinger he indicated the border separating the state of Maine from the province of New Brunswick. "There is a CPR bridge that crosses the St. Croix into New Brunswick at Vanceboro, Maine, which carries heavy traffic from Canada and the United States. Most of these trains carry war supplies destined for the port of Saint John, where they are loaded onto ships. When the St. Lawrence is frozen, the bridge provides the CPR with the shortest link between Saint John and Montreal."

"I see." The Count could understand the logic of the plan. "Who did you recruit for the job?"

"Werner von Horn. A reliable man," said the captain. The Count doubted that very much but didn't say anything.

Von Papen replied defensively, "He was a German reserve officer in Guatemala. He was available. He knew explosives. And he volunteered to do the job."

"How much did he ask for the job?" demanded the Count.

"Seven hundred for expenses."

"Was he successful?"

"Yes, the bridge was destroyed," replied the captain with a touch of pride.

"Very good. If he is reliable, we can use someone with his skills."

The captain pursed his lips. "He is not available."

"Why?"

"He is currently in jail," said the captain with a scowl. "He was captured by the Maine authorities shortly after he destroyed the bridge. And the Canadians have been demanding that the Americans extradite him. They are arguing that he placed the bomb on the Canadian side of the bridge, therefore it was a Canadian crime and the Canadians should try him. I've convinced von Bernstorff that we must fight the extradition. Von Horn is a German army officer and the attack on the bridge was an act of war, not a crime."

"Was von Horn aware of the embassy's involvement prior to his arrest?" The captain reluctantly admitted this with a slow nod. "So, it's possible he could tell the American authorities of the embassy's role in the attack?"

"He's a loyal German — he wouldn't do that," retorted the captain hotly.

"I didn't mean to imply otherwise," responded the Count quickly. The captain glared at him. The Count gave him a wry smile, but he knew his question was valid. How loyal was von Horn? Would he tell the Americans all he knew? How much *did* he know? Now he understood why Ambassador von Bernstorff did not want any of their "special activities" to be linked to the German embassy.

"So where is he now?" asked the Count.

"He was sent to an Atlanta penitentiary after he admitted that he had planted the bomb as a German military officer. We were successful in convincing the Americans not to extradite von Horn to Canada."

"Well, at least he is not in Canadian hands," muttered the Count. "Now, I still don't have a clear picture of the Irish in our plans."

The captain leaned forward in his chair and grinned. "Captain Boy-Ed has been in contact with various Irish groups in New York and has been using them to plant bombs on Allied ships in the port. Boy-Ed will meet you in a few days and provide the details of his part of our operations."

"Very good," said the Count. The chair creaked as he leaned back to balance it on two legs. "What other plans do you have to disrupt Canada?"

The captain pointed to Lake Ontario. "One of our other plans was to obtain motorboats and man them with interned German-American naval crews. Arm them with rifles and machine guns then attack local shipping and mount raids on Toronto, Sarnia, Windsor, and Kingston from the American side of the border. A few Canadian lives would be lost, but the public hue and cry would pressure the government to keep Canadian troops at home to guard against future raids."

"Interesting," replied the Count. The chair's front legs thumped as he leaned forward to examine the map again. The plan was audacious and operationally feasible. Buying boats and guns and recruiting men he didn't view as a problem. There were plenty of German sailors stranded in the States because of the American internment of German civilian and military ships. The only problems he would face would be getting the equipment and men to the appropriate locations along Lake Ontario without attracting the attention of the American or Canadian authorities. If a single German sailor were discovered along the U.S.–Canada border, the entire operation would be blown.

"You presented this plan to von Bernstorff?"

"Yes. Of course," replied the captain with a slight wave.

"And?"

"He turned it down."

"Did he give a reason?"

The captain simply shrugged. The gesture irritated the Count, because he had a good idea why the ambassador refused to sanction the operation. The political fallout from such an attack would be immense. The Canadians would waste no time and spare no resources trying to locate the attackers. They would demand the Americans' help.

Up to now, Ambassador von Bernstorff had been able to argue that any acts of sabotage against Allied interests in the U.S. and Canada were the results of the zealousness of patriotic Germans. Although such actions were understandable, considering the circumstances, the German embassy did not sanction them or provide the perpetrators of such acts with any support. Of course, the Americans strongly suspected that the embassy was involved; otherwise Franz von Papen and Karl Boy-Ed would not have been declared *personae non gratae*. Even if none of his men were killed or captured, Ambassador von Bernstorff would be placed in an untenable position. Whether von Bernstorff had knowledge of the operation or not, the Americans simply would not believe his denials. At best, the Americans would demand that the ambassador be recalled. At worst, the Americans might enter the war on the Allied side. That was something that had to be avoided at all costs.

"Are there any specific military targets?" the Count demanded.

The captain pointed to the sliver of land between Lake Erie and Lake Ontario. "All shipping must pass through the Welland Canal to avoid Niagara Falls. That waterway is the only artery for the supply of grain coming from the Northwest."

"So you want to destroy the locks," observed the Count.

"Yes. We've already made one unsuccessful attempt, I'm afraid."

The Count was not surprised. "What happened?"

"The agent I recruited to lead the mission, Horst von der Goltz" — the Count gave a start when he heard the name — "indicated that the operation was betrayed."

"How?" The Count scowled.

"We don't know," admitted the captain reluctantly. "I had sent him to recruit men from the crew of a German ship in Baltimore. When he came back to New York, he picked up three additional men I had recruited for him for the job."

The Count returned to the map and imagined the concrete and steel used in the construction of a massive series of locks. "You're going to need a substantial amount of dynamite to severely damage the locks," he remarked.

"We had three hundred pounds, courtesy of Du Pont Chemicals," replied the captain in a self-satisfied tone.

The Count's chin dropped in surprise. "How did you manage that?"

"Through Captain Tauscher. He ordered the dynamite from the company for us."

"And they delivered it!" exclaimed the Count in disbelief.

"Yes," said the captain with a smirk. "It's quite amusing, actually. Von der Goltz had gone to the Du Pont barge near Black Tom Island, which is near the Statue of Liberty, to get the dynamite. He stored the explosives in his home before he and the other men left for Canada."

The Count shuddered. He didn't find the idea of sleeping above three hundred pounds of explosives at all amusing. "How was he going to get the dynamite to Canada?"

"Von der Goltz had the dynamite packed it into three steamer trunks when they took the train to Niagara Falls."

"They didn't check the trunks at the border?" demanded the Count in amazement.

The Captain shook his head. "When Von der Goltz got to Canada he said that he made a reconnaissance of the canal by making several flights over it."

"He flew over the canal in an aeroplane?" blurted the Count. This strained credulity. Where had he managed to get an aeroplane?

"That's what he said," replied the captain defensively.

"So what went wrong?"

"Von der Goltz aborted the mission. He claimed that he was being followed," answered von Papen.

The Count gave him a sharp look. "By whom?"

"He didn't say. It could have been the Americans or the Canadians. We don't know."

"Was he being pursued or did he get cold feet?"

"Von der Goltz is a trained military officer," replied the captain testily.

"I see," said the Count drily as he examined the map again. "Where is von der Goltz now?"

"In October, he sailed for Europe under a false passport. I gave him a letter of introduction to the German consul in Genoa. The last I heard he had reached Berlin safely. What happened to him after that I don't know."

The Count gave the captain a grim smile. "Actually, I do. He came to England, and he got himself arrested in mid-November. He's in the Tower awaiting execution."

"That is most unfortunate."

"Yes, most unfortunate, for him." The Count glanced back at the map of Canada. "About the United States? What kind of operations have you been running?"

"Nothing directly against the States. What we have been doing is buying American war supplies and trying to tie up companies' production capacity."

"How have you been doing that?"

"It's easy enough. We set up false companies. One of our more successful companies was the Bridgeport Projectile Company. We hired Americans to act as the company's officers then hired employees to manufacture the guns and ammunition. We paid them at a higher wage than the real companies to drive up those companies' labour costs. Bridgeport then ordered all the gunpowder it could to keep any from reaching the Allies. We also accepted orders from the Allies and kept them waiting for the deliveries that never came." The captain chuckled.

"And we used their money to supply our own troops," said the Count with a sardonic smile.

The captain smirked. "If it wasn't for the damn blockade... It's extremely frustrating that the Allies can buy and ship any type of war supplies, but we cannot."

"I know."

"I was glad when Berlin authorized operations to disrupt the American shipping of war supplies to the Allies." Von Papen pulled out his pocket watch to check the time. He frowned. "I did not realize it was so late. I'm going to have to leave soon."

"What time is it?"

"Ten."

"I believe I have a good idea of what we are doing. Have we covered everything?" asked the Count.

Captain von Papen was about to rise then scowled in irritation. "I forgot to mention that we have been trying to encourage labour disruption at American factories."

"How?"

"What we have been doing is creating labour organizations such as Labor's National Peace Council in Washington that are ostensibly for peace. What they are actually trying to do is create an embargo against munitions shipments. They were relatively successful, claiming they represented over a million labour votes and four and a half million farmers and got a fair amount of publicity. As we saw it, if the organization could actually represent organized labour, it could enforce an embargo, either by its potential voting power and influence or by a nationwide strike."

"Did they?"

"They once tried to get a special session of Congress to promote universal peace. They attacked the Federal Reserve Bank as munitions trusts. They even chastised the New York harbour master for allowing munitions ships to sail out of the harbour."

The Count grinned. "I like that very much. I like that a lot."

"I thought you would. There is more, but we don't have the time tonight," said the captain as he pulled out his timepiece again.

"As you wish. We'll have to arrange another meeting to finish our discussion," the Count said.

The captain pursed his lips. "We have to do it early next week. I'll be in Washington on Thursday."

"Are you available Tuesday, then?"

"I believe so. If not, I'll let Müller know. I'll also let him know to arrange this apartment again."

"Has this apartment been used for previous meetings? If it has, I don't think that it's wise to use the same place very often. We will need a new location," stated the Count with a raised eyebrow.

"That is most inconvenient. Where will we get one on such short notice?" said the captain, rubbing his moustache in irritation.

"We will have to manage, won't we?" remarked the Count. "When you come to the next meeting can you also bring any papers or records you have?"

The captain hesitated for a moment. "Would that be wise? I prefer not to carry such papers on my person. Especially after Dr. Albert's experience."

"I understand, but I'll need your papers to efficiently take over when you leave," insisted the Count, glaring at him.

"I would prefer that you come to my office," said von Papen, returning his stare.

"In all probability your office is being watched by the security services." Was the captain's reluctance to hand over the papers more than his worry about security — was he trying to hamstring the Count? "Could you have Müller bring them to me?" the Count suggested finally.

The captain's gaze finally broke away as he considered the Count's suggestion. "That would be acceptable. I'll get them to Müller at the earliest possible convenience."

"Good. And we will meet next Tuesday?" His instincts told him that the captain was not going to pass over his papers. But maybe von Papen would surprise him.

"As you wish," said von Papen with little enthusiasm.

CHAPTER 9

INSPECTOR MACNUTT'S OFFICE, EAST BLOCK,
PARLIAMENT HILL, OTTAWA
11:30 A.M., SATURDAY, DECEMBER 11, 1915

MacNutt was sitting at his desk, glaring at the work schedule and the vacation schedule, trying to make them balance. Christmas was always an administrative nightmare. At this time of year the workload was very light. Parliament was not in session and would not be recalled until mid-January — January 12 this year. The MPs and their staff were usually back in their ridings, visiting family and taking care of any constituency business. Normally, with the MPs gone, he could give his officers time off so they could spend time with their own families during the holidays.

However, this year it was not to be. Sir Robert and Lady Borden had decided that they would rather enjoy some warm weather rather than endure Ottawa's cold December. They were leaving next Monday, the thirteenth of December. They would spend two weeks travelling through the States. On the 21st, the PM, with Sir Charles Davidson, would attend a Canadian Club meeting in New York City. After that Borden and his wife would vacation in the southern states. They were slated to return on December 27. He was considering whether he should have one of his men accompany the PM or request the Pinks assign one of their men to guard him. Either way, he had to decide whose Christmas to upset.

The door opened and Lacelle hurried in with a frown. "Good morning, Sergeant," MacNutt said, welcoming a distraction from the schedules.

"*Bonjour*, Inspector, I have a telegram you might want to read," Lacelle declared, handing MacNutt a piece of paper.

"Who is it from?" the inspector asked as he accepted it. His forehead wrinkled in curiosity.

"The New York Pinks."

MacNutt ripped open the telegram. It was relatively long one. "You've read this?" he demanded when he finished. The sergeant nodded. "They lost von Papen the other night!"

"Yes, but according to the Pinks he was back in his office on Broadway yesterday morning," Lacelle stated.

"I know." MacNutt scowled as he leaned back in his chair. "But they didn't know where he was the night before. Who knows what mischief he was involved in."

"You would think he'd be too busy packing to have time to plot any new adventures," said Lacelle.

MacNutt snorted. "So what the hell was he doing that night?" he muttered as he reread the telegram.

"They checked his mistresses' places — he wasn't with either of them. So where in the hell was he?" Lacelle shrugged.

MacNutt glanced down at the vacation schedule on his desk. Then a thought struck him. "When is von Papen supposed to leave the U.S.?"

"There is no definite date as far as I know, but the first week of January seems to be when everyone expects him to be placed on a ship."

"So he'll need to brief his replacement over the next several weeks, won't he?" said MacNutt as he returned to the calendar.

"Seems logical," answered Lacelle.

"So where is his replacement?"

Lacelle bit his lower lip then suggested, "Maybe Germany hasn't sent him yet."

MacNutt started drumming his fingers on his desk. "I think they have, and he's already in New York. That is why von Papen lost his watcher. He was meeting with his replacement."

Lacelle brightened when he began to get the drift. "Wouldn't his replacement be a member of the consulate?"

"With the parade of people around the consulates? Our people, the Pinks, the New York Bomb squad, and the American Secret Service? I don't think so. You'd want to find someone as far away from the consulates and embassies as possible."

"If he is not going to have a direct connection with the embassies, he will be difficult to uncover," Lacelle pointed out.

"Yes, he will. However, though he might not visit the embassy, they will still have to be in contact with him. To give him his orders, contacts, and money."

"So if we watch the comings and goings of the embassy staff, they will lead us to him," concluded Lacelle.

"I hope so," said MacNutt with a predatory smile. "I certainly hope so."

"*Bien.* I'll let our people in New York know," Lacelle said as he turned towards the door.

"And let them know not to lose him this time," ordered MacNutt.

"Yes, sir."

"Good," MacNutt said, returning to the vacation schedule. "Oh, Sergeant!"

Lacelle paused at the door. "Yes?"

"I think just for my peace of mind we'll have Constable Briggs accompany the PM and Lady Borden on their vacation."

"He won't be happy," warned Lacelle.

"I know," conceded MacNutt, raising his eyes from the schedule.

"I'll let him know," Lacelle said as he closed the door behind him.

MacNutt went back to glaring at the schedule. With Briggs gone for two weeks, he'd have to do the entire damn schedule over again.

OTTAWA COLLEGIATE INSTITUTE, LISGAR STREET, OTTAWA
7:30 P.M., SATURDAY, DECEMBER 11, 1915

Bittersweet memories threatened to overwhelm Katherine as she passed through the grey sandstone-and-glass entrance to the Ottawa Collegiate Institute's foyer. Her grip on Andrew's left arm tightened, so that he winced. He murmured, "Are you all right?"

"Yes-yes. I'm fine," she stammered. "It just brought back memories."

Andrew understood. They had been so proud the day they enrolled Jamie as a student at the Ottawa Collegiate Institute. When the school opened in 1843 in Centretown, at the corner of Waller and Day, it had only forty paying students. By 1874, the school had moved to Lisgar Street to accommodate its expanding enrollment. The school was a progressive one, with high academic standards. It was one of the first schools to admit girls, around 1859, and some twenty years later it was the first public secondary school in Ontario to hire a female teacher. The school offered courses in classical and academic subjects. Most of the students were expected to go on to university. Jamie had done well in his studies and was at the top of his class. Andrew and Katherine had high hopes that he would attend one of the elite universities in the States or in England. But that was now not to be.

"If you wish, I'll take you home," suggested Andrew.

"Don't be silly. I'll be fine. What will people think if we just leave?"

"We can make our apologies," he replied.

"No, Andrew," she said firmly, straightening her shoulders. "I'm fine."

"Okay," he said, offering her his arm as they joined the line of club members waiting to get into the hall where the Canadian Club meeting was being held. The Canadian Club of Ottawa had been established to further Canadian patriotism through the study of Canadian institutions, history, politics, and economics. The association held periodic luncheons at which speakers of note were invited to deliver speeches on topics of interest. The men's Canadian Club was established in 1903 and the women's in 1910, and the MacNutts had been members since the clubs' inception. As a rule, the clubs held separate luncheons once a month and the slate of speakers reflected the particular interests and tastes of the club members. From time to time, when an invited speaker was of interest to both clubs, they held a joint luncheon. That was the case with this evening's invited speaker, Rustom Rustomjee, the former editor of the *Oriental Review of Bombay*, India.

They had barely joined the crowd when a voice behind them made Andrew stiffen. Katherine knew the voice well, and she gave her husband a "you behave now" glance before turning to face Mrs. Ramsey.

"Why, Mrs. Ramsey, this is a pleasant surprise," she said, feigning cheerfulness. She heard her husband snort under his breath. Mrs. Ramsey was not a member of the Canadian Club — she was an imperialist through and through — and Katherine hadn't expected her to be here this evening.

Mrs. Ramsey gave Katherine a quizzical glance. "I've always been fascinated with India."

Katherine nodded, which Mrs. Ramsey mistook for agreement. The real reason was that His Royal Highness would be attending this evening's speech. Beside the fact that the governor general was the clubs' patron, the Duke of Connaught had spent a number of years in India as the commander of the Bombay army. Mrs. Ramsey took every opportunity to ingratiate herself with the Royals. She viewed Andrew expectantly.

"Mrs. Ramsey," he said stiffly.

"I was pleasantly surprised you came this evening," she said brightly. Andrew knew what she was really trying to say. *You have time for a Canadian Club meeting, but you can't find the time to take my concerns seriously.*

Before Andrew could respond, Katherine quickly interjected. "Andrew, waiting in line has given me a thirst. Be a dear and get me and Mrs. Ramsey some fruit punch."

"Of course," he said with relief.

When he left to get the drinks from the bar, Mrs. Ramsey turned to Katherine and said, "I've heard from Count Jaggi."

"Oh, yes," responded Katherine in a neutral tone.

"He sent a telegram to inform us he will be in next week. Will you be available?"

"What day next week?" inquired Katherine cautiously.

"Tuesday."

"That should be fine," Katherine replied as the line moved closer to the sign-in and ticket table. "Where will the meeting be held?"

"I'll make the arrangements and let you know. But we will need some design samples of the posters promoting the event."

"I'll see what I can do," replied Katherine.

"Very well. I think that we should meet a half hour prior to the meeting with the Count to discuss our arrangements," said Mrs. Ramsey.

Katherine nodded. She felt a tap on her shoulder. Andrew was back with two glasses of fruit punch. Katherine would have preferred a glass of wine, but as the war went on it was frequently frowned upon to serve alcoholic drinks at public functions. "Here you go," he said.

"Thank you, Andrew," Katherine said as she took the glass. "Mrs. Ramsey was just telling me that Count Jaggi will be in Ottawa next week."

"Who?"

"Count Jaggi. Belgian Relief. I have mentioned him to you several times already," Katherine said with irritation.

"Yes, of course." Katherine didn't believe that he remembered. "So why is he coming back to Ottawa?"

"He's in New York fundraising for Belgian Relief. The Count has agreed to give a speech in January as a special fundraising event. He's coming up to attend a planning session, and the Belgian Relief sale being held next week at the Château," said Mrs. Ramsey.

"That is interesting. I wouldn't mind attending the speech."

"I'll make sure that you do," said Katherine firmly.

"Yes, dear." There was an awkward pause then Andrew said, "If you don't mind, Katherine, could you get my ticket for me? I need to check on the governor general's security arrangements."

This was news to Katherine, but she managed to keep the surprise from her face. She knew what he really meant was, *If I don't leave now, I'll strangle her.*

"Go ahead, dear. Don't take too long."

"I won't be but a few minutes." Andrew gave her a glance before heading for the side entrance where the head table guests were meeting. She understood his message: *And* don't *let her sit at our table.*

The Count sat at a table in the relatively upscale saloon he had found just off Broadway. He could have taken a seat at the bar, but he wasn't inclined to make conversation with relentlessly cheerful Americans. He needed a few moments alone to gather his thoughts, and he had a lot to think about. The last few days had been very busy, chaotic even. On occasion, he felt overwhelmed by the task that his superiors had assigned him. He mentally reviewed the list of items before him. At the top of his list was the problem of personnel. Most of the men that Captain von Papen had recruited, while they were for the most part enthusiastic, were not very reliable. The quandary he faced was how to get rid of them without them running to the Americans or British. He had two options: to keep paying them, even if they did nothing, or to put a bullet in their heads.

He sighed as he motioned to a waiter for another glass of Jack Daniels. He still couldn't believe his discovery that von Papen was paying his agents with cheques. Of all the silly and stupid things to do, that was the most idiotic. He shuddered at the thought of an agent being caught with a cheque in his pocket. Incredible.

"Good evening, may I join you?" asked Müller. The Count peered at a fatigued Müller, as he took off his overcoat and draped it over the empty chair to his right. He placed his hat on the coat and tossed his gloves into the hat.

"Go ahead," said the Count.

"So how was the meeting with the captain?" asked Müller. The waiter splashed a hefty shot of whiskey into a glass.

"Informative," replied the Count. "A number of questions have arisen."

"I'm not at all surprised." Müller grimaced slightly as the liquid passed his lips.

"I have to ask. Does the captain make a habit of paying his agents with cheques?" asked the Count in a matter-of-fact tone.

Müller's head whipped up, and he stared at the Count. Then he flushed as the implications of the question sank in. "That was mentioned at the meeting?"

The right corner of the Count's mouth twitched but he remained silent.

"How did you discover?" asked Müller.

"That is unimportant," said the Count tersely. "What is more important is that we stop it immediately. All agents should be paid in cash so that they cannot be traced to us."

"I agree. But until the captain transfers control of the accounts, there is very little we can do," Müller pointed out.

The Count swore. "I need a copy of all the captain's accounts, cheque books, and any other papers that he might have, now!"

"Did you ask the captain for his papers?" asked Müller. The Count's eyes met Müller's. "I asked. He said he would provide them. But I got the impression that he really wasn't very receptive to the idea."

"I see," said Müller. He did understand. He'd had his difficulties with the captain himself. "So what do you want to do? Would you like me to ask the ambassador to order von Papen to give us the papers?"

The Count started to speak then stopped to consider his options. After a few moments he ordered, "Wait till I get back from Ottawa next week. I asked him to provide them to you, because I really don't want to go near his office. If he hasn't provided you with his papers, then you will have to take it up with the ambassador. Von Papen will be gone in a couple of weeks and the damage has already been done. Does von Papen have the only copies?"

"I'll have to dig into it. I believe that he has the only copies," answered Müller sourly.

"Please find out. We will have to set up new accounts and move the money into them just to be on the safe side."

"Agreed. But it will take some time," Müller warned. "And do you have someone reliable to do the work? There is a lot of money involved."

The Count gave a resigned sigh. It came back to recruiting good, reliable people. "We'll have to do what we can and as soon as we can. If the British get their hands on his papers, we will be in serious trouble."

"Agreed again. But the likelihood of the British getting their hands on his papers is extremely low," said Müller confidently. "He knows the importance of keeping documents safe after Dr. Albert had his papers stolen on a train. No one is likely to forgotten that incident where the

British Secret Service stole Dr. Albert's papers on the subway. I'm also certain that before he leaves he will provide us with all his papers."

"If you say so," replied the Count skeptically.

"I'll see to it," Müller announced. "When do you want to arrange the next meeting? Didn't you say that you will be in Ottawa a few days?"

"Yes. I have some Belgian relief work to do there."

"Is it important?" asked Müller.

"It is," replied the Count. It was true that one of the main reasons he was going to back to Ottawa was because of Katherine MacNutt, who intrigued him. But he did have an operational reason for going. If his own instincts could be relied upon, there was a chance he could turn Katherine, which would give them access to the local security forces' information. That access would be priceless. However, until he had turned her, he wasn't about to explain his motivation to Müller. That she was desirable was icing on the cake.

Müller saw that the Count was not in the mood for an argument. Resignedly he said, "Who do you want to meet with next?"

"I need to meet your forger. I need a new set of identity papers,"

"Why?"

"I always like to have a second set of papers, just in case things go wrong."

"I see," replied Müller.

"Good," said the Count. "Also, when I get back, we will need to sit down and discuss what we can do concerning our British friends."

"What do you have in mind?" asked Müller warily.

"I would like to have a clearer picture of the American and British security forces that we are facing and what measures we need to take to thwart them," said the Count with a cold smile.

"I like it," replied Müller, now grinning.

"It came to me when I passed 60 Broadway, and with all those agents standing out in front, that we need to do something," explained the Count. "We can't have uninvited guests crashing our little parties, don't you agree?"

Müller laughed. "I agree."

"Good. Let's finish our drinks then, before we go," the Count said, and he poured more Jack Daniels into Müller's glass, then his own.

CHAPTER 10

Count Jaggi was sitting at a conference table strewn with papers and posters of various designs. The expectant faces of Katherine, Mrs. Ramsey, Kim Crane, the association's treasurer, and Nicole waited tensely.

"Quite nice." The Count beamed at the ladies. "Quite nice indeed."

"I'm glad that they meet your approval," Mrs. Ramsey said in a satisfied tone.

"Nicole, have we received all of the poster samples from the printers?" asked Katherine.

Nicole's lips pursed. "I'm afraid not. I spoke with him this morning. He'll try to have them by this afternoon. He's doing them for us for free. So if he gets a paying job, we drop to the bottom of his priority list."

Mrs. Ramsey snorted in disgust. "You tell him, young lady, to stop profiteering from the war. It's a disgrace putting money ahead of one's duty to one's mother country and king. I'll have a word..."

The Count saw Katherine's lips thin slightly before she interjected. "Mrs. Ramsey. Nicole is pushing him as far as she can."

From the corner of his eye, the Count caught the glare Mrs. Ramsey shot at Katherine.

"But he's been very kind and generous to us. I don't want to upset him," Katherine said, returning Mrs. Ramsey's glare with a formidable one of her own. Despite himself, the Count felt his opinion of Katherine rise. She solicited the table for comments. "So is there anything else?" she asked a touch sharply.

The rest glanced surreptitiously at each other. Feeling somewhat intimidated, they didn't speak up. Besides, everything that could possibly have been said was said during the meeting.

"Excellent then. Everything seems to be going well. Don't forget the meeting next Tuesday," Katherine said with a smile in an effort to reduce the sting of her tone.

Count Jaggi gently coughed to get their attention. "Mesdames and mesdemoiselles, I must say a few words of thanks for the hard work you have been doing on my behalf." He was pleased by the women's reaction to his compliment.

Nicole rose gracefully from the table. "Thank you, Count. I think we've accomplished a lot today."

Kim said, "Yes, we did." She cringed when she turned toward to Mrs. Ramsey and whispered, "Oh, Mrs. Ramsey, I just remembered that the vicar asked if you'd have a moment after the meeting to discuss the Christmas party."

Kim's mouth opened slightly in surprise when Mrs. Ramsey cheerfully answered, as she pushed herself heavily from her chair, "Ah yes. I was hoping to have a word with him. I'll be back in a few minutes, and then we will have some tea."

The Count acknowledged with a raised eyebrow. Once they left the room, he turned his attention to Mrs. MacNutt. She held his eyes a touch longer than what might have been proper for a married woman before lowering her gaze to the papers on the table. She began shuffle the samples into order.

"Everything appears to be going well," he said, trying to draw her out.

"There are a few minor problems, but nothing we can't handle," she replied, studying him again. He felt her blue orbs touch him in a way he hadn't felt in a long time. He turned the feeling off.

"It's a pity about Borden not being able to attend," she said.

"I didn't know that. Is there a particular reason?"

"He and Lady Borden are vacationing in the southern United States for a few weeks," explained Katherine.

"Is that why Madame Ramsey does not seem to be herself today?" He was only mildly interested in why Mrs. Ramsey was more abrasive than usual.

"More the fact she also sees spies under her bed. As to why they would be under *her* bed, I wouldn't know. There hasn't been anyone in or under her bed in years." Katherine blushed slightly. "That was a dreadful thing for me to say."

The Count was amused by her display of modesty. "But accurate, I believe." He paused for a moment. "Excuse me, Madame MacNutt. Count Jaggi is so formal. Please call me Lucien."

"If you wish," said Katherine, pleased.

The Count looked at her, trying to convey warmth and affection through his eyes. His gaze made her uncomfortable, forcing her to turn away.

"You-you will be attending the Daughters of the Empire sale on Thursday?" Katherine stammered.

"I really would like to but I'm not certain at the present time. I have some commitments in New York, and I was planning to take the 4:45 p.m. train that evening."

"Oh, you must attend!" she exclaimed. "The Madeleine de Verchères Chapter is organizing it. The Royal Highnesses have announced that they will be attending. We will have several tables were we will be try to sell items that we managed to get donated. Mrs. Goor, the wife of the Belgian consul, will be there. Of course, she will be selling Belgian objects. There will even be an evening dance."

"A dance, you say?" Count with interest.

"Yes," Katherine said shyly.

"With a proposal like that, how can I refuse? I can always take the train in the morning," the Count said with a suggestive grin.

Katherine blushed. "My husband will be accompanying me."

"Your husband is a most fortunate man," the Count proclaimed.

"I suppose," replied Katherine with a hint of doubt. "So I'll see you there on the Thursday."

"I'm certain that I will be seeing you much sooner than that," replied the Count.

"You've received your invitation to the New Year's levee?"

The Count froze a moment in fear and suspicion. He kept his tone neutral. "I received my invitation a short while ago. How did you know that?"

Katherine gave him a knowing smile. "Dear Count." She paused for dramatic effect. "Lucien. There are few secrets in Ottawa!"

"I will have to remember that," said the Count, his grin returning. "I have not yet decided. I may if I can come back from New York. Will you be attending?"

Katherine's smile waned slightly before she said, "I'm not sure at the moment — I will have to check with my husband. He may be working." Andrew had told her that he would be supervising security just the day before.

"On New Year's Eve?" he asked. What could be so important that he would be working on New Year's Eve?

"Unfortunately, it may be so."

He sensed she didn't want to discuss it further. "If you have a need of an escort, I would be delighted to offer my services."

"Thank you. I'm flattered, I think my husband may not be," she teased.

She didn't move away when he stepped closer. His nostrils flared when he caught the whiff of her perfume, exciting him. At the sound of the door opening, she stepped quickly away. Irritated, the Count was starting to scowl as he turned towards the interruption.

Mrs. Ramsey was viewing them beadily. The way she stared at them seemed to imply that it wasn't proper for a married woman to be alone with a single man. Appearances were important; he knew well how fragile a woman's reputation was.

The Count turned his scowl into a friendly grin as he said cheerily, "Ah, Mrs. Ramsey, just the person we wanted to see. Perhaps you can settle something that Mrs. MacNutt and I were discussing."

"Of course, if I may be of service," she asked suspiciously.

"Excellent," exclaimed the Count as he drove over Mrs. Ramsey's suspicions. "Mrs. MacNutt and I were discussing the merits of having a slide show. What is your opinion?"

Mrs. Ramsey instinctively started to say no. Then she bit her lip when she saw the Count's beaming face. She wasn't a great fan of the new fangled slide shows. She reluctantly said, "I think that it is a splendid idea. We will have to bring this up at our next meeting."

"By all means. Can you place it on the next meeting's agenda?"

Mrs. Ramsey couldn't completely hide her distaste when she agreed. "It would be my pleasure."

"Capital," the Count declared. He pulled out his pocket watch and checked the time then frowned. "I'm afraid that I must take my leave. I have another appointment at noon."

"Who are you meeting?" Katherine asked curiously.

"One of the governor general's aides. I'm meeting him at the Parliamentary Restaurant," replied the Count.

"Which aide?"

"A Major Simms."

"Ah yes. Major Simms," muttered Katherine coolly. She winced when she glanced at Mrs. Ramsey.

The Count caught the glance. Was the aide a friend of Mrs. Ramsey's? He decided to ask her. "You know of the major?"

"Oh, yes. He is a dear friend of mine," answered Mrs. Ramsey brightly. "I'm sure that you will find his company quite enjoyable. He's a fine gentleman."

"Excellent," said the Count. He did not put much faith in Mrs. Ramsey's recommendation, but one never knew. Simms could be a fine gentleman with bad taste in women.

"Count Jaggi, why don't I escort you to the Hill? I would like to see if my husband's available for lunch, and his office is on the Hill as well," Katherine suggested. The Count thought he saw the hint of an encouragement.

"I would be extremely pleased to have your company," he said grandly. He was certainly pleased to have a chance to speak with Katherine alone without interruptions.

"I'll get my coat," she said as she left the room.

"Mrs. Ramsey," the Count said with a nod, "until our next meeting."

INSPECTOR MACNUTT'S OFFICE, EAST BLOCK,
PARLIAMENT HILL, OTTAWA
12:30 P.M., MONDAY, DECEMBER 13, 1915

Katherine entered her husband's office without bothering to knock. Sergeant Lacelle was sitting at his desk with his back towards the door, hunched over his typewriter and muttering curses under his breath. The top of the typewriter was opened, and from the stains on his hands, Katherine knew that he was trying to replace the typewriter's ribbon.

"*Bonjour*, Sergeant. Still having trouble with it?" said Katherine.

Startled, Lacelle snapped his head towards her. "Ah, Madame Mac-Nutt. *Oui*, it's always the same problem," he muttered as he raised his ink-stained hands.

"I'll let you work on it peace," she said amused. "Is Andrew in?"

Lacelle pointed at the inspector's door.

Katherine opened the thick, leather-padded door to her husband's office and slowly poked her head in. Andrew was at his desk, his cheek propped on his left hand, staring at the folder open before him. He looked up, irritated, when he felt the slight breeze that meant someone had entered his office without bothering to knock.

His eyes widened when he saw Katherine. She rarely visited his office. They had an unspoken agreement that she'd only come when the job required it, or in an emergency.

"Katherine, is there something wrong?" he asked with concern.

"Everything's fine," she answered with a smile.

"Aren't you supposed to be at a meeting for Belgian relief?"

"Yes. But we finished early. It's past noon."

"It is?" Andrew pulled his watch from his vest and grunted when he saw that she was right. "So the meeting went well?" he asked as his attention returned to the papers on his desk.

"The meeting was fine. We got a lot done," Katherine replied, irritated by her husband's lack of interest.

"Because of or despite Mrs. Ramsey?" he said absentmindedly. Katherine regarded him with annoyance, which Andrew caught with the corner of his eye. As he closed the folder to focus his attention on his wife, he suppressed his own irritation. Of late he simply never knew what would make her mood change. "And this Count?"

"Jaggi. Count Jaggi," she said warmly.

Andrew cocked an eyebrow. "Ah, yes. What is he like?"

"I like him. He seems to be a nice man. He doesn't seem to have the same arrogance that some of the British have," she explained. Andrew couldn't help noticing the way her face lit up when she spoke about the Count. He felt a pang of jealousy, and now his curiosity was piqued.

"Why don't you take a chair and tell me about it," he suggested.

"I can't. One of the reasons I came was that I couldn't get to the bank, and they are closed for the rest of the day," Katherine replied defensively.

"You've spent your stipend already?" Katherine nodded. "Not a problem, dear," MacNutt said, removing two five-dollar Bank of Montreal bills from his wallet and handing them to her. "Christmas is coming up quickly, and we need to talk about gifts for the family."

Andrew noticed a shadow crossing Katherine's face. She sighed. "I know. I've been wracking my mind as to what to get everyone this year. Maybe wandering around the Market will give me some ideas."

"I suppose," said MacNutt. He was really curious about this Count, but now was not the right time to interrogate his wife. He suggested instead, "Well, make sure that you are bundled up warmly. Winter's nearly here."

"I'll keep warm." Katherine left the office.

PARLIAMENTARY RESTAURANT, CENTRE BLOCK,
PARLIAMENT HILL, OTTAWA
12:45 P.M., MONDAY, DECEMBER 13, 1915

After he escorted Katherine to the East Block, the Count hurriedly headed towards the Centre Block for his meeting with Major Simms, one of the Duke of Connaught's aides-de-camp. When he was about twenty feet from the main entrance, he heard the first gong of the tower's clock bell ring. He glanced up at the clock face, reminiscent of London's Big Ben, and saw that it had struck 12:45. He would be late but doubted the aide would start without him.

At the entrance, the duty constable, Constable Edwards, stopped him. "May I help you, sir?"

"*Bonjour,*" the Count said, touching his hat with his fingers. "Yes, you can. Can you tell me where I can find the Parliamentary Restaurant?"

"Is someone expecting you, sir?" Constable Edwards earnestly demanded.

"*Oui*, I believe that someone is," replied Count, amused by how seriously the youth took his duties.

"Your name, sir?"

"Count Jaggi."

"A moment please." Edwards checked names on a clipboard he retrieved from under the desk. He grimaced and blurted, "You are here to meet Major Simms?"

"*Oui*, monsieur."

Edwards scowled. "If you'll wait a moment I'll get a messenger to escort you. I apologize for the inconvenience, sir. The restaurant is on the fourth floor. You will need to take the first corridor on your left, and once past the House of Commons there will be a set of elevators. The messenger will walk with you and direct you to the restaurant."

"Is this necessary?"

"I'm afraid so, sir. It's part of our security measures," said Edwards. He was not about to explain the various security measures that had been put in place since the war started. One of the first things Edwards was taught was that the Centre Block was under two separate administrations, one for the House of Commons and one for the Senate. Each had its own protection service and fire watchmen for its side of the building. The Senate had felt it would be able to protect with their available staff, as did the House of Commons. Edwards' commissioner, Sherwood, felt that the protection was inadequate, so he suggested that all the entrances be closed, except for the main one. He had seven uniformed constables assigned and stationed at key corridors in the building when the House was in session. Two plainclothes sergeants roamed the building to supervise the constables and to keep a sharp look out for suspicious persons. Edwards' job was to ensure that all visitors not on the list were escorted by a messenger. The MPs and senators were required to provide

FRANK ROCKLAND

the main entrance with a list of expected visitors. God help him if he didn't follow procedure.

"Please have a seat, sir," suggested the constable. "A messenger will arrive shortly." He held open the large wooden door. Inside Jaggi found himself in the marble white foyer with three hallways radiating north, east, and west. On the floor he saw eight provincial coats of arms inlaid in the marble, one of which was blank.

A blue-uniformed messenger, in his mid-forties and balding, appeared before the Count. "Count Jaggi?"

"Yes."

"Please follow me, sir," the messenger ordered briskly.

He turned on his heel and took the hallway to the Count's left. The Count examined the portraits that lined the hallway. They were quite badly painted, but he supposed they were all Canadian statesmen. Once of the corridors that ran towards the north was lined with pine-panelled wardrobes.

When the messenger saw the Count looking around the corridor, he said, "That's the House of Commons, sir. If you wish, you could have a tour after your meeting with Major Simms."

"Thank you, I will," replied the Count. The messenger continued to the lifts just past the House of Commons chamber.

"Hi, Phil. Which floor?" asked the tired lift operator, a boy of sixteen.

"The Parliamentary Restaurant," declared Phil. "He's meeting Major Simms."

"Okay," the operator replied. He pulled the lever and the elevator rose to the fourth floor. The boy pulled open the elevator doors. "Watch your step!" Phil and the Count followed the corridor to their left that took them to the Parliamentary Restaurant.

"*Merci*," Jaggi said. He reached for a coin in his breast pocket.

Phil raised his hand in polite refusal. "*Il n'est pas nécessaire*," he said with a wave. The Count acknowledged with a slight nod.

"Ah, Count Jaggi," the *maître d'* said cheerfully, "how are you today?" The Count regarded the man with surprise. He didn't recall having met the man before. The *maître d'* just gave him a beaming smile.

"I'm well today, *monsieur*. I'm to have lunch with a Major Simms."

The *maître d'* nodded. "He has been expecting you, sir. Please follow me." He led the way to a table set near the window. Through the windows Jaggi saw the mist from the Chaudière Rapids rising in the afternoon sky. The mist slightly obscured the small cluster of buildings that belonged to the city of Hull.

The Count's attention, however, was focused on the khaki-clad officer already seated at the table. The major rose slightly and offered his hand. The Count quickly assessed the major. He appeared to be a typical, arrogant, high-handed British officer. If he had any ambition — and the Count was certain he did, because the major's uniform fitted too well to be anything other than custom-tailored — he would chafing at being stationed in a backwater town like Ottawa. The Count saw the major's grey eyes surveying his Brooks Brother suit with approval. He knew what the officer was thinking: *For a foreigner, he knows how to dress well.*

"Ah, Count. It's a pleasure to finally meet. I've heard so much about you. I'm an aide-de-camp to their Royal Highnesses, the Duke and Duchess of Connaught," Simms boomed. From the accent, the Count placed him as country gentry. Not well off but doing admirably.

"I apologize for being late. I was delayed at the front entrance. But, it is a pleasure to meet with you," the Count said, shaking the man's hand.

"You were delayed at the front entrance, you say?" inquired the major with a frown, gesturing to a seat.

"Yes," answered the Count as he sat uncomfortably across from Simms. He never liked having his back to the room. "It seems that security is quite tight. They wouldn't let me in unless I stated my business and with whom I was meeting."

The major scowled. "I did leave instructions at the front entrance."

"They did have me on their list. They indicated to security that I needed to be escorted."

"I will have a sharp word with them. The escort was unnecessary," the major said tartly.

The waiter interrupted. "Would you like to order a drink?"

The major glared at him. "I'll have a glass of red wine."

"I would like a glass of red wine as well." The Count would have preferred a beer. He doubted that ordering one would impress the major, who was vetting him before arranging a meeting with the Royal Highnesses.

"I'll be back in a moment," said the waiter with hint of contempt.

"How are the Royal Highnesses? They are in good health, I hope?" the Count inquired.

"They are quite well. The climate here is quite healthy."

"The weather is quite invigorating," the Count observed.

"That it is. That it is." There was a hint in the major's tone that he would have preferred a warmer climate.

The conversation paused for a moment, then the Count asked at last, "Is there any news from the front?"

The major grunted. "I'm afraid nothing new for the moment. I've seen some dispatches concerning the First Canadian Battalion. They recently suffered losses, 68 dead and 149 wounded." There was a note of satisfaction in Simms' voice that caught the Count by surprise.

"How are the Canadians performing?"

"Well enough for colonial troops. Contrary to what the Canadians believe, they are not on par with the Imperial troops, but they are improving. Were you in the army?" asked the major with raised eyebrows.

The Count grinned briefly. "Cavalry."

The major gave him an understanding nod. "The war has played havoc with the cavalry."

"You were wounded?"

"Yes. I was in a skirmish near Ypres early in the war," answered the major, touching his left shoulder. "During my recovery they posted me here to Canada," he added bitterly.

"And you are a liaison with the Canadian military?"

"Actually, Colonel Stanton is responsible for liaison with the Canadians."

"What is he like?"

"I find myself working with one of the two best soldiers that I have ever had the privilege of serving under. The other is the Duke," said the major proudly.

"The Canadians must be pleased to have such distinguished soldiers to assist them," Jaggi said.

"You can say that," the major replied without much enthusiasm.

The Count noted this and realized that the major didn't particularly care for Canadians. That perked his interest. Was there a rift between the Duke and the Canadian government, or was it only this officer's problem? He recalled the smug tone when Simms related the Canadians' battle loses. There was a hint of vindication.

"I have met with Sir Borden. He seems be quite able. He was not quite what I expected for a politician," the Count commented.

"You have, have you," the major said coldly.

It was obvious what had happened. The major had tried to give the

Canadian prime minister what he thought was sound military advice, and the PM had ignored him. Jaggi strongly suspected that he ignored the colonel's and the Duke's advice too. Knowing the British, he suspected that their advice was given with high-handedness and arrogance. Borden appeared to be an orderly, solid man without much imagination. It would take a considerable amount of effort to upset him. Somehow they had managed to do so.

"Oh, yes. We briefly discussed the December 20 meeting with the presidents of Canadian railways and banks concerning Belgian Relief. He mentioned that his Royal Highness was the committee's patron," the Count stated with a smile, putting the major in an awkward position.

Simms tightened his lips when the Count mentioned that Borden had attended the meeting. "The Duke is quite pleased to offer his patronage to such a worthy cause," he said stiffly.

Sensing he was losing the major, the Count took a different tack. "I'm most grateful that his highness has extended his patronage to our cause. I've also spoken to the Belgian consul here, and he is quite grateful for the Duke and Duchess's patronage as well."

"I will relay the consul's kind words to the colonel," said the major, mollified.

"It is my understanding that the Royal Highnesses will be attending the Belgian fundraiser on the fourteenth."

"That is true. The Royal Highnesses will be in attendance," Simms confirmed.

"Would that be an appropriate time for introductions, or would it be more suitable that they are made privately?"

The major's stiffness softened. "I believe that may be a suitable time for introductions."

"Will Bor ... the prime minister be in attendance?" The Count thought it might not irritate the major so much if he used Borden's title instead of his name.

"I'm afraid not," the major answered with a disdainful scowl. "The prime minister will be vacationing in the southern United States for the next few weeks. You would think there wasn't a war on."

"What!" exclaimed the Count. "So who will be in charge when he is on vacation? The defence minister?"

The major stared at him in horror. "Oh my God, no! Borden may be a fool, but he's not that much of a fool."

The Count was puzzled. "I have heard a great deal about the

minister of militia and defence, a Major-General Samuel Hughes. I just assumed that he would be in charge."

"Obviously, you have not met the general," the major sneered.

The Count shook his head. "I have not had the pleasure."

"Believe me, it is not a pleasure," said the major, sounding disgusted. "You will have to meet the man to fully comprehend my meaning."

The major seemed to feel the need to elaborate further when he saw that the Count continued to be confused. "How do you think he was promoted to major-general?"

"The usual promotion list?"

"He promoted himself from colonel to general!" the major grumbled.

"You are not serious!"

"Yes, I am," replied the major.

"How did he get away with it?"

The major shrugged. That explained a great deal. It was not surprising something like that would affront the sensibilities of British officers.

The Count grimaced sympathetically. Changing the subject, he asked, "Will the prime minister be available for the December 20 meeting?"

The major frowned. "I don't know."

The feeling the Count got was that if Borden did not make the meeting, it would not be a great loss.

The waiter caught the major's attention. "Let's order something to eat. The one thing about Canada is that there is excellent beef here."

"By all means," replied the Count.

CHAPTER 11

The Count was tired. It had been a hectic two days of meetings, luncheons, and dinners, and yet he faced another potentially deadly boring evening. Boredom was a slow way to die but preferable to being in a cold, wet trench on the Western front. At least he was warm and dry as he watched the Château's ballroom fill with people entering to view the items for sale on the various tables. A maze of tables ranged across the room's hardwood floor. There were several tables for baby items, a tobacco and cigarette table for the gentlemen, a fancy goods and bag table, a doll table, more homemade jam tables than he cared to count, a fancy work table, and even a fortune-telling booth.

In the corner near the fishpond Madame Goor, the wife of the Belgian consul general, was talking with Mrs. Yada, the wife of the Japanese consul general. He hadn't seen the women's husbands yet. He suspected that they were in the bar fortifying themselves for the long evening ahead.

The Count had been somewhat apprehensive meeting Goor, the Belgian consul general to Ottawa. He was confident that his cover was relatively secure; his Belgian French was impeccable, and he had spent his youth in Belgium due to his father's business interests. He had taken the precaution of sending a telegram from the London offices of Belgian Relief with several references to forestall any inquiries concerning his background. What concerned him most was the remote possibility that the consul general had actually met the real Count. However, the meeting went very well. He and Goor had a long discussion concerning the local brews. The consul general recommended several brands that were passable.

He clasped his hands behind his back as he scrutinized the room for Katherine. She was to have arrived a half hour ago. He finally spotted her at the main entrance, where she had paused to scan the room. In a black crepe dress, with a matching shawl draped over her shoulders, she was so stunning he couldn't help but stare at her. Her eyes locked on his for a long moment, then she flashed a small smile. She began to make her way through the maze, scrutinizing items on various tables. From time to time, she smiled warmly and greeted people with a touch of her hand as she headed in his direction. While she gave him the same smile she had given the others, her pupils seemed to brighten slightly as she neared him. At that moment, he knew he could have her if he wanted. He was surprised at how much he did.

"Good evening, Count," she said warmly, offering him her hand.

"Good evening, Katherine. You look quite lovely this evening." He took her warm hand in his, brought it up to his mouth, and gave it a gentle kiss. It gave him the opportunity to catch a glimpse of the top swell of her breasts. When he returned his focus to Katherine's face, a small twitch of amusement crossed the left edge of her lips. Several men at the nearby cigarette table gave him envious stares, which he ignored.

"Why, thank you, Count." She reluctantly released his hand, and he moved to stand beside her. They watched the crowd in awkward silence for a moment until the Count finally observed, "The event is attracting a fair number of people."

As she smoothed her long, loose hair and then adjusted her shawl, Katherine agreed. "The turnout is greater than expected."

"How much are they expecting to raise?"

Katherine gave him a glance, then said, "They are hoping to raise about $200. We might do better than that."

The Count seemed impressed. "The people of Ottawa are very generous."

Katherine turned serious. "Thank you. It's our Christian duty to help the less fortunate."

The Count declared, "The people we will be helping here tonight will be most grateful for your support." Pleased by his comment, Katherine's expression softened slightly.

"So did you enjoy your visit to New York?" she asked as she returned someone's greeting with a small wave.

"Yes, I did. Unfortunately, I did not see very much of New York, as I was kept quite busy with appointments and meetings."

"That's a shame. You should make some time to visit the sights, such as the Statue of Liberty."

"You've been to New York?" he asked with a raised eyebrow.

Katherine beamed happily. "A number of times. I really enjoy the theatre there. It's been a while since I've been. Where did you stay?"

"At the Waldorf Astoria."

Katherine regarded him with disapproval, which forced the Count to say defensively, "One of our American patrons was kind enough to provide me with the accommodations. I must admit that the lodgings are quite luxurious, which I'm a bit uncomfortable with." Katherine appeared skeptical. "The money that is being spent on my room for a day could feed a family for a month. I'm currently looking for more modest accommodations."

"What will your patron think about that?"

"I really don't want to offend him but my main concern is the welfare of my people, especially since I'll be spending more time there."

"Why?"

The Count smiled. "I've received a telegram from London informing me that I am to remain in New York and to help raise American funds. I will have to rent lodgings and an office as well that is more in keeping with my position."

"So we will be seeing more of you then?" asked Katherine, casting him a sideway glance.

"That is a possibility. Canada is included in my responsibilities, so I will be making frequent trips here," he conceded with some amusement.

"But you will be spending most of your time in the States," she said as she teased lock of loose hair.

"Yes."

"That's too bad."

The corner of his mouth twitched. "New York is not that far. If you are ever in the city, I would be quite pleased to have supper with you. And your husband," he added as an afterthought.

"Thank you," murmured Katherine. She sighed regretfully. "It's been quite awhile. Before the war we would go two or three times a year. With the war, my husband has not been able to make the time."

"That is most unfortunate," replied the Count. "And as I mentioned, if you ever decide to come I would be quite pleased to see you." Katherine acknowledged this with a wistful smile.

She changed the subject. "By the way, did you have any trouble at the border?"

"None entering the United States. However, entering Canada was a different matter."

Katherine frowned. "There was a problem?"

"Not a problem really. Just your customs officers were more stringent in reviewing my travel documents."

"I'm not surprised. There have been a number of attempts by Germans to enter from the States to commit acts of sabotage," she explained.

"Really?" he exclaimed in mock surprise. He took a moment to consider how to take advantage of the opening she had given him. He didn't want to raise any suspicious by appearing eager or by asking too many questions about her husband's business. He suspected that over the years she would have developed a fine sense of when someone was trying to pump her for information. Hoping that he had the correct tone, the Count probed, "Have here been many of these incidents?"

Katherine leaned towards him. Her perfume distracted him for a moment. She spoke in a soft tone to ensure that their conversation would not be overheard. "Unfortunately yes. But, we really don't like to talk about it much."

"I assure you I will not tell anyone."

"Of course you won't. I trust you," she responded, touching his arm again. "But we had several scares. One in New Brunswick, where they tried to blow up a railway bridge."

"Was it serious?"

"We were lucky. No one was hurt, and there was only minor damage to the bridge." The Count noted that this account didn't match the information von Papen had given him the previous week, when he had said that the bridge was destroyed. Given the possible source, he trusted Katherine's statement more than von Papen's.

"Also, a German tried to destroy a factory in Walkerville," Katherine continued.

"Excuse me, Katherine. Where is Walkerville?" asked the Count, trying to locate it on a mental map.

"Oh, sorry — it's near Windsor, which is across from Detroit."

"Is that near the Welland Canal?"

Katherine gave him a speculative look. The Count hoped he appeared as innocent as possible as he wondered if he had made a mistake. "No. Niagara Falls is closer to Toronto than Windsor," she corrected.

"Ah." The Count was relieved that she hadn't seen anything amiss.

"Where was I?" Katherine paused to think. "Oh yes. The factory in Walkerville. It seems that a former night watchman, I can never remember his name, planted a bomb, and blew up the Peabody Factory. Fortunately, no one was hurt because it happened during the night."

"If I may ask, what did the factory manufacture?"

"Uniforms."

"Uniforms!" blurted the Count, surprised. "Why in the world would one destroy a uniform factory?"

Katherine readjusted her shawl. "The company had a large contract, a million dollars I think, to make military uniforms, gloves, and the like for the British army." The Count kept himself from shaking his head with disgust. No wonder von Papen had not informed him. Did he really think bombing a coat factory would help Germany win the war?

"Did they capture the night watchman?"

"Oh, yes, they did. He's been sent to the Kingston Penitentiary for ten years. He had also planted a bomb at the Windsor Armoury. Fortunately, that one did not detonate."

Before the Count could say another word, Katherine straightened slightly as a commotion at the ballroom's entrance caught her attention. "The Royals are here."

Katherine watched as the Count turned his attention to the Duke and Duchess of Connaught. Accompanying them was their daughter, Princess Patricia. Katherine watched with interest as the Royals make their way around the various tables.

The Duke, as usual, was dressed in the khaki uniform that was the current military style. On the left breast of his tunic he wore his ribbons above stars that represented his royal honours. He was a tall, slender man with a large, snowy-white walrus moustache that nearly touched the fringe of white hair surrounding his bald scalp. Even though he was sixty-five, he still had a youthful stride.

Katherine knew that everyone was excited when it was announced that the Duke of Connaught would be the next governor general of Canada. Much was made of the fact that back in the 1870s, as a young army officer, he had spent a season in Montreal. He supposedly had expressed a desire to return some day as governor general. Katherine did believe the story until Andrew told her the real reason why the Duke was given the governor generalship of Canada.

It seemed that King Edward wanted him out of England. Andrew also said that the Duke had become something of an embarrassment ever since he abruptly resigned his position in Malta in 1909. That he had accidentally shot the feathers off the Queen of Italy's hat at a shooting party didn't help. He had been sent to Canada to get him out of England for a while. Most Canadians didn't know any of this and were all too happy to have someone of the royal blood as governor general. The Duke wasn't all that happy about his job in Canada, but he didn't have a choice in the matter.

Katherine didn't hold this story against the Duke, since she liked him. She suspected that his marriage was not a happy one, though it was hard to tell with the Royals. Considering to whom he was married, she wasn't surprised.

She glanced at the Princess Louise Margaret of Prussia, Duchess of Connaught, the daughter of Prince Friedrich Karl of Prussia, who strolled beside her husband dressed in a dark dress with a small black hat. While Katherine respected the Duchess for doing her duty, she had never really warmed to her.

However, the one thing that condemned the Duchess in the eyes of many Ottawans was the Kreuger incident. As a young German, Kreuger had immigrated to Canada. He had settled in Ottawa, where he became the premier supplier of champagne and fine spirits. He and the Duchess had become quite close, since she was glad to have someone with whom she could speak Prussian. Days before he was to be interned as an enemy alien, he disappeared. It was subsequently discovered that he had made his way to Germany via New York. Everyone had strong suspicions that the Duchess knew her friend would be interned and had warned him to leave Canada as soon as possible.

There was much speculation about the amount of secret information that the man took back with him to Germany. After all, he had known everyone in Ottawa, since he was the supplier of champagne and beverages to nearly everyone of note. Well, if he had stayed he wouldn't be making much money now, since Rideau Hall had declared that for the duration of the war, the Hall would be dry.

The tall, attractive woman in her late twenties who followed on their heels was Princess Patricia, one of the Duke's three children and his favourite. She wore a gown of blue and gold trimmed with sable fur. A hat of black with steel ornaments covered her dark hair. The Princess was a great favourite of Canadians. At the outbreak of war, Captain Andrew Hamilton Gault of Montreal had approached General Hughes with the offer that would personally recruit members for, and contribute $100,000 to equipping, a regiment for the Canadian army. Princess Patricia was asked whether she would give permission that the regiment be named the Princess Patricia's Canadian Light Infantry and she be its colonel-in-chief. She was delighted. She even designed the regiment's badge and colours. Katherine also knew how hard she had worked for the past months to ensure that every Canadian soldier would receive a card and a box of maple sugar for Christmas.

The Royals made their way around the various tables, followed by a rather large entourage — a couple of officers in khaki uniforms, one of them Major Simms, escorting the Princess Louise; the Princess's ladies in waiting; and the evening's organizing committee. The sales people at each table rose and curtsied to the Royals. The Royals smiled then studied the items on the table. If an item struck their fancy, they indicated it to their aide-de-camp, who handled the actual transaction.

At one of the tables, Katherine saw Major Simms give her and the Count a glance. He bent over and spoke in the governor general's ear. The Duke glanced first at Katherine, who he acknowledged with a slight nod, then turned his attention to the Count. It took a couple of tables, but it eventually became clear that the Duke was heading in their direction. When the governor general passed the last table, he headed straight for the Count, with Major Simms at his heels.

"Your Royal Highness, I would like to present to you Count Jaggi of Belgium," said Major Simms.

"Your Highness," said the Count nervously. It was one thing to talk about meeting a Royal; actually doing it was quite another. He bowed from the hips as he had been instructed. The Royals did not like being touched.

"Count," acknowledged the Duke with a regal nod. "How are you doing this evening?"

"I'm quite well," was the only thing the Count could say.

"And you, Mrs. MacNutt, how are you this evening?" the Duke asked warmly.

"I'm well, Your Highness," replied Katherine, as she curtseyed.

"Very good. If you would be so kind, would you inform your husband that I'm grateful he accompanied my daughter to Montreal. It was most kind of him."

"I will, Your Highness."

The Duke returned his gaze to the Count. "So, Count Jaggi, what is your opinion of the Americas?"

"It has been an adjustment," answered the Count truthfully.

The Duke gave a brief smile. "That is true. Very true. Major Simms has informed me that you are involved in Belgian Relief."

"Yes, Your Highness. A small role, I assure you, but one must do what one can," blurted the Count. "And I would like to personally thank you for your patronage, Your Highness. It is most appreciated."

"I, too, play a small role," declared the Duke. "But I am quite happy to assist the Belgian people in their time of need."

"Thank you, Your Highness," replied the Count.

"Very well. I'm sure that we will see each other from time to time in the course of our duty," the Duke stated as he prepared to leave.

"Of course," croaked the Count.

"Excellent. Good evening to you, sir."

"Your Highness," replied the Count, bowing again. The Duke turned and headed towards one of the doors that led into the ballroom where the dance was being held.

HAMBURG-AMERICAN STEAMSHIP, BROADWAY,
MANHATTAN, NEW YORK CITY
12:30 A.M., FRIDAY, DECEMBER 17, 1915

Inspector Tunney stood in front of the Hamburg-American steamship offices on 125 Broadway, studying the building that had become quite familiar of late. More familiar than he really cared for. He glanced at the four plainclothes detectives who stood beside him, Barnitz, Cory, Terra, and Corell, to see if they were ready. The members of the New York City Bomb Squad were primed and ready to go.

He sighed as he stroked his moustache. When his squad was formed and he was given command, he had never dreamed that they would be in this position. The Bomb Squad was created in 1914 in response to an assassination attempt against John D. Rockefeller, a retaliation for the Ludlow massacre. It was most fortunate that the three anarchists who were attempting the assassination were killed when the bomb they were making blew up. He really didn't have much sympathy for the anarchists, especially since a number of them had bombed several police stations that same year. He and his squad had spent the last two years infiltrating a group of Italian anarchists in New York to forestall their bomb plots. Their most spectacular success had been the arrest of Abarno and Carbone for their plot to blow up St. Patrick's Cathedral.

"So he is inside then?" Tunney demanded.

"Yes, sir," Detective Barnitz said.

"Good. About time, don't you think," Tunney said with a predatory grin.

All four detectives returned his grin. Tunney understood his squad's impatience and their satisfaction that they finally had the bastard, Paul Koenig. Koenig had been a tough nut to crack.

It was along the waterfront that one of Tunney's men first noticed

Koenig. What piqued the detective's interest was that even with most of the Hamburg-American's ships tied up at the Hoboken dock, Koenig was extremely busy for someone who really had nothing to do. The German-owned liner's ships were tied up on the docks because of accusations that they were supplying food, ammunition, and other war supplies to German naval raiders in the North Atlantic, a direct violation of the United States' neutrality. It was true that Koenig did visit the ships where some of the crews lived, since they couldn't afford a place in the city. It just seemed that Koenig was spending more time on the docks than he needed to. They'd thought at first that since Koenig had once been a detective and superintendent of police for the Atlas line, a subsidiary of the Hamburg-American line, he was helping some of the line's ships make a run for the open sea. That idea was unrealistic, since it would take a number of days to get the boilers heated up enough to build the steam they'd need, and with the British warships patrolling just outside American waters, they would not have got very far.

Suspicious, Tunney had contacted the Department of Justice at Government House. His contact had informed him that they knew Koenig, but he wasn't sufficiently interesting for them to waste any time on. If Tunney wanted to take a run at him, that was fine. Tunney ordered his men to keep a close surveillance on Koenig. His squad's surveillance turned up some interesting items. As a superintendent, Koenig had supervised the dozen or so men who watched the company's employees against theft and investigated customer complaints. Therefore, he had extensive knowledge of the sailors, tug skippers, wharf rats, longshoremen, and dive keepers along the waterfront. None of them wanted to talk about the man they called the "Bull-Headed Westphalian."

As part of their surveillance, they had tapped Koenig's phone and listened in on his conversations. Their big break came when one day a man telephoned Koenig and got into a shouting match with him on the phone. It was the second phone call that allowed the Bomb Squad to trace the phone number to a public telephone at a bar. The bartender didn't know the fellow's name, but he couldn't help overhearing, since the person was screaming into the phone at the top of his lungs. Based on his description, they canvassed the neighbourhood and soon identified the irate caller as George Fuchs. He turned out to be a distant cousin of Koenig.

Since Fuch was looking for work, Tunney had one of his undercover police officers contact him, posing as a wireless telegraph company's representative with a possible job offer. It wasn't until a third meeting, though, that Fuchs was comfortable enough to confide to the officer the details of the Welland Canal sabotage operation and how he came to New York to work for Koenig. He told the officer that Koenig had fired him.

Tunney's men picked up Fuchs, who broke down and gave the bomb squad all he knew about Koenig's activities on the docks.

"Let's do it then, lads," ordered Tunney as he led his men into the building. He went up to Koenig's office and didn't bother to knock. They found Koenig sitting at his desk with one of his thick, apelike hands holding the phone.

"*Ja.* I will talk with you later," he yelled into the mouthpiece, and hung up.

"So, Inspector, what can I do for you today?" Koenig asked. He appeared confident that Tunney had nothing on him.

Tunney despised the man. What galled him most was that Koenig never went out in daytime without one or two of his agents trailing him to determine whether he was being shadowed. He used to turn a corner, suddenly, and stand still. When one of the officers ran around the corner, he would come face to face with Koenig, betraying his identity. Koenig would then laugh at the detective.

This had forced the inspector to come up with a new system of shadowing him. He had a team of detectives follow Koenig. One detective would start ahead as the "front shadow," who would be signalled by his teammates, who followed in the rear, whenever Koenig turned a corner. The man in front would run down side streets to get ahead of Koenig. If Koenig boarded a streetcar, a detective would hail the car several blocks down to avoid suspicion. In several instances, the detectives, guessing which car he would get on, would already be on board when he got on.

"You will have to come with us," ordered Tunney.

"And if I don't want to come?" said Koenig as he rose to feet and leaned his muscular arms on the desk.

Tunney said scornfully. "Suit yourself. Either way, you are coming in."

"You don't have anything on me," bellowed Koenig, raising a fist in Tunney's face.

"Oh, I have one or two things," warned Tunney, allowing a satisfied smile to appear.

Koenig glared at the four burly detectives in his office, then his shoulders slumped. "Take him downtown," commanded Tunney. One of the detectives twisted Koenig's arms behind him. Koenig grunted in pain when one of the other detectives handcuffed him then led him out of the office.

"You want me to search the place?" asked Corell.

Tunney peered at the two wooden filing cabinets that lined the wall then turned to Terra and Corell. "Fuchs said he liked to keep records. So they will be here or at his apartment."

"Surprising, him keeping records," said Corell as he pulled out a drawer. He frowned at the files he found.

Tunney shrugged. "He was a cop once. Difficult to lose the habit."

"I guess you're right, Inspector. I'll take the place apart," Corell replied as he started pulling files out of the cabinet.

"Good. I'll be downtown in a few hours," replied Tunney as he left to accompany Koenig on his ride back to his office. He was going to enjoy interrogating the "Bull-Headed Westphalian." Now they'd see how bull-headed he was.

CHAPTER 12

The wet, cold wind blew straight into Müller's face as he walked down the narrow street. He looked longingly at the Lido Hotel across the road, where he could get some relief from the inclement weather. Located a few blocks north of the Hoboken piers, it had seen better days, though even then, it seemed to Müller, it would have had the same battered and dreary look. From the type of traffic that moved through the hotel he was fairly certain it was more of a brothel than a place where one went to rest weary bones. Most of the men he saw entering its doors had that rolling gait sailors developed from spending most of their lives on board ship. He really should not have been surprised, considering who had picked the hotel for their meeting tonight.

Müller shivered as he walked past the Lido. He hoped that he would not get the grippe on account of this, but there was nothing for it. He had to take additional precautions because of recent events. He had taken a circuitous route which he hoped had shaken any surveillance, and he had arrived about a half hour earlier than planned. With so few people around, he didn't dare stay in one place for long in case he attracted attention, so he walked a short circuit around the hotel. He couldn't stray very far from it, because he needed to intercept the Count before he entered the hotel. He had sent a message warning the Count that the meeting was off, but he hadn't received confirmation. It was imperative that the Count not enter the hotel. He cursed Koenig again for his carelessness, which put them all at risk — as if they weren't already at enormous risk! As he made his circuit, he kept an eye peeled, and a couple of times he thought he spotted the Count. It was amazing how many men resembled him. When he was dressed in a business suit, the Count's 5' 11", tall, lean frame and streaked grey hair gave him an aristocratic air which allowed the man to move easily in middle and upper class circles. Dressed in slightly oversized workman's clothes with a day's growth of beard stubble, the Count mirrored the emaciated sailors who worked with backbreaking effort on the deck of a ship with poor food. In this area of New York he would blend in.

After spending a futile half hour, Müller finally decided to call it a night and headed towards the Hudson and Manhattan Railway Station to catch a train back to Manhattan. It seemed that the Count had received the message and would not be coming tonight. Which was good — but Müller was still irritated. Why hadn't the Count acknowledged receipt?

He had travelled a couple of blocks when someone softly called out, "Müller."

Müller twisted his body towards the voice that came from a doorway. His right hand fumbled for the .38 Smith & Wesson in his pocket. "It's you!"

"Who else would it be?" snorted the Count.

Müller's initial relief quickly evaporated. "With all that is happening the last couple of days, I thought it might be the police!" he retorted angrily.

"Koenig."

"Yes, *Koenig*. What the hell are you doing here? Didn't you receive my message?"

"I got it."

"Then why are you here, and why didn't you let me know that you got it?"

"I wanted to see who would be stupid enough to show up," said the Count, scanning the street. "Also, I really didn't appreciate having to learn about his arrest in the paper," he continued with undisguised disgust.

"I know," replied Müller, glowering. He wasn't happy that he too had only learned about the arrest when it hit the newspapers the next day.

"What's worse, it appeared in the *Canadian* papers before you managed to inform me! They could have been waiting for me at the border."

"I did send you a message by general delivery, as you directed," Müller argued, his voice rising. "There isn't much I can do if you don't keep me informed of your whereabouts."

The Count stared at Müller for a moment then checked the street again. "How much damage has been done?" he said after a moment.

"Considerable. Let's talk as we walk to the subway. We don't need to attract attention by standing around whispering in a doorway. I've been hanging around enough already, and I need to get out of these wet clothes," snarled Müller.

The Count gave another glance along the street then studied the wet, miserable Müller. "Agreed." He stepped out from the protection of the doorway into the brisk wind gusting down the street. Water from the canvas awning over the store entrance splashed down onto his wool fedora and overcoat. The Count glared at the canvas, annoyed. "So, what's considerable mean?"

Müller shivered as he chose his words carefully. In the end, he couldn't sugar-coat it. "He kept detailed notes about his contacts and the sums that he paid."

"Scheisse!" The Count kicked at some refuse lying on the street. "Why the fuck did he keep notes?"

Müller shrugged his ignorance and tightened his collar, trying to stop trembling. The Count fixed his eyes on Müller. "How much did he know about me?"

Müller returned a miserable gaze. "I only told him that you were going to take over when von Papen leaves for Germany."

"Hmm," grunted the Count. Müller knew that the Count was weighing the information, thinking about people he had met in the network and how reliable they were.

"So, all of his people have been compromised?" said the Count sourly.

"I'm afraid so."

"Did he know about all our other operations?"

"No. But he's not stupid. He has his own sources, and he may have guessed about a few on his own," answered Müller weakly.

"Right. Müller," said the Count as he tugged his fedora down, "I need to think about what we do next."

"What is there to think about?"

"There is a *great* deal to think about."

"When and where?" asked Müller.

"Tomorrow noon. Pick me up in front of the Pabst Hotel."

"Yes, sir."

At the station entrance the Count stopped abruptly. "I'll leave you here. I'll get a cab home. It's best that we go our separate ways."

"As you wish."

The Count nodded brusquely then walked off. Müller stared thoughtfully at the Count's receding back as he disappeared into the railway terminal. What was the man planning? Well, he would find out tomorrow, but he hoped that it wasn't too spectacular. As he entered the subway station, he figured he'd better make his own plans, just in case.

Katherine was sitting with her legs crossed on the red Turkish rug in her living room, leaning back against the settee, surrounded by boxes and bags. In front of her on the coffee table ribbons and bows lay in a tangle, and sheets of green, gold, and red wrapping paper fanned out across the surface. A steaming cup of Earl Grey tea sat amid the clutter. Katherine's frown was a little haggard; she had spent most of the day shopping for Christmas gifts. Her parents were always difficult to buy for, but this year it was proving to be more difficult than usual. She was at her wits' end trying to buy just the right thing.

She had managed to find a seafoam dress that she knew her sister, Emma, in Vancouver would like. It was wrapped now and ready for tomorrow's mail. For Irene, her other sister, who lived in Winnipeg, she had ordered a Japanese chocolate set out of the Eaton's catalogue to add to the one she had sent last year. So that was another present to strike off her mental shopping list.

Andrew's brothers — Hank, who was living in New England, and Simon, who was aboard a Canadian Navy patrol boat in the North Atlantic — would not be able to make it to Ottawa for Christmas this year. She had picked out warm wool coats for each of them. They were both wrapped and ready to go, too. She thought Simon, especially, would appreciate the gift this year.

She groaned as she stretched her stiff legs under the coffee table then reached for her cup. Her mood lightened when she thought of her parents. They coming in by train from Kingston, Ontario, and were going to be in town for Christmas and the New Year's holidays. Andrew's parents, out in Brandon, Manitoba, could not make it this year. Earlier this afternoon she had gone to the butcher shop and ordered a turkey for the Christmas day meal. The butcher had promised to get her a nice plump one. She was glad that her mother was coming. Christmas was going be hard this year with Jamie gone. She remembered Christmases past when Jamie was growing up and fondly recalled the times when he helped her bake Christmas cookies. The memory of her son's beaming face flashed before her, and she could feel tears welling. She pulled a handkerchief from her dress sleeve and wiped her eyes.

With a shake, she was back to glaring at the mess of gift wrap. She had had enough wrapping for the afternoon. She began to carefully wind the festively coloured ribbons back onto their spools, then folded the wrapping paper into neat squares. As she picked up a green sheet of paper from the table, she uncovered the list of gifts she still needed to buy. She had managed to get little knick-knacks for most of her friends. *I even managed to find something for Mrs. Ramsey,* she thought with a grimace. The woman was always a trial, but it was not wise to forget her. Katherine had also had to invite her to the Christmas party she and Andrew had planned for next week.

The face of Count Jaggi sprang momentarily in her mind, bringing a half-grin. Should she invite him or not? She wasn't sure if he would be in Ottawa next week. She sighed wistfully then made up her mind to invite him. It was the Christian thing to do, after all, and it *was* the Christmas season.

CHAPTER 13

Katherine was putting the finishing touches on her toilette when the first guests arrived — there were always a few who arrived early, before she was quite ready.

She really hadn't wanted to hold their usual Christmas reception this year. With Jamie gone, the holiday season this year would be hard, but she had not imagined how truly difficult it would be. There was a limit to how much Christmas cheer she could take, and she hoped to God that she could hold on till the season was over in two weeks.

She heard Isabelle, her part-time maid who had come in to help for the evening, greeting guests at the front door. Katherine had instructed Isabelle to direct the female guests into the front parlour and the male guests to Andrew's study. There was a rap at the master bedroom door.

"Katherine, the guests are beginning to arrive," Andrew said through the closed door.

"Yes, dear, I'll be right along," she called out.

"I'll go down now," she heard Andrew say, then she could hear the stairs creak as he went down to the foyer to welcome the first guests.

Katherine smoothed her hair one last time then fiddled with her earrings, delaying the moment when she too would have to descend the staircase. What she really wanted to do was crawl back into bed, draw the down comforter over her head, and make the world go away. But all the wishing could not help her. She gave herself a final critical check in the mirror, twisted her lips into a smile, and left her sanctuary.

As Katherine made her way to the ground floor, she could hear several women already chatting in the front parlour. She knew that Isabelle would be pouring out tea into the best china cups for the ladies. In the drawing room, across the hall, the husbands were sequestered. From the stairs she could smell their cigar and cigarette smoke. The men were on their best behaviour at the moment, but she knew they would soon be quite boisterous. Andrew would be offering some harder refreshments to a few select guests — what with the war and the temperance movement, it was politic to be discreet. She would have preferred not to serve any liquor at all, but Andrew would not have it. There was nothing wrong with a man having a drink or two was his position. The doorbell

125

rang as Katherine was coming down the stairs. Isabelle appeared and quickly opened the door, which sent a frigid blast of air sweeping up the stairs. Katherine's gown rippled slightly against her skin. She was delighted to see the beaming face of Lady Zoé Laurier. "*Joyeux Noël*," Lady Laurier called.

"*Joyeux Noël, Madame*," welcomed Katherine, "*et Monsieur Laurier*."

"*Joyeux Noël*," said the impeccably dressed Sir Wilfrid Laurier as he entered the hallway. Katherine hurried over to help Isabelle with their coats. She assisted Lady Zoé with her luxurious fur coat while Isabelle took Sir Wilfrid's top hat and his coat with its fox fur-trimmed lapel.

The hallway became quite crowded when a third person entered. "Merry Christmas, Mrs. MacNutt," said Mackenzie King pleasantly. Katherine's eyes widened in surprise when she saw King. She knew that the Liberal party was holding a policy session on Monday to map out its strategy for the coming parliamentary session; King still had a powerful influence on the party, although he was spending most of his time in the States. She had assumed he would be in New York attending to the Rockefellers, but obviously not. She had never particularly liked the man. There were always rumours going around in the Market about his dalliances, which she somewhat discounted because of his devotion to this mother.

"I hope you don't mind that I have come to your home uninvited," he said. "I was meeting with Sir Wilfrid and Lady Laurier, and they told me that they had been invited to your home for the evening. Since your home was a short walk away, I insisted that I escort them myself."

"Not at all. Please do come in and warm up," she said with a welcoming wave. It would have been impolite not to extend the invitation. "I hope that you are having a good Christmas season."

"It's been quite pleasant. How is your husband?"

"He is fine," she replied. She called, "Andrew! Andrew!"

"Yes," came Andrew's voice from his study. A moment later he emerged from the smoke-filled room. When he saw Laurier, he broke into a broad smile. No one but Katherine would have noticed how his smile dimmed a little when he saw King. She wondered why. She would have to ask him about it later this evening.

"Sir Wilfrid, it's a pleasure to visit you and your lovely wife this evening," Andrew said as he bowed slightly towards Lady Laurier.

He turned and as he shook King's hand somewhat hesitantly, he said, "Mr. King, it is an unexpected pleasure to see you again."

126

"Mine as well."

"Please come into my study, gentlemen," MacNutt said, indicating the room with the sweep of his arm. "Lady Laurier, my wife will take care of you. Won't you, dear?" he said congenially.

Sir Wilfrid touched his wife's arm. When she gave him permission with a slight nod, he headed for the study. King shrugged and followed his leader.

"Lady Laurier, do come into the salon and meet the other guests," Katherine said. Seated in the salon were six women ranging from their mid twenties to early forties. Lady Laurier greeted each of the ladies warmly. She had already met most of the women in the room at political functions she and Sir Wilfrid had attended. Lady Laurier took the empty chair near the fireplace. The logs burning on the grate gave sufficient heat to make the room comfortable but not stifling.

When she was seated, Katherine inquired, "Would you like tea or coffee?"

"Coffee, please," she replied in heavily accented English. Katherine remembered well the first days when Zoé first came to Ottawa. She was a shy person and dressed rather dowdily at times, especially when compared with Laurier's lady friend Émilie Lavergne. Over the years, Lady Laurier had improved her English, but she still preferred to speak in French.

Katherine took a seat on the settee beside the wing chair. She noticed Lady Laurier inspecting the room. When Lady Laurier spotted the black-framed picture of Jamie, she became sombre. She leaned over and touched Katherine's hand. For a moment, when Lady Laurier started to speak, Katherine thought that she might mention Jamie. But instead she said, "You have decorated your home beautifully."

"Thank you. You are so kind," replied Katherine, blushing at the compliment and relieved at the change of topic. "It was difficult to decide whether to put Christmas decorations up this year."

Lady Laurier chuckled. "Sir Wilfrid and I had the same discussion."

The doorbell pealed and the ladies in the salon could hear the booming voice of Mrs. Ramsey. Katherine gave a sideways glance at Zoé Laurier. She hoped that there would not be fireworks. Mrs. Ramsey did not have a high opinion of Lady Laurier. There had been much talk about the relationship between Sir Wilfrid and Émilie Lavergne. To Mrs. Ramsey, it was not conjecture but fact that Émilie's son was fathered by Sir Wilfrid. "Anyone with eyes can tell that Laurier is the father," she would snort when the topic came up. It was true that there was a remarkable physical resemblance between thirty-five-year-old Armand Lavergne, when he was a boy, and Sir Wilfrid. What amazed Mrs. Ramsey was that Lady Laurier put up with the cad: *she* would have sent the man packing a long time ago.

Now another voice at the door, a man's voice, made Katherine start slightly, and she moved expectantly to the edge of her chair. A moment later Mrs. Ramsey made her grand entrance into the salon. "Merry Christmas!" she practically bellowed.

As Katherine greeted her, Mrs. Ramsey's eyes flickered to Lady Laurier then returned to Katherine. "It's a cold evening. It feels like winter will never end." Katherine knew how much Mrs. Ramsey detested the Ottawa winters. "But I have quite a Christmas gift for you."

"Oh!"

"Do come in, sir," she urged the man standing in the hall.

When Count Jaggi entered the room, he said cheerfully, "Merry Christmas, Mrs. MacNutt." Katherine clasped the hand he offered. It was still cold. She felt her cheeks heat slightly.

"Count Jaggi, this is quite a pleasant surprise. I thought you were in New York?"

Jaggi gave her a brief smile. "Some of my meetings fell through, so I decided to come up a few days earlier. I hope that you don't mind my intrusion."

"Not at all. Not at all. I did send you an invitation," Katherine stammered. "When I didn't receive an RSVP, I assumed that you would not be attending."

"You did?" said the Count with a slight frown. "Of course you did. You must have thought me a boor. My dear Katherine, I never received your kind invitation. If I had, I would have certainly responded."

"Well, no matter," replied Katherine, delighted. "I'm glad you could come."

"It's my pleasure."

"Let me introduce you to my guests," said Katherine. "Count Jaggi, I would like you to meet Lady Laurier; Lady Laurier, Count Jaggi."

"*Joyeux Noël*," said Lady Laurier, offering her hand. The Count took it and kissed it. Lady Laurier's eyes twinkled with merriment at the man's gallantry.

"*Je suis enchanté de faire votre connaissance, madame*," said the Count.

128

"Lady Laurier is married to Sir Wilfrid Laurier. He was the previous prime minister of Canada," Katherine explained.

"I'm honoured," the Count said with a bow.

"So you are providing help for *les pauvres Belges?*" Lady Laurier said.

"*Oui, madame,*" replied the Count with a raised eyebrow.

Lady Laurier smiled and said, "Ottawa is a small town." Katherine saw Mrs. Ramsey stiffen; whether Lady Laurier had intended to deliver a message to Mrs. Ramsey or not, the busybody had taken it that way. "Sir Wilfrid is with my husband in the study. I'll take you to him."

The Count followed Katherine to the study. He admired Katherine's backside as it swayed back and forth before him. He had the mischievous urge to reach out and pat it, but he knew that wouldn't be wise with her husband so near.

Katherine paused at the study's door. "Andrew. Andrew!"

When the Count scanned the book-lined room, he counted seven men. A man pouring whiskey into a portly fellow's glass paused at the sound of Katherine's voice.

"Yes, dear?" he inquired.

"Andrew, I have a special guest for you," she announced, indicating the Count with her chin.

The Count saw MacNutt's puzzlement, then they locked gazes. Although the man was smiling, the Count could tell that he was being assessed with a policeman's scrutiny. The Count picked up a note of displeasure in Katherine's voice when she added, "Andrew, this is Count Jaggi from Belgian Relief. Count Jaggi, I would like to introduce you to my husband."

"Merry Christmas, sir," said the Count, making the first move by entering the room and offering MacNutt his hand. "It is a pleasure to me you, sir." He was pleased that his voice didn't crack with nervousness, intermingled with a small amount of fear, and that he was able to give MacNutt a firm handshake. It was an enormous risk he was taking, but he knew that sooner or later he would have to meet the chief inspector. He'd rather do it on his own terms than on MacNutt's. But Inspector MacNutt seemed familiar. Jaggi had seen him before, and he was trying to remember where.

"I you, Count Jaggi," MacNutt declared. Katherine appeared to doubt her husband's statement, but she took her leave with a nod and returned to her female guests.

"Have we met before? You look familiar," MacNutt wondered.

129

"I was going to say the same," replied the Count with a chuckle. "I've visited your Parliament buildings on a number of occasions. We may have seen each other in passing."

"That could be it." MacNutt introduced the Count to the other men in the study. Count Jaggi quickly forgot most of their names, since it soon became apparent that these men held no interest. He was, however, keenly interested in the last two gentlemen MacNutt introduced him to.

"Last but not least, let me introduce you to the Honourable Mackenzie King." MacNutt paused as the Count shook King's hand. "And the Right Honourable Sir Wilfrid Laurier, the leader of the Liberal party and former prime minister of Canada."

Sir Wilfrid rose from the brown wing chair and extended his hand. "Pleasure to make your acquaintance. *Joyeux Noël.*"

"*Joyeux Noël, monsieur*," returned the Count. "I hope that I'm not intruding."

"Not at all, my dear sir. I would be interested in hearing your perspective. Please do have a seat." Laurier indicated the seat beside him. The Count took the seat, which faced the other six men in the room. "Andrew, please do get the Count a drink."

The Count could not tell how Andrew felt being ordered about in his own home, but in any case he complied with Laurier's request.

The Count turned his attention to Laurier as MacNutt went to get him a brandy. The Count's first impression of Sir Wilfrid was that here was a lion in winter. At seventy-four, his eyes were bright and he still had a sharpness of mind. Age was beginning to make the tall man stoop slightly. He was immaculately dressed in what passed for Canadian fashion: a tailcoat with black trousers over a waistcoat, a white shirt with starched, winged collar, a white bow tie. Cufflinks showed at his wrists. Spats covered his pointed boots. In one of his hands he held a cane with a silver knob.

Laurier waited until MacNutt handed Jaggi his drink. What Laurier said next dumbfounded the Count. "Just before you arrived we were having a discussion concerning our country's efforts to maintain or even increase our rate of enlistment."

Médéric Martin, standing with his back to the fireplace, clarified. "What we were actually talking about was the rumour that Borden will announce he wants to increase the Canadian Army Corps to half a million men." Martin was the liberal MP for the federal riding of St. Mary in Quebec. He also happened to be the mayor of Montreal.

"The British are already talking about the possibility of conscription," declared MacNutt.

Laurier turned to the Count and asked, "What is your opinion, sir? Will England impose conscription?"

The Count surveyed the room, trying to assess his audience before composing his answer. He decided he might as well stir the pot slightly. "It is my feeling that they will bring conscription in soon."

Laurier winced. "The latest news that I have indicated the British government would not invoke conscription."

King placed his hand on Laurier's shoulder. "You must have better sources of information than we do?" he suggested to the Count.

"How many casualties have the Allies suffered during the last year and a half? Over a million men dead and wounded. Those men will have to be replaced. The figures for the enlistments have been going down. They will not have any choice if they can't get enough volunteers," the Count said. What he was saying was the truth. Unfortunately, it was also true for the German Imperial Army.

"That is a bleak assessment, Count," Laurier replied sadly. "I hope that we will not find ourselves in that situation. Otherwise, I fear for my country."

"I don't understand," said the Count, puzzled. "Wouldn't conscription help the Canadian war effort?"

Laurier frowned. "How many men will conscription bring in? Just a few slackers, farmers, and schoolboys. Conscription will sow disunity in the dominion at a time that we need it most. It will encourage the extremists on both sides." The Count's ears perked up at the word "extremists".

"I and the Liberal Party support the war effort. We must discover another solution. Conscription is not the answer," Laurier said strongly.

As Laurier was speaking, the Count was watching King. From his body language, it was obvious that King did not agree with Laurier, but he wouldn't publicly disagree with his party leader.

The Count didn't have a full grasp of Canadian politics, but he had a sense that Laurier was maintaining a delicate balance by supporting the war but not conscription. How this would play out was anyone's guess.

The Count noted that Médéric was pleased with Laurier's statement. But the reactions of several others in the room confirmed that there was opposition to Laurier's position. How strong was the opposition in the Liberal Party and could Laurier continue to hold the party together?

Only time will tell, thought the Count.

King, trying to forestall one of the men from reacting, turned to the Count with a rapid change of subject. "Andrew's wife said that you are working for Belgian Relief?"

"Yes," replied the Count. He hid his irritation; he had wanted to learn more about Laurier, but there was very little he could do when all the men in the room turned their attention to him. "The London office felt that they needed someone in the Americas to coordinate things, and I was asked if I were interested."

"Are you based in Canada?" asked King.

"I'm currently based in New York. I'm mainly responsible for fundraising efforts in the United States. Since Canada was so close, it seemed a good idea to include your country as well. I have to do a lot of travelling, which I like. I do enjoy meeting new people and exploring new vistas. With the war, travelling can be problematic."

"That is true," King admitted sourly. "I have to travel quite a bit myself since I'm called to New York quite often."

"Oh, what do you do?"

"Currently, I'm an industrial consultant," answered King, giving Laurier a glance. The Count got the impression that he was waiting for Laurier to jump on this remark, but Laurier kept his own counsel.

Médéric interjected. "He works for the Rockefellers in New York. He's helped them resolve some labour issues."

"I'm most impressed," remarked the Count. He had done his homework on King too. It was ironic that King was born, of all places, in Berlin, Ontario. Laurier had made him minister of labour in his government, and King held the post until the Liberal party was defeated in 1911. For a couple of years after his defeat, he managed to scrape together a living until he was hired by the Rockefellers to help them deal with the after-effects of the Ludlow, Colorado, massacre and continuing labour strife.

"Are you here visiting family for the Christmas season?" asked the Count.

"I'm afraid not. My family currently resides in Toronto. I'm a member of the Liberal party, and the party is having a two-day session to plan the strategy for the next parliamentary session."

"I see," murmured the Count. He was already aware of that, and he was hoping to get himself invited to some of the sessions or even to some of the various gatherings and parties. Otherwise, the trip would be a total waste of time. Well, not a total waste, considering how Katherine had viewed him a few moments ago.

"Are you in town for long?" asked Laurier.

"For a couple of days. Then I'll be returning to New York by mid-week, depending on how well things go," the Count replied. He needed to get back to New York as soon as he could. He knew that his time was well spent in Canada, but his priority was America. He needed to quickly try to save what he could of the dilapidated German networks there and rebuild them. They were critical to the German war effort.

"Will you be attending the Belgian Relief meeting next week?" asked King.

"I would very much like to if I may, but I have not been invited to the meeting," the Count stated with a hint of a scowl. He was aware of the meeting. It was also one of the reasons he had come up. A committee had been organized by a group of distinguished men to come to the aid of Belgian Relief. His Royal Highness was the patron, and the committee included Sir Robert Borden and Sir Wilfrid Laurier. What intrigued the Count was the other members of the committee: the heads of the CP, Grand Trunk, and CN railways, and the presidents of four banks — the Bank of Montreal, the Merchants Bank, the Royal Bank, and the Chevalier Crédit Foncier — would be in attendance.

King questioned Laurier with a look. Laurier answered him a nod. "If you would provide me with the name of your hotel in Ottawa, as well as the address of your office in New York, I will see what we can do to get you an invitation to the meeting."

"Excellent — I would be most pleased. Also, it would be a pleasure, if you happen to be in New York, to dine together," replied the Count.

"That would be enjoyable," said King, lifting his glass.

"What do you think of the Americans' mood concerning the war?" demanded Médéric.

The Count paused and considered his reply. "It appears that the Americans are not very enthusiastic about being drawn into the war. They are very sympathetic to the Belgian Relief, and I am obtaining a great deal of local support." He was observing the men's reactions and was pleased that they were impressed.

"I'm assuming that you will be buying your supplies on this side of the Atlantic. How will you be getting the supplies to Europe?" asked MacNutt.

"I'm currently planning to book a ship in New York to transport the supplies to England," explained the Count. In truth, the supplies would not end up in England, but instead would be funnelled to a desperate Germany. A benefit of his Belgian Relief cover was that it provided a plausible explanation for his spending so much time on the New York docks. Also, his visits provided needed intelligence on pinpointing for sabotage those ships that were carrying strategic cargoes or for identifying the U-boats to target in the North Atlantic.

"It will be difficult with the British blockade, will it not?" Laurier suggested.

"Yes, it will. But I'm hoping that the British and the Germans will let us through because we're providing humanitarian aid."

"You are a courageous man," Laurier said approvingly. "So, how many tons of supplies do you intend to ship to Belgium?"

"It entirely depends on how well my fundraising campaign does," replied the Count with a concerned frown.

He noticed that King kept hovering within earshot, as if Laurier might do or say something untoward. After a moment King leaned over to Sir Wilfrid and whispered in his ear.

Slightly irritated, Sir Wilfrid turned to King. "We can be a few minutes late, can't we?"

"I'm afraid not, Sir Wilfrid," replied King apologetically. "It wouldn't be wise."

Sir Wilfrid sighed. "I'm afraid that I must take my leave, sirs."

"So soon?" exclaimed Andrew.

"Unfortunately, I have other engagements to attend."

"I understand. Thank you for coming, Sir Wilfrid."

Sir Wilfrid rose gracefully from his chair. "It was a pleasure to meet you, Count Jaggi," he said. The Count rose partially from his chair and shook Sir Wilfrid's proffered hand. Sir Wilfrid continued, "I hope we will be able to meet and talk within the next week or two. I'm very interested in your Belgian Relief plans."

"Of course, sir. I would enjoy that," replied the Count.

"I'll escort you to the front door," offered MacNutt.

"You are most kind, Andrew," said Sir Wilfrid. He said his goodbyes to the rest of the room with a wave of his hand.

"Come along, Mac," commanded Laurier, and he led Mackenzie King and MacNutt out of the study.

CHAPTER 14

Katherine had hoped that Christmas day would be a quiet one. In other years, she had always enjoyed the hectic pace leading up to it as she hurried to finish shopping for gifts, bought the last items for the Christmas dinner, and put up the decorations or at least cajoled Andrew into putting them up. This year she was only going through the motions. What once gave pleasure and satisfaction now brought bitter sweetness.

It really hit home when she and Andrew went to the train station to pick up her parents, Walter and Ada Lowan. The train station was a madhouse. There were long lines for those travelling to the States as they went through U.S. Customs. People were also waiting anxiously for late trains bringing family or friends. Others were rushing down the platforms, harried Red Caps trailing behind them, in their eagerness to secure a seat, ready to bound up onto the train almost before it had fully stopped. A four-hour train trip would feel a good deal longer if one had to stand all the way.

Her parents had telegraphed a few days earlier, giving the day and time of their arrival. Katherine would have loved to have had Andrew's parents, Helen and Henry, come from Brandon, but Helen was not feeling very well and Henry was concerned that the long train trip would be detrimental to her health. Predictably, Katherine's parents' train was late, but thankfully Andrew had taken the precaution of calling the general manager of the Grand Trunk to find out if it was on schedule so they wouldn't have to spend two hours waiting at the station. She and Andrew managed to retrieve her parents' luggage in short order from the tender mercies of the Grand Trunk. When they finally arrived home, her parents headed straight to bed, exhausted after nearly eight hours of train travel.

By mid-morning, Katherine knew it wasn't going to be a quiet day. She really needed Isabelle's extra pair of hands, but the maid was tending her own family's needs. Katherine was grateful for her mother's help; without it, the day would have ended in complete disaster. Andrew and her father were not much help. It took nearly an hour to clean up after they opened the large pile of gifts that had been placed under the tree. It was the family tradition to open the gifts first thing in the morning.

When Jamie was a little boy, he had suffered through waiting impatiently until all the grown-ups were up before attacking his gifts, tearing the wrapping off in great anticipation of the goodies inside.

This Christmas there was no strong sense of anticipation, no real surprises. Everyone waited until they had some breakfast before they made their way to the living room and the tree. Everyone received articles of clothing to get them through the winter ahead, and books and records for the Victrola. Katherine unwrapped Andrew's gift of some expensive stationery that had caught her notice, and a beautiful jade fountain pen. Her mother didn't complain about the grey pleated skirt Katherine gave her, which meant she liked it. Walter grumbled about the cost but kept fingering and examining the gold pocket watch she and Andrew had bought to replace Walter's plain mechanic's timepiece. Andrew was pleased with the fur-lined chocolate leather jacket she had picked out for him. He was even more pleased with the 12-gauge Browning double barrel he received from her father. He and Walter enjoyed going out hunting in the fall.

After they had cleaned up, it was nearly nine o'clock. Later, Katherine and Ada prepared a light lunch of cold roast beef sandwiches, Macintosh apples, and freshly baked butter tarts for dessert. That afternoon, the Russell Theatre was showing a moving picture that Katherine's parents particularly wanted to attend about the war. Before they left for the theatre, the two women cleaned and stuffed the turkey and put it in the oven to start cooking. It was an eight-pound bird, with lots of stuffing, so it would need the full afternoon to cook. They put the peeled potatoes, carrots, and turnips into saucepans and covered them with cold water so they wouldn't dry out while the bird cooked.

When they got back from the theatre, it was nearly three o'clock, and Katherine was in a sombre mood. The moving picture they had watched had disturbed her greatly. It was not what she'd been expecting. The *Ottawa Journal* had promoted the picture as a "thrilling and graphic" war film made in France, with "stirring scenes that would give tremendous support to the Allied cause by stimulating interest in recruitment." But the scenes had the opposite effect on her. Seeing the devastated and denuded landscape projected onto the screen in all its horror, all she could think of was that Jamie had died in such hell. At one point, she had to leave her seat to weep into her handkerchief as quietly as she could in the privacy of the women's washroom.

Then, still feeling emotionally raw, for the next few hours back at the house she had to endure friends and relatives who stopped by to offer their Christmas greetings. It was nearly six o'clock when the last of the guests finally left.

As she and her mother made the final preparations for dinner, Katherine realized how comforting it was to have her mother with her for the holidays. While she loved her mother dearly, usually after a few days of being treated as if she were still a little girl she felt relief when her parents returned home. This year she didn't mind the mothering. She took a moment to really see her mother as she was peeking into the oven to check on the bird. She saw the lines on her mother's face and noticed that her hair was now more white than chestnut. She was getting old. The thought someday that she wouldn't be here any more came unbidden. A tear welled up and rolled down Katherine's cheek.

Her mother straightened up from her inspection and wiped her hands on her apron. "The turkey is nearly done. We can start on the..." She stopped when she saw the tear on her daughter's cheek. She smoothed her hair with her hand as she said, "I know, dear. It's quite all right. It's been a long day."

"Yes, Mom," sniffed Katherine as she wiped her eyes.

"How are things between you and Andrew?" her mother asked with a level gaze.

Katherine averted her own gaze. She really didn't want to answer the question, but if she didn't she would have to endure her mother's inquisitiveness until she got every detail. Playing it safe, she replied, "We are doing fine."

She read her mother surreptitiously and noted the disbelief. To deflect her next question Katherine asked, "Is Dad feeling better?" Her father had been suffering poor health of late.

"That man can be trying at times. The doctor said he needed some rest. But do you think that he will?" Ada waved her hands in frustration. "No! He still goes into the store every day. I keep telling him that Peter can take care of things when he's not there." Peter was the store manager. "But he won't listen to me. I don't know what I'm going to do with the man."

"Andrew is having the same problems with his mum," commented Katherine sympathetically. "Was business good this year?" Katherine's father ran a farm equipment company that supplied most of the Massey-Ferguson farm equipment in Waterloo.

"Actually, with the war it has picked up. Like everyone else, your dad's finding that hiring staff is difficult. We may be forced to hire women, if it continues."

"Dad would like that," replied Katherine sarcastically.

Her mother snorted. "He may not like it but he may not have a choice."

Katherine turned her attention to the potatoes boiling on the stove.

Ada watched her for a moment. Her hands were smoothing her apron. They stopped when she made a decision. "Piece of advice, dear," she said. "It's best to settle this between you and Andrew as soon as possible. If you don't, marriage can be very long and trying."

Katherine peered intently at the potatoes, poking one with a fork. "I know, Mom. I just can't."

"Katherine. Look at me when I'm talking to you," Ada commanded.

Katherine reluctantly faced her mother. "What!"

"Don't take that tone with me, missy," scolded Ada, sternly shaking a forefinger.

"Yes, Mom," murmured Katherine more respectfully.

"That's better. One more thing. You're still young. You should consider having another child."

"Mom!" replied Katherine, her mouth dropping open in shock.

Ada put up her hand and said, "I know. I know. You're hurting right now and the last thing you are thinking about is having another child. And having a child will not guarantee that you and Andrew will patch things up. God knows in some families it makes things worse. However, if we hadn't lost your brother to polio, we wouldn't have you."

Ada sighed wistfully. "I still think of him from time to time. I wonder what he would have been like as a grown man. But he will always remain five, just as Jamie will always remain seventeen, the last time that I saw him before left for the army."

After a moment's awkward silence, her mom indicated, with her chin, the boiling pot. "Are the potatoes ready?"

Grateful for the distraction, Katherine picked up the fork again and pricked one of the potatoes in the pot. "They're done," she announced.

"Good. You'd better call your father and husband," her mother ordered.

"Right, Mom," Katherine said obediently.

As Katherine moved toward the kitchen door, Ada spoke again. "Katherine — just keep it in mind. You don't have to decide right away."

Katherine acknowledged her mother with a glance and a half grin. Then she left the room to summon the men to supper.

In the study, Andrew was having an enjoyable drink and a cigar with Katherine's father, Walter. They had always gotten along, since they had similar interests: hunting, fishing, and hockey, despite Walter being a fan of the Toronto Blueshirts hockey team.

"It was a pretty good game. Seven to one. It was tight the first period. Nighbor was showing good form," said Andrew smugly.

"Percy LeSueur has made some spectacular saves," Katherine's father pointed out. "But Toronto needs some strong defence."

"Still, from what I read, Toronto was giving some pretty good body checks. Unfortunately, in the second period they were beginning to sidestep them."

"I wish that I could have been at the game," said Walter with a longing sigh.

"It would have been fun if you had been able to come earlier. I've been so busy of late that I haven't been able to get to many games. From time to time, I walk past as the team is getting into shape along the canal," said Andrew.

"Really? I would like that," said Walter, brightening with interest.

"Sure, they usually run along the canal. We probably will see them when we take a constitutional."

"Good!" exclaimed Walter. "I just want to make sure that Toronto wins the cup this year."

"We will have to wait and see, won't we," teased Andrew in a good-naturedly. Walter chuckled as he finished his glass. "You want another one?"

"Of course," replied Katherine's father.

As he went to refresh his father-in-law's glass Andrew said, "By the way, did I mention that I got a new pistol?"

"Really?" Walter interest was piqued.

"I didn't tell you?" said Andrew, handing him his glass. "Here, take a gander." Andrew went to the gun cabinet. From one of the drawers, he pulled out a wooden case, which he placed on his desk. His father-in-law grunted as he got up from his chair and came to the desk. In the box, against the dark coloured felt lining, was a Colt revolver.

"Very nice. May I?" he asked.

"Of course. Go ahead."

Walter reached in and picked up the gun. The first thing he did was check whether the weapon was loaded by opening the cylinder. Once he was satisfied that the gun was safe, he hefted it then stared down the barrel. "Nice balance," he said admiringly. "When did you get it?"

"It's government issue. We ordered about five thousand of them. I got one assigned to me," MacNutt informed him proudly.

"Very nice. Very nice indeed," Walter murmured enviously.

"Dad, Andrew," said Katherine behind them. "Dinner's ready."

Both men turned to Katherine, who was standing in the doorway. "Thanks, Katherine."

"Thank, you dear," said Katherine's father, grinning. "We will be along in a moment."

Katherine glared at the gun. "Can't we have one day without talking about guns?" Before the two men could say a word, she turned and stomped down the hall.

Walter turned to his son-in-law. "I'm sorry, lad, but you are in deep."

Andrew sighed as he put the gun back in the case. "I know."

TENEMENT BUILDING, RIVINGTON STREET, LOWER EAST SIDE,
MANHATTAN, NEW YORK CITY
9:00 P.M., SATURDAY, DECEMBER 25, 1915

Count Jaggi would have rather been sitting at the Ritz having a decent Christmas supper. Instead, he was sitting in a safe house meeting with Captain von Papen, who was beginning to try his patience. It didn't help that he was tired, since he had spent most of the day reading telegrams, letters, and reports. He was glad for his cover, otherwise he would have had a hard time trying to explain the volume of mail he was receiving. He thought briefly about getting someone to take some of the load from him, but the problem was finding someone trustworthy and reliable. Considering that most of the people in the network had been recruited by von Papen, it was not a good idea until he determined their reliability.

"So it's official?" he asked von Papen, who was sitting across from him.

"I'm afraid so," replied von Papen remorsefully.

When the Count had arrived at the safe house, he found a sombre and dejected von Papen waiting for him. It didn't take a genius to figure out why. Von Papen was being sent back to Germany in disgrace. It was an embarrassment to the German government.

"When do you set sail?" asked the Count, keeping his delight that this incompetent was out of his hair out of his voice.

140

"Next Wednesday the 28th," grumbled von Papen, sipping the brandy that the owner of the safe house had left out for them.

"Is Boy-Ed travelling with you?" asked the Count. He was well briefed about Captain Karl Boy-Ed, who since 1911 had been serving as Germany's naval attaché to the U.S. It was well known that Boy-Ed was a protégé of Admiral Alfred von Tirpitz. He had also worked with the German naval secretary to increase the size of the Imperial Navy, as a counter to the British Navy. However, so far the navy, except for the U-boats, had not been as effective as hoped.

Von Papen grimaced. "He has not been officially asked to leave yet, but he will be sent back shortly."

"Very well then. I'll have time to chat with him before he leaves," said the Count. He had not yet had the chance to talk with the naval captain, but he would have to meet with him soon, because they would be working closely together. He hoped that Boy-Ed would prove more competent than von Papen.

"As you wish," was von Papen's subdued reply. "You've also heard about Franz von Rintelen's capture in England?"

"No, I did not." The Count was not terribly surprised by the satisfied gleam in von Papen's eyes. He knew the history between the two men. "That makes things difficult."

Von Papen nodded.

"I was hoping to salvage something from our operations," the Count continued. Von Papen frowned at the word. The Count cursed himself for the slip. He was trying to manoeuvre von Papen into a comfortable position. In truth, the Count would write off most of von Papen's operations, but he wouldn't tell him that. When von Papen found that out, he would already be in Berlin, too far away to do anything, even if he wanted to. He hated to lose any good men, but if they had been compromised, which was most likely, then they were not of much use to him, except to distract the American authorities from his real operations. Still, von Papen had some useful contacts and knowledge of past operations that could be of interest. Of particular interest to the Count was the captain's access to funds that the Count desperately needed to finance any future operations.

"Unfortunately, there is very little that I can do to help," said von Papen.

The Count gave him a reassuring smile. "What you can do is give me a further briefing on your operations. Especially those that have been successful."

Von Papen directed his attention away from the Count as his hand rolled the cupped bowl of the brandy glass. The glass stopped moving when he made his decision. "As you wish."

"Good," replied the Count. "Can you give me an update on the present political situation?"

"I'm afraid that it's not good. The damn British have turned the Americans against us."

"But don't we have any friends in the U.S. government at all?"

"We do, but they have been keeping a low profile lately," said von Papen.

"They want more money?"

Von Papen waved his right hand dismissively, which told the Count that was indeed the case.

"What have we done to date to help the political situation?"

"In Chicago we set up the Labor Peace Council, with the express purpose of recruiting and using the workers' and farmers' votes to put pressure on the American politicians to enforce an embargo of weapons and military supplies to the Allies."

"Sounds promising. What did you actually tell the workers and farmers?" asked the Count, frowning.

"That we wanted to promote universal peace," said the captain, smirking. "Response was promising enough that we set up an office in Washington, and we did have a number of conferences and meetings to promote universal peace. The Council raised quite a bit of money, which we used to bribe elected officials."

"Are American officials easy to bribe?"

The captain snorted. "They are quite easily bought, but the problem is that they don't stay bought."

The Count understood the problem. Once they got their money, one could never trust that they would actually deliver what they promised. "How long did it last?"

The captain shifted uncomfortably in his seat, then reluctantly said, "I'm afraid that the details were in Dr. Albert's satchel when it was stolen by the British."

The Count gazed at the captain for a long moment. "How big was this satchel? Did he carry all of his important papers in it?"

Von Papen glowered then said defensively, "He was worried that the British would break into his office and steal his papers. He thought it was best to carry them with him at all times."

"What was he planning to do if the British decided that it was more convenient to take his satchel by putting a bullet in his brain?" Expressionless, the captain didn't speak. "What's done is done. What happened to the Council?"

Sourly the captain stated, "After the American authorities got hold of Dr. Albert's papers they shut it down. It was a real shame. We got a fair amount of attention — we estimated we could deliver a million labour and half a million farm votes. We used the Council to attack the Federal Reserve Bank as a munitions trust, and attacked the collector for the port of New York for allowing munitions ships to sail from the harbour."

"There was no suspicion that it was connected to us?"

"No, not really," von Papen answered with a shrug. "Though when we tried to entice Samuel Gompers, the head of the American Federation of Labor, to join the Council, he flatly refused to meet with us. It's possible that he suspected it was a front."

The Count made a note of the name. In the next few days, he would endeavour to confirm what the captain was telling him. He didn't quite trust the man to give him everything. After all, it wasn't in von Papen's best interests to help him succeed. He might not go out of his way to betray Jaggi, exactly, but he could conveniently forget details of importance.

"There were other allegations linking the Council to us, but the Council's lawyers denied there were any. After the doctor's papers were published, there was little we could do. People started to withdraw their memberships and the funding dried up."

The Count stroked his temple thoughtfully then asked, "Do we have any influence on Henry Ford's peace plan?"

"I'm afraid not. The ambassador has met Ford on a number of occasions. For such a rich, powerful man, he is rather naive about politics."

"He's leading the peace group that is in the Fatherland now. I'm sure that Berlin is planning to take full advantage of it."

"I'm sure that they will."

There was an awkward moment, then the Count asked, "Are you all packed for your trip back to Europe?"

"I still have a great deal to do," the captain answered dryly.

"I just want to remind you of my request that any papers and documents related to current operations be forwarded to me."

Von Papen couldn't keep the irritation from his voice. "I have not forgotten."

"Just a friendly reminder. After all, we don't want them falling into British hands."

"All important documents will be left behind. I will only be bringing personal papers back with me. Also, I still have diplomatic immunity, and we have been given assurances that the British will not interfere," assured the captain.

Since when have the British followed the rules? thought the Count. He said instead, "Very good. If I don't see you again, have a safe trip."

"Thank you," replied the captain. "It will be nice to be back in the Fatherland."

CHAPTER 15

The Count felt pleasantly tired and drained when he left the apartment for a rendezvous with Müller. He pulled out his watch, noted the time, and sighed. He would be late and Müller would be upset. He really didn't want to upset the man too much. He had to keep him reasonably happy since he was the only one in the German network who was competent, reliable, and discreet. He was even more essential with the network in shambles. Paul Koenig was sitting in an American jail while Franz von Papen was on his way across the Atlantic to Germany. The loss of Müller would cripple the network for months until a suitable man, if there was one, could be found.

A block from the apartment he waved down a cab and ordered the driver to take him to the corner of Broadway and 22nd Street. When the cabbie dropped him off, he spotted Müller immediately. It wasn't difficult — there were not many people out on the street and Müller had posted himself on the corner. Though he had an impatient air about him, Müller did blend in with the little pedestrian traffic there was. He was dressed in a dark business suit, over which he wore a tan overcoat and a black homburg. A battered brown satchel dangled from his left hand.

"Good morning, Müller," said the Count pleasantly when he reached him.

"You're late," said Müller brusquely.

"I was unavoidably delayed."

"Blonde or brunette?" asked Müller.

The Count studied him for brief moment then laughed. "A bit of both," he answered. The woman whose bed he had just left wasn't particularly sophisticated, but she made up for it with plenty of vigour and enthusiasm. She was the wife of one of the American contributors to his Belgian Relief fund. At a fundraiser the previous week, he had caught the gleam in her eye. When he had approached her and nonchalantly stroked her backside, she didn't move away. She gave him a knowing smile and her card. It was obvious that it wasn't her first time, because she showed no hesitation to quickly get undressed as he entered her apartment when her husband was away.

Müller looked at him, puzzled.

"Let's just say that the mount was of a different colour," the Count explained wryly.

Müller frowned as he remarked, "Women will be the death of you."

The Count raised an eyebrow in amusement. "True, but considering the alternatives I can't think of a better way to go. Shall we take a stroll?"

Müller acquiesced and they strolled towards Fifth Avenue. The Count preferred to talk in public places rather than in the paper-thin tenements they had used so far. The neighbours were more likely to notice and speculate about the comings and goings. He could have used a hotel, but there was cost involved this way, and the hotel detectives were just as suspicious as the tenement's neighbours.

"I have some mail for you," Müller said.

The Count glanced at the satchel Müller was carrying. "Were you able to set up a new mailbox yet?"

"Not yet," replied Müller.

"Did you pick it up or did someone pick it up for you?" the Count demanded sharply.

"Someone picked them up for me and delivered them. I made sure that I had no surveillance when I did. I am looking into getting a new one soon," Müller answered.

"Someone reliable, I hope."

"Of course," replied Müller testily.

The Count smiled. "So what happened to the rubber shipment?"

Müller cast a sour glance at the Count. "Simply bad luck, it appears. The British were doing an ordinary search and found the rubber in the mail bags."

With the British blockade of German ports and the internment of much of her merchant navy in allied ports, Germany began to use neutral ships to transport essential war supplies she needed. However, the British soon extended their blockade and began regularly to stop and search the neutral ships that were bound for Germany, even American ones, for war supplies. Since then the Germans and the British had been playing cat-and-mouse smuggling games. The latest had involved sending rubber in large mail bags to Germany via Holland using the American postal system.

"We are not having very much luck, are we?" the Count said with a matching sourness.

"Not at the moment," answered Müller.

"So we will have to create a new route then."

"I'm afraid so."

"Do you have any ideas?"

"We could use your Belgian Relief shipments to transport supplies," Müller suggested.

"It's not a bad idea, but I'll have to give it some thought."

"What is there to think about? It's a good idea," Müller pressed. "The shipments get less scrutiny than normal cargoes would. They would be addressed to neutral countries, which would then ship them on to the Fatherland."

"That is true," sighed the Count. "But we have to plan it out carefully. It wouldn't do to have a poor starving Belgian open a box expecting porridge and find bullets instead."

"*Ja*, Herr Count."

"The question is whether it is worth blowing my cover. How many runs can we get before the British stumble on our scheme? Two or three?" asked the Count rhetorically.

"More than that," insisted Müller.

"If you say so. The shipments will help the Fatherland, but they may be insignificant compared to providing the Imperial General Staff with political, economic, and military intelligence that will go a long way to winning the war."

"You have a point," Müller agreed reluctantly.

"I still can be of use."

"How?"

"I'm a representative of Belgian Relief, and I need to hire ships to carry relief supplies. I will be spending quite a bit of time at the port. I may be able to find ships that would be interested in carrying contraband. And during my visits I might be able to pick up information on ships that could be carrying cargo we don't want to reach the Allies."

"We do have people on the docks that provide us with information already," Müller pointed out.

"With Koenig in jail, how many of our people have been compromised? We need to verify the information that is provided to us before we take action. I don't want an operation to fail because we didn't check that the information we obtained was from a reliable source."

"I understand," replied Müller. "When are you are going back to Ottawa?"

"In a day or two. I haven't decided yet. It's a backwater, but still there is useful intelligence there," said the Count. "The Canadians announced over the holidays that they will increase their army corps to over 500,000, which is interesting."

Müller whistled. "Where are they going to find the men? You'd think they'd already be scraping the bottom of the barrel."

"I have no idea, but their defence minister, Hughes, says they will do quite nicely with volunteerism," said the Count skeptically. "On another topic, were you able to find information about their head of secret police?"

Müller frowned. "I checked my sources, and they don't have very more than you already have on him."

"A pity. I guess I'll have to get more from other sources," answered the Count as he resumed walking.

"What sources?" Müller skipped a few steps to catch up.

The Count evaded the question. "Do you have a date when our cigars will be delivered?" He was amused by the use of the word "cigars" in reference to pipe bombs, which were the weapon of choice in sabotaging Allied shipping leaving the New York harbour.

Müller stared at the ground as he considered the Count's question. "We supplied the cigars to the Irish last week. They should be in place by now. At least some of them. I'll check with them to make sure everything went well. By the way, they've been asking about arranging a meeting with you."

"They have, have they," muttered the Count. He had concerns about meeting with the leadership of the Clan na Gael, the local Irish secret society. The Irish were extremely useful, since, unlike most of the German workers on the docks, they had free access to the cargo ships. The Count had explicit orders from Major Nicolai about the Irish. He was to provide them with money and weapons but under no circumstances was he to indicate to them that Germany would provide troops or advisors in their struggle to liberate Ireland from the British.

"Isn't Boy-Ed dealing with them?" he asked.

"Yes," replied a sullen Müller.

"Is there any reason why I need to meet with them?"

The question caught Müller off guard. He reset his homburg as he paused to think about it. "I just thought you might want to meet the players involved."

"I agree, but only if I need to. They are already familiar with Boy-Ed, and therefore they are comfortable with him. Let's not add any more complications. Also, the fewer of our people they meet, the better our security."

Müller frowned. "Boy-ed may not be happy about it."

The Count snorted derisively. "Have you arranged a meeting with him yet?"

Müller sighed as his briefcase gently bumped his leg. "Boy-Ed said that he will be in New York next week. We might be able to arrange a meeting then."

"That sounds good. I'll leave that in your capable hands."

"That will be fine," answered Müller. "Don't forget your mail." He gave the Count the battered satchel. The Count took it and watched as Müller waved down a cab before he started heading for the nearest subway station.

MEETING ROOM, EAST BLOCK, PARLIAMENT HILL
1:45 P.M., WEDNESDAY, DECEMBER 29, 1915

MacNutt watched Commissioner Sherwood as he closed his copybook and slipped his reading glasses into his shirt pocket, signifying the end of their meeting. "Going back to the office?" he asked MacNutt as he rose from the table.

"Yes, sir," replied MacNutt amiably.

"Good. I'll walk with you," replied Sherwood as he held the door open for MacNutt. In the hall he asked, "By the way, have you completed your review of the Enemy Alien Act?"

"I've gone over it and made some comments and minor changes," answered MacNutt. "Why?"

"Justice Minister Doherty would like to have all the comments by the end of the week. He wants to get the final draft ready for the next session of Parliament on the fifteenth," explained the commissioner.

"I understand, sir. It's sitting on my desk. If you want to stop by my office, you can pick it up right now."

"That would be fine."

When they entered MacNutt's outer office, they found Lacelle rapidly striking the typewriter keyboard with his two index fingers. They were a blur; he could hit sixty words a minute. It took a few moments for their presence to break his concentration. When he recognized the commissioner, he immediately rose and stood at attention.

"At ease, Sergeant. I'm sorry that I've interrupted you. That was quite a display," said the commissioner as he gestured to the sergeant to sit down.

"Thank you, sir," replied Lacelle, pleased.

"I'm glad that someone is actually doing some work for a change," said Sherwood.

"Yes, sir," replied Lacelle. "How can I help you, sir?"

"It's all right, Sergeant. The commissioner wanted to get my comments on the latest draft of the Enemy Alien Act," answered MacNutt.

"Yes, sir. However, I think you need to read this right away, sir," Lacelle said as he snatched up the telegram on his desk.

"It can wait for a moment," retorted MacNutt.

"No, it's important, sir. It came in the morning mail," blurted Lacelle as he thrust the telegram at MacNutt. Annoyed, MacNutt jerked the telegram out of Lacelle's hand. What could be so important that it couldn't wait a moment? When he finished reading the telegram, he looked at Lacelle then handed the telegram to the commissioner.

When Sherwood finished reading it, he said dryly, "Well, that solves your budget problems."

MacNutt gave a start, then just a hint of a smile appeared. "Not what I had in mind." He turned to Sergeant Lacelle. "I want you to send a telegram back to MI5 asking them to send everything they've got on this on the next available ship."

"Yes, sir. That is what I been working on," Lacelle muttered, indicating his typewriter.

"You are a good man, Sergeant," complimented MacNutt as he turned to the commissioner. "Now as long as we can get MI5 to cooperate…"

Sherwood sighed. "Let's wait for their reply before we start rattling cages."

"Do you want me to inform the PM?" asked MacNutt.

Sherwood rubbed his chin for a moment as he considered it. "The fewer people who know, the better, otherwise we'll have a witch hunt. I'll mention it to the minister, and he may have a quiet word with the PM. Besides, what can we tell him? That MI5 has provided proof that there is a German agent in Canada. We don't have any more solid information than this. Until we do, let's keep it as quiet as possible for the moment."

"We'll try. It will be difficult once the Mounties and Customs learn about," MacNutt stated.

"I know. But let's try to keep it as low as possible."

"Yes, sir," replied MacNutt. Then he remembered. "What about the Royals?"

Sherwood grimaced. "I doubt that the Huns are silly enough to strike at the Royals, but we should increase security just the same."

"That should make Simms happy," replied MacNutt.

Sherwood snorted. "Well, it seems as if you have everything in hand, so I'll leave you to it."

As the commissioner turned to leave, MacNutt said, "Just a moment, sir. Do you still want my notes?"

"Yes, of course. Thank you for reminding me," replied a relieved Sherwood. MacNutt quickly entered his inner office, returned with a manila file folder with a diagonal red stripe across it, and handed it to the commissioner.

CALLOT'S DRESS SHOP, BANK STREET, OTTAWA
2:30 P.M., WEDNESDAY, DECEMBER 29, 1915

Katherine was struggling to put on an evening dress, but there wasn't much space in the change room, so she kept banging her elbows on the cubicle walls. She finally got the gown on, but she couldn't reach the buttons running down the back, so she left it unfastened till Nicole could help her.

She found Nicole in Callot's Dress Shop's main showroom studying a dress that Shelley, the slim, auburn-haired middle-aged salesclerk, was holding up for her attention. Nicole turned when she heard Katherine's footsteps.

"Can you help me with the buttons?" Katherine requested as she turned to face the full-length mirror.

"I'll do it, ma'am," interjected Shelley. She hung the dress up on a nearby rack and went to Katherine's assistance. When Shelley was done, Katherine released her breath. The bodice was somewhat tight, but it wasn't interfering with her breathing.

"So what do you think?" Shelley asked as she gauged Katherine's reaction. "It's the latest fashion in New York and London."

Katherine smoothed a wrinkle on the bodice and tugged gently so that it covered more of the tops of her breasts. The neckline was barely within the bounds of modesty. She turned sideways and viewed her profile. It was quite flattering to her figure, but she had doubts about the pale taupe colour.

"I don't know." Katherine frowned. She turned to the mirror again. The dress was more ornate than she liked. She favoured dresses with simpler lines. But it *was* the latest fashion.

"What do you think?" she implored Nicole.

Nicole rose slowly from the upholstered chair then circled her friend, tapping her lips with her forefinger as she examined the dress critically. "Hmmm, it's okay, I like it," she replied unconvincingly.

Katherine raised an eyebrow then eyed her reflection again. She had gone shopping for dresses because she had absolutely nothing to wear to the opening of Parliament, and all the accompanying luncheons and dinner parties she had to attend. Nicole had already had enough shopping and was patiently waiting for Katherine to reach the same point.

"What's wrong with it?" demanded Katherine.

Nicole glanced in the direction of Katherine's breasts and said with a smirk, "Well, Andrew will no doubt appreciate it."

Katherine glowered at Nicole. She returned to the mirror, seeking another reason to reject the dress.

Shelley, sensing a sale slipping away, spoke up again. "It's a *beautiful* colour, so rich. It's the absolute latest in New York and London."

Katherine decided. "No, it doesn't suit me. I prefer a darker colour."

Shelley's smile did not waver. "Yes, ma'am. I have something in the back that you may like better. Be back in a moment." She hurried to the back of the shop.

Katherine turned her back to Nicole. "Can you undo me, please?"

"Are you going to the governor general's levee?" Nicole asked as she undid the buttons.

"I haven't decided yet. Andrew will probably be attending, because he will be taking care of security," Katherine replied before she entered the change room. She left the door slightly ajar so she could continue talking with Nicole. "Are you going?" she asked, raising her voice slightly.

"Yes. I wouldn't miss it for the world," Nicole said. "Why aren't you coming?"

As Katherine stepped out of the dress, she paused to consider her reply. She had attended quite a few New Year's levees at Rideau Hall. She remembered the times when she and Jamie had attended. Jamie never lasted more than a few hours; he always complained that it was too boring just watching strangers stand in line.

"I don't know," Katherine muttered, lifting the gown carefully. She gave it a couple of shakes to remove any wrinkles, then slipped it back on its hanger.

"What did you say?" asked Nicole.

Katherine stuck her head around the change room door. "I said I don't know."

Disappointment crossed Nicole's face. "Aw, Katherine, please do come. It will be awfully dull without you."

Katherine ducked back into the change room. "So have you heard anything from Michael?" she asked, changing the subject. Michael was Nicole's husband.

"I received a letter from him yesterday. He's still on the Salisbury Plains. He's trying to reassure me that everything is fine, but I can tell from the tone of his letters that he's having a difficult time. He doesn't know when he will be sent to the front, but he says that they will be going soon," replied a worried Nicole.

"Well, you could let him know that he will be getting some company soon," said Katherine.

"What do you mean? Don't tell me that Borden finally decided to let your husband volunteer?" exclaimed Nicole.

Katherine popped her head out again and gave Nicole a sharp look. "No. I mean that Borden will announce that they are increasing the Canadian corps to half a million men."

"The poor boys," cried Nicole softly.

Katherine was disappointed by Nicole's reaction, especially with her husband being a major in the corps in England. She had hoped her friend would be pleased by the news that the Canadian government was getting serious about prosecuting the war. She knew that her campaign to encourage recruitment by handing out white feathers was a bone of contention between them. Nicole had handed out a white feather only once. The man's reaction had such a deep impact on her that even with Katherine's reassurance and cajoling, she refused to hand them out again.

"So are you going to the opening of Parliament?" asked Katherine, quickly changing the subject.

"Duty calls. But I don't think it will be as enjoyable as in previous years," Nicole said.

"You may be right," acknowledged Katherine wistfully.

Shelley finally returned from the back of the shop with several new dresses draped over an arm. "What do you think of these?" she inquired.

"Let's see." Katherine held up a light apricot one and considered it in the mirror. "This colour's better. I'll start with this one."

"Of course, Mrs. MacNutt," said Shelley. Katherine entered the dressing room and exchanged the dresses that were hanging there with the new ones Shelley had brought.

Nicole cast an eye at Shelley then winked. "By the way, have you heard from that Count of yours?"

Katherine abruptly poked her head out and gazed at Nicole, her mouth open in shock. "What do you mean?"

"Well, he did come to your Christmas party."

"And your point?"

"Are you inviting him to come to Parliament?" asked Nicole. She gave Shelley another wink.

"Whatever for?"

"For one, he's a handsome man," teased Nicole.

Katherine replied, scandalized, "I'm a married woman!"

Shelley had a difficult time trying to keep a straight face. Nicole laughed. "You may be married, but you are not dead."

Katherine didn't reply.

"Kath. Katherine?" said Nicole as her smile creased in concern.

Katherine's reply was muffled by the dress she was pulling on over her head. When she emerged, she stood in front of the showroom mirror again. She raised her hair so that it was out of the way. "Can you help, please?"

"So are you?"

"Am I what?"

"Going to invite him?"

"I don't know about that. He's a busy man. I don't think he would be interested in the opening of Parliament," Katherine said as she examined herself in the mirror.

"Now *that's* nice," said Nicole. This time her tone was genuine. Katherine agreed. She liked what she saw in the mirror.

"I'll take this one, Shelley," said Katherine.

"Excellent," replied the saleswoman. "I'll get a box for you." She bustled off to the back of the store again. Katherine inspected the shop then sighed, dispirited. "Nothing else here really appeals to me."

"You want to go someplace else?"

"We've been to every shop in Ottawa already. There isn't very much," Katherine lamented.

154

"We could always go to Montreal," countered Nicole, "or even New York."

"That is a thought," said Katherine.

"Why not. We need to get away for a couple of days to have some fun. Why not?"

"I'll have to ask Andrew about it. I don't know that he'll want me to go."

"I'm sure if you ask him nicely," Nicole said with a smirk.

Katherine rolled her eyes.

"Wonderful!" said Nicole excitedly. "I know exactly where we can go in New York. We'll get the night train and then..." As Nicole began planning the trip, the thought entered Katherine's mind that she might be able to see the Count while she was there. She liked the thought. She liked it very much.

CHAPTER 16

The Count was sitting in a small coffee shop a couple of blocks south of Broadway, feeling tired and hung over. Unfortunately, the hangover was from spending the previous evening in a dive on the waterfront trying, successfully, to outdrink a young German sailor he wanted to recruit from the ship *Vaterland*.

He drank the terrible-tasting coffee he had ordered in the faint hope it would sharpen his wits, which he needed in full working order for his morning appointment. It was too early in the morning, but he had picked neither the time nor the place. He had had very little choice because the naval attaché would be out of town the following week. Besides, it was politic to go along. It was a good idea to be on good terms with Captain Karl Boy-Ed.

As he waited, the Count reviewed what he knew of the captain. The man was in his mid-forties, a product of a German-Turkish marriage. He couldn't remember if the father was the Turk, or the mother, but that was of little consequence. Boy-Ed had entered the navy at a very young age and rose quickly through the ranks. Eventually, he caught the notice of Admiral Alfred von Tirpitz, who made him his aide. As the admiral's aide, he had carried out several highly successful press campaigns to increase the size of the imperial navy, to the great pleasure of the Kaiser. As a reward, he was given the posting as a naval attaché to Washington. Before the outbreak of the war, Boy-Ed had cut a swath through Washington, politically and socially, with his charm and cultivation.

Jaggi missed Boy-Ed's entrance into the shop, so he gave a start when the chair in front of him was pulled out and the captain sat down.

"Good morning, Herr Count," said the captain cordially as he stuffed his leather gloves into the pockets of a grey overcoat, which he then draped on the back of the empty chair to the Count's left.

"*Guten morgen*," returned the Count courteously. He signalled to the waitress that he needed his cup refilled. It tasted vile, but it should help him keep his senses alert. When the Count returned his gaze to the captain, he noticed that Boy-Ed had been unobtrusively appraising him. Boy-Ed was cut from a different cloth than von Papen. Anyone who had been a protégé of von Tirpitz was certain to have a degree of competence.

After the waitress filled their cups with more bad coffee, the Count spoke again. "So, it was finally time that we meet in person."

"*Ja*," said Boy-Ed as he leaned back in his chair, waiting for the Count to continue. The Count was well aware of the captain's strategy. With von Papen on his way back to Berlin, there would be a reorganization of their clandestine activities. If the Holland-American liner SS *Noordam* had set sail when it was scheduled, on the 22nd of December, it should be near Falmouth, England, by now. The English had given assurances that von Papen would be allowed to continue his voyage to Rotterdam, but one never knew with the English. At least with von Papen out of the way, they could reorganize their activities in a more efficient manner. Which brought the Count back to Boy-Ed. As the naval attaché, Boy-Ed was responsible for collecting, collating, and reporting back to the *Kaiserliche Marine* the U.S. Navy's intentions and capabilities. Which meant that the captain had contacts and informants that would be useful, even essential, in the campaign against the Allies. The captain was waiting for the Count to outline his strategy before he committed himself. The Count liked Boy-Ed's approach; it was the same way he would have handled the situation.

"As you are aware, I'll be taking over some of von Papen's duties now that he is no longer with us," began the Count.

"Some of his duties?" asked the captain as a crease of concern appeared on his forehead.

"Yes. His unofficial duties. I will not be attached in any official capacity with the embassy," explained the Count.

"I see. So what do you expect of me?"

The Count snorted. "Due to the haste with which the captain was forced to leave, I unfortunately did not get as complete a briefing as I would have liked. I was hoping that you would be able to fill in some critical gaps."

The captain frowned as he considered the request. "I would like to clarify one point. Are you reporting to the ambassador for your orders?"

The Count understood instantly what the captain was concerned about. One of the issues with Rintelen was that neither von Papen nor Boy-Ed recognized that Rintelen was in command and refused to take orders from him. This confused chain of command was an issue that needed to be addressed.

"That is one of the issues I will take up with Berlin. As a naval captain, you will understand quite well that there can only be one on a ship."

Boy-Ed agreed. "The question is, who will be the captain?"

"All I can do is contact Berlin for orders. In the meantime, we can arrange to meet regularly to discuss some of our operations so that we minimize any potential problems."

The captain stared off into space for a while. "That sounds agreeable. Until we get confirmation from Berlin."

"Good." The Count hoped that his face didn't betray what he was thinking. Essentially, they had a race on as to who could contact Berlin first. Boy-Ed had the advantage because he could use the embassy's telegraph and wireless facilities. From Müller, the Count had learned that the United States had ordered the closing of all private wireless stations, which included the German-built Sayville Station on Long Island. Also, all interned German ships had been ordered to shut down their wireless and remove and dismantle their aerials. However, the German sailors were quite inventive in rebuilding wireless radio aboard the interned ships. They erected hidden aerials throughout parts of the ships, such as in the funnels, so they could continue to receive and transmit messages to and from Berlin.

The Count leaned towards the captain. "So, Captain, I understand that it is your task to take care of the German sailors that have been interned here in New York."

The captain leaned forward as well. "Yes. Quite a number of ships have been interned. We would like to get the interned ships out, but with the British Navy sitting just outside American waters, there is very little we can do," he said with a touch of frustration in his voice. "I was able to resupply some of our battleships and cruisers with coal and food. With the British just outside the legal limit, it was not enough. After a couple of resupplies the British would always locate our ships."

"How were they able to do that?" asked the Count.

"I don't know," answered Boy-Ed soberly.

"Do we have an informant?"

"I have not been able to find him. *If* we have one."

The Count let the captain's statement slide for now. "Can't we sneak our ships out at night?"

Boy-Ed shook his head. "It takes time. First, the ship's captain needs to recall his men. Quite a few sailors live on board ship, but many are onshore in boarding houses. Once he gets his men on board he needs to make sure that the ship is seaworthy, especially if it has been sitting docked for several months. That means he has to acquire the necessary equipment to make repairs. Then he needs to fill his bunkers with coal and get provisions for his men. Once he has all that, the ship will need at least a day to build a good head of steam. With British spies everywhere, it is next to impossible for all that activity to go unnoticed. When the ship finally sails, there will probably be a British squadron waiting for it."

"So you've been getting German sailors back to the Fatherland?"

"It's the least I can do. Many sailors wanted to get back to Germany to get into the fight. Quite a few were in dire financial straits." When the captain saw the Count's expression, he cracked a grin then explained. "The sailors are only paid when they are at sea. With the ship tied up in the harbour they are not earning money. Many sailors are living on board ship because they cannot afford to live onshore. The ship's owners have helped out, but every day that the ship is tied up at the dock they are losing thousands of marks."

"How have you been getting them home?" the Count asked.

"It's fairly straightforward. Any sailors who want to get home can go to an office I have set up specifically for that purpose. I provide them with false passports and passage on a neutral ship — preferably Norwegian or Swedish, but we have been routing them through the Caribbean and South America of late. We also provide them with some spending money."

"Why South America?"

"The British have been stopping neutral ships in the North Sea and have been extra diligent checking papers, and they have been arresting more of our men. They haven't been checking them quite as much when the ships' destinations are Portugal or Spain. Once they get there, the German consulates help in getting them back into Germany."

"What about the American navy?"

"The American navy has a fleet of about 150 ships. The fleet is comprised of 50 destroyers, 10 dreadnoughts, 40 cruisers, and 23 pre-dreadnought destroyers, and 27 modern submarines."

"A formidable force. If the Americans enter the war, how many ships can they send to Europe?"

Boy-Ed took a sip of coffee as he considered the question. "It depends on the fuel supply. Their coal-firing ships would be most suitable because England has a plentiful supply of coal. Their oil-firing ships are a different matter. They could send several squadrons, which would relieve some of the British units for other duties."

The Count grimaced. "Are they continuing to build up their navy?"

Boy-Ed nodded. "They currently have a number of capital ships being built. They have a rather large industrial capacity, since they are also building replacement ships for the British and Russian navies, as well as merchant ships to replace those being lost to our U-boats."

"Is there nothing we can do to stop them or slow them down?"

"We tried several projects, but their capacity is such that it would be a minor disturbance at best."

"What about the Canadians?"

"They are of little consequence," Boy-Ed said dismissively with a wave.

"Why?" asked the Count in surprise.

"When the war started, they had two tired pre-dreadnought destroyers with 250 sailors. The British Navy is currently taking care of the defence of the Canadian coasts and ports. They did acquire two subs about a year ago. What they will do with them I have no idea."

"What about them?"

"They are coastal subs. They were built in Seattle for the Chilean government, but the deal fell through and the Canadians acquired them."

"Interesting," said the Count. "And the Welland Canal?"

"It would be extremely useful to shut down the canal, because it would have a significant effect on the British supply situation, but it's now next to impossible. You'll never get large enough explosives at critical points in the locks to be able to put the canal out of commission. Security is too tight. Why the interest in Canada?" Boy-Ed added curiously.

The Count paused to think about it for a moment before answering, then he decided it was worth the risk. "I'll be in and out of Canada for the next few weeks and I was wondering what information would be useful to us."

"By any chance are you going to Ottawa or Montreal?"

"Why?" asked the Count. Now he felt that he had already given the captain too much information about his movements. Was the captain setting him up for betrayal to the authorities?

"I've heard that the Canadians are having some kind of enquiry in Ottawa into the boats they acquired. If you can get information on that, I would appreciate it."

"And Montreal?"

"It appears that the Canadians are building submarines for the British Admiralty in Montreal at the Vickers shipyard. I believe that they are Electric Boat Company designs. If you can confirm the type of subs and the number they have built and who bought them, it would be of interest to the *Kriegsmarine*."

"I'll see what I can do."

"Excellent." Boy-Ed glanced at his watch. "I have to leave now, or I'll be late for an appointment. We will talk again."

"We will," replied the Count as he watched the captain leave the restaurant.

PORT OF FALMOUTH, ENGLAND
11:00 A.M., SUNDAY, JANUARY 2, 1916

Inspector Owens watched as the dock workers secured the grey-painted passenger liner *Noordam* to the Falmouth dock. The inspector studied the ship. In places, the ship's original black and white paint was faintly visible. With the threat of being attacked and sunk, passenger liners had been repainted grey to make it more difficult for German submarines hunting in the North Atlantic to spot them.

Once the ship was secured, the crew swung the gantry into position. Owens had to wait until a steward released the metal chain on the gantry's entrance. With a tip of his fedora to Sergeant Connell and the two constables, he marched up the gantry.

Before he could step onto the ship, he was met by its chief purser.

"Good morning," he said. "Welcome aboard."

"Good morning," replied Inspector Owen, taking his warrant card from his breast pocket and holding it up for him to view. "I'm with Scotland Yard's Special Branch."

The purser visibly stiffened and became more alert. "Yes, sir. What you do need, sir?"

"Can you take me to Captain von Papen's stateroom, please?"

The purser said briskly, "Yes, sir. I know the way quite well." The purser led the Special Branch detectives through the well-appointed corridors. It took about five minutes to get to von Papen's stateroom on the port side of the ship.

Sergeant Connell knew that the inspector had been waiting impatiently ever since the ship had sailed from New York. The British government had given assurances, due to von Papen's diplomatic status, that he would have safe passage to Germany. It would be interesting if the man matched the picture they had developed.

Connell knocked on the stateroom door. He waited a moment then knocked again.

"Yes," said an irritated von Papen when he opened the door. He glanced quickly at Connell and Owens.

"Captain von Papen?" Connell demanded.

"Yes. How can I help you?" replied von Papen suspiciously.

"Scotland Yard, Special Branch," stated Connell, showing his warrant card.

"Please come in, gentlemen. Please have a seat."

"We will stand," said Connell stiffly. Owens and Connell inspected the stateroom. The room was made up of a sitting room with a door that let into a bedroom. Considering it was wartime, it was well furnished.

"As you wish," said von Papen as he took a seat and lit a cigarette. "So how can I help you gentlemen?"

"We would like to inspect your luggage," said Owens.

Von Papen gave him a sharp look. "That will not be possible."

"Why not, may I ask?" said Owens.

"Your government has given assurances that my passage back to Germany would be unhindered."

"That is correct, but it does not apply to your luggage or your papers," replied Owens.

Von Papen glared at Owens for a moment. "Sir, that is outrageous. I have diplomatic immunity. It also includes my luggage and my personal papers."

"Unfortunately, the Foreign Office disagrees."

"This is outrageous! I will speak with the ship's captain," von Papen shouted, pointing to the purser. "You, sir, please call the captain."

The purser goggled at Owens, then at von Papen. "Yes, sir."

It took about five minutes for the captain to appear, and he listened to von Papen's complaint. "I'm sorry, sir. There is very little that I can do. We are in British territorial waters, and they have a legitimate warrant. I'm afraid you must surrender your luggage and papers to Scotland Yard."

Von Papen was visibly furious, but there was very little he could do. "Very well. My government will lodge a protest with your government concerning this treatment. I also demand a receipt for the luggage." He knew quite well that the protest would fall on deaf ears.

"That is acceptable," sneered Owens.

Owens turned to the ship's captain and ordered, "Captain, can you please see to it that Captain von Papen's luggage is brought ashore."

"Yes, sir," said the captain.

"One of my constables will stay with you until we have gone through your luggage and until the ship leaves the port."

Von Papen gave Owens an angry nod.

"And we will search you again before you leave British waters to make sure that you are not leaving with contraband," Owens said. Von Papen was grinding his teeth as he was escorted from the room.

CHAPTER 17

When MacNutt entered his office, he noticed that Lacelle was not at his desk. He tried to recall if Lacelle was scheduled to be out of the office but nothing came to mind. MacNutt shrugged and went through the pile of letters in the in-basket on Lacelle's desk to determine whether there was anything urgent. He was scanning a memo when a haggard Lacelle trudged into the office.

"Good afternoon, sir." MacNutt peered at the clock on the wall and then back to the sergeant. "I apologize for being out of the office," Lacelle said stiffly. "I had a family matter to attend to."

"You look terrible. Nothing serious, I hope?" asked MacNutt.

"It's just the kids, sir," replied Lacelle glumly as he removed his overcoat and put it on the hanger behind the door.

When Lacelle mentioned his kids, MacNutt knew why the sergeant was upset and he cursed himself for not realizing it sooner. MacNutt had heard of the riot at the Guigues School where Franco-Ontarian parents, objecting the replacements of the Desloges sisters, had clashed with the Ottawa police. Several officers were injured in the fracas. He had planned to ask the sergeant whether they needed to investigate the matter.

"Were they at the school today?" he asked, his forehead creased with concern.

Lacelle's demeanour lightened a touch. "Marie had them at home. Pierre had the grippe, and she was afraid that something like this might happen."

"So what are you going to do?"

"I don't know," answered a dejected Lacelle as he made his way to his desk. "The kids love Béatrice and Diane. I just don't know what I can do. They need to learn French. I don't mind if they learn English, but I don't want them to lose their heritage."

MacNutt was aware, somewhat dimly, of the bind that his sergeant was in. Lacelle was fiercely proud of his culture, his heritage, and his language. He became somewhat prickly when someone told him to speak English. There had been a number of occasions when there was pressure from certain quarters to have the sergeant replaced with someone who was English and Protestant. MacNutt resisted the pressure, pointing out

164

that because of Lacelle's language skills he could conduct investigations in places where someone who only spoke English could not. MacNutt really didn't want to lose Lacelle; he was a good officer and would be extremely difficult to replace.

"You can always get them tutors," suggested MacNutt lamely.

"It's an added expense, and I really can't afford it," replied Lacelle gruffly.

"I'm sure that you will work it out one way or another. If you want, you can take some time off to take care of your family, go ahead. I can manage."

"No, that's okay, sir. Marie's at home with the kids. I'd rather be working," said Lacelle.

"As you wish. When you are settled, come in and take some notes for me," said MacNutt.

"Yes, sir."

"I wouldn't worry too much, Lacelle. Things will settle down, and the kids will be back in school as if nothing has happened. You'll see," said MacNutt weakly. He was at a loss as to what else to suggest.

He couldn't be more wrong.

REGENT THEATRE, BANKS AND SPARKS STREETS, OTTAWA
7:45 P.M., WEDNESDAY, JANUARY 5, 1916

Katherine admired the elegant lobby of the new Regent Theatre and smiled with pleasure at Andrew. They had been invited to the Regent Theatre's grand opening on New Year's Eve but with Andrew taking care of security at the governor general's levee, they couldn't make it. This evening was the first opportunity they had to come out and view the new theatre, and Katherine had wait impatiently for this evening to arrive, though she had to drag Andrew out of the house. When they arrived, they ran into Nicole and her brother, Denis, who had decided to come to the same show.

Nicole and Katherine had eagerly taken a quick tour of the theatre while Andrew and Denis went into the smoking room to have a cigar, and Katherine was sure that they would chat about politics. And she could guess what the topic would be. The recent announcement that the government promised to raise and put into the field an army corps of 500,000 had everyone in a buzz.

Nicole and Katherine agreed that the Regent was impressive. It was quite large, with 1,600 seats, about 100 fewer than in the Russell Theatre. It had some amenities that the Russell didn't have.

"So what do you think about the show?" asked Nicole as she came back from the refreshment counter with glasses of fruit punch.

Nicole's cheerfulness dimmed when she saw Mrs. Ramsey approaching them. "Katherine, you look lovely this evening."

"Thank you," replied Katherine with a side glance at Nicole.

"A splendid evening," Mrs. Ramsey said slyly to Nicole.

"Yes, it is," acknowledged Nicole with a brief crooked smile.

"Oh, have you heard about the German who was sent to the internment camp?" said Mrs. Ramsey, turning to Katherine.

Katherine flashed an irritated frown. A number of people seemed to gloat, telling her the story of the German who had escaped an internment camp and found employment in a war munitions factory in Hamilton. It was embarrassing for her husband, but what was done was done.

Mrs. Ramsey sniffed then asked, as she adjusted her shawl, "So how is Count Jaggi?"

"He seems to be fine," replied Katherine patiently.

"He's back in New York?"

"So I understand," interjected Nicole.

"Do you know when he will be returning?" Mrs. Ramsey asked Katherine with a raised eyebrow, ignoring Nicole.

"I have no idea," Katherine replied truthfully. "Why?"

"Oh, nothing…" Mrs. Ramsey said in a tone that belied her words. Before Katherine could inquire further, someone caught Mrs. Ramsey's attention, causing her to stiffen. Katherine turned too, and when she spotted Rebecca Bates, she understood Mrs. Ramsey's reaction. Mrs. Ramsey had never forgiven Mrs. Bates for denying her the presidency of the Order of the Imperial Daughters. When Rebecca spotted them she trailed over. She was in her early sixties, in an elegant black gown, with her silvery grey hair done up in an elegant chignon.

"Good evening, Katherine. Nicole." She gave both of them a smile and Mrs. Ramsey a polite nod. She didn't particularly care for Mrs. Ramsey either. "So how is your Belgian Relief work coming along?" she asked. "I understand you have a fundraiser soon?"

"Oh, yes," interjected Mrs. Ramsey. "Count Jaggi will be our guest speaker." Mrs. Ramsey stressed "our". Katherine knew that Mrs. Ramsey thought Rebecca might try to poach their speaker and was warning her to back off.

"Ah yes. The famous Count Jaggi. Is he here this evening?" Rebecca studied the crowded lobby.

"He's in New York," Katherine said. She could feel Mrs. Ramsey's eyes drilling into her.

"Oh, really?" replied Rebecca with a hint of skepticism. "I wouldn't mind meeting him, if it would be possible." Rebecca was now deliberately goading Mrs. Ramsey.

Katherine felt trapped. Whatever she said would end up offending one of the ladies. She hedged. "I don't know. He mentioned that he might be in town next week." In her peripheral vision, she saw Mrs. Ramsey clench her jaw.

"Just in time for the opening of Parliament," suggested Rebecca with a cheerful wave of her hand. "Excellent. Do you know which hotel he will be staying at?"

Katherine shook her head. "No, I'm afraid not." She almost blurted out that she and Nicole would be in New York this weekend, and if she saw the Count she might ask him. She held back because she had not found an opportune time to discuss the trip with Andrew.

"When you find out, could you could let me know — I'd be ever so grateful. I would like to invite him to a soirée I'm hosting to mark the opening," said Rebecca.

"I'd be happy to," replied Katherine.

"Delightful! Now, where did I lose my husband?" Rebecca announced as she scanned the lobby. "That man is probably in the smoking room. Lovely to meet you again, my dear," she trilled to Katherine before sailing towards the smoking room.

When she was out of earshot Mrs. Ramsey hissed, "You're not going to tell her where the Count is staying, are you? You know that ... that woman will try to poach him for her own fundraiser."

"Why not? What's the harm?" Katherine said with an innocent expression. She just wanted to tease Mrs. Ramsey. The strength of the other woman's reaction surprised Katherine.

"You don't see any harm!" Mrs. Ramsey sputtered. "Don't be naive!"

Stung, Katherine retorted, "I'm not naive."

"Really?" Mrs. Ramsey said with a raised eyebrow. Katherine didn't like the gloating smile. "What do you think our dear Count was doing in the Market the last time he was here?"

"I have no idea. What are you getting at?" demanded Katherine sharply.

"It seems that someone saw him with one of those unspeakable ladies in the Market one evening," Mrs. Ramsey asserted as she adjusted her shawl. She glanced at Nicole then continued. "You know, the ones who sell their wares."

"What do you mean, *seen with*?" exclaimed Katherine.

"Anyway, it certainly *looked* like him, from what Mary said."

"And what was Mary doing in the Market late at night? Never mind. What did she actually say?" asked Katherine with distaste.

"She said she saw him go into a house with one of *those women*." Mrs. Ramsey couldn't bring herself to say the word "prostitute".

"I don't believe it," said Katherine stoutly.

"I suppose Mary could be mistaken," said Mrs. Ramsey, losing interest in the story in the face of Katherine's disbelief. "Oh dear, it is nearly time. I do need to freshen up before the show begins. I'll see you both after the show." She turned and headed for the women's washroom.

Nicole watched Mrs. Ramsey leave then spat, "Vile woman."

"I know. I know," Katherine said.

The lights began to flicker on and off. It was time to return to their seats. Andrew emerged from the smoking room and scanned the room for Katherine. She waved. They went into the theatre to find their seats.

MACNUTT RESIDENCE, LAURIER AVENUE WEST, OTTAWA
11:00 P.M., THURSDAY, JANUARY 6, 1916

When MacNutt arrived home, he picked up the day's mail from the foyer table. The house was quiet. He glanced up to the second floor as he ran his finger along the torn edges of the envelopes and noticed an edge of light along the slightly opened door of their master bedroom. He sighed and went into his study. He tossed the mail onto his desk then went over to the sideboard and poured himself a glass of rye. He brought the bottle with him when he returned to the desk and lowered himself into the chair before it. He sipped the whiskey gloomily as he reflected on the day's events. As he refreshed his drink, he heard the stairs creaking and the soft padding of slippers.

He didn't turn towards the door, but he could sense Katherine's disapproving gaze. "Couldn't sleep?" he asked before turning towards her. Katherine stood in the doorway dressed in a white bathrobe that she held close with crossed arms over her breasts. Underneath, she was wearing a woollen nightgown that kept the cool air away from her soft skin. It had been a while since he had caressed her, and from her expression, it was unlikely he would tonight either.

"You're drinking too much," Katherine complained.

"If the temperance folks had their way, this might be the last one," he declared as he downed the shot. He saw Katherine's lips tighten. "So, is there something you want to talk about besides my drinking?"

She appeared to hesitate, as though this was not the right moment to ask. "Yes, there is," she finally admitted.

Andrew paused a moment to pour another shot. He picked up the glass and waited for Katherine to get to her point.

"Nicole and the girls are planning a trip to New York," she proclaimed.

His first reaction was no, out of the question. But he hesitated, and when he recalled his conversation with Lacelle that morning concerning the New York papers, he was glad he had paused.

"When do you want to go?" he replied, swirling the contents of his glass.

"We were thinking of going this weekend," she answered.

Andrew regarded Katherine wearily. "Shopping trip?"

"Yes!"

"It's fine by me. In fact, I think it might do us some good to be apart for a couple of days," he replied, subdued. Katherine had not expected that he would agree so easily, and he was pleased by her surprise. He would wait just before she left to ask that she bring home the New York papers. He'd probably get them before Lacelle did. And truth be told, he really did need a couple of days of peace and quiet.

CHAPTER 18

It was late morning when the Count entered the National Bank's main branch on Broadway and quickly scanned for surveillance. Except for the uniformed guard, with a holstered .38 on his right hip, who scrutinized everyone who entered the bank, the Count attracted no attention. There were quite a few customers trying to get their banking done before it closed for the day. He lined up impatiently, clutching his briefcase. It weighed heavily in his right hand while he supported his weight on a silver-tipped cane in his left. This was the third bank he had visited today. He had just come from the Morgan Bank, where he had withdrawn nearly $20,000 from each of the three special accounts set up to fund activities in New York.

The Count sighed as he tried to keep his irritation to a minimum. But he silently cursed von Papen and his stupidity for putting him in this situation in the first place. When he had awakened this morning, he had a busy but orderly day planned. He had several important meetings arranged with some wealthy New Yorkers concerning Belgian Relief as well as a clandestine meeting concerning the Russians. The meeting was to get an update on the status of the latest scheme to disrupt the Russian supply of arms. The Russians, like all the Allied countries, had set up offices in New York to monitor their munitions contracts. He had been enjoying his morning breakfast of steak and eggs in the hotel's restaurant, impressed by the large portions that the American eateries provided to their customers, when a messenger approached his table.

"Count Jaggi. I have a telephone message for you," he announced as he placed the message slip on the table.

"*Merci*," replied the Count, giving the young boy a ten-cent tip.

His day turned into chaos the moment he read the message. "Aunt Beatrice is not well. Please come urgent."

The message was from Müller. It was an emergency code phrase telling him that something had gone seriously wrong and to meet at the agreed-upon rendezvous point as soon as possible. The thought entered his mind that his cover was blown and that he would have to run. But when he reread the message he realized that the code phrase indicated a serious problem, but it was not the "stop what you are doing and run

170

immediately" code. What the problem was he had no clue, but he would learn soon enough. He regarded the meal in front of him unenthusiastically. He had lost his enjoyment in eating. He kept eating, for fuel, feeling that it was going to be a long day.

The Count met Müller on the East Manhattan side of Central Park's lake. The Count had taken the usual precautions before he approached Müller, who was gazing out over the water. "Müller! What the hell's going on?" he demanded.

Müller turned to the Count with a worried frown. "I received an urgent telegram from Berlin."

"That was quick. I didn't expect to hear from Berlin that soon…" The Count stopped when he saw Müller's expression.

"It's von Papen."

"What happened, did a U-Boat sink his ship?" quipped the Count. He couldn't help the hopeful tone in his voice.

"He's still alive, I'm afraid."

"So what did he do?"

"It happened when his ship docked in Falmouth."

"Don't tell me the idiot got off the goddamn ship," the Count exclaimed, nearly shouting. Realizing that he might be attracting attention, he dropped his voice.

"He didn't leave the ship. Even with diplomatic immunity he didn't trust the British that far. He knew they were out to get him," said Müller

"So what the hell is the problem?"

"The British confiscated his papers."

"What do you mean they confiscated his papers? How did they confiscate his papers?" bellowed the infuriated Count.

"It seems that when his ship stopped at Falmouth the British were waiting on the dock. They boarded the ship, and they took them all."

"I don't understand. Didn't he have diplomatic immunity?"

"He did. But the British said that it didn't extend to his luggage."

"You are not serious?"

"I wish I wasn't."

The Count scowled. "Was there anything in his papers…?" He paused when he saw Müller's expression. "Don't tell me!"

"They have his bank records with all the payments he made to his confidential agents," croaked Müller. All that Müller could do was appear abashed while the Count cursed. *How could the man be so stupid?* Hadn't he learned a thing from the Dr. Albert incident?

"Do the Americans know about this yet?" asked the Count as he tried to calculate the damage.

Müller shrugged in resignation. "If they don't, they will soon."

"Is there anything we can do to warn any of our people to lie low?"

"I know some of them, but I don't know all of von Papen's agents."

"Damn."

"What is important is that we need the money in those accounts for our operations," stated Müller emphatically.

The Count glanced at Müller sharply. "What are you proposing?"

"I have the details for the bank accounts and the names they were set up under. All we need is the appropriate documents to withdraw the funds."

The Count rubbed the back of his neck. He grimaced skeptically. "It seems rather risky, don't you think?"

"We're talking about nearly a million American dollars," Müller pointed out.

"That much?" said the Count, raising his eyebrows. Müller nodded. "Still, it will not do us much good if we end up in jail."

"It's going to take the Americans a few days to get organized. If we can do it today and tomorrow, we can clear out most of the accounts before they know what is happening," Müller asserted.

"How many banks are we talking about?"

"About a dozen. If we take six each, we can get it done in a day," answered Müller.

"And identification papers?"

"Not a problem. I've spoken with our counterfeiter. He's working on them as we speak. They will be ready when we get to his place. In about an hour and a half."

Count Jaggi glared at the lake for a moment, weighing the merits of the plan. A million American dollars were well worth the risk. "Let's go meet your counterfeiter."

Müller smiled as he turned and headed out of Central Park with the Count at his heels.

PHOTOGRAPHY SHOP, BROME STREET,
LOWER EAST SIDE, MANHATTAN, NEW YORK CITY
7:15 P.M., MONDAY, JANUARY 3, 1916

"Is this forger reliable?" questioned the Count as he and Müller approached a dilapidated office building. He was glad that Müller knew where they were going, because he was totally lost. They had taken the subway from the 98th Street Entrance and gotten off on the Lower East Side. After wandering for the last half-hour down back alleys, the Count didn't have a clue how to get back.

"He's a very good forger, but he's a difficult man to deal with," admitted Müller.

"Why are we still using him?" retorted the Count.

"He volunteered."

The Count was not impressed. "Did you tell him why we need the papers?"

"No. But because of the nature of the papers we asked to create, he will be able to figure it out," replied Müller.

"Can we replace him?"

"I have been trying since Rureoder was arrested. It's been difficult. It's not as if I can put an advert in the paper," muttered Müller.

"Who's Rureoder?"

"He was our forger until he was arrested by the police last year. They arrested his assistant and four men he was getting passports for," explained Müller as he opened the door for the Count. In the building Müller headed for the stairs.

"They didn't pick up your forger?"

"No. He wanted nothing to do with Rureoder. He had worked for von Wedell, who was our forger before Rureoder."

"What happened to von Wedell? Was he arrested as well?"

"He was on his way back to Berlin when his ship struck a mine and sank. Or so I have been told. Here we are." When Müller opened the door to the fourth floor, he headed straight for a door with PHOTOGRAPHY spelled out on it in flaking gold letters. When he opened the door, the bell fixed to the door frame jangled. The room was empty except for a six-foot banker's desk set against the far red-brick wall. Beside it was a small window through which the only view was another brick wall of the adjacent building. The plaster wall to the right was painted with a pastoral mural, which was partially obscured by an ornate blue-gold curtain and large camera with a flash pan set beside it.

To the Count's left a door opened and a man with a slight stoop emerged to investigate who had entered the office. "Can I help you?" he asked. When he saw Müller he stiffened. "Oh, it's you."

"*Guten morgen*, Meyer."

Meyer's eyes flickered to the Count.

"It's quite all right — he's with me."

"Is he?" Meyer asked suspiciously as he moved to lock the door. "Who is he?"

"*Guten Morgen, Herr Meyer*. I'm Count Jaggi." He offered the man his hand.

Meyer ignored him. He repeated his question to Müller. "Who is he?"

"Count Jaggi is replacing von Papen," answered Müller. The Count looked sharply at Müller. He really didn't want that bandied about.

Meyer grunted. "Are you sure he is not from the police?" he asked, turning his gaze to the Count.

"I'm sure."

"So was Ruroeder until the man he was dealing with turned out to be a police agent," retorted Meyer.

Müller was losing patience. "Enough. I don't want to hear about it again. Are the papers ready or not?" Meyer glared stubbornly at Müller. "Well?"

"Yes. They are ready," Meyer spat out.

"Well, get them."

Meyer turned abruptly on his heels. "Come." He led them into the next room. It was set up as a darkroom. There were wires strung across the room punctuated by wooden clothespins holding a dozen or so drying photographs. Along the wall were a couple of tables on which were set trays filled with development fluids. Against another wall stood a six-foot-tall cabinet safe, closed and locked. Meyer went to the cabinet and spun the lock's dial, pulled on it, and opened the cabinet. From one of the shelves, he pulled out some papers and handed them to Müller.

Müller studied the papers critically. "They're good."

Affronted, Meyer retorted, "They are more than good — they are perfect."

Müller handed the papers to the Count, who glanced at them. One of the papers stated that his new name was Mike Brown from New Jersey.

"They will pass inspection?" the Count questioned Müller.

Meyer answered tersely. "Of course they will. Didn't I just say they're perfect?"

"How much?" asked the Count.

A glint of avarice entered Meyer's eyes. "We agreed on $35."

Müller nodded and pulled a wallet from his jacket pocket to get the money.

174

"I have need of a passport," said the Count as Meyer counted the money Müller had handed to him.

As the money disappeared in Meyer's pocket, he smirked. "What kind of passport?"

"What do you have?"

Meyer dove into the metal cabinet and came out with a number of passports. He shuffled them then said, "I have a Mexican, Swiss, Norwegian, and an Argentinian."

"Do you have any American ones?" the Count requested.

"Of course." He handed the Count the passports as he went back to the cabinet. The Count gave them a curious glance then handed them back to Meyer as the forger gave him an American passport. The Count flipped the passport's pages. He stopped and examined the photo and description. They were for a much shorter man. "How much?"

"For the Mexican and Argentinian ones, $40. The Swiss are going for $80 and the American ones for $100."

Müller snorted in disgust. "That's extortion and you know it." Turning to the Count, he said, "The going price is about half of what he is asking for, between twenty and fifty dollars."

"I need at least $80 for the American one. Getting the South American ones is easy. Getting the American ones is harder, and harder to forge," protested Meyer.

"Why?" asked the Count.

"We get most of our passports from sailors and immigrants in the Lower East Side. There are plenty of people who need money and are willing to sell their papers. As for the American ones, we actually get them from the government. We get people to send in a passport application and then in a couple of weeks we get a new passport. They used to do minimal checking. But they caught on quickly, so now you have to provide a description, and you need to give them a photograph that they put on the passport."

"How do you get around that?"

"That's the tricky part. We have someone send in an application with their photo. But the description is general enough that it practically applies to anyone. When we get the passport back, we carefully replace the photo on the passport with a new one. That's the tricky part, exchanging the photo without any sign of tampering," responded Meyer with pride.

"How soon can I get this done?" asked the Count as he waved the passport.

"In a week or two. I have to find a passport that matches your general description, and I will need a photo of you to put in the passport," explained Meyer. The Count was uneasy about having his photo taken. If Meyer were arrested then the police would have an easy time identifying him.

"I'll give you the $80."

"That's way too much," argued Müller. But before he could continue, the Count cut him off.

"Under one condition — that you destroy the plates and no copies are made of my photograph."

"Agreed," said Meyer quickly. Rather too quickly for the Count's taste. "Do you want to have your photo taken now or do you want to come back later?"

"No time like the present," replied the Count, pointing at the camera.

NATIONAL BANK, BROADWAY,
MANHATTAN, NEW YORK CITY
11:00 A.M., FRIDAY, JANUARY 7, 1916

The Count had just left the bank, happy that he could drain the account without a hitch. He must admit that the papers Meyer forged worked like a charm. The bank manager didn't have any qualms about giving the money in cash. He even offered a guard to escort Jaggi back to his office because of the large amount of cash he was carrying, but he declined.

He was just a block away from the bank when a large man hidden in an alley tried to grab his bag. The Count refused to let go and was dragged into the alley by the man's superior strength. The Count didn't dare to yell for help. How was he going to explain the large sums he was carrying?

When the man yelled in German, "Let the fucking bag go!" the Count knew that this was not an ordinary robbery. He let go of the briefcase. He still had the presence of mind to retain his cane. He twisted it and the knob at the top came off, along with six inches of sharp steel. He stabbed the man in the right shoulder, pinning him against the wall. The man yelped in pain.

"Who sent you?" hissed the Count in German.

The man groaned in pain as he grasped his shoulder around the blade. "Who sent you? Müller or Meyer?" repeated the Count.

When the man didn't answer fast enough, the Count twisted the blade. "Meyer — Meyer sent me."

"The forger?"

"*Ja. Ja!*" the man yelled, his eyes wide with fear.

"That's too bad," sneered the Count as he withdrew the blade from the man's shoulder, then stabbed him through the throat. He held the blade in until the man collapsed on the hard concrete, then pulled it out. He used the man's clothing to wipe the blood off the blade. He stared at the corpse, trying to figure out what to do next. He noticed four large metal dustbins nearby and dragged the body behind them. He knew that he would have to pay Meyer a friendly visit. It was most unfortunate that the forger had proved to be so unreliable.

CHAPTER 19

MacNutt was glad that the holidays were over and that he was getting back into a routine. Unfortunately, that also meant that after a three-week hiatus, the regular intelligence committee meetings were resuming today. He was apprehensive about the morning's meeting. He had an issue he needed to discuss, one that he'd deliberately left off the agenda. It wasn't even in the notes he'd prepared that lay on the conference table before him. At least it was his turn to host today's meeting, since the RNWP hosted the last meeting in December.

The usual committee members were in attendance except for Atwell from External Affairs, who had been called away for an urgent matter in Washington. He had sent Scott Houle, a short, thin man dressed in brown tweed in his place.

"Are we the only ones attending or will there be others?" Houle avoided MacNutt's gaze as he examined the room.

MacNutt glanced at Stephens, who shrugged.

When Colonel Denny, the army's military intelligence representative, took his seat. MacNutt said, "As you can tell from the agenda, we have a lot on our plate. Does anyone have any problems with the minutes from our last meeting. Nothing? Good. By the way, thank you for providing the list of agents I requested at the last meeting." The list of names he had received was helpful in managing the network they were building and in reducing duplication of effort. "It has been very helpful. Remember, if you have any changes, let me know right away."

It was about an hour before MacNutt finally worked through all the items on the agenda. He sat back. "Okay, round table. Let's start with Mr. Houle. Anything new and exciting from External Affairs?"

Mr. Houle regarded the other men in the room as he took a sip of lukewarm coffee, then announced, "Mr. Atwell needed to attend to several issues with the Americans concerning security at the Windsor bridges and ferries."

"What kind of problems?" broke in Mike O'Neal, the customs inspector, alarmed. "We have been taking care to ensure that immigrants of Teutonic descent do not escape to the United States. As you know, a great number of them have managed to get back to Germany and Austria and are currently serving in the army."

"Yes, you're right, we know all that," remarked the colonel, slightly irritated as he shifted his bulk.

Mr. Houle flushed but continued. "The Americans are now becoming more co-operative. Especially after the recent sinking of the *Lusitania* by German U-boats. The Americans' patience is starting to wear thin with the German shenanigans."

All the men at the table nodded.

"And they did finally deport von Papen and Boy-Ed and they arrested that Koenig chap in New York too," declared Commander Stephens, the head of Canadian Naval Intelligence, with some satisfaction.

"They only deported von Papen. Boy-Ed is still in the States," pointed out MacNutt.

"Shit," blurted the commander.

"I would have liked both men gone. But of the two, I'd have preferred Boy-Ed gone rather than von Papen."

"Why?" asked Houle, startled.

"Boy-Ed is more dangerous," explained Stephens. "He's an experienced naval officer who knows how to go about hurting us at sea. Von Papen is merely an army captain."

The colonel snorted.

"Sorry, Colonel," Stephens said with a grin when he realized how his comment could be taken. The colonel waved his hand for the naval commander to continue.

"We are still very concerned about the number of ships we've been losing," explained the commander.

"Why so many ships?" asked Houle with a concerned frown.

"The U-boats seem to have fiendishly good intelligence," Stephens stated wryly.

"I certainly hope that we don't have any Hun spies in Halifax," commented Hewitt of the RNWMP.

Before MacNutt could respond, Houle asked with widened eyes, "Have there been?"

The commander took a moment to consider his reply. "All the troublemakers have been interned. We keep a close surveillance on anyone of Teutonic birth in the city. We make sure that they are not privy to any sensitive information."

"What about the crews of the ships that enter and leave the harbour? Could any of them be German agents?" fretted Hewitt.

The commander sighed. "We try to check the reliability of the ships' crews. But with the large number of ships we can't check everyone. We inform the crews of the importance of secrecy. But if they are in a bar and have one too many, there is very little we can do."

"What about U-boats watching the harbour traffic?" Houle suggested.

"We do have regular patrols keeping a close eye out for subs," Stephens replied defensively.

MacNutt knew that Admiral Kingsmill and Commander Stephens had grave concerns about the threat of German subs operating in Canadian waters. They had been struggling to build a proper naval service. Both men wanted the fleet to have true warships capable of defending Canadian waters and shipping from marauding cruisers and subs. Unfortunately, circumstances were forcing them to make do with jury-rigged auxiliary vessels, such as donated and converted private yachts, manned by far-from-professional crews. Also, the Canadian government wasn't interested in spending large sums of money to build warships. It was mainly interested in shipbuilding for the Royal Navy, though these contracts had not yet materialized. What frustrated the commander most was the attitude of the British Admiralty. When the Canadian government sought advice from the Admiralty, it discouraged the expansion of the Canadian Navy. The Admiralty said it didn't have the resources to provide instructors and trainers to the Canadians. However, with the German sub threat, the demands on the Royal Navy were such that the Admiralty was beginning to demand the Canadian Navy take over patrols of Canadian waters — to free up Royal Navy vessels for more pressing duties.

The commander faced similar frustrations when he dealt with the Admiralty on intelligence matters, and with British intelligence in London and in New York. As part of his mobilization plans, he had established an intelligence centre in Halifax to collect and disseminate intelligence for British and Canadian vessels operating along the Canadian and U.S. east coasts. But the Admiralty had established a similar centre in St. John's, Newfoundland. Stephens was furious: two intelligence centres, doing the same work! What made matters worse was that neither of them provided him with regular reports. A case in point: neither he — nor anyone else in Ottawa — had been informed that a squadron of Royal Navy ships had been stationed in the Gulf of St. Lawrence to convoy the Canadian Expeditionary Force's first sailing for England.

"Speaking of U-boats, isn't Admiral Kingsmill going before a defence committee concerning those subs of his?" wondered the army colonel. Kingsmill was the Director of the Royal Canadian Navy.

"Yes, he is."

"What's the matter with the subs?" blurted Houle. "I didn't even know that we had subs."

"There is nothing wrong with the subs," replied Stephens testily. "We're damned glad to have them. However, some of the MPs got into their heads that our new subs are not up to par — but they are!"

Hewitt said, "But I heard that they can't go into deep water!"

"They are not designed for the open sea," Stephens conceded. "They are coastal defence subs and have limited range. They are well suited for the task they were designed for. We have them stationed in B.C. because there are concerns German surface raiders may be operating out on the West Coast."

"That is also why you have some agents in Seattle?" asked Houle.

MacNutt regarded Houle intently. "Atwell told you that, did he?"

Houle picked up MacNutt's tone. "Yes. But only me. And I don't have loose lips. I don't even speak with my wife."

"That makes for a rather quiet marriage," said the colonel, getting a chuckle from the men at the table.

"Mr. Atwell felt that I needed to be fully informed in the event I should have to take over his duties," replied Houle stiffly.

MacNutt signalled with his chin for the commander to continue.

"You have to understand the German imperial navy's strategy is cruiser warfare. Cruiser warfare mainly strikes at an opponent's economic lifelines by sinking its merchant shipping. However, it also encompasses hit-and-run operations, attacks by landing parties, and bombardment of communications, as well as of industrial facilities along the coast. About ten or eleven years ago, the German patrol cruiser *Falke* visited all important points on both of our coasts on an intelligence-gathering mission. Around the same time, the Kaiser sent the gunboat *Panther* on a lengthy voyage that we believe was to search for secret anchorages. In time of war their cruisers could use these anchorages to hide out, and to replenish their supplies of coal, food, and ammunition from German sympathizers. Then, in 1907, the German cruiser *Bremen* visited Halifax, Saint John, and Quebec City on a goodwill tour. It is a given that during that trip they would have gathered intelligence on our harbour defences.

"We have agents in Seattle and Tacoma because there are large German populations there. The Germans had years to plan, and it would have been easy enough for them to station secret commercial agents there. We've had reports of supplies being stockpiled for German raiders, and we've been investigating. However, we haven't found anything untoward so far."

"If you do send anyone else out there, make sure that you keep me informed. I may need to keep the Canadian consulate in Seattle in the know. They might be peeved if they're not informed," MacNutt advised with a sigh.

"As you wish," said the commander.

"And Colonel Denny, how are things going on your side?" asked MacNutt.

The colonel gave him a grin. "Pretty well. On the whole, nothing really unusual to report. We've been having some problems with our military census. Especially in Toronto."

"Is that why Hughes is out there then?" asked MacNutt.

"Yes," answered the Colonel with a half-smile. "He wants to assure the public that the government will not adopt conscription."

"If recruiting continues to drop, won't we eventually have to?" argued Houle.

"Regrettably, despite Hughes's assurances, it seems that way to me," the colonel responded with lips pinched. "The government called for half a million men for the Corps. Meeting those numbers is not going to be easy."

"It's for the government to decide," answered MacNutt. The men at the table nodded. "By the way, I heard that the States are gearing up for the war. Their secretary of war announced they were planning to increase their armed forces to two million men and increase their budget to two hundred million dollars."

"Good for them," said Hewitt. "But they are not coming into the war any time soon, no matter how much German provocation there is. There's a strong peace movement in the States." He was well informed on American matters because he was good friends with the American consul general in Ottawa, who kept him abreast of the American political scene.

182

"And, last but not least," MacNutt said, turning to Hewitt.

"Actually, I have very little to say."

Everyone was startled. "You have nothing?" questioned MacNutt. He couldn't keep the surprise from his voice.

"Yes. Everything is under control. Nothing unusual is happening currently," Hewitt explained. "We have been keeping surveillance on certain German aliens out west, based on recent information we've received."

"Mrs. Ramsey?" suggested MacNutt with wry smile. Hewitt simply shrugged.

If the horsemen want to waste time, money, and manpower it's up to them, thought MacNutt. At least Mrs. Ramsey was out of his hair for now.

"Well, Andrew," inquired the colonel. "Do you have more to add?"

"Not at the moment," answered MacNutt. He had discussed with the commissioner whether to inform the other members of the committee of the telegram they had received from MI5. The commissioner had left it up to his judgement.

"Do you have information on who's replacing von Papen?" asked Hewitt.

"I've been seeing some signs that they have a replacement in place, but I've not seen any report that identifies who it might be yet," said MacNutt. He knew what Hewitt's next question would be.

"What kind of sign?" demanded Hewitt on cue. MacNutt tried to read Hewitt's face to gauge how much he knew. Hewitt's expression revealed nothing, but MacNutt's instinct told him Hewitt knew. It was tough to keep things secret in this town.

Because he suspected that Hewitt knew, MacNutt decided it would be best if the revelation came from him. "We did receive a telegram indicating that there may be a German agent operating in Canada." MacNutt caught the glint of satisfaction in Hewitt's eyes. "MI5 tells us they discovered a letter in the possession of a German agent they arrested in London that had been mailed from Ottawa."

"Do you know who it is yet?" inquired Stephens. He had sat up at attention when he heard MacNutt's news.

"Not yet. We've opened a file and are investigating," answered MacNutt.

"Why were you keeping it quiet?" asked Hewitt pointedly.

MacNutt hated being placed on the defensive. He stared directly at the inspector. "Some people can be quite excitable about such things.

Particularly if this news found its way in the papers. We can censor the local papers but the American ones..." MacNutt let the sentence hang for a moment before going on. "By the way, it should go without saying, this conversation is not to leave this room." He paused again until each man at the table indicated he would comply. "I want the man identified but not arrested or detained."

A startled Houle demanded, "Why not? We don't want him loose, wandering around."

"That is exactly what we want," said MacNutt firmly.

Hewitt drummed his fingers on the table. "You want to uncover who he talks to?"

"Yes. I want to know who may be leaking secrets to the Huns. The only way is by letting him have free rein while we have him under surveillance."

"Risky," suggested the colonel. "If he gets away and blows up something critical, there will be hell to pay."

"There is an element of risk. But as long as we can keep him in our sights, it's worth it," argued MacNutt. From their expressions, the men around the table did not seem very enthusiastic about the idea.

"Well," responded Hewitt as he leaned forward in his chair, "we don't have to decide right now. How we proceed is all conjecture until we identify the man. When we know who we've got, we can make our plans."

"Agreed," said the colonel briskly.

Seeing the other members of the committee nodding, MacNutt acquiesced. "As you wish. If no one has any further business, let's call it a day, shall we?"

PLAZA HOTEL, FIFTH AVENUE AND 59TH STREET,
MANHATTAN, NEW YORK CITY
2:20 P.M., SATURDAY, JANUARY 8, 1916

Katherine was humming when she entered her hotel room. She continued to hum as she dropped her packages onto one of the queen-size beds. She took off her hat and coat and dropped them beside the packages.

"You seem to be in a happy mood," said a voice from the general direction of the window.

"Oh, hi, Nicole. I didn't see you there," gasped a startled Katherine. "What are you doing?"

"Enjoying the view."

"Anything interesting?" asked Katherine as she walked to stand by

Nicole. The Grand Army Plaza was just below their window. The shadow from the surrounding building dulled the gold statute of the American Civil War general William Tecumseh Sherman that stood in the middle of a semi-circle of pear trees. To their left, behind the gold statute, was an entrance to Central Park. The only flaw in the scene below was the clutter of construction at the plaza's southern end, to their right. When they had inquired about it at the front desk, the clerk had told them the late Joseph Pulitzer left $50,000 for a fountain to be built there. The fountain was near completion, awaiting only the statue that was to sit atop the tier of six graduated granite bowls. The clerk also said that he had heard the statue would be of a Roman goddess. He couldn't remember which one.

Katherine was pleased that the girls had decided to stay at the Plaza Hotel. It was exactly as it had been advertised in the *Citizen* and the *Journal*. At five dollars a day it was expensive, but sharing two double rooms, Katherine and Nicole in one with Beth Winslow and her sister, Nancy Nolan, in the other, helped save some of the Canadian gold dollar coins they carried in waist money-belts concealed under their clothing. The gold coins were becoming rare because of the government's decision to withdraw them from circulation. At the beginning of the war, there had been heavy gold withdrawals from the banks. There were fears that there would be a run on the banks if depositors could not withdraw their funds in gold. The government agreed that the banks could meet their obligations in paper for the duration of the war. It was unfortunate, because the dollars were readily accepted at par by the American shopkeepers. They were the same weight and quality as the American gold coins. Many shopkeepers refused to accept Canadian paper bills because they couldn't be sure the banks would redeem them.

Katherine caught Nicole studying her in amusement. "What?"

"It's been quite a while since I've seen you this happy," Nicole remarked with a wink.

"What do you mean?"

"You've been humming ever since you came in."

"I have not!" Katherine protested.

"Yes, you have," teased Nicole. "I haven't heard you humming for quite a spell."

It took Katherine a few minutes to realize that Nicole was right. She gazed out at the plaza, watching the traffic come and go on Fifth Avenue. She had felt the difference ever since she got off the Grand Trunk train at

Central Station, but it had taken her a while to understand it. The young men in New York City didn't have the wariness that the young men in Ottawa had when a woman approached them. Was she interested, or was it a white feather? In New York, the men had not been subjected to that constant pressure, because the Americans were not yet in the war. Katherine felt a weight had been lifted from her shoulders. She didn't feel the need to hand a white feather to every man she met in New York.

"So what did you buy?" asked Nicole as she inspected the packages.

"I'll show you," offered Katherine. She went over to her bed and opened one of the packages. She pulled a beautiful wheat-coloured brocade gown and held it up in front of her. "What do you think?"

"It's beautiful," replied Nicole as she admired the dress. "Where did you get it?" Katherine picked up the bag, which read "Macy's". "Oh, so you went back then."

"Yes."

"Was the snotty sales girl still there?" Nicole asked.

Katherine frowned at the memory then her smile dimpled her cheeks. "I found someone else. She was quite good. Besides, I really wanted the dress."

"How much did you pay for it?" inquired Nicole as she reached out and touched the material.

"Twenty dollars, and it was a bargain," replied Katherine proudly.

Nicole grimaced. "At the rate we are spending, our husbands will be quite vexed with us."

Katherine laughed when she saw Nicole fighting her grimace from turning into a grin. "I'll buy Andrew a couple of shirts, maybe a suit at Brooks Brothers. He won't complain too much."

Nicole finally gave in and chuckled. "We can give it a try. So what do you want to do tonight? Where would you like to go for dinner? Shall we pop in to the tea room downstairs?"

"It's rather expensive — you know Nancy won't go for it," said Katherine. "How about that little Italian place we saw down the street instead? I've never had Italian food."

"Okay, Italian it is. But let's do try the tea room at least once before we go home. I'll go gather the girls," said Nicole. She walked around the bed and checked her face in the mirror hanging beside the door. She put her hand on the doorknob then turned back to Katherine. "By the way, have you heard from the Count?"

"No," replied Katherine as she turned away from Nicole's questioning gaze. "I sent a message to his hotel, but I haven't had a reply yet. I was hoping that I could have a brief word with him before I left."

"I'm a bit surprised he hasn't been in touch," said Nicole sympathetically. "Oh well, you did give it a try. And we still have a couple of days left."

"You're right, there's still time," agreed Katherine with a disappointed frown as she followed Nicole through the door.

CHAPTER 20

It was nearly two thirty when Katherine and Nicole returned to the Plaza Hotel in a taxi. The friends were tired but satisfied from the day's bargain hunting in the Ladies' Mile district along Fifth Avenue. The porters were heavily laden with the dress- and hat-boxes which they extracted from the cab. With the ladies' trophies held firmly in place with their chins, they followed Katherine and Nicole into the hotel.

"I love the lobby," gushed Nicole as she looked up and examined the ceiling.

Katherine craned her neck and couldn't help but be impressed. The French decorators would have been pleased that their Louis XVI-style lobby, enriched with marble pillars and pilasters embellished with gilt bronze, lush tapestry, mirrors, and fittings were impressive to the hotel's guests. They would not have been happy to know that she would never know the name of the French decorating firm of L. Alavoine et Cie and the work of the great decorator Allard, who also crafted the interiors of other notable New York landmarks, such as the Marble House and the Breakers.

"So do I. I wish that we could stay longer," said Katherine.

"You had to remind me!"

"Sorry." It was fun having a few days without a care in the world. But tomorrow evening they would be taking the Grand Trunk back to Ottawa and going back to the war. She did feel a slight letdown that she had not heard from the Count, and she had only one more night left in New York.

"Let's get our room key and allow the poor boys to rest their arms," suggested Nicole.

"Thank you, ma'am," grunted one of the porters, his voice slightly muffled behind the stack of boxes.

When Katherine approached the reception desk, one of the clerks said, "Good afternoon, Mrs. MacNutt."

"Good afternoon." Katherine was impressed that he remembered her name, but for the life of her she couldn't remember his, though she had dealt with him several times. "My room key, please."

"Of course. I hope you had a pleasant day shopping?" he inquired as he turned to the key rack. When he turned back to the counter, he held a key and an envelope.

"Your room key, ma'am," he stated as he handed it to her, along with a folded card. "And a message was left for you this morning, ma'am."

"There is?" questioned Katherine as she took the card. Her hand trembled slightly with nervous excitement.

"Yes, Mrs. MacNutt," replied the clerk.

"Who's the message from?" demanded Nicole as she stretched her neck to peer at the envelope.

"It's from Andrew. He said to pick up some New York papers if I can find the time," answered Katherine as she read the card. Her face burst briefly with delight before she extinguished it.

Nicole stared at her. "He sent you a telegraph to tell you to pick up newspapers?"

"That's my husband," Katherine grumbled.

Nicole snickered. "I'm glad it's you who's married to him, and not me!"

Katherine laughed as she and Nicole and the porters headed towards the lifts.

* * *

"Are you feeling ill, Kath?" asked Nicole, her forehead wrinkling with concern. Katherine was lying on one of the beds with a comforter pulled up to her neck. Katherine had been fine half an hour ago when Nicole popped down to Emily's room on the floor below.

"To be honest, I'm not feeling that well," said Katherine hoarsely as she squinted up at Nicole.

Nicole sat on the bed and put her hand to her friend's forehead. "Well, at least you don't have a fever. Touch of a cold?"

Katherine groaned. "I certainly hope not. The train back to Ottawa will be pretty bad if it's the grippe. No, I think that I must have eaten something that didn't agree."

"Maybe we shouldn't have had that pretzel from the street vendor," suggested Nicole. Katherine waved the suggestion away listlessly.

"So I guess you're not going to make it to supper tonight?" Nicole sighed. "I'll let the girls know that we won't be able to make it." She stood up from Katherine's bed and straightened her dress.

"Oh, no, Nicole!" exclaimed Katherine. "Don't miss dinner on my account! It's your last night in New York, and I'd feel terrible if you were stuck here with me when you could be having fun."

"I don't know, Kath," Nicole said doubtfully. "Will you be all right on your own?"

"I'll be fine. A good nap will be the best restorative," replied Katherine firmly.

"Well, if you're sure," said Nicole, still reluctant. "But I don't like the idea of leaving you alone. What if you need a doctor?"

"Don't worry. It is nothing serious. I'll be fine," Katherine said.

"If you insist." Nicole reluctantly reached for the winter coat she had bought earlier in the day on Fifth Avenue. "Shall I turn off the light?"

Katherine shook her head. "Leave it on, please."

"Good night and take care, then," said Nicole as she closed the door.

As soon as Nicole was gone, Katherine sat up in bed, listening intently.

She moved off the bed and over to the floor-length mirror near the closet, and weighed the dress she was wearing critically. She wasn't happy with it and decided to change. She opened the closet and pulled out one of the new dresses she'd bought that morning. It was very pretty, soft pink with a pattern of roses, but as she held it up to her, she frowned, then returned it to the closet. She pulled out another of her purchases, this one in alabaster, and checked the mirror again: better. She carefully hung it on the closet door. She slipped off her dress and put on a dressing gown, then went into the suite's bathroom to draw a bath. Katherine was grateful that the Plaza's individual rooms had bathrooms — in most hotels guests shared bath facilities with the other guests on their floor.

She had nearly finished her preparations and was just dabbing a touch of perfume behind each ear when she heard a knock. "Hello," she called, turning towards the door.

A young man's voice said, "I have a message for you, ma'am."

"Just a moment," shouted Katherine, giving herself a last critical once-over in the mirror. When she opened the door, she had to drop her gaze to a freckle-faced boy dressed in a hotel uniform. "You have a message for me?"

"Yes, ma'am," he replied. "A Count Jaggi wishes to inform you that he has arrived and he is waiting at your convenience in the lobby."

"Oh, thank you. Just a moment," she said, reaching for her purse and retrieving a nickel. "Here's something for your trouble."

"Thank you, ma'am. Would you like me to deliver a message in return?"

"Yes," answered Katherine. "Please let the gentleman know that I will be down shortly."

"Yes ma'am," said the boy as he turned and walked briskly away.

Katherine stepped back into the room and closed the door softly. She waited another thirty minutes before she gathered her coat and purse and pulled the door shut behind her. She took a deep breath before entering the elevator. She asked the operator to take her to the lobby.

* * *

Women, everywhere, were all the same, he thought: they loved to keep men waiting. He was sitting in a wing chair trying to read a newspaper. Two of the chairs that surrounded a low coffee table with a vase of arranged flowers were occupied. The occupants held little interest. He held the paper in front of him, but he was too busy watching the flow coming and going to give it much attention. He had taken the corner chair with the best view of the lobby. Some of the women were quite impressive, and a few gave him lingering glances as they made their way to the hallway that connected the lobby to the hotel's public rooms.

It took him a moment to realize that Katherine had finally arrived. She was standing a few feet from the elevator scanning the lobby for him. It was certainly worth the wait, he admitted. He viewed the dress she was wearing. It was very becoming, complementing her skin and hair, and showing off her figure to great effect. *Ah*, he mused, *the skills of a New York dressmaker*.

He put the paper on the coffee table and rose to greet her. Her back was towards him when he approached.

"Welcome to New York," he said.

"Oh!" she exclaimed, moving her right hand to her neckline. "You startled me."

"I apologize. I didn't mean to startle you," pleaded the Count as he took her hand and gave it a light kiss.

"It's a pleasure to see you again," she said, her voice sounding a little breathless.

The Count smiled and took a step back to admire her dress. "You look lovely this evening. That's a beautiful dress."

Katherine blushed. "Do you think so?"

"Of course, madame has excellent taste." For once, the Count was truthful; she did indeed have excellent taste.

Katherine laughed. "You do know how to flatter a woman."

"True. And you are a woman, are you not?" teased the Count with a hint of amusement.

Katherine was taken aback for a moment then tapped him gently on the arm. "Do behave."

"As you wish, madame. Will any of your friends be joining us?"

"I'm afraid that they have other plans," replied Katherine.

"In that case, shall we proceed?" He offered her his arm.

Katherine shyly tucked her arm into his. "Where are we going for tea?"

"Why don't I surprise you," suggested the Count as he led her down the corridor away from the lobby. The corridor ended at the entrance to the Plaza's tea room.

Katherine gave the Count a stern glance before laughing. "It's the best tea house in New York," said the Count, smiling at her as he led her deeper into the restaurant.

The maître d' lifted his focus from his appointment book and smiled. "Good afternoon, Count Jaggi." He gave Katherine a discreet glance then returned his attention to the Count. The Count was pleased with the man's discretion, a requirement of the job. It was not the first time, nor the last, that he would see a man with a married woman other than his wife.

"Table for two?" he suggested.

The waiter led them through a spacious room that was filling rapidly. The tea room was quite popular with the upper and middle classes of New York. The table assigned to them was strategically placed near the dance floor and the orchestra. Tea dances were all the rage. The potted palm tree gave them some privacy from the table next to them. The waiter pulled out and held the chair as Katherine seated herself. Once the Count had taken his seat, the waiter handed them menus.

The Count noted that in between glances at the menu Katherine was unobtrusively goggling at the room, taking in its large, mirrored walls, the Venetian glass ceiling, and grey marble floor.

"I'll be back in a moment to take your order," said the waiter. Across the room, the orchestra players began to tune their instruments.

"I hope that this is suitable," said the Count, placing his menu on the tablecloth and gazing at Katherine.

192

"Oh yes, quite suitable," replied Katherine. "My friends and I have been meaning to have tea here, but we have been so busy shopping, we haven't had the opportunity." She didn't mention that two of the women thought it was too expensive and preferred to eat at the cheapest places they could find.

"Do you come here often?"

"I've been here a number of times to meet some important people who might be interested in donating to Belgian Relief."

"Oh, really? Do tell me who," asked Katherine curiously, leaning towards the Count.

"The Morgans, the Rockefellers, and the Vanderbilts." The Count was naming the most prominent citizens of New York.

"Then the fundraising must be going well?"

"Yes, indeed. Better than my expectations." It was true that the fundraising was more successful than he'd anticipated.

They were interrupted by the waiter pushing a tea cart to their table. He carefully set two teacups imprinted with the Plaza's logo on the table in front of them. After he filled the cups with tea, he said, "The dessert cart will be along in a few minutes. Enjoy your tea."

"Thank you," said Katherine. As the waiter departed with his cart, she turned to the Count, but before she could continue their conversation, she heard a male voice beside her.

"Mrs. MacNutt, this *is* a pleasant surprise."

Katherine gazed in surprise at the man standing beside their table. "Sir?"

"You don't remember me, do you?"

"I'm afraid, sir, that you have me at a disadvantage."

"That's quite all right, madame. But I do remember you quite well. At the British embassy party in Washington two years ago. You and your husband attended."

"Ah yes," recalled Katherine, her face brightening at the memory. "I do remember you now. Captain Guant! You're the naval attaché."

The Count nearly choked on his tea when Katherine said the man's name. He was well aware who the captain was. He was the local British naval intelligence station chief. Müller had briefed him on the Australian-born captain. The Count knew that he worked out of the consulate offices on 44 Whitehall Street. Unfortunately, he appeared to be more competent at the game than their own operatives, von Papen and Boy-Ed. The Count suspected that some of their previous operations had gone awry because of Guant's efforts. However, he seemed to be subject to the same weakness as von Papen. Everyone knew he was a spy, but he loved the social scene and the other perks of the Big Apple.

The Count's coughing to clear his throat caught Katherine's and the captain's attention. "Are you all right?" asked Katherine.

"I'm fine. The tea was hotter than I expected."

"Captain, I apologize for not introducing you. This is Count Jaggi from Belgian Relief," she said.

"Ah yes, pleasure to meet you," said the captain, shaking the Count's hand.

The Count could sense the man evaluating him and passing judgment. He was hoping that the man would conclude, quite correctly, that he was after Katherine, and dig no deeper. "Here on business?"

"I'm afraid so. Nose to the grindstone and all that." The captain turned his gaze back to Katherine and smiled at her. "Did your husband accompany you to New York?"

"Andrew was unable to make the time," she said.

"That's a pity," said the captain with disappointment in his voice. "Well, enjoy your tea. I have to return to my guests."

The Count kept an eye on the captain through the thin screen of the palm trees as he made his way where two men were seated. He didn't appear to be too happy when he sat down at their table.

I wonder if they are Mansfield and Wiseman? he thought. Müller had briefed him on the Dictaphone operation involving the captain. It was well known where Guant stayed when he visited New York. Müller's agents had rented the hotel rooms next to British attaché's so they could listen in on his meetings.

They discovered that a Sydney Mansfield and William Wiseman had arrived from London with orders from Smith-Cummings, who was the head of Military Intelligence's sub branch 1c, commonly known by the acronym MI1c, to set up a station. The Captain reported to Reginald "Blinker" Hall, the chief of Naval Intelligence and Smith's opposite number.

From the swearing on the Dictaphone recordings, Gaunt was not pleased. For the last several years he had built a successful network of agents who were quite effective in thwarting the schemes of von Papen and Boy-Ed. With von Papen gone, he was working hard to get Boy-Ed sent home too. What he didn't need was the two amateurs messing about on this side of the pond. Guant had made it clear the British needed to tread carefully, because although he had some support for his activities from the American government, it was limited. The Americans were sensitive about Europeans meddling in their backyard. With his diplomatic cover, the worst that could happen was that he would be unceremoniously shipped home. Mansfield and Wiseman did not have that luxury, because they were not officially attached to the embassy, and there would be little the embassy could do if they got into trouble and were arrested, tried, and jailed.

Hmm, that is something I need to suggest to Müller, the Count thought. Just then feminine shrieks from a large table to his right caught his attention. He recognized members of the Russian Supply Committee among the shrieking woman's male companions. They had been sent by the Tsar to buy essential supplies for the Russian army's fight against the Germans. Unfortunately, the Committee's reputation was one of corruption and incompetence, with some justification. Rintelen had swindled the Russians out of large sums of money for non-existent war supplies. He and Müller were working on another similar scheme.

When he returned his attention to Katherine, the dessert cart had arrived, and they spent a few minutes considering the various scones, cakes, and pastries before settling on a vanilla cake for Katherine and a slice of chocolate cake for the Count.

As they enjoyed their tea and cake, the band began to play, and one by one couples joined the dance floor. The Count noticed Katherine tapping her foot in time to the music.

"Would you like to dance, Katherine?"

She hesitated.

The Count stood up and silently offered her his hand, then led her onto the dance floor. His hand found the small of her back, but she stiffened her arms slightly when he pulled her too close. The Count began to lead her through several sedate waltzes and foxtrots. He was pleased that Katherine was a good dancer. Very pleased. The night was young and promising.

PLAZA HOTEL, FIFTH AVENUE AND 59TH STREET,
MANHATTAN, NEW YORK CITY
11:12 P.M., SUNDAY, JANUARY 9, 1916

The Count was lying naked on his right side, resting his cheek in the palm of his hand. He was watching Katherine's chest rise and fall. Her eyelids were closed, but he knew that she wasn't sleeping. She was simply trying to recover from some energetic lovemaking. He hadn't expected much in the way of skills or sophistication, but he had been pleasantly surprised by the woman's performance. And unlike many of the women he had had in the past, Katherine appeared to truly enjoy making love. She was rather hesitant at first, and he suspected that other than her husband, she had not bedded many men.

Katherine's lashes flickered open and she smiled sheepishly as she raised the covers to her neck in a vain attempt to cover her bare skin. The Count used his left forefinger to gently move a lock of her brown hair that was falling on her cheek. "How are you feeling?"

"I'm fine," she answered.

"I'm pleased."

There were a couple of seconds of awkward silence before Katherine suggested, "I think that I have to go." She didn't make any attempt to get up.

"Are you sure?" he wondered, running his finger down her cheek, then along her throat, coming to rest at a spot between her breasts. She shivered slightly, and her nipples became visible through the sheets. Her gaze moved from his face, down to the hair curling over his chest, stopping at the juncture between his legs. Her eyes widened slightly when she saw him twitch and stir. The Count glanced down then gave her an amused smile.

"Do you really want to go?"

She blushed then began to rise, dragging the sheets off the bed with her. "I have to go. Nicole will be wondering where I am."

"Nicole?" he asked as she bent over to gather her underclothes lying on the floor, intermingling with the Count's trousers and shirt.

She glared at him sharply as she snatched up the garments. "I just need to get back to my room." She picked up her dress that the Count had thoughtfully placed on the paisley-patterned chair as he had unrobed her.

The Count understood that Katherine wanted to keep this aspect of their relationship private. But he couldn't resist the temptation to gently tease her. "By the way, I'll be in Ottawa next week."

Katherine's turned sharply towards him. She stuttered, "I-I thought you weren't coming until the end of the month?"

"The opening of Parliament is too good an opportunity to pass up. Besides, I can't wait to see you again." When he saw her anxiety, he asked, "Is there a problem?"

"No. No problem. I'll be glad you're in Ottawa. I just didn't expect it so soon," she replied with faint enthusiasm.

The Count was pleased that he had planted a seed of concern. He knew she would be worried that one of them might make a slip, some little thing that would make her husband doubt her fidelity.

"That's wonderful," he explained as he rose from the bed. He ignored the clothes scattered on the carpet as he walked over to Katherine and kissed her gently on the lips. "You'd better get dressed. You don't want to give your friend any ideas," he said, gently running his hand over her naked bottom.

INSPECTOR MACNUTT'S OFFICE, EAST BLOCK,
PARLIAMENT HILL, OTTAWA
9:16 A.M., MONDAY, JANUARY 10, 1916

MacNutt was reading the weekly intelligence reports from Esquimalt when he heard the phone ring in Lacelle's office. MacNutt became annoyed when it continued to ring. Lacelle must have stepped out of the office. He got up from his chair and went out to silence the irritating ringing.

"Yes," he shouted into the phone's mouthpiece.

"May I speak with Inspector MacNutt," said the voice on the other end of the crackly line.

"Speaking. And who is this?" shouted MacNutt again.

"Hallo, Andrew. It's Keith McKenna from the *Ottawa Journal*."

For some reason, MacNutt hadn't recognized the voice of the *Journal*'s parliamentary reporter, though he knew him quite well. Like most reporters, McKenna was especially keen on intelligence matters. As a rule, he was nearly as well informed as MacNutt. From time to time, they traded information, to their mutual benefit.

"Hi, Keith. A social call?" MacNutt knew damn well that it wasn't a social call when he glanced at the wall clock. It was nearly time for the paper to be put to bed. Keith probably had a hot story and he wanted MacNutt to confirm or deny it.

"I'm afraid not," replied McKenna. "I'm calling to get confirmation on a story we're about to print."

"What story is that?"

"The New York papers are publishing von Papen's personal papers," stated McKenna.

"They are?" MacNutt let slip his surprised tone. He was thinking furiously. What the hell was Keith talking about?

"Hallo, hallo," yelled McKenna through the phone. "Are you there? Are you there?"

"Yes. I'm still here, Keith. What kind of papers are we talking about?"

"You really don't know?"

"Of course I know. I just want to confirm exactly which ones we are talking about."

"Well, the New York papers are printing von Papen's personal papers. Apparently, the British confiscated them when they stopped him in Falmouth. The story is that they provide full details of German agents in America."

"I see." MacNutt frowned as his mind raced. *What the hell is going on?* Of course, he was well aware that the British had stopped and interrogated von Papen when he was en route to Germany and that some papers had been confiscated — but to have them published in the New York papers? That could only mean that the British had decided they were worth more as propaganda than as information that could further any investigation. And they had done it without giving him so much as a warning or a copy of the papers. There was only one thing he could say. "Well, Keith. You know that I really cannot discuss an on-going investigation."

"Did you receive a copy? Have you arrested anyone?" McKenna fired right back.

"Come, come now, Keith. You know better than that. I would like to, but I can't really say until the investigations have been completed."

McKenna laughed. "You can't fault a man for trying." MacNutt could hear some rustling of papers on the other end of the line. "But I have to write something for my article."

MacNutt grunted. He knew what game McKenna was playing. "Keith, I would really like to..."

"Yeah. Okay, Andrew. What if I just say that you cannot confirm or deny for now?"

"Sounds good," returned MacNutt, wondering what it would cost him.

"But you will let me know first when you have an item that may be of interest," McKenna continued.

"Agreed," said MacNutt quickly. "When I have a story that may interest you."

"Fuck," said Keith when he realized what he had just agreed to. Then he laughed. "Okay, okay, Andrew, but you better make sure that it's juicy."

"I'll do my best," chuckled MacNutt.

"You'd better," McKenna retorted, then MacNutt heard the receiver click.

"Who was that?" asked Lacelle, who had entered the office just in time to catch the tail end of the conversation.

MacNutt told him, then gave a tired sigh. "It seems that the New York papers are publishing von Papen's secret papers."

"*What* secret papers?"

"How the hell do I know!" exploded MacNutt. "I'm only a chief inspector of the Dominion Police." Lacelle kept his face carefully neutral, waiting for MacNutt to continue. "Sorry. But Borden will be livid when he finds out."

"There's nothing we could have done. It's not our fault," protested Lacelle, throwing his hands up in supplication.

"I really don't want to be the one to tell him," grumbled MacNutt as he leaned on Lacelle's desk. "Let's make sure that we have our backside covered. We did send a telegram requesting that if there were information of interest, they forward it on to us?"

Lacelle nodded.

MacNutt shrugged. "We need to get the latest copies of the New York papers. If we can't get them in Ottawa, we'll need to send a gram to New York and get them sent to us."

"That may take some time," Lacelle pointed out.

"I know. But I have to tell Borden something when he finds out. It would be nice if the news came from us for a change." MacNutt noticed Lacelle's skeptical expression. "Yes, I know, bad news travels fast."

"Why did the British leak the papers to the American press?"

"Why do you think? It puts the Germans on the defensive. We have been claiming for months that the Huns have been planning sabotage, and now we have proof. Or at least the goddamn British do! It also puts pressure on the Americans to take action."

"Do you think the British gave the Americans advance notice?"

"I certainly hope so," replied MacNutt. "I wouldn't want to upset President Wilson."

"*Oui.* I'll get started on that," said Lacelle as he reached for a sheet of paper and inserted it into the typewriter. "Do you still want me to attend Bourassa's speech tonight?"

MacNutt's gaze was pensive as Lacelle's fingers began to furiously work on the typewriter's keys. He had some concerns about Lacelle monitoring Bourassa's speech tonight, especially since it was in response to the Guigues school incident. MacNutt knew that Lacelle was sympathetic to Bourassa's point of view. His children were caught in the middle of the Regulation 17 dispute. But it wasn't clear to Andrew exactly how sympathetic he was. However, he hadn't much choice since he needed someone to be there and report on the speech. And no one else was available.

"Get what you can done before you leave. I need someone there to keep a watch on Bourassa. I'll need a report the first thing in the morning."

"Yes sir," replied Lacelle.

CHAPTER 21

Andrew was seated at the meeting table dressed in his ceremonial uniform of dark navy blue, every brass button on the jacket brightly polished, being briefed on the opening of Parliament scheduled for three o'clock this afternoon. At his left breast hung two silver Boer War campaign medals, the King's South Africa Medal, with two bars, and the Queen's South Africa Medal, with three bars. On the table was his officer's hat with the Dominion Police badge gleaming. A second hat rested on the table, this one belonging to Sir Percy Sherwood, the commissioner of the Dominion Police.

Across from Sherwood sat Thomas Flint, the clerk of the House of Commons, dressed in black legal robes. He was leading the meeting. Sitting beside him was his assistant similarly dressed. At the foot of the table sat Senator Thomas Sproule, who had been invited to the discussion as a courtesy. Normally, senators were not invited to sit in on House of Commons briefings, since the Senate had their own. However, before yesterday's announcement by the Prime Minister's Office that Sproule would be appointed to the Senate, he had been the speaker of the House and therefore the most familiar with the planning that had been done for the afternoon's event.

His appointment had caused some consternation. The official opening session of Parliament was delayed a day because when the Black Rod had summoned the House at three to the Upper Chamber, there had no longer been an elected speaker. When they arrived at the Senate, the senate clerk had informed them that the governor general had expressed his view that since there was not an elected speaker with whom the Crown might have official discourse, the House had to go back and elect one. Once they had elected a speaker, the governor general would re-summon them.

Borden had not been in the House the previous day, nor today for that matter, because he was sick with the grippe, but he put forth Albert Sévigny as his candidate for the speaker of the House. With Laurier's support, Sévigny was acclaimed and then ceremoniously dragged to the Speaker's chair at the front of the House.

Sproule was a bit stiff and correct with the new speaker. Andrew was not particularly surprised, although both men were members of the Conservative Party. Sproule was in ill health and the demands of the speakership had taken its toll. But the main reason was that Sproule was an Orangeman who opposed French language rights. He was no ordinary Orangeman. For five years he had been the Most Worshipful Master and Sovereign of the Order, and in 1906 he had been elected president of the Imperial Grand Orange Council. His loyalty to the Order was such that he had broken with the party on the Manitoba Schools question in 1890.

In contrast, Sévigny was elected as the representative of the Dorchester riding in Quebec and was a member of Henri Bourassa's Nationalist Party. The party had actively campaigned against Laurier's naval bill because of the fear that it would involve Canada in imperial wars. Bourassa had hoped that the Nationalist Party would hold the balance of power, but the Conservatives had won sufficient seats to form the government. Sévigny, as had most of the Nationalists, joined the Conservative Party because he detested Laurier and the Liberals.

"The governor general and his consort will arrive at approximately 2:30 p.m. at the Senate. Once they have entered the building they will make their entrance in the Senate at three o'clock, when the Gentleman Usher of the Black Rod will call the House to the Senate. When the House arrives at the Senate, Speaker Sévigny will be presented. Once you have completed your speech and left the Senate, the members of the House will return to the House for the evening session. Do you have any more advice to add, Senator Sproule?"

Sproule shook his head stiffly. "You have taken care of all the details as always, Mr. Flint."

"Any questions?" asked Flint, giving each man at the table a glance. No one put one forward. "Thank you all for attending this meeting. I'm reassured that the opening will go smoothly without any further incidents?"

Sir Sherwood spoke. "I give you my assurance that there will not be any incidents."

"Very well then," Flint said, closing a polished, tanned leather binder. "We don't have much time, and we have quite a bit of work still to do."

"When will your family be settling in?" Inspector MacNutt asked Sévigny as they rose.

"In the next few days," replied Sévigny, who seemed slightly overwhelmed by his new position. "We just have to arrange the quarters for the children."

"It will take a while getting used to living in the Centre Block," MacNutt said.

One of the perks that came with the position was the speaker's apartment. The speaker, being critical to the smooth functioning of the House of Commons, needed to be available at a moment's notice. The apartment was located on the north side of the Centre Block, opposite the House of Commons, facing the Ottawa River. The living quarters occupied two floors. On the ground floor were the speaker's offices, a dining room where the speaker could entertain guests, and a kitchen. A private staircase led to the second-floor parlour, three bedrooms, and servants' quarters. The rooms nearest and above the Reading Room were being converted into children's bedrooms to accommodate the speaker's two young girls, one a baby of ten months and the other five years old. The speaker's family, including two nannies, would be moving into the quarters in the next several days. The apartment's employees — a steward, a cook, and a housekeeper — were quite excited about the prospect of young children being in the household. "*Oui.* We will manage," declared the new speaker.

"If you have a need, let my people know and we may be able to accommodate you," said Sir Percy.

"*Merci*," replied Sévigny.

Sir Sherwood exited the meeting room with MacNutt at his heels, as per protocol. As they walked down the corridor Sherwood ordered MacNutt, "Do a final inspection to ensure that the security details are in place."

"Yes, sir," replied MacNutt. "I have a couple of men escorting the governor general to the Senate entrance. We will have a constable with the Royals the entire time they are in the Building. I've provided the entrance security the details, including the latest list of undesirables, to ensure that they do not cause any incidents."

"Very good. I have to go. I have an appointment with General Hughes at his office," stated Sir Sherwood with a grimace.

"Hughes will not be attending the opening?"

Sherwood gave him a wry smile. "He's indicated that he has some urgent matters to deal with, so he can't be there."

"I see," muttered MacNutt.

"To change subjects, how is the investigation progressing?" Sherwood asked briskly.

MacNutt shrugged. "We are following up some promising leads at the moment. And we've got the Pinks doing some background checks."

"Where are they doing the checks?"

"Detroit, Rochester, and New York."

"You couldn't get the New York British consulate to do the enquiries?" asked Sherwood.

"I would rather not deal with the British ambassador, Commissioner."

The commissioner snorted. "We all have our crosses to bear. I understand that Mrs. MacNutt was recently in New York. Did she enjoy her stay?"

"Yes, sir. She said she enjoyed it very much. She was very impressed with the Plaza Hotel where she stayed. Unfortunately, my pocketbook suffered somewhat because of it."

"That was to be expected, was it not?" said Sherwood in an amused tone.

"Yes, sir," replied MacNutt, cracking a smile.

"I'll keep the Plaza in mind next time I make a trip to New York. I've heard some good comments about it. By the way, is Mrs. MacNutt attending the opening today?"

"She is, but she is escorting that Belgian Relief fellow to the opening."

"Hmm..." replied Sherwood with a slight frown. "If I don't see her, please give her my regards. And please keep me informed whenever you have news regarding the investigation."

"Of course, Commissioner."

Sherwood gave him a curt nod and made his way to one of the nearby staircases. It would lead him to the underground tunnel that connected the Parliament Building with the East Block, so that he could avoid going out into the cold.

MacNutt made his way down the corridor to the Parliament Building's foyer, where he met Sergeant Lacelle, also in his dress uniform. With a critical eye, MacNutt inspected the sergeant but found nothing amiss.

"The commissioner asked that we check the security arrangements," MacNutt answered without preamble.

"Of course, Inspector. Where do you want to start?"

"With the House entrance," replied MacNutt. "Also, the commissioner asked how the investigation is going."

Lacelle winced. "May I ask what you said to the commissioner?"

MacNutt briefly recounted his conversation. "Do you have more to add?"

"Yes, sir. I got a telegram from the Pinks deciphered this morning. It appears that one of the names on our list does not check out. MacQuinty. He stayed at the Russell between Christmas and New Year's. Claimed he was a business traveller. I could not locate anyone in Ottawa who has done business with the man. The Pinks checked the address in New York and they never heard from him either. Unfortunately, the description we have is rather vague. There was nothing memorable about the man."

"He could be a Fenian in league with the Germans," remarked MacNutt thoughtfully. "Unless he uses the same name again, it will be tough to catch him. I'll have a chat with Denon. He may have heard something of interest."

"I don't think that he will be very co-operative," stated Lacelle.

It took a moment for MacNutt to remember why. A friend of Denon who worked for Ottawa's Public Works department had taken exception to some remarks made by his parish priest concerning the German war conduct and had caused an incident. It was sufficient to catch his attention, requiring that MacNutt investigate and lay charges. It resulted in the man losing his job.

"What else is new," muttered MacNutt. Denon was likely to be even more unhappy with him when he showed up on his doorstep. "Well. Let's get this day over with so we can get back and do some real work."

VICTORIA TOWER ENTRANCE, CENTRE BLOCK,
PARLIAMENT HILL, OTTAWA
2:30 P.M., THURSDAY, JANUARY 13, 1916

Katherine was walking with the Count up the freshly shovelled pathway that ran along the East Block. It was late afternoon, and by the sun's position in the sky above the West Block, she estimated that it would be dark in about an hour or so. She couldn't help glancing to her right at the windows that peered into her husband's office on the ground floor. She then scanned to her left, past the Count, at the crowd that lined the roadway that wound past the East, Centre, and West Blocks. Blue-uniformed constables kept a careful watch on the crowd. She noted that the crowd that had come to view the Royals' arrival was the smallest she had seen in recent years.

"Quite a crowd," observed the Count.

"I've seen larger. They're waiting for the arrival of the governor general," grumbled Katherine. "They love the pomp and ceremony."

"In this weather?"

"Yes. It isn't that cold," she teased. "Do you want to view it from here? It's quite a sight, and you're dressed for it." The Count had learned from his previous visits to Ottawa that he needed to dress warmly. He was wearing a taupe grey woollen coat with a bright red plaid scarf and a black fur fedora. Katherine was wearing her fur. Underneath it, she wore the wheat-coloured dress she had bought in New York just the week before. She glanced at the Count, wondering if he thought of the night they had spent together. Unfortunately, she had not found a private moment to talk to him about it.

"I used to love watching the governor general arrive in his horse-drawn carriage with his escort of soldiers. They were dashing in their red coats and bright metal helmets, and riding beautiful horses," Katherine recalled fondly.

The Count said gallantly, "If you would like, we can wait outside." It was the last thing he wanted to do, and Katherine picked up his reluctance.

"No, I've changed my mind. Let's wait inside — otherwise we may not be able to get a seat."

The Count flashed her a charming smile, then they headed towards the Centre Block, the jewel of the three buildings that comprised the Parliament Buildings complex. All three buildings surrounding the snow-covered courtyard were in the Gothic revival style, though adapted for the harsh Canadian weather with steep roofs to keep weighty snow from accumulating, and thick stone walls provided some protection from the cold. The Centre Block was five stories high, 472 feet long, and, including the Parliament Library, 575 feet in depth. The exterior of the imposing and ornate building was constructed of light-coloured local Nepean sandstone, with grey Ohio sandstone mixed in to provide relief in colour. Accents were provided by red Potsdam sandstone in the door and window arches.

The focal point of the building was the 180-foot-high Victoria Tower. Intended as the grand entrance to the Centre Block, the three arches at the base of the square tower were wide enough for a carriage to pass through them. The arched windows of the tower's second and third floors complemented the windows of the east and west wings of the building. The east wing housed the Senate, while the west wing housed the House of Commons. On the fourth storey of the tower were two tall, slender arched windows that nearly touched the large clock dial and its eight-foot hands. Above the clock, the tower was topped with an iron crown. The crown contained a powerful white lamp, visible for twenty miles when lit, which was only when Parliament was in session.

The mansard roofs of the House and Senate wings were covered with green-and-grey slate, now partly obscured by patches of white snow. The roof was topped by wrought-iron railings and ornaments. The roof line was also broken by chimneys, from which smoke was gently being carried by the wind easterly towards the Ottawa River.

As the Count and Katherine walked towards the Victoria Tower, the Centre Block's intricate architectural details became more apparent. The local carvers had used their skills and craft on various cornices, corbels, and colonettes scattered about the building's facade. Far above grimaced the intricately carved faces of gargoyles.

When they reached the Victoria Tower, they had to wait in line with the rest of the crowd. One of the constables spotted Katherine and waved to her to come forward. She left the line to talk to him, the Count in tow.

"Good evening, Constable Briggs. You have to work tonight?" asked Katherine sympathetically.

"I'm afraid so, madame," the constable replied, eyeing the Count suspiciously.

"Constable, this is Count Jaggi of Belgian Relief. He's my guest this evening." Katherine knew that a report would go shortly to her husband, though he knew of her plans. The constable waved them through the main entrance's large, panelled oak doors.

Still leading, Katherine walked through into a large hall. On the mosaic floor were inlaid eight shields, seven of them depicting the coats of arms of the provinces that had comprised the Dominion when the building was built. The blank shield had been intended for the next new province admitted to the confederation. However, in 1905, when Alberta and Saskatchewan were created, it was politically impossible to insert the coat of arms of one province but not the other. It was decided to leave the eighth shield blank.

Before them they had a choice of two semi-circular landings, one leading east to the Senate, the other west to the House. To get to the staircases, they needed to pass through Arnprior marble arches supported by six Nepean sandstone columns. Behind the arches was a series of arched stained-glass windows. Instead of taking the dozen steps up to one of the landings, Katherine led the Count underneath the staircase to the Senate, through an archway to a lift. They waited for the operator to open the gate. As they stood close together to make room for the operator in the close quarters of the small chamber, Katherine's and the Count's bodies brushed each other. The Count winked at her and Katherine could feel herself blushing. The operator, oblivious, secured the gate and pushed the lever to raise the car. When they reached the second floor a few seconds later, he pulled the lever to stop the lift then opened the gate for them.

"Where are we going?" wondered the Count.

"The Senate's visitor's gallery, so we can watch the throne speech," answered Katherine as she led the way down a north-south corridor lined to mid-height with intricately carved wooden panels. Sandstone blocks ran the rest of the distance to the ceiling.

When they arrived at the end of the corridor, they were greeted by the Dominion police duty constable, who waved them through when he saw Katherine.

Katherine took a couple of steps down the east-west corridor then opened the door into the visitor's gallery. There were still spots open in the first of the three rows of benches. Once they had seated themselves and placed their folded coats beside them on the smooth wood, the Count took a careful view of the Senate Chamber.

Galleries for spectators, as many as a thousand, rimmed the chamber, which the Count estimated to be about eighty feet long and about half as wide. The gallery above the throne was reserved for reporters. Stained-glass windows and a corrugated glass ceiling, fifty feet above the Senate floor, provided plenty of natural light. The glass ceiling was supported by stone arches atop columns of light Portage du Fort and dark Arnprior marble. Artificial light was provided by suspended electric lights and lamps dispersed among the three rows of chairs on the Senate floor.

At the south end of the chamber hung portraits of King George III and Queen Charlotte. At the north end were two arched doorways used by the clerks and pages to enter and leave the chamber. Centred between the two doorways was a very ornate valance, festooned with draperies, below which sat the governor general's throne. Also set in the middle of the chamber were six chairs for the Chief Justice and the Puisne Judges of the Supreme Court of Canada.

The gallery was filling quickly, and the crowd talked quietly as they waited for the ceremony to begin. As Katherine and the Count passed pleasantries, the Count noted that in the visitors' gallery on the far side were seated various consuls general and their wives. He could recognize Goor from Belgium, Bonin from France, Likatcheff from Russia, Kada from Japan, and Foster from the United States.

At three o'clock, the Duke and the Duchess of Connaught entered the Red Chamber. The governor general was dressed in a court uniform: a red tunic with gold embroidery on epaulets and arm sleeves, white trousers, and polished black boots. His military campaign medals hung on his left chest over a sash that ran from his left shoulder to his right hip. Gold braid also ran in a loop from his right shoulder to a button just below the uniform's straight collar. Below the campaign medals were four stars that represented the honours he was entitled to display: Extra Knight of the Most Ancient and Most Noble Order of the Thistle, Knight Grand Cross of the Most Distinguished Order of St. Michael and St. George, Knight Grand Commander of the Most Exalted Order of the Star of India, and Knight of the Most Illustrious Order of St. Patrick.

The Duchess was dressed in a black satin dress with a matching black tunic of spangled net. The tunic's collar was made of pink chiffon and lace. The black tunic contrasted well with the white pearl necklace and diamond ornaments she was wearing. Also, on her left breast, decorating her bodice she wore her honours: the Companion of the Order of the Crown of India, Member of the Royal Red Cross, Dame of Justice of St. John, and Lady of the Royal Order of Victoria and Albert.

The Princess wore a rich gown of bright sky-blue panne velvet, topped with a short tunic of dark blue tulle, spangled with silver. The sleeves were the same shade of tulle over a cream-coloured shadow lace. She also wore a pearl necklace and diamond earrings. She, too, had orders decorating the bodice of her tunic, the Order of Victoria and Albert, St. John of Jerusalem, and the Crown of India.

The Royals were followed by the Gentleman Usher of the Black Rod, the Clerks of the Senate, the pages, and finally by the senators, who flowed into their assigned seats.

When the Duke and the Duchess were seated, the governor general nodded to the speaker of the Senate. Speaker Landy, in the traditional dress of black silk robes, white tabs and gloves, rose and said in a voice that carried to the back of the Senate, "Gentleman of the Usher of the Black Rod!" He waited until the Black Rod rose to his feet and bowed respectfully to the speaker.

"Proceed to the House of Commons and acquaint the House that it is His Royal Highness the governor general's pleasure that they attend him immediately in the Senate," he ordered.

The Gentleman of the Usher of the Black Rod bowed, and holding the ebony rod, the symbol of his office, turned and left the Chamber. When he exited the Senate, he turned left and walked down the short corridor to the Grand Lobby. He crossed the lobby, climbed the steps, turned to his right, and walked down the corridor to the entrance to the House of Commons. The corridor was lined with pine wardrobes where the members hung their outerwear before entering the Green Chamber. The doors, as was traditional, were closed, a custom since the days where the Commons feared Royal displeasure and barred the doors against intrusions. He knocked three times with his staff. On the third knock the door opened, and he was admitted by the sergeant-at-arms. The Black Rod walked to the bar of the Chamber and bowed to the clerk of the House of Commons three times.

"It is his Royal Highness the governor general's pleasure that they attend him immediately in the Senate so you may hear the cause of the summoning of Parliament," he commanded, his voice carrying to the back of the room. When he finished speaking, the Black Rod turned and left the chamber. On his heels, he was followed by the sergeant-at-arms, who was carrying the ceremonial mace, the Clerks of the House and his assistants, and the newly elected speaker, followed by the assembled members of the House.

Once the procession arrived at the Senate, the Speaker of the House, Sévigny, mounted a low platform, removed his tricorne hat, and announced in a firm voice, "May it please Your Royal Highness, the Houses of Commons has elected me as their speaker, though I am but little able to fulfil the important duties thus assigned to me. If in the performance of those duties, I should at any time fall in error, I pray that the fault may be imputed to me, and not to the Commons, whose servant I am."

The speaker of the Senate rose from his chair and replied, "Mr. Speaker, I am commanded by His Royal Highness the governor general to assure you that your words and actions will constantly receive from him the most favourable construction."

The governor general smiled, then his aide handed him several sheets of paper. He rose to his feet and began to read his speech, which extolled the virtues of the Canadian government's war effort and the government's plans for the coming session.

When he completed the speech, he handed his papers to his aide and rose from his throne. He offered his arm to his consort, and with the Princess trailing them, the Royals left the Senate. The Count knew that they were heading to a state dinner to which he was not invited.

With the departure of the Royals, the visitors' galleries began to empty. Count Jaggi helped Katherine with her fur. She gave him a smile as they headed for the exit. The Count and Katherine had been invited to another event that he hoped would be more useful. He noted that a few of the visitors were staying to watch the Senate proceedings, but the Count was not particularly interested in Canadian senators discussing a railway bill. Not that he wasn't interested in Canadian railways, but he doubted that the senators' discussions about legal technicalities would provide any tactical information he could employ in the planning and execution of railway sabotage.

In the Centre Block's Central Hall, Katherine spotted her husband standing in the corner, scanning the crowd. "Excuse me for a moment," she said to the Count. She walked over to her husband and whispered in his ear. He peered at the Count curiously then nodded. When she returned she said, "Shall we go then?"

"Everything is acceptable with your husband?" inquired the Count as they left the Centre Block.

"Yes." She didn't elaborate.

RUSSELL HOTEL, ELGIN AND SPARKS STREETS, OTTAWA
5:30 P.M., THURSDAY, JANUARY 13, 1916

Katherine and the Count spoke very little as they walked carefully along the East Block to Wellington Street, the main street that ran east and west in front of the Parliament Buildings. They had to cross and walk past the Langevin Building, a government building styled along Italian Renaissance lines and which housed the Department of the Interior and the Post Office, before they could reach Sparks Street. They had to wait a few minutes for the traffic to clear before they could cross over to the Russell Hotel.

The Russell was the premier hotel in the city and an Ottawa landmark. Built in 1865, it had expanded over the years to the point that it occupied a full city block on the corner of Sparks and Elgin. The hotel was a four-storey structure that in summer sported red and white awnings. In the late 1800s, Canadian prime ministers, including Sir John A. Macdonald, Tupper, and Laurier, had lived at the Russell during their tenures. It was also the first hotel in the city to have bathrooms and steam heat. Attached to the building on the Queen Street side was the opulent 1,500-seat Russell Theatre. It was built in 1897 but rebuilt in 1901 after a fire. The stature of the theatre was such that it attracted the likes of Lillie Langtry, Oscar Wilde, and Sarah Bernhardt.

There was an entrance on the corner of Elgin and Sparks, but they chose to go in the main entrance doors further down Elgin Street. The rotunda inside was decorated with a number of deep plush chairs and lounges for the comfort of the hotel's guests. The room's dome was decorated with stained-glass depictions of the coats of arms and flowers of the Canadian provinces. Branching off one side of the rotunda were carpeted stairs and elevators. Hallways also branched off to the theatre to a bar which was regularly attended by MPs and Senators, a dining room with a seating capacity of 250, a reading room, and the Russell Café. The café was famous for its buckwheat cakes.

The Count had been invited to the Grand Trunk's meet-and-greet being held in the hotel's bar by David Mahoney, one of the railway's vice presidents. It was at the December meeting of the presidents of the railways and banks to discuss Belgian Relief that the Count became acquainted with Mahoney, who had said the railway used the opening of Parliament as an opportunity to lobby MPs, bureaucrats, and important business leaders. If the Count were interested, he could come to promote Belgian Relief. The lobbying was not surprising, since the Canadian government had been subsidizing the Grand Trunk and the other railways since Confederation. With the war, the railways had been doing well with government contracts to move Canadian troops and military supplies to the ports of Montreal and Halifax.

As they approached the bar, Katherine paused. The Count raised questioning eyebrows. Katherine smiled at him ruefully. "I'm afraid that ladies are not allowed in the bar."

"Oh," replied the Count, "I'm sorry. I thought you had been invited?"

"I have been invited," exclaimed Katherine, "but to the Russell *Café.*" She indicated the restaurant on the other side of the rotunda.

"I didn't know," replied the Count, disappointed.

"I'll see you tomorrow at nine o'clock," Katherine said, touching his arm.

"Yes, I have not forgotten," answered the Count with a slight bow. Katherine acknowledged him with another smile then left him standing in the rotunda. The Count watched her backside until she disappeared into the café. He sighed at the memory of her naked hips swaying as she walked into the Plaza Hotel's washroom. Her behaviour had been totally chaste in Ottawa. He understood why she didn't want any whispers that might destroy her reputation. He was seeing her tomorrow, and one never knew when an opportunity would present itself.

When he entered the bar, it was already nearly filled to capacity. Free drinks always made it easy to fill a bar. A waiter dressed in evening clothes greeted the Count. "Good evening, sir, may I help you?"

"Yes, I'm Count Jaggi. I'm to meet Mr. Mahoney."

"Very good, sir. Please follow me." The waiter led the Count deeper into the bar. Standing at the end of the bar was a group of three men. The waiter approached them and tapped the shoulder of one of the men, who had his back to the Count. When he turned and saw the Count, he smiled broadly and headed over.

The Count's first impression was of a jovial, happy-go-lucky man. He was in his mid-sixties, dressed in a dark suit with a white shirt and a striped club tie. His moustache connected with his sideburns, and his beard was neatly trimmed.

"Ah, Count Jaggi! I'm glad that you could come." Mahoney offered the Count his hand.

"The pleasure is all mine," replied the Count, shaking the hand. "David, I'm glad we have this opportunity to talk about Belgian Relief."

Mahoney waved the statement away. "It's a worthy cause, and the Grand Trunk would be glad to provide you any assistance. Come, let me introduce you to some gentlemen who might be of interest to you." He led the Count to his three colleagues.

"Toronto beat the Sens last night, one zero," declared one of the men in the foursome.

"Damn," groaned another.

Mahoney snorted. "The Maroons will win the cup this year."

"Do you want to make a wager?" chimed in the third man.

Mahoney laughed. "Easy money! Easy money! Gentlemen, let me introduce you to Count Jaggi. Count Jaggi, the gentleman here with a poor taste in hockey teams is Nigel Hawthorne. He's a manufacturer from Toronto."

"Pleasure," Hawthorne said. He was in his mid-forties with sandy blond hair, amber eyes, and a firm handshake. Even in the low light one could tell his suit was well tailored.

"And this reprobate is Keith McKenna, the Parliamentary reporter for the *Ottawa Journal*." Mahoney indicated him with a grin. The reporter's fingers had ink stains and he was dressed in a ten-dollar Eaton's suit. He scrutinized the Count with keen interest.

"Ah, Count," he chortled, grasping the Count's hand and pumping it. "It's a pleasure to finally meet you. I've heard your name mentioned on the Hill a number of times. If you have a few minutes, I would like to interview you."

"Good God, man! Let the man have a drink before we bring on the inquisition." Mahoney motioned to the bartender. "What'll it be?"

"A beer, thank you," replied the Count.

After ordering beers all around, Mahoney turned to McKenna. "I've got to ask you, Keith, what have you heard about that massacre in Mexico?"

McKenna shrugged and took a swig of his beer. "It seems to be getting worse. The Americans have moved about five thousand troops along the border. Wilson hasn't officially announced what he is going to do yet. But it's likely that the American army will be crossing the border into Mexico."

"Really?" asked the Count. He was quite pleased with the news. Anything that would distract the Americans from German activities was a very good thing.

"Yes. They are not likely to take this lying down, especially when Americans are massacred on American soil," declared McKenna.

"How many people were killed in the attack?" asked Hawthorne.

"The latest reports over the wire say at least eighteen. Two were British women. The rest were Americans."

"Jesus, all we need is another war," blurted Hawthorne in disgust.

"Well, things have been pretty chaotic in Mexico for the last few years. They seem to change governments on a daily basis," Mahoney pointed out.

"And what do you expect the Americans to do?" asked McKenna.

"What the devil was that Villa fellow thinking he was doing, attacking the Americans? He must be mad," Hawthorne barked.

"Mad or not, he has a peasant army backing him. It could get messy," said Mahoney.

"The American general they have down there, Pershing, is supposed to be one of their better ones," argued Hawthorne. "He should make short work of Villa."

"Let's hope so," grunted Mahoney. He gestured with his beer mug at the Count. "What do you think?"

Before the Count could frame a reply, Hawthorne interjected. "David, why are so interested in Mexico? You never were before. Does the Grand Trunk have any interests there?"

When the men turned their attention to Mahoney, he returned their gaze sheepishly. "My wife and I have a vacation planned in February down south."

"Where?" asked McKenna.

"The Bahamas."

"Very nice. But what does that have to do with Mexico?" asked Hawthorne.

"Exactly. That's what I've been telling my wife. But she's got it into her head that Florida is going to be invaded by hordes of Mexicans."

The men started laughing.

"It isn't that funny."

"Sorry," said Hawthorne. Buzzing behind the Count had caught his attention. "Oh my God. Hughes just walked in."

All heads turned towards the door. Two gentlemen dressed in khaki overcoats and dress caps stood in the entrance. The older of the two gentlemen removed his coat and handed it to the other man, his aide. The aide disappeared with it into the cloak closet. Hughes was dressed in the Canadian version of the standard British military uniform. A gleaming black Sam Browne belt with a leather strap ran from his right shoulder to his left hip. His collar tabs and epaulets indicated that he held the rank of major-general.

This was the first time that the Count had seen the minister of militia and defence in the flesh. He quickly reviewed the facts he had accumulated about the man. In 1866, Hughes had joined the 45th Durham Infantry Battalion of the Canadian Militia. He saw action in the Fenian raids in 1870, where he had been awarded a medal. In 1899, he volunteered for South Africa and had served as a lieutenant-colonel. While he was a decent commander of irregular troops, his temperament and boasting eventually resulted in his dismissal due to a lack of military discipline. He had been bitter with the British for denying him a Victoria Cross for his service in the Boer War, which he felt he had earned and deserved. In 1911, he had ridden the wave of Borden's election sweep and was appointed minister of militia and defence. Hughes was promoted to major-general in 1914 and was knighted in 1915.

When Hughes spotted Mahoney, he marched immediately across the room.

"Great. He's coming over," muttered Hawthorne.

Mahoney turned to him and ordered, "You behave."

"Don't I always," Hawthorne replied with a smirk.

Before Mahoney could reply, Hughes was upon them. "Ah, Mahoney. Just the man I wanted to see," he declared. He ignored the rest of the men.

"Good evening, Sir Hughes. It's a pleasure seeing you again," Mahoney said. The Count noted that the man's smile was hiding his dismay. "I was not expecting you this evening. I thought you were in Ludlow reviewing the troops."

"Yes, I was, and I was helping with the recruiting drive," answered Hughes.

"How is the recruiting coming along?" inquired McKenna. The Count was glad McKenna had asked, because he was interested as well.

"It's coming along quite nicely. We will not have any problem getting half a million men in the field," boasted Hughes.

"Sir Hughes, would you like some tea?" asked Mahoney. Hughes was a confirmed teetotaller.

"Please," said Hughes. He studied the Count curiously for the first time.

"Excuse my manners, Sir Hughes. Let me introduce you to Count Jaggi. Sir Hughes, minister of militia and defence."

"Pleasure," said the Count with a slight bow.

"Likewise. I understand that you work for Belgian Relief." The Count was startled by the minister's statement. He didn't like the implications. "Belgian Relief is a good cause. I applaud your efforts," continued Hughes with a sharp nod.

"Thank you, Minister," replied the Count. Hughes gave him a final glance then ignored him again.

"Minister, I've read in the paper that they may be moving one of the Ross rifle plants to Lindsay," said Hawthorne with mock innocence.

The Count felt a sudden tension among the men. Mahoney seemed especially displeased.

"Yes. If Quebec doesn't want the plant, the people of Lindsay will gladly take it," replied Hughes tersely. The Ross Rifle Company's main production plant was in Québec City. His tone carried a mixture of pride and a bit of watchfulness.

Hawthorne continued calmly. "I just was a bit surprised, since I have been hearing reports that there are problems with the rifle."

"That's a lie. The Ross rifle is the finest military rifle in the world," Hughes said hotly, waving a finger at him.

"So there have not been any problems with the rifle jamming after repeated firings?" Hawthorne returned, unfazed by Hughes' theatrics.

"If the Canadian round is used, there are no problems," declared Hughes.

"Really? I understand that the Canadian troops prefer the Lee-Enfield because it is more reliable."

Hughes turned an apoplectic purple. "As long as I'm the minister, the troops will use the Ross." His demeanour indicated that he would not suffer further discussion on the issue.

"Excuse me, gentlemen. May I have a word with Mr. Mahoney privately?" Hughes barked as he turned, fully expecting Mahoney to follow him.

"Of course, Minister," replied Mahoney. He glared at Hawthorne then rushed off with the minister to mollify him.

McKenna turned to Hawthorne and whispered, "For a moment I thought he was going to have you shot."

"Unlikely, if he used a Ross," quipped Hawthorne.

McKenna scowled. "I wouldn't want to upset Hughes. Especially if you want government contracts."

"Am I getting any? Haven't you noticed that most of them are going to his friends and cronies?" Hawthorne noticed the Count's confusion. "You don't know what I'm talking about, do you?"

"I must confess that I do not follow the conversation," replied the Count. He was familiar with the Mauser and the Lee-Enfield but not the Ross.

Hawthorne shook his head sadly. "The Ross rifle is the Canadian Expeditionary Force's standard infantry rifle. It's a fine hunting rifle. It's my favourite. But it is simply not a military rifle. Hughes liked the rifle and we have been stuck with it ever since."

"Now, now let's be fair. The rifle had problems," said McKenna, "and they have been trying to fix them."

"Like I said," Hawthorne interjected, "the Ross is a good rifle but not a military rifle. It's too delicate. Dirt in the breech causes it to jam.

Also, it is far too easy to put the bolt in backwards, and when you do, it can blow your face off when you squeeze the trigger."

"My God," exclaimed the Count.

"Everyone but Hughes recognizes that there are problems with the Ross," grumbled Hawthorne.

"Does not the prime minister have a say in the matter?" asked the Count.

"One would think," sighed McKenna. "I personally think Borden is afraid of him and that is why he won't fire him. But sooner or later Hughes will step over the line and Borden will have no choice."

Mahoney finally rejoined them. He jabbed at Hawthorne angrily with his finger. "I told you to behave."

Hawthorne raised his hands in mock surrender. "What did he want?"

"He wasn't too happy with you, my friend. You may have lost any chance of contracts."

"As if I stood a chance in hell anyway," Hawthorne scoffed.

"That's not fair. The contracts are rewarded fairly and to the lowest bidder," retorted Mahoney. He had to defend his party.

"I know the companies that won those contracts. They are making a tidy profit by overcharging and cutting corners," snapped Hawthorne as he downed the last of his beer.

"Sadly, that's too common a story. Like what happened to Admiral Kingsmill over there," suggested McKenna, pointing to a man in a Royal Navy dress uniform, with rear-admiral gold epaulets on his shoulders and stripes on his sleeves. On his left breast were the African General Service Medal, Egypt Medal, Khedive's Star for service in Egypt, Grand Office, Order of the Crown of Italy, and the Legion of Honour from France. His cap was under his arm. He wore a neatly trimmed moustache and goatee beard. "He has to appear before the defence committee to talk about his new subs."

"Subs?" exclaimed Hawthorne. The Count couldn't believe his luck. Information concerning subs would be of interest to Berlin.

"Yes, those two that McBride bought," explained McKenna.

"What's wrong with them?" demanded Hawthorne.

McKenna responded, "There was a reason why the Chilean government was wrangling with the shipbuilder about the subs. My information is that the subs have a tendency to lose buoyancy and go into uncontrollable dives. If I understand correctly, that's not very good for subs!"

218

"How do you know all this?" asked Hawthorne.

McKenna shrugged. "I have my sources. What is not common knowledge is that if a German cruiser did attack the West Coast, the subs would be useless anyway."

The Count couldn't help himself. "Why?"

McKenna snorted. "They were so intent on buying the subs, they neglected the torpedoes. They thought the sub came with them."

Hawthorne closed his eyes in disbelief. "You're joking?"

"I wish I was. They tried to buy the missing torpedoes from the Americans, but unfortunately, their neutrality laws prevented them from selling them to us. Even if the neutrality laws were not in place, they would not have sold them to us, because they were upset that we stole the subs, so to speak, right under their noses. They found some torpedoes that fit the subs in Halifax, which they had transported to B.C. by train."

"What is Kingsmill going to say?" asked Mahoney.

"What can he say? He may be the director of the Canadian Naval Service, but it wasn't his idea to get the subs in the first place."

Again, the Count couldn't help himself from asking a question. "Why did the Canadian government buy the subs in the first place?"

McKenna turned to the Count and explained. "It wasn't the Canadian government's idea." He saw the Count's confusion and continued. "In a nutshell, what happened was that when the war was appearing to break out, British Columbia was essentially defenceless. England had recalled most of its ships back to home waters and left the Pacific to the Americans and the Japs. Rumours that the Germans had a couple of cruisers as raiders scared the British Columbians. We only had one ship in the Pacific, an old light cruiser we got second-hand from the Royal Navy. The Germans would have blown it out of the water in seconds."

Mahoney sighed. "And to think of all the ruckus caused by Laurier's Naval Bill." He was referring to Laurier's Liberal government bill that had created the Canadian Naval Service. Laurier was trying to balance the interests of both the anti-imperialists in Quebec and the pro-imperialists in Ontario. However, by insisting that the fleet be under Canadian control, he had alienated both sides. The anti-imperialists believed building a fleet was a waste of money. Rear-Admiral Kingsmill had been named the director of the service when it was created. It was a curious piece of fate that the director of the Naval Service was a Canadian. Kingsmill was born in Guelph, Canada West, in 1855. At the age of fifteen he had joined the Royal Navy and then rose steadily through the ranks. In 1908, he was promoted to rear-admiral and sent to Canada to run the Marine Service of the Department of Marine and Fisheries. The Marine Service performed coastal water protection and search-and-rescue operations.

"McBride heard that the America shipyard was having problems with the Chilean navy about the payments for the subs. He inquired if the subs were for sale, and the shipyard said yes, for a million dollars for both. McBride decided to buy the subs. What he didn't know at the time was that the shipyard had named him a higher price than what they had agreed to sell the subs for to the Chileans."

"How much higher?" asked Hawthorne.

"I heard anywhere from $200,000 to $500,000. I never got an exact number. However, McBride had to get the deal done and the subs in Canadian waters before war was actually declared. Once war was declared, American neutrality laws would kick in and at that point the shipyards would be violating U.S. neutrality by selling the subs, and the boats and the money could be confiscated."

"Good God. I'm surprised that they could manage it," exclaimed Hawthorne.

"The shipyard was in Seattle. It's only a couple hours away from Victoria," explained McKenna. "They sailed the subs into Esquimalt hours before war was officially declared. McBride was on the dock with the money. He handed them the cash, and they gave him the subs.

"The deal nearly ended in catastrophe," he added. "It happened so fast that they neglected to inform the shore batteries that the subs were coming, and they nearly blew the subs out of the water!"

Mahoney said, "Once it was a done deal, Borden had no choice but to buy the subs from B.C. Defence is the federal government's responsibility. We can't have the provinces with their own armed forces, can we?"

"So that is why Borden has a bee in his bonnet about subs," said Hawthorne with new understanding.

Mahoney added, "It gets worse."

"How can it get worse?" Hawthorne exclaimed.

"What people don't know is that we have been building subs for the Royal Navy at the Vickers shipyard in Montreal."

"*What?*" exclaimed McKenna.

Mahoney turned to him. "You can't write any of this!"

"Oh, come on." Seeing Mahoney's seriousness, McKenna grumbled, "All right, all right, I give."

"So this is what happened: London wanted to build up their sub fleet. The Electric Boat Company in the States sold the Royal Navy and Churchill on a plan to build ten subs, with the first to be delivered in six months' time. The problem was the subs couldn't be built in the States because of the neutrality laws, but they could be built in Canada, with the Electric Boat Company providing the blueprints, equipment, and supplies. In January of last year, the British government took over the Vickers shipyard in Montreal. They also cancelled an important icebreaker contract in the process."

"They built and delivered the subs?" said McKenna in wonderment.

"Yes," replied Mahoney. "They did. But Ottawa didn't know about it. When Borden found out, he was absolutely furious — I never saw him so mad! All along he had been saying that we were full partners with the British in fighting the war. It sure didn't feel like it. He then suggested that it be a shared operation so that subs could be supplied to the East Coast and they could be used to defend the eastern provinces. The Admiralty refused."

"That helps explain why he gives Hughes so much leeway," noted Hawthorne. "And why he was upset with Churchill. He was publicly defending the Gallipoli campaign in December — then we found out they were pulling out of Gallipoli this month with nothing to show for it."

"That's true," said McKenna. "But what added salt to the wound was that the Electric Boat Company had made the offer to the Canadian government first. Borden and Kingsmill had forwarded the proposal to London. The Admiralty turned it down, saying that the subs were of an older design and not much use."

"Good God!" said Hawthorne.

"Right. Next thing Borden knows, they are building the damn subs a couple of hours away by train and he can't have any of them!" Mahoney scowled.

"You know, sometimes it's difficult to tell the difference between your friends and your enemies," McKenna said.

"Welcome to politics," said Mahoney. As a lobbyist for his train company, he knew all too well.

Turning to the Count, he said with a half-grin, "I'm sorry to bore you with such talk."

"Not at all. I found it quite interesting," the Count said truthfully. He had found the conversation very interesting indeed.

RUSSELL HOTEL, ELGIN AND SPARKS STREETS, OTTAWA
11:45 P.M., THURSDAY, JANUARY 13, 1916

The Count was weary when he entered his hotel room. He dropped his overcoat on the chair near the window that overlooked the canal locks. He gazed down on the empty locks and then stared for a few minutes at the brightly lit East Block before closing the blinds. He was feeling slightly drunk, but he needed to make some notes from the party he had just left while it was still fresh in his memory.

He took off his waistcoat and rolled up his sleeves, then went into the bathroom to get a glass of water. He set it on the writing table then pulled from the briefcase lying beside the desk some sheets of onionskin paper, fountain pens, and a black cloth button. He dropped the button into the glass of water.

He tested one of the pens, and when he was satisfied with the flow of ink he began to write on the onionskin in a quick hand. The party had provided him with nuggets of information that he was now panning for gold. Nuggets that could be of interest to Berlin. As he wrote, ideas and questions began percolating in his mind. Could they intercept the subs built in Montreal in Canadian waters; could the widening rift between the Canadians and the British be further widened; could they exploit the Mexican crisis?

When he filled one sheet, he took a fresh one and continued to write out notes in point form. By the time he completed the fourth and last sheet of notes, his handwriting had degenerated into a scrawl that was barely legible, but he was pleased he had managed to get everything down. What he needed to do now was organize the notes in a coherent and logical order.

He broke from his work for a moment when he saw that the ink from the black button had discoloured the water and was ready. He filled a second pen with amber-coloured ink.

He picked up the black-ink fountain pen and began to write his second draft, this time condensing the text into two handwritten pages. His fatigue and the drink were taking effect, and he was having trouble focusing on his task. The next step was the most time-consuming and needed his undivided attention, but he was having trouble keeping from dozing. He decided that the remaining step could wait for the morning, when he would be rested and fresh.

He put the papers and pens aside, rose from the desk and dropped onto the bed, still dressed. He fell asleep as soon as his scalp touched the pillow.

CHAPTER 22

When the Count awoke the next morning, he felt a bit groggy but his mind slowly cleared as he stared at the ornate ceiling. He squinted down and saw that he was still dressed. He sat up, and as he yawned his gaze was drawn to the papers on the desk. He fell back onto the bed and wrapped the comforter around him, closing his eyes in the hope that he could catch a few more minutes of sleep. After a couple of minutes he gave up hope, got up off the bed, and undressed. He padded into the bathroom to shower and shave.

When he was freshly dressed, he read the papers on his desk again then checked his watch. He was running late now and needed breakfast before he met Katherine at eleven. He sat down and converted the previous night's notes into his cypher. As he wrote the notes with the fountain pen he had prepared the night before, they gradually faded and disappeared into the paper. When he finished the last sentence, he let the paper rest for a few moments.

He switched pens and wrote a London address on the manila envelope. He licked and carefully set a stamp in the right corner. He folded the two sheets of paper twice, slipped them into the envelope, and sealed it. He then took up the drafts he had written and one by one held them to a wooden match. The onionskin paper flamed and twisted in the ashtray till nothing was left except traces of carbon.

Now in a hurry to meet Katherine, the Count emptied the glass of inky water into the bathroom sink and set it beside the faucet. In the hotel room, he put on his jacket, which he'd left lying on a chair near the writing desk. He picked up the envelope and slipped it into his inside jacket pocket. He slid one of the pens into his briefcase. The other pen had rolled out of sight under one of the sheets of paper.

He picked up his overcoat from the chair near the window and the briefcase from the chair in front of the writing desk. He glanced around the room with a nagging feeling he had forgotten something, but he couldn't identify what it was. He shrugged and left the room.

Count Jaggi emerged from the elevators and headed for the front desk, his usual routine. The lobby had some traffic, and there were several people sitting in the armchairs reading newspapers, their faces obscured. By the time Jaggi had given the lobby a cursory glance he had reached the front desk. Donald, the desk clerk, saw him approaching and had already retrieved his mail, handing it to the Count with a cheerful good morning. The Count smiled at Donald and shuffled the envelopes to determine whether there was anything of importance, then put them in his overcoat pocket. He gave Donald a wave as he headed for the exit and his meeting with Katherine.

As the Count exited, one of the newspapers in the opposite corner of the lobby lowered. Inspector MacNutt had been waiting in the lobby for half an hour for the Count to descend from his room. He had a rough idea of when he would come down, because his wife had mentioned there was a Belgian Relief meeting this morning. As he headed for the elevators that led to the guest-room floors, he was glad that the Count had decided to go for breakfast in the Grill rather than order room service. He had been just about to give up and head for his office.

Just as he got to the elevators, the doors opened, and he stepped in.

Just as he stepped in, Katherine entered the lobby. Due to the angle of the elevators, he could not see her, but from her angle Katherine spotted her husband. Her mind raced. Why would Andrew be at the Russell? She was relieved that Andrew had not noticed her. She paused for a moment. Should she stay? It wasn't difficult to decide that it would be best to leave as quickly and quietly as possible. She would meet the Count later, at the Belgian Relief meeting.

* * *

Inspector MacNutt exited the elevator and walked down the corridor until he reached Count Jaggi's room. He looked up and down the corridor before pulling a passkey from his pocket. His office had passkeys for all the hotels in Ottawa. He knocked on the door. Once he was sure that no one was in the room, he slipped the key into the lock and swiftly let himself in.

A quick perusal of the room confirmed that it was empty. He had a story prepared if he were interrupted by the hotel staff. It was that he had some information implying someone was out to harm the Count. He was already quite familiar with the hotel's staff routine, and he was confident that he would not be interrupted.

He quickly began to search the room. He wasn't sure what he was searching for. He had seen how the Count leered at his wife the previous evening, and he was unhappy about it. Katherine had talked of having lunch with the man while she was in New York. His feelings about his wife's relationship with the Count aside, something about the man was not quite right. It also bothered him that ever since Katherine had met the Count, she seemed like her old self again.

He went through the closet in which the Count had hung a jacket, a pair of trousers, and a couple of white shirts. In the bathroom, nothing in the medicine cabinet caught his attention, nor did the empty glass on the sink.

He left the desk for last. He checked the pedestal drawers, which were empty, as was the centre stationery drawer. The black carbon in the ashtray made him curious. What had the Count burned and why? He shrugged then went on to examine the papers and postcards on the desk. He picked one up and turned it. The back of the postcard was blank. He didn't notice the fountain pen, the one the Count had not put in his briefcase, roll off the desk and fall to the floor.

He rose from the desk and did a survey of the room to be sure that he had not left any traces. He carefully opened the door and checked the corridor. It was empty. He locked the door and headed for the elevators.

BELGIAN RELIEF, BANK STREET, OTTAWA
12:30 P.M., FRIDAY, JANUARY 14, 1916

The white-oak table was so old it had lost its true colour decades ago. The constant slamming of cups and other implements had left countless dents and scratches on its surface, but Belgian Relief was a volunteer organization, and a battered table was just as serviceable as a fine, polished one. At the moment, most of its elderly surface was covered with typewritten notes and copies of the Count's speech.

Katherine was sitting at the far end of one side of the table, and the Count was sitting beside her at the front, reviewing lines on a sheet of paper. His briefcase was on a chair at his other side.

The Count spoke. "Excuse me, is this phrase correct?" He tilted the page toward Katherine.

She turned her attention from the paper she was studying and leaned closer to get a better view. She caught the Count staring at her. She glanced at him and smiled knowingly. She didn't say anything, but the Count knew that she knew what he was thinking and that he'd better stop it.

"Yes, the wording is fine, but your structure is French. Move this clause to here. It will make more sense." She pointed at the offending sentence.

They were interrupted by knocking on the meeting room's thin door. The door opened, and Anna poked her head in. "Sorry to bother you," she said hesitantly.

Katherine was amused. She knew that the slight, pretty brunette still had a crush on the Count, ever since she first meet the man at the December Belgian Relief at the Presbyterian Church. Normally, she was an articulate woman, but around the Count she was tongue-tied. "Do you have a minute?" Anna continued.

Katherine glanced at the Count then chuckled. "Certainly. Come in, we're almost finished. Do you need the room?"

Anna glanced at Katherine then back to the Count as she blushed. "Go ahead, Anna."

"I was hoping..." She paused. Katherine waited while she gathered her thoughts. "I was hoping … that the Count could do me ... a favour?" she blurted.

"Anna!" Katherine was scandalized.

The Count touched Katherine's sleeve. "It's quite all right. How can I be of assistance?"

Anna spoke rapidly before her courage failed her. "We have some women in the sorting room who would like to meet you. I mean, it would mean so much to them if you would have a word with them."

The Count smiled and rose from his chair. "It would be my pleasure."

Anna beamed. "Oh, thank you, Count. Thank you. They would be so honoured."

Count Jaggi turned to Katherine. "I shall return in a few minutes." He left the room with Anna leading the way.

Katherine decided to tidy some of the files that were sprawled across the table as she waited for the Count to return. She began arranging them in order. When she picked up the paper the Count had been working on, she began to read it. She shook her head at the story that was unfolding on the page. "The poor Count," she muttered sympathetically.

She picked up her fountain pen and began to edit the Count's phrasing. After a couple of strokes her pen ran dry. She shook it carefully in the hopes that it might make the ink flow again. She tried again, but it was still dry. She had forgotten to check the pen before she left home. There appeared to be no ink bottles handy to refill it. She spotted the

Count's attaché case on the chair — perhaps he had a spare pen. She hesitated for a moment then picked up his case and opened it to check. She saw a folded newspaper and some letters and postcards in a couple of the smaller pockets, then, at the bottom of the case's main divider, she found what she was searching for. She reached in and took out the gold-accented black pen. She unscrewed its cap and tested it on a blank sheet of paper. The ink was an unusual colour, amber; she normally used washable blue or red ink, depending on the task at hand. Perhaps this was the latest fad in Europe.

She had made only a few edits before the meeting room door opened and the vicar stepped in. He was a tall, thin, handsome man in his early sixties. "Hello, Katherine. I'm sorry to disturb you, but do you know where the account books are?"

"Yes," replied Katherine with a smile. She liked the vicar very much and considered him one of the few men of her acquaintance who believed what he preached. "Mrs. Ramsey was taking a gander at them. They should be in Anna's office."

"That woman..." the vicar sighed. He blushed when he realized he had spoken the thought out loud. Katherine smiled at him again to let him know that she understood.

"I'll give you a hand, Father," said Katherine. She placed the paper on the desk with the Count's fountain pen on top as she rose from the table.

"Thank you, Katherine, I would greatly appreciate it."

When Katherine resumed her seat at the old oak table a few minutes later, it took her a moment to remember what she had been doing: editing the Count's notes for his speech. She reached for the sheet of paper she had been proofreading then stared at it in bewilderment. There were no edits on the sheet. Hadn't she made a few changes before the vicar had interrupted her? She checked the other papers on the table to make sure that she had not picked up the wrong one. None had edits.

She picked up the Count's pen and began to mark up the text again. When she finished, she began to reread the sheet. As she read, she blinked in surprise. As she watched, the ink was slowly fading, then disappearing altogether.

"What..." she exclaimed, bewildered. "I'm sure that I..."

She stared at the paper in disbelief.

The door opened and the Count entered the room. His smile dropped slightly when he saw Katherine's wide eyes and his pen in her hands. He closed the door gently behind him.

Katherine lifted her puzzlement from the paper into Count Jaggi's watchful gaze. "That's odd," she said.

"What's odd?" asked the Count, approaching her quietly.

"The ink — it disappeared!"

"Really?" replied the Count. He studied her reaction. He caught the moment that she realized the significance of her discovery. Her eyes widened more then she leapt up from her chair and took a step back.

"Katherine, it's not what you think," said the Count, his voice calm and reassuring.

"You're a spy!"

"No. I'm not a spy," he answered swiftly. He knew that killing her was not an option, because that meant a certain death sentence. He needed to convince her that he wasn't a spy and then ensure that she would not mention this incident to her husband. "Please, Katherine, let me explain," he said urgently, his mind working rapidly to create a plausible story.

He saw that the tension in his voice was creating doubt in Katherine's mind. She crossed her arms protectively across her chest and ordered, "Explain! Why do you have invisible ink? Only spies use it."

"Yes, I do have invisible ink," said the Count, taking a deep breath, deciding on his approach. He would have to remain calm and talk her through this. "I need to use it when I send correspondence to Belgium. You do not understand how terrible it is living under the Huns. The Belgian people don't know from one day to the next where they will get their next meal. When I need to inform my people that a shipment is arriving, I have to send them a telegram or a letter. When I write them, I must do so in code. If we did not do this, then all the good that you and your wonderful women have done would be lost. We must be as cunning as the enemy to protect ourselves."

The Count studied her gravely and waited. He could sense that his words were having an effect as Katherine's stance softened somewhat. He then recalled the article he had read over breakfast at the Russell. Inspired, he reached into his briefcase and extracted the *Ottawa Journal*. He flipped the pages until he found the story. "Look," he said handing her the paper, "look at this." He pointed to the headline "U.S. Gov Bans Telegram Codes."

"I don't understand," said Katherine, confused, after she read the article. It concerned the American government's ban on the use of commercial and personal codes in telegrams. The new regulation required that all telegrams entering and leaving the States be written in clear text.

"Most commercial enterprises send sensitive information in code to ensure that prying eyes — competitors and undesirables — cannot read their messages. Belgian Relief ships and supplies are extremely valuable, so we need to ensure that our messages can only be read by our people. In this manner, we can avoid having unscrupulous people hijacking our supplies."

"I didn't know," whispered Katherine.

The Count smiled gently. "It is not information that one wants to publicize."

"Don't your people run the risk of being arrested as spies?" She frowned.

The Count's laugh was hollow. "No. We have informed the authorities, so they are well aware of our activities and codes. They can read the messages whenever they wish."

"The Germans too?"

The Count gave Katherine a false grimace as he added another lie. "I'm afraid so. Unfortunately, we need their co-operation to get the supplies in." When he saw her look of protest, he put up his hand to stop her. "I know, the propaganda says they are inhuman, but some that I have met are very decent. They no more wish the people to suffer than we do. They allow us to get our supplies to those who need it most."

"I see," she acknowledged with a nod.

He knew he had her when she handed him the pen. He had bought himself some time. If she were to ask her husband to verify his statement, he would be in serious trouble. However, an expression crossed her face that he could not interpret. It was as if a thought had entered her mind that she had not considered before, and she was debating what to do next. Her next question caught him completely off guard.

"If you are in touch with the Germans, can you find out about my son?"

"I thought you said your son was dead?"

Katherine shuffled some paper. "I said that, but they never found his body. He could be in a German prison camp, and we wouldn't know it."

He paused thoughtfully. "Does your husband feel the same way?"

Katherine replied simply. "No. He does not, so I would prefer not to mention this idea to him for now."

"I understand," said the Count. He hoped that he had kept the relief he felt out of his voice. Given MacNutt's feelings, it was very unlikely that she would reveal this conversation to him.

230

He had only a moment to savour the feeling of having survived a near miss when the door opened suddenly and Mrs. Ramsey entered. "There you are, Count Jaggi!" she boomed. "How are things going with you two?"

The Count gave Mrs. Ramsey a charming smile then turned towards Katherine and arched an eyebrow. "Everything is quite all right. Isn't it, Mrs. MacNutt?"

A flicker of a grin appeared at the corner of Katherine's lips. "Yes. It's all right. What do you think, Count? A few weeks?"

"A few weeks. A month at the most, Mrs. MacNutt."

"That is all that I can ask," replied Katherine.

Mrs. Ramsey peered at them bewilderment. "Are you quite well, dear?" she asked Katherine with false concern. She had finally noticed that Katherine was not quite her usual self.

Katherine broadened her smile to reassure Mrs. Ramsey. "Just a touch of the sniffles."

"We must not have that, dear. You go home straight to bed. A strong hot toddy will take care of those nasty sniffles," she commanded.

"I will take your advice," replied Katherine. She kept the old oak table between her and Count Jaggi as she left the room. A moment later, after a few pleasantries, the Count packed his briefcase and escorted Mrs. Ramsey out.

BASEMENT, EAST BLOCK, PARLIAMENT HILL, OTTAWA
5:15 P.M., FRIDAY, JANUARY 14, 1916

The room in the basement of the East Block was hot and stuffy because Constable Briggs had an annoying habit of putting on too much coal in the fireplace, claiming the room was always never warm enough. Briggs was seated at a narrow table, dressed in his dress uniform, while the other two men sitting at the table with him, Sergeant Lacelle and Constable Gary Gillan, had their jackets off and their shirt sleeves rolled up. All three were poring over hotel logbooks, police ledgers, and train passenger lists.

"Good morning, lads," MacNutt said cheerfully.

"Good morning, sir," answered Lacelle as he closed a ledger tossed onto the completed pile.

"Inspector," replied Gillan, his chubby red face weary from working too many hours. His uniform was creased as if he had slept in it.

"Doing a double shift again?" asked MacNutt.

Briggs snorted as he rubbed his neck. "Yes, Inspector. Another shipment arrived last night for Finance. It's unfortunate that we don't get a percentage."

"I would be careful who you say that to — Finance does not have a sense of humour," quipped MacNutt with an understanding smile.

It was one of the most closely guarded secrets in the government. Six years ago, when they added a new addition to the East Block, they also built six vaults in the basement for the Department of Finance's storage of the Government of Canada's gold reserves. By law, Finance was required to hold one gold dollar for every four paper dollars up to $30,000,000, and a gold dollar for every dollar above that. This meant that the vaults contained approximately 4.2 million ounces of gold bullion and coins worth approximately $90,000,000. There were an additional 330,000 ounces in gold worth $7,000,000 held in the Royal Post Office savings accounts and other public accounts.

At the beginning of the war, Parliament had authorized Finance, if it required, to draw down on the gold bullion to pay for war expenditures. Also, the Department of Finance was an authorized trustee for the Bank of England. This meant that if a North American company or a foreign government wanted to liquidate its debts, it could do so by shipping its gold to Ottawa rather than risk sending payments by cargo ship across the North Atlantic. In addition, the Royal Canadian Mint, on Sussex, was producing gold bullion and coins from Canadian and South African gold ore for both the Canadian and British governments.

Since the Dominion Police were responsible for the gold, once it arrived on the Hill they were kept busy supervising the gold shipments that regularly entered and left the vaults. The Mint shipments were guarded by the Mint's own security force, while private guards were hired to protect the train shipments being transported to and from the Hill.

"Sir," acknowledged Gillan. He suppressed a yawn, but he appeared relatively well rested.

"Are you making progress?" the inspector demanded.

"We're halfway through, sir," reckoned Gillan. "We haven't found nothing yet."

"He's right, sir," added Lacelle.

Andrew noted the man's tired air. Lacelle needed a rest. So did he, as a matter of fact, but that was not going to happen any time soon. Lacelle's voice was hoarse, with what sounded like the onset of a cold.

"We're doing a search of dossiers to determine if we missed something. We really need the Mounties' and the Customs and Excise files."

MacNutt knew that Lacelle was correct, but there was no love lost between the Mounties and the Dominion Police. The Mounties would love to embarrass the Dominion Police by bringing in the German spy before they did.

"I'll have to talk with the commissioner," MacNutt said.

"As you wish. It is more difficult this way," Lacelle returned with a shrug.

"Do what you can. If we have to, we will ask them at the appropriate time."

"I'll try. But it would be easier if we knew why he was here."

"The spy?"

"Yes, sir." MacNutt wondered about it himself. While Canada had an important place in the war effort, it was not that critical, no matter how much people tried to convince themselves that Britain couldn't survive without the Dominion's help. But still, a German agent could wreak a lot of havoc.

"I have no idea, but the Pinkertons believe he's in Ottawa at the moment," answered the inspector.

Lacelle blurted, "Do they know who he is and do they have a description?" MacNutt shook his head. Lacelle said in a resigned tone, "If we knew that, it would make searching for him easier."

"He may be getting the lay of the land," MacNutt said thoughtfully.

"It would be a great coup if we caught him," Lacelle emphasized.

"Yes, it would." MacNutt didn't like what he would have to do, but he had little choice. "I'll really have to have a chat with Denon. He may know something."

"You have not spoken with him yet?"

"It's been on my list, but I haven't had the chance," replied MacNutt.

"You should, since he's a fucking Hun, after all," said Briggs in disgust.

The inspector gave Briggs a cold stare. After a moment Briggs broke away then said, "Begging your pardon, sir."

"Is there anything else?" asked MacNutt as a general question.

"Have you seen this morning's papers?" said Lacelle.

"Yes," said MacNutt. He had read the paper at the Château.

"So you saw the article concerning Lavergne's speech last night?"

MacNutt frowned. "I must have missed it. What did he have to say? Is it about the Guigues school affair?"

Lacelle said, "He said that every cent spent on enlistment was money stolen from the French of Ontario. If the *franco-ontariens* win the justice they deserve, then the English can ask them to go and fight for liberty in Europe. Also, he said that the Canadian government would never impose conscription, because if it did, French Canadians in Ontario and Quebec would revolt. He went on to say that since we have shipped every single rifle or bayonet in the country to France, if the U.S. decided to invade Canada, they could simply walk in. We don't have the means to defend ourselves. But Germany is not a threat to us, since they can't invade us. Even if they tried to, the U.S. would protect us."

Briggs couldn't resist interjecting. "You can't have it both ways! On the one hand, the U.S. will invade Canada, so we don't send soldiers over the pond — while on the other hand they will protect us if Germany invades? That doesn't make any sense!"

"That is what the paper reported," retorted Lacelle with an angry gesture.

"Well, we all know how reliable the papers are," grumbled Gillan.

"Great! Just great," groaned MacNutt. He didn't like where this was going, but there wasn't much he could do about it since he knew damn well that Borden would not authorize him to place Lavergne in protective custody.

MacNutt glanced at Briggs and Gillan. What he had to discuss with Lacelle he wanted to discuss in private. He motioned to Lacelle that they needed to talk outside. The two other men wore curious expressions when Lacelle rose and followed MacNutt out of the room. Briggs and Gillan knew not to ask questions.

In the empty corridor MacNutt got to the point quickly. "I want you to do a background check on Count Jaggi."

Lacelle blinked at the turn in the conversation. "Is there a particular reason?"

"Yes. He seems to have ingratiated himself into some pretty high circles awfully quickly," replied the inspector.

Lacelle was trying to understand MacNutt's sudden request. "Yes, sir."

"I know that you are busy. It isn't a priority, but whenever you can make some time..."

"Understood, sir."

"Call me when you find something in either case," ordered MacNutt.

"Yes, sir," replied Lacelle, understanding that he was dismissed. He headed back to the room to work on the hotel logbooks and train lists while the inspector headed for the stairs that led to his office on the ground floor. As Lacelle regarded the inspector's back, the image of Mrs. MacNutt and the Count at the opening of Parliament entered his mind. He then knew why MacNutt had asked to check on the Count. From what he could recall, he got the sense that there was something between them, but he wasn't going to say so to his superior. However, he had seen the look the inspector gave the Count when he saw him with Mrs. MacNutt. It was the look of a jealous man.

RUSSELL HOTEL, ELGIN AND SPARKS STREETS, OTTAWA
8:15 P.M., FRIDAY, JANUARY 14, 1916

Count Jaggi entered his room and locked the door behind him. He automatically gave the room a careful study. It was difficult to tell whether the room had been searched since the maids had been in. The bed had been made and the bathroom had been cleaned, as evidenced by a clean glass on the sink. He set his briefcase on the writing desk's chair. Then he went to the soft brown leather valise, closed and fastened with its double straps, which sat on the luggage rack beside the bed. He undid the straps then flipped open the top. He opened the closet and pulled out his clothes, tossing them onto the bed. As he folded the clothes neatly and placed them in the valise, his thoughts turned to Katherine.

He was concerned about her. It had been a mistake to leave the pen filled with invisible ink in his case, a stupid mistake. For now, she appeared to believe his story, no matter how illogical it might be, but how long would she continue to believe it? The hook that was planted about her son would give her some pause. His instinct was to run as fast and as hard as he could. It was fortunate that he was scheduled to leave Ottawa by train this evening, because his departure would not raise any alarms.

When he had packed the last items in his valise, he went over to check his briefcase to ensure that he had everything. He noticed that the letters and cards he had prepared in the morning were still in his case. He had been in such a rush that he hadn't had time to put them in the mail before his Belgian Relief meeting. And after his encounter with Katherine he had been so rattled that he forgot. He needed to mail them before he left, because he didn't want them on him in the event he was stopped and searched by Customs, but there was bound to be a mailbox at the train station. He also noticed that one of his pens was missing, because it wasn't on the desktop. When he checked the drawers it wasn't there either. He finally spotted it under the desk.

As he picked up the pen, various scenarios entered his mind. Was it a simple case of the pen rolling off the desk while the maids were cleaning the room, or was there a more sinister cause, such as the room being clandestinely searched by the secret police? He forcefully stopped his mind from racing. He knew that he was in danger of over-thinking, and that was just as dangerous as not thinking enough. It was more likely that it had rolled off when the maids cleaned the room. The incident with Katherine was serious, but not serious enough that her husband would be involved this soon. Besides, he told himself, he had not left any traces of incriminating evidence in the room before he left this morning. He put the pen into his jacket pocket and snapped his briefcase shut. He put on his overcoat and hat and tightened the straps on the valise. Taking the heavy valise in one hand and the briefcase in the other, he gave the room a last inspection before heading out of the hotel for the train station.

GRAND TRUNK RAILWAY TRAIN,
OTTAWA TO NEW YORK CITY
11:00 P.M., FRIDAY, JANUARY 14, 1916

The night train to New York was crowded, but it wasn't full. The Count had booked a ticket in the first-class car because a sleeper was not available. The seats were wide and comfortable, and he had plenty of legroom. The seat beside him was empty, but the two seats across from him were occupied by a couple in their mid-forties going to New York to attend a Broadway show. The woman displayed no interest in him, so he didn't attempt to use his usual charms. He chatted amiably for a short period, but the conversation petered out once they exhausted subjects of common interest.

Around eight o'clock, he felt hunger pangs. He used the need to stretch his legs as a convenient excuse to avoid having supper with the dull couple. When he entered the dining car, some of the women gave him quick glances. Two were not particularly attractive, but a blonde in a hunter green dress had potential. What brought him up short was a male face he had seen before but which he couldn't readily place. The man, however, recognized him. He smiled and waved the Count over.

"Good evening, Count Jaggi." Sensing the Count's confusion, the man added, "We met at MacNutt's Christmas party."

"Ah yes," replied the Count as he recalled the party. The man with his brown hair parted down the middle was one of them. The man was attired as he had been on the earlier occasion, in a white shirt, tie, brown wool vest, and jacket. With the recollection came his name. "If I recall correctly, you accompanied Sir Laurier and his wife. It's Mr. King, is it not?"

"You have a good memory, sir," answered King.

"In my line of business it is a necessity."

"As in mine," asserted King. "Please join me. I would be pleased to have some company. Train travel can be tiring." King pointed to the chair across from him.

"Thank you, Mr. King," the Count replied as he took the seat.

"Please call me Rex; most of my acquaintants do."

A waiter appeared promptly and placed two trays with menus and pencils on their table so that they could make their meal choices. On the Count's last trip, he had found the food on the train to be very good. He quickly checked the items on the card and handed it to the waiter. The waiter took their menu cards with a flourish and then left.

"So, Rex, are you going to New York for work or pleasure?" inquired the Count. The waiter had returned and poured water in the glass goblets on the white linen-covered table.

King smiled. "I'm living in New York currently."

"What do you do in New York?"

"I'm the Director of Industrial Relations for the Rockefeller Foundation."

The Count gazed at King in confusion. "I understood that you were a Canadian politician?"

"I am," replied King, sipping his water. "I'm the Liberal candidate for York North. It's near Toronto," he added, recognizing that the Count would not know this. "My employer allows me to engage in political activities."

"You have an understanding employer," stated the Count with a touch of interest. "How did you become involved in industrial relations for the Rockefellers?"

The Count had done some background work on William Lyon

Mackenzie King after the MacNutts' party. What amused him was the fact that King was born in Berlin, in 1874. It was Berlin, Ontario, not Berlin, Germany. Berlin was considered the German capital of Canada, but since the outbreak of the war, anti-German sentiment had been putting pressure on the city to change its name. One name being bandied about was Kitchener, in honour of Field Marshal Lord Kitchener, the British secretary of state for war. Obviously, they were trying to curry favourable public opinion, thought the Count in disgust.

"About two years ago I was contacted by John Rockefeller to help him with the striking miners in Ludlow, Colorado. Several workers and their families were killed during the strike. As a former labour minister I have some experience dealing with labour issues," explained Mr. King. He paused as the waiter placed a china plate with a rack of lamb, baked potatoes, and vegetables in front of him. The waiter also placed a plate before the Count. He had ordered the rainbow trout with mashed potatoes and carrots.

"So have the labour problems improved?"

"Oh, yes. I suggested to him that if he wanted to avoid or at least minimize labour strife he should institute reforms for the mines and towns, such as paved roads and recreational facilities for the miners. Also, I suggested that he have worker representation on committees dealing with working conditions, safety, health, and recreation. Conditions are not perfect, but the workers are much better off. Rockefeller's reputation has recovered as well from those dark days."

"I'm impressed. But you are still involved in Canadian politics. Correct me if I'm wrong, but you were in Ottawa for the opening of Parliament, were you not?"

"Quite right. I was helping the party on its strategy for the upcoming parliamentary session. Normally, we would be preparing for an election, but it is being postponed," King beamed.

"Why is it being postponed?"

King humphed then gave the Count a brief lecture on Canadian parliamentary practice. "Traditionally in Canada, an election is called once every four years, but it is the prime minister who decides when to call one. If his prospects are poor, he may delay calling an election for an additional year. Due to the war, Borden has already governed for five years. Without an agreement from Laurier he would be forced to call an election. He had spoken with Laurier about extending Parliament for another year. Borden felt calling an election now would have been a distraction from the war effort. Laurier felt that it would be prudent to agree. We're hoping that the war will be over by then, otherwise Borden will be in a very strong position when he calls one."

"Will conscription help or hurt Borden's election prospects?" said Count Jaggi, studying King's reaction.

"What makes you think Borden will bring in conscription?" demanded King sharply, squinting at the Count.

The Count needed a moment to gather his thoughts. There was a bright mind here, and he needed to take care. "From some of the conversations I've overheard and comments some have made, they feel it will be inevitable. I must point out Britain has already imposed conscription."

King relaxed. "That is, unfortunately, true. I'm hoping that the war be over soon so it will not be necessary. If Borden tries to impose conscription it will divide the country along language lines. It also may break the Liberal Party."

Count Jaggi stared at King in surprise. "I had no idea. I'm not very familiar with Canadian politics."

King scoffed. "I've been involved in a number of labour negotiations. Business leaders make the mistake of forgetting that men are ruled by self-interest. They treat their employees horribly and then don't understand why the workers do not accede readily to their demands. I pride myself in finding a middle ground that allows both sides to reconcile their differences. Unfortunately, there is very little middle ground in Canadian politics, as both sides are bitterly attacking each other. I fear that it's going to get worse before it gets better."

"That's a rather bleak assessment," replied the Count.

"I'm afraid it is," agreed King. The Count noticed King glancing over at the blonde sitting across from them from time to time. When he did, a strange expression crossed King's face, one that the Count had seen before in London, on the faces of men who with religious fervour went out into the streets to save prostitutes from depravity. As if the fallen women really needed saving, thought the Count in amusement. He suspected most of them wanted to sleep with the women but simply didn't know how to go about it.

Changing the subject, King asked, "So, are you working with Herbert Hoover's Commission for Belgian Relief work in New York?"

The Count blinked in surprise. He took a moment to collect his thoughts as he carefully removed a bone from the trout on his plate. King appeared remarkably well-informed about Belgian Relief. When the German armies cut through Belgium in an attempt to quickly knock France out of the war, they had had a devastating impact on the Belgians. It wasn't long before news of the Belgians' desperate plight leaked out and caused a worldwide charity campaign to help alleviate their plight. Herbert Hoover, a mining engineer, had helped stranded Americans in Europe return home at the start of the war. When he returned to the States, he became the chairman of the Commission for Relief in Belgium. He then set out to co-ordinate the various organizations, committees, and church groups providing relief. Since America was a neutral country, he was able to position the Commission as the sole channel through which supplies could be sent through to the occupied territories. He got the British and the Germans to provide guarantees to ensure that the supplies got to the Belgians and were distributed to Belgians. Millions of dollars flowed through the Commission. The New York office co-ordinated the activities in the States while the office in London co-ordinated the activities in Britain, the British Commonwealth, and committees in other countries.

King gave the Count a simple shrug. "The Foundation is providing the Commission with support." The Rockefeller Foundation was one of the major contributors to Belgian Relief in New York. Not only did the Foundation supply funds, but it also bought food and provided warehouses to store it and ships to transport it.

The Count caught King's undertone. "You don't approve."

"Oh, no, I approve," answered King quickly. What the Count did not know was that King had been heavily involved in the creation of the Rockefeller Foundation in November of 1914. Among the first activities the Foundation discussed was Belgian Relief. "I was just thinking that Belgian Relief aided me in my work in industrial relations," he offered.

"Really? How so?" asked the Count. He didn't see an obvious connection between the two.

"Last year I received a telegram from a miner requesting aid from John Rockefeller Jr. to help starving miners in Colorado. At first Rockefeller felt that he should only help current and former employees of his mining company. I helped persuade him that it was a relief project. It was consistent with his Foundation's aims to enhance labour relations. It was no different from the work being done to help the Belgians."

"Well, some good may come out of this war," stated the Count.

"I certainly hope so," replied King. He fished around in his coat pocket, took out a card, and handed it to the Count. "Here's my card, with my office address. It's in the Standard Oil building on 26 Broadway. Give me a call and we will arrange lunch at the Whitehall Club."

"Thank you," said the Count as he put the card into his coat pocket. It was unlikely he would visit the office, but one never knew when a bit of information might come in handy. He picked up his cutlery to finish his rack of trout, which was getting cold. For the rest of the meal, King and the Count engaged in small talk. All things considered, it was one of the more enjoyable meals the Count had for quite some time.

CHAPTER 23

ROYAL POST OFFICE,
ELGIN AND WELLINGTON STREETS, OTTAWA
11:15 A.M., SATURDAY, JANUARY 15, 1916

The Royal Post Office national headquarters and main post office were at the corner of Elgin and Wellington Streets. Four storeys of the building's arched windows were visible above street level. The floor below street level that ran along the canal was only visible if you stood on Sapper's Bridge and looked down at the two arched windows set on both sides of a carriage entrance. Fred drove past the post office down Elgin Street and turned left on the street that ran past the canal. At the carriage entrance, he honked his horn. When the doors opened he drove the truck into the building up to the loading dock. He got out and pulled the tarpaulin towards the front of the cab. He then began to unload the crates and the mailbags.

"Hi, Fred. Need a hand?" offered one of the loading dock workers.

"Sure, Kev," Fred panted as he pulled a wooden-wheeled crate over to the truck. Kev handed the sacks to Fred, who put them into the crate. The red canvas sacks were last since the contents were fragile and needed extra care. He put the sack that contained the railway station mail on top.

"That's it?" asked Kev.

"Yep," answered Fred as he pulled the tarpaulin back in place. "I'll see you in a couple of hours."

"Till then," replied Kev as Fred got into the truck and put it into gear.

Fred pulled the cart from the edge of the loading dock, turned it around, and pushed it down a corridor to the sorting room. The room was well lit, but it was filled with blue smoke. Most of the sorters had a cigarette hanging from a corner of their mouths. There was very little conversation; talking was frowned upon because it interfered with production efficiency. In the room were several tables surrounded by male sorters of various ages. He wheeled the cart up to the closest table and started to empty the sacks. The sacks full of the *Globe* and *Toronto Star* newspapers he left in the cart, since they would be handled by the mail carriers. As he emptied the sacks onto the table, he turned them inside out to ensure that no piece of mail was caught at the bottom.

Once the contents were on the tables, the sorters quickly went through the mail. The Eaton's and Simpson's mail orders were quickly sorted and prepared for the local truck delivery runs. Letters and postcards were separated. Local mail was tossed into the mailbags for the letter carriers to sort. The House of Commons mail was tossed in sacks unsorted, because it would be sorted by the House of Commons and Senate mail rooms. Many did not have stamps — Canadians could send mail to MPs and senators postage-free. Letters were quickly sorted into various piles: local mail, Toronto and Western mail, Montreal and East Coast mail, mail for the CEF in France, and international mail. The international mail was re-sorted again into U.S. and British piles.

Any mail addressed to German-sounding names was pulled and put into a separate pile that would be sent to the Mail Censor unit, where the envelopes would be opened and the letters read for any seditious material that might be considered a threat to Canadian security. German-language magazines and newspapers were also sent to the censors for sanitization. If mail were found that was suspicious, seditious, or treasonous, it would be forwarded to the Dominion Police for investigation. At the beginning of the war, outgoing German-language mail to the U.S. or to Germany that contained money was confiscated in order to deny Germany potential funding for the military. Few letters that contained money were forwarded on after confiscation. The senders of the few that did get delivered needed to provide assurance that the money was intended to support a family.

As the British pile was being sorted, a sorter frowned when he read an address on a postcard. He put it aside then pulled out a handful of letters from the sorted mail bag he had just filled and shuffled through them. When he didn't find what he was seeking, he tossed the sorted letters into another bag and grabbed another handful from the sorted bag beside him.

"What's the matter, Greg, lose something?" joked one of the other sorters.

"This address." Greg held up the postcard. "Seems familiar. Ah, here it is," he exclaimed when he found the envelope. He then went over and checked a typewritten list that hung on a clipboard beside the sorting table. He flipped a couple of pages until he came to the address he was searching for. He compared the two addresses.

"Just as I thought. It's on the list," he declared as he casually tossed the Count's letter and postcard into a leather sack. The leather sack was destined for the Dominion Police Secret Service. Because of the hour, it would not be delivered to Parliament Hill until the next morning.

READING ROOM, CENTRE BLOCK, PARLIAMENT HILL, OTTAWA
1:45 P.M., SATURDAY, JANUARY 15, 1916

Lacelle made his way through the Reading Room to a set of open iron doors that opened into a short, arched corridor. The corridor connected the Parliamentary Library to the Centre Block. When the heavy doors were closed, they isolated the Library from the rest of the building. The chief librarian had insisted the library building be as fireproof as possible during its initial construction. Fire was a major concern to the library because it could easily destroy the collections in a matter of hours. Unfortunately, the library had already gone through that experience. In 1849, the Parliament Building in Quebec City was destroyed by a blaze, its precious library entirely consumed. It had taken years to replace the collections. The library, Lacelle noticed, was busier than usual for a Saturday afternoon. He could see about a dozen or so people doing research on the three concourses.

The library had a spacious and airy feel. It was a circular room, approximately 90 feet in circumference. It was capped by a doomed ceiling that rose 120 feet above the white marble statute of Queen Victoria centred in the middle of the room. The Parliamentary Library was modelled after the National Library in London. The room's centre was reserved for the staff, about half a dozen clerks and three librarians.

The walls on the three concourses were constructed of white pine. Every wooden surface was hand-carved with designs of flowers and leaves. On some of the panels mythical faces, partially camouflaged by fauna, gazed at the patrons with wooden eyes. The shelves, floor to ceiling, were crammed with books. Black wrought-iron railings kept the researchers from falling off the walkways as they conducted their research. Eight alcoves jutted from the walls towards the centre. On each corner of an alcove, on the second concourse, were set the coat of arms of the seven original provinces. The eighth was blank; it had originally been intended for the addition of the next province to the Dominion. Like the eighth shield in the Centre Block's foyer, it remained empty for political reasons.

The library's collection was too large to be contained on the main concourses, so there were additional subterranean floors that contained the rest. The collection was the largest in the country, with over 100,000 books, newspapers, and magazines, and was reserved for Hill staff.

Lacelle paused at the wooden railing, waiting for the one of the clerks to recognize him. After a minute Michael MacCormac, the clerk nearest to him, sighed and rose to serve Lacelle.

"How can I help today, Sergeant?" inquired MacCormac pleasantly. As a Parliamentary Library clerk, one of his duties was to conduct research for MPs and senators. On occasion he had done some research for the Dominion Police.

"*Bonjour*, Michael," Lacelle said cheerfully. "I'm researching information on peerages."

"May I ask why?"

"I'm afraid that it is confidential," answered Lacelle.

MacCormac raised an eyebrow then pointed to second alcove on the right of the main entrance. "They are located on the second floor."

"*Merci*," Sergeant Lacelle said with a brief grin.

He took the stairway that led to the second concourse. It was hidden by the jutting alcove. On the second concourse, on the second shelf, he found *Debrett's Peerage & Baronetage*. He flipped through it and found that it listed mostly the British nobility. He couldn't seem to find anything concerning Belgium or other European nobility.

Out of the corner of his eye he caught one of the other library clerks keeping a surreptitious watch on him. Police officer or no police officer, he was not exempt from their suspicion that he might walk off with one of their precious books. He was tempted to do just that but decided that would be pushing it a tad too far. He replaced the *Debrett's* where he had found it and made his way to ground level.

As he walked out of the library's connecting corridor, he turned left and pushed through the reading room's swing doors. In the room he spotted Keith McKenna, the *Journal* reporter who had called Inspector MacNutt last Monday for information on von Papen. He was standing beside one of the six long tables that occupied the fifty-foot long by twenty-foot wide room. The walls were lined with beautifully ornate, carved, brightly varnished pine. There were wooden racks set beside the wall nearest to the library, filled with newspapers and magazines from across the country. Bookcases filled with twenty thousand volumes lined the first and second floors. A glass ceiling provided natural light. Electric lights were available to provide illumination when the sun went down. The reading room was restricted to MPs, senators, and Hill staff. Since McKenna was a member of the press gallery, he had access to the facilities. McKenna had a lit cigarette in his mouth and was reading the paper on the table.

"You like to live dangerously, Monsieur McKenna?" Lacelle joked.

McKenna looked up. "What did you say?"

Lacelle touched his lips, indicating the cigarette, then pointed to the *No Smoking* sign on the table.

McKenna laughed and made a dismissive gesture. "So, *mon ami*, how can I help you?"

Lacelle arched an eyebrow then smiled. "You know me too well. I have some questions for which you may know the answers."

"Usually it's the other way around, Sergeant. I do the asking," McKenna quipped.

Lacelle lifted his shoulders slightly then inquired casually, "What do you know of Count Jaggi?"

Keith's eyes narrowed. "Why do you want to know about him?"

"Just satisfying my curiosity," said Lacelle, straight-faced. He had to be careful with McKenna. He was one of the sharpest reporters around and one of the toughest. McKenna would eventually extract his pound of flesh.

"Just satisfying your curiosity?" He sat back and regarded Lacelle shrewdly. "Mrs. MacNutt is an attractive woman."

"Yes, she is," acknowledged Lacelle.

"But I don't think she is the type."

"What type is that?" remarked Lacelle with a touch of annoyance.

Keith arched an eyebrow then shrugged. "Yes, Count Jaggi. I met him on Thursday night after the opening of Parliament at the Russell Hotel. I've been checking up on him," he said. He absentmindedly fished into his tan tweed jacket for a packet of cigarettes. He shook a new one out.

"You have?" asked Lacelle in surprise.

"Of course. I'm planning to write an article on the man," explained Keith. "I've checked our newspaper morgue and the peerage books but essentially there isn't much to tell. What I have been able to gather is that he is one of the poor aristocrats. When Belgium was overrun, he managed to escape through German lines before the border became a no man's land. He made it to England, and he became part of the Belgian Relief agency there. Has helped to raise a great deal of money, I understand. Also, he was quite a hit with the ladies, so I have heard from several sources."

"So he is really a count then?"

"I suppose so. It's difficult to tell nowadays because a lot of people are calling themselves counts and countesses," answered McKenna.

Lacelle grimaced. "Is that all you have?"

"Maybe," McKenna said coyly. "If I have more, you'll have to read it in the paper, won't you? But I do find it interesting that you and MacNutt are investigating him. What am I missing?"

Lacelle put on his best poker face. He would have to inform the inspector. "It's just routine."

"Ah," exclaimed McKenna, not believing a word of it. Lacelle sighed.

McKenna smiled cynically then held the butt of his cigarette up to his mouth for one last drag. "Let me know if something comes up, *mon ami.*"

Lacelle left the reading room. There was nothing more to learn there, from *Debrett's* or that hack McKenna. Next step: a telegram to London to MI5, who might have a dossier on the mysterious Count.

CASTOR HOTEL, SUSSEX STREET, OTTAWA
4:15 P.M., SATURDAY, JANUARY 15, 1916

Major Simms sat in the Castor Hotel's small, elegant bar, drinking single malt Scotch, trying to drown his sorrows before making his way through the frigid cold to his digs. To his disgust, it was beginning to snow before he entered the bar. Another reason for a stiff one. What he wouldn't give to be warm again. He signalled the bartender to pour him another round.

He was feeling somewhat melancholy tonight, unusual for him. It was nearly three years since he had last requested a foreign posting. He had hoped for India or Hong Kong — one could make one's career and fortune in those colonies. He had been told that the posting would be in the Americas. He hadn't realized it was going to be Canada, rather than the United States, until it was too late for him to refuse. That he was an aide-de-camp to His Royal Highness the Duke of Connaught took away a little of the sting.

The outbreak of the war in Europe brought home to him quite clearly that he could never aspire to a marshal's baton. Some of his classmates from Sandhurst had already received their general's pips, while he languished in this godforsaken town thousands of miles away from the front. He had hoped that at least a commission would be made available for him in the colonial forces. The Duke had hinted as much.

In the early days of the war, he woke every morning telling himself that today would be the day, but his hopes were dashed by the falling-out between Borden and the Duke. Borden insisted that the Canadians fight as a unit and that they be led by Canadian officers. At the time, Simms didn't think much of the idea, because if Colonel Hughes, now General Hughes, was any indicator of the Canadian officer corps, he felt in his bones that they would request his services. Unfortunately, the Canadian General Staff didn't view it that way.

His musing was interrupted by a voice behind him. "How are you this evening, Major?"

Simms turned and broke into a smile when he saw Charles Templeton standing behind him. "Good evening, Charles. Good of you to come! Join me for a drink?"

"Don't mind if I do. Thanks." Charles occupied the space that Simms made for him at the bar. "I'll have the same as the major," he informed the bartender. The bartender poured a glass of single malt for him and left the bottle at the colonel's signal. Charles tossed the Scotch back and heaved a contented sigh. "I really needed that."

It was a shared love of single malt that had united the men in friendship. When Simms learned that Templeton ran CP's telegraph operations in Ottawa, he made a point of cultivating the man; one could never have too many contacts. And Templeton proved to be quite valuable to him by passing along interesting tidbits of information that Simms used to his advantage. One tidbit, while amusing but not very useful, was the fact that the very bar they were sitting in was one of Sir John A. MacDonald's favourite haunts.

"Tough day at the office?" Simms asked, topping up Templeton's glass.

"More than usual." Charles turned towards the colonel. "God! I need to get away for a while."

"We all do," Simms said sympathetically, splashing a finger of Scotch into his own tumbler.

"It's unfortunate there is a war on; I would have loved to visit England again."

"I miss her too," replied Simms dutifully. In truth, although he detested Ottawa, he really didn't miss merry olde England very much, but he'd noticed that many a native-born Canadian became so earnest in his admiration for all things British, it sometimes verged on the farcical. Templeton was an ardent British imperialist, a fact Simms used to gain access to the Dominion Police's Security Services telegram traffic. It took some time to convince Templeton that His Royal Highness's security was too important to be left in the hands of the locals. Simms also took some pleasure in the fact that he was one up on MacNutt.

Both men sat silent for a moment. Finally Templeton spoke. "Interesting piece of information came through today."

"How interesting?"

"Count Jaggi."

Simms' glass paused halfway to his lips. "Count Jaggi?"

Charles nodded sombrely.

"What about him?" Simms croaked, his glass still suspended.

Templeton shrugged. "No idea. All I know is what is in the telegram. They requested a background check on him in London."

"Hmm," Simms murmured. His instincts were to defend the Count's character. He was aware of Jaggi's work for Belgian Relief. His sister in London had mentioned him in glowing terms, too glowing, he sometimes felt. The Duchess found the man charming and appreciated having someone to talk to in German. However, if there were to be even the slightest whiff of scandal about the Count, he would need to distance the Duchess and the Duke from him. Whatever the state of the royal couple's marriage, the Duke was loyal enough to complain about any criticism levelled at his wife on account of her German birth. Of course, the wine merchant incident hadn't helped. The Duke pointed out that his wife devoted considerable energy to the war effort, such as helping to raise money for the Red Cross, Belgian Relief, and the Patriotic Fund. She was also slated to visit the wounded soldiers at Wallis House the next week. Her good works managed to mute some of her critics, but not all.

"If you hear of something else, let me know," Simms advised.

As their conversation turned to the latest war news, Simms was trying to work out a way to use this latest information. A smile began to creep along his face as an idea slowly formed.

CHAPTER 24

Andrew MacNutt was not very happy when he arrived at his office. He was curt as he passed Lacelle, who was, as usual, already at his desk and working. When he reached his own desk, he slapped the newspaper he was carrying hard on its surface.

Lacelle had sprung up and followed him, knowing that something was wrong. "What's the matter?"

"Did you read today's paper?"

"No, not yet."

"Well, read this." MacNutt shoved the paper at him.

Lacelle's eyes jumped to the headline. "Von Papen paid money to the thugs, made payments to person charged with blowing up munitions plant."

Lacelle skimmed the article then made a sound of disgust. "How did this happen?"

"How would I know! Remember, I'm only the chief of the Secret Service!" MacNutt took the paper back then snorted, "When McKenna called I thought it was a fishing expedition, since he had heard that the British confiscated von Papen's papers. I didn't think they would provide all this detail to the papers."

MacNutt growled. "It says that von Papen made frequent payments to persons charged with the responsibility of blowing up munitions works and bridges in the U.S. It would have been nice if some idiot over there would have sent us the same damn copies."

He went back to reading the paper. "'One entry shows that Captain von Papen gave $700 to Werner Horn, who was arrested for blowing up a Canadian Pacific railway bridge at St. Croiz, N.B. The day before the German embassy paid $2,000 to von Papen's account at the bank — Riggs National Bank of Washington. Cheque stubs, books, and letters listed 500 items, many routine expenditures. Others have figured prominently in the activities of German agents in America and to at least one spy who committed suicide in a cell in an English prison.'

"Didn't anyone from MI5 think of sending them to us first, so that we could read them and use them for our investigations? For God's sake! With this being blurted from every street corner by every newsboy in the country, you can bet that any agents remaining in Canada have all gone underground and are running for home. They are probably crossing the border as we speak!"

They were interrupted by a knock at the door. "What?" barked MacNutt.

Austin Blount, the PM's private secretary, peered around the door. "Am I disturbing you?"

MacNutt found Blount annoying at the best of times, and this was not the best of times. He fixed a stern gaze on Blount.

Unruffled, Blount delivered his message. "The PM wants a word with you, Inspector MacNutt, if you can spare a moment from your busy schedule."

MacNutt knew that this was not a request but an order. He took a deep breath before he answered. "Of course. I'll be glad to meet with the PM. May I ask what he would like to discuss?"

"You may," Blount advised him. "It's concerning the very topic you were just now discussing. I could hear you from the outer office."

MacNutt ground his teeth. "When?"

"In fifteen minutes, if you don't have anything pressing."

"Will the minister or the commissioner be there?" inquired MacNutt. It was standard protocol that if the PM needed information on a topic, the PMO would forward the request to the minister of justice's office. His staff would review it and send the request to the commissioner's office. The commissioner would then forward it on to MacNutt. Once he had researched and prepared a report, he would send it back to the commissioner's office, which would review and comment. Once the revisions had been made to the commissioner's satisfaction, the report would go through the same process in the minister's office before the document was forwarded to the PMO. Nothing went to the PMO without the minister of justice and the commissioner seeing it first. The war had loosened some of the protocols, but it made MacNutt uncomfortable to be meeting the PM without one of his superiors present.

The secretary shook his head. "I'm afraid they have other pressing matters to attend to."

"Understood," said MacNutt. "It would be my pleasure."

"You'll be there in fifteen then." Blount left the room.

Once they were sure that Blount was no longer in earshot, Lacelle asked, "So what are you going to tell the PM?"

"The truth, I guess. That we don't know what the hell is going on and we can't find our asses with both hands."

Lacelle frowned. "Well, that's one approach."

MacNutt said soberly, "I'd like to know how they got this past the censors. And why on earth wouldn't they inform me before releasing this?"

"Perhaps it's in today's mail," suggested Lacelle.

"Has the mail arrived yet? No? Well, let me know if there is as soon as it gets here," ordered MacNutt. With a glance at the clock he lurched out of his desk chair and left for the PMO.

PRIME MINISTER'S OFFICE, EAST BLOCK, PARLIAMENT HILL
10:15 A.M., MONDAY, JANUARY 17, 1916

Several minutes later, on the second floor of the East Block, MacNutt tried to conceal his impatience as he watched Borden wield his pen over a stack of papers that Blount had presented to him in a red leather-bound portfolio. When the PM had signed the last one, he returned the cap to his fountain pen, closed the portfolio, and handed it to his secretary.

"Prime Minister, you have a cabinet meeting at 10:30," Blount reminded him. Borden acknowledged this with a brisk nod then waved Blount out. When the door had closed behind him, Borden turned his full attention to MacNutt.

"I'm not very happy," announced Borden firmly.

"Prime Minister?"

"You did read today's papers, did you not?"

"Yes, Prime Minister, I did," replied MacNutt, a hint of dread in his voice.

Borden sensed MacNutt's tension. "Relax, Andrew, I know that you are not to blame. But we still have to deal with the fall-out. My office is getting calls from the papers asking for comments. And we all know that all we can say is that my government is co-operating fully with the British and American authorities to the fullest extent possible."

"Yes, of course, sir," said MacNutt with a touch of relief.

Borden grinned. "We both know that is a load of horse manure, don't we?"

MacNutt's mouth almost twitched into a smile. "What can I say?" he replied truthfully.

"So what do you think is really going on?" demanded Borden, leaning forward.

MacNutt took a moment to gather the thoughts that had teemed through his mind since first reading the news. "What I think is that the British are using the von Papen papers to help win the propaganda war in the States. As an investigative tool and evidence they would be invaluable to our investigations, but we are at best a secondary interest. If they have so much as considered the impact on my operations, I would be really surprised."

Borden nodded with a frown. "What can we do about it?"

MacNutt scowled. "There is very little I can do, if they don't want to co-operate with me."

"Let me take care of that," said Borden. "I'll add it to my list of grievances that we will send to London."

"I appreciate that, Prime Minister."

"Don't get your hopes up," warned Borden. "I don't think they will listen to me either. I'm just a colonial politician." There was frustration in his voice. "Keep me informed," ordered Borden, standing up. "I have to go to my cabinet meeting. If I don't keep an eye on them, God knows what trouble they will get into."

MacNutt stood up too and walked with the prime minister as far as the hallway outside the PMO, at which point the PM turned left and headed for the Privy Council office in the southwest corner of the East Block. MacNutt turned right for the staircase that led to the ground floor. He needed to brief the commissioner on his meeting with Borden.

INSPECTOR MACNUTT'S OFFICE, EAST BLOCK,
PARLIAMENT HILL, OTTAWA
10:45 A.M., MONDAY, JANUARY 17, 1916

Nearly a half-hour later, MacNutt got back to his office to find Lacelle brimming with excitement. "What's going on?" MacNutt asked.

"I got these in the morning mail," said Lacelle, handing MacNutt the intercepted letters and postcards. "They're from the mail censors."

MacNutt glanced at the letters and cards. He was about to hand them back to Lacelle when he read the address on one of the postcards. It took a moment for it to register. When it did he whistled. "These are from our German agent."

"Yes, sir," agreed Lacelle.

"So we really do have a live one then," said MacNutt, controlling his excitement. He examined the cancellation on the stamp. "Posted two days ago, and here in Ottawa."

"Yes, sir," answered Lacelle, his own excitement hardly contained. "Are you going to open them, sir?" Lacelle handed him the letter opener from his desk.

MacNutt selected one of the letters and carefully slit it along its edge, leaving the flap untouched. He pursed his lips and blew gently into the envelope to separate it from its contents. He then pulled a folded letter from the envelope and unfolded its three pages. He began reading and as he finished each sheet he handed it to Lacelle, who seized them eagerly. The penmanship was quite good, the text quite legible, and in English. MacNutt turned to the other two letters and slit them open in the same manner. When he had finished reading them, he examined the postcards.

"That's it?" Lacelle whined a few minutes later after they had digested everything.

"I'm afraid so," stated MacNutt. "They are rather mundane." He had been expecting to find some kind of cypher or code in the text, but they appeared to be ordinary, touristy descriptions such as one would send home on a vacation trip. But upon reflection, his expectation seemed unrealistic: would a German agent make his letters so suspicious by using an obviously cryptic code?

MacNutt picked up the first letter and reread it. Something about the paper bothered him. He raised the letter to the light bulb in the ceiling in order for the light to filter through the paper. Then he thrust the paper at Lacelle and headed to his desk in the inner office, where he rummaged for a moment in a drawer. He emerged in Lacelle's office with a magnifying glass, took the paper back, and smoothed it flat on the sergeant's desk. He positioned the desk lamp to throw light directly on the sheet. Then, bending over the letter, he examined it closely with the glass. "There is something between the sentences. Take a look," he indicated, handing Lacelle the magnifier.

Lacelle peered at the line MacNutt pointed to. "Invisible ink?"

"I think so," replied MacNutt.

"Shall I get a candle, sir?" Some invisible inks became visible when subjected to heat.

MacNutt shook his head. "I think this may be more sophisticated than milk or lemon." Those were the standard invisible ink techniques that every schoolboy knew.

"What now?" asked Lacelle.

MacNutt strode to the coat rack and pulled on his overcoat. "I'll give Foster a visit. He may have some ideas. I'll be back as soon as I can. We won't notify the commissioner until we see if Foster can help. Meanwhile, start on the copy books from the hotels. And get the latest train passenger lists. We'll go through them one more time. A name may pop up." He carefully placed the letters and postcards in his briefcase and fastened the straps. He paused before he closed the door behind him. "If anyone needs me, I will be over at the Langevin Block."

LANGEVIN BLOCK, WELLINGTON ST., OTTAWA
11:05 A.M., MONDAY, JANUARY 17, 1916

Across the street from the East Block on the corner of Wellington and Elgin Streets was the Langevin Block. The four-storey Empire-style building, completed in 1889, was constructed in response to the growing demand for civil service office space. It was the first government building built off the precincts of Parliament Hill, and located as it was on prime downtown real estate, it caused some political headaches for the Ottawa City council due to the property tax revenue it represented. It was named after the minister of public works who had started the project, Hector Langevin. The civil service quickly outgrew the building. With the war, the pressure on office space was acute. Now civil servants were scattered throughout the downtown area in a number of different buildings. The Langevin Block currently housed, in cramped quarters, the Department of Interior and Indian Affairs, the Department of Agriculture, the Patent Offices, and the Dominion Police's National Fingerprint Bureau.

MacNutt took the fourteen steps up to the building's main entrance, which was richly ornamented with pilasters, carved panels, and moulded cornices. He pulled on the heavy wooden door and walked through a short corridor to the central staircase. The staircase's elaborate wrought-iron balustrades swept all the way from the ground floor to the fourth. Each floor had stairway lobbies framed by arches, supported by polished granite. He ignored the elevators, which were situated in the four corners of the lobby, and instead took the stairs, two at a time, to the second floor and followed a familiar route to the door marked Dominion Police Fingerprint Bureau.

The bureau was a large room, its walls lined with filing cabinets. Light was provided by the overhead electric fixtures and by the sunlight that streamed through three round top windows. There was an oak desk at the front of the room, and situated in the centre were another eight desks. These eight were set in two rows facing each other and butted together. At each desk sat a fingerprint technician poring over stacks of fingerprint cards.

Inspector Foster, dressed in civilian clothes with a white smock overtop to protect them from fingerprint dust and ink, was seated at the big oak desk examining a fingerprint card with a magnifying glass.

Foster led the Dominion Police's Criminal Investigation Division, with about forty men under his command. He was so focused that it took a minute before he realized someone was standing in front of him. When he recognized MacNutt, he smiled. "Good morning, Andrew. What can I do for you?"

"I need a favour," said MacNutt. "What do you know about invisible inks?"

Foster leaned back and grinned at MacNutt. "Not my area of expertise — now, if you wanted to know about fingerprints, I could help you."

That was an understatement. Inspector Thomas Alfred Edward Foster was one of the foremost fingerprint experts in North America. In 1904, he had been assigned by Commissioner Sherwood to protect the gold exhibit that the Canadian government was sending to the St. Louis World Fair. It so happened that the International Association of Police Chiefs was having a convention in St. Louis at the same time. A Sergeant J. H. Ferrier of the London Metropolitan Police gave a speech on a new criminal identification system, fingerprinting.

Intrigued by Ferrier's speech, Foster requested permission from Sherwood to stay in the States to learn more about fingerprinting from Sergeant Ferrier. He came back convinced that fingerprinting was the wave of the future. He then set out to promote the merits of fingerprinting, since it was simple and cost-effective to train officers in taking proper fingerprints. In 1908 an Order-in-Council sanctioned the use of fingerprinting for criminal identification. In 1911, the National Fingerprint Bureau was officially established. Foster was promoted to inspector and named its head.

The biggest obstacle he faced was training police officers in the use of fingerprints as an investigative technique. Many old-school police officers were highly skeptical of fingerprinting. It wasn't until 1911, when he testified as an expert witness at the Thomas Jennings murder trial in Chicago, that he was able to put most of those doubts to rest.

The Illinois Supreme Court ruled for the first time that fingerprints were admissible as evidence.

"Invisible ink," mused Foster, "not my area, as I said, but I do know someone who might be able to help you. One of my technicians is quite keen on the topic. Come with me." Foster led MacNutt to the far side of the room and stopped in front of a young man in his twenties. He was thin, with oval wire-framed glasses perched on his nose. He was concentrating on two sets of fingerprint cards. He examined one set and then the other, attempting to perform a match. Then he looked up. "Inspector Foster, I believe that it is a match — that these prints are from the same man."

"Good. Fill out the appropriate forms and let the Toronto Police know that the man they have in custody is Leopold Bernhard," Foster ordered.

"The escaped prisoner from the Kapuskasing internment camp?" asked MacNutt.

"Yes, the prints match those from Kapuskasing," explained Foster. It was standard practice that all Germans and Austrians sent to the internment camps were fingerprinted. All Canadian internment camps, prisons, and police forces were required to send their fingerprint cards to the bureau for cataloguing and for storage.

"He escaped from the camp last month," recalled MacNutt. "Good to know that we finally have him back."

"Yes, sir," said the technician, relieved that the inspector was pleased with his work. His gaze flickered from MacNutt to Inspector Foster.

"Ken," Foster informed him, "Inspector MacNutt wants to know what you can tell him about invisible inks."

The young man brightened. "I know a great deal on the subject, sir. It's a hobby of mine." He pushed his glasses up on his nose and began. "Invisible inks come in two types: those developed by heat and those developed by chemical reactions. Inks developed by heat are usually organic and acidic. That's why milk, lemon juice, onion juice, and vinegar work rather well — as do diluted sugar solutions. With these 'inks' you write on a piece of paper and later, when you want to reveal the writing, you apply heat to the ink and it will appear, usually as a brownish ink."

"What kind of heat?" asked Foster.

Ken turned to Inspector Foster. "Any heat source will do — a light bulb, a hot iron, or an oven. You just have to be careful that you don't burn the paper."

"And the other method?" asked MacNutt.

"Yes, sir, inks that appear as a result of chemical reactions. Chemical-reaction inks cannot be developed by heat. You must either spray the paper with an atomizer or soak it in a chemical solution for the writing to appear. Vinegar and ammonia-based inks can be developed using red cabbage water and copper sulfate inks by using sodium iodide, sodium carbonate, or ammonium hydroxide solutions. Depending on the particular chemical formulation of the ink, you may need a different chemical developer."

"I see," MacNutt said. "How can you tell whether an invisible ink has been used?"

"There are tell-tale signs you have to check for. Pen scratches from a sharp pen, or sections of the paper may be rougher and reflect light differently from the surrounding surface. The visible ink may have some bleeding, if the person who used it wrote over it with the invisible ink text. And if a chemical ink is used, it may give off a chemical odour," answered Ken.

"I see," the inspector said again. He peered at Ken, then at Foster. He put his briefcase on the desk, undid the leather straps, and pulled out the letters and postcards.

"I would like your opinion on these letters," he requested, handing them to Ken, who carefully examined the postcards first then turned his attention to the letters. He took the folded letters out carefully from their envelopes. He held the pages up to the lamp on his desk. He caught his breath and gave a quick glance at Inspector MacNutt. He set the sheets of paper on the desk then took out a magnifying glass and examined the letter again.

"My God, sir," he exclaimed, barely containing his excitement. "Is this for real?"

"May I?" asked Foster, putting out a hand for the letters.

Foster examined them minutely then turned to MacNutt, whose shrug told Foster all he needed to know.

"So, how can I help, sir?" asked Ken.

"Can you develop the writing for me?"

"To be honest, Inspector, apart from some experiments I have never done this before." Ken paused as MacNutt waited.

"But then neither has anyone else in Ottawa, sir," he added hurriedly before MacNutt changed his mind. "I'm willing to try, but I cannot guarantee success. The Germans are great chemists. I could end up destroying the letters in the process. If I have to bathe the letters, the visible ink may get washed out. Even if I did manage to make the writing visible, the writing could be in cipher."

MacNutt considered the risks. "This is what I want you to do. Have the letters copied. Once that has been done, try raising the ink. How long will you need?"

Ken's forehead furrowed a moment before he responded. "A couple of hours to have the letters copied. Then I'll need to get the appropriate equipment and chemicals. Maybe till tomorrow morning, till Friday at the latest."

"That long?"

"If you want it done properly, sir."

MacNutt nodded then turned to Inspector Foster. "Can I borrow Ken for a couple of days?"

"As long as you return him, I don't have a problem. He's a very good worker, and I need him," stated Foster. Ken blushed at the inspector's praise.

"I'll try to return him in one piece," replied MacNutt. He turned to Ken again. "I'll leave the letters and postcards with you. Call me when you have anything."

"Yes, sir," promised Ken. He carefully picked up the letters and placed them in a manila folder on his desk.

Before he turned away, MacNutt fixed his gaze on the man and said quietly, "I hardly have to mention that you are not to discuss this business with anyone."

"Understood, sir," Ken assured him quickly. He was fully aware of the consequences if he should be indiscreet.

"Good," MacNutt said. He and Foster turned and headed for the exit.

BROOKLYN FEDERAL BUILDING,
WASHINGTON AND JOHNSTON STREETS,
BROOKLYN, NEW YORK CITY
1:00 P.M., MONDAY, JANUARY 17, 1916

Frank Johnson and Ignatius Timothy Trebitsch-Lincoln stepped out of the main entrance of the white-walled Brooklyn Federal Building. Trebitsch-Lincoln, on the right, made way for several people who were entering the building. One of them, a man busy shuffling letters, bumped Trebitsch-Lincoln's leather portfolio, bulging with papers, as he passed. Ignatius glared, irritated, as he watched the man hurry towards the U.S.

Postal Service office located on the building's ground floor. The upper floors housed the federal courts and other federal government offices and agencies.

The dark suit Trebitsch-Lincoln was wearing had seen better days, as had the threadbare coat over it. He shivered when a brisk wind swirled down Washington Street. He had a slight pallor, which indicated he didn't spend much time outdoors.

He turned to Johnston and asked, "Do you think that we could stop to get a bite to eat?" He spoke English with a thick Hungarian accent. The years he had spent living in Britain, Canada, and the U.S. had done little to soften it.

Johnson paused to consider his prisoner's request. It was past noon, and he was hungry too. Having lunch at the Raymond Street jail didn't appeal to him either. "Sure, why not," replied the U.S. Deputy Marshal. "I know a couple of places where the food is cheap and there is plenty of it."

Trebitsch-Lincoln smiled. "Very good. If we are passing your motor car, do you think I could leave this in it?" He lifted his leather portfolio up to his chest. The portfolio contained German cyphers and chapters for the book he was writing on German espionage.

"Not a problem," the marshal replied as he led the way to his car. He kept a close watch on Lincoln as they walked. Lincoln was his prisoner, one with unusual and special privileges, but all the same a prisoner.

Ignatius Timothy Trebitsch-Lincoln had been arrested and was being held on forgery charges. He was born Ignaz Trebuchets in 1878 and was the son of orthodox Hungarian Jews. At the age of eighteen he emigrated to England, one step ahead of the law. In England, he converted to Christianity and became a Presbyterian minister. In 1910, after becoming a British citizen, he was elected to the British Parliament as a Liberal MP. Due to some financial improprieties he didn't run for re-election. Again, just one step ahead of the law, he decided to take his usual luck to the States.

Since August he had been fighting a losing extradition battle. He claimed that he was innocent of the forgery charges and that they were part of the British government's plot against him. Johnson took the man's claim of innocence with a grain of salt: *all* prisoners, in his experience, claimed they were innocent. Johnson conceded that there might be a kernel of truth in Lincoln's accusation against the British government, because the charges had been laid at the request of the New York British consulate. However, Lincoln had brought them on himself, because the British government was unhappy with the pro-German letters he had written and then published in the major newspapers. Also, his claim that he was a German agent certainly didn't help. The book he was writing was an exposé of the German spy network in Britain and the United States.

Once they had dropped off the portfolio, they crossed the street to the Brooklyn Daily Eagle building at the corner of Washington and Johnston Streets, which housed the *Brooklyn Daily Eagle* newspaper offices. Above the main entrance was a rampant eagle with a globe in its claws. The restaurant was just on the Johnston side of the triangular building.

When the men entered the restaurant, the waiter asked. "You want a table?"

"Yes, for two," replied Johnson.

"Sure," the waiter said, canvassing the busy restaurant for a table. "Hey, Ethel. Is table five ready?" he asked a plump blonde waitress in a pink uniform.

"Yeah. They're gone. Give me a minute to clean it up, Sam," she replied as she bustled off to the kitchen.

Sam turned to the two men. "If you want to take the empty table near the window, she'll clean it up for you in a minute."

"Sure, why not," answered Johnson. The men made themselves comfortable at the table, pushing the dirty dishes aside to make room for their elbows. A moment later Ethel appeared. She handed them each a menu, brushed a lock of hair back around her ear, and then started removing dishes. "The special of the day is roast beef sandwiches with baked potatoes. I'll be back in a minute to wipe the table and to take your orders," she rapidly informed them before she rushed off again,

"Thanks," replied Johnson sarcastically as he opened one of the menus.

Trebitsch-Lincoln was disgusted with the table. "I need to wash my hands. Do you mind if I go to the restroom?"

The marshal scrutinized his charge for a moment. He had been escorting Lincoln to and from the Raymond Street Jail to the Federal Building two or three times a week since August. An office had been made available to him there in which he could decipher German codes for the American government and complete his book. During that time, there hadn't been any incidents.

"Go ahead. But make it quick," he ordered.

"Of course. Order me the special, if you don't mind?" Lincoln requested as he headed for the washroom.

Frank Johnson saw him go to the back and enter the washroom. He then turned his attention to the menu and was reading it when the waitress arrived to wipe the table with a damp cloth. She set the table with fresh cutlery, coffee cups, and glasses. Then she pulled out her order pad. "What'll it be?"

"A beer for me and I'll have the special," he demanded.

"Any dessert?" she said, her pencil poised over the pad.

"Apple pie."

"What about your friend?"

"He isn't my friend."

"Whatever!"

"He went to wash his hands. He wants the special."

"Apple pie for dessert?" she asked.

"I don't know. Ask him when he gets back," answered Frank.

"Okay. I'll bring your beer," she said, picking up the menus.

As he waited, he watched the people in the restaurant and the crowd on the street through the glass window. It took nearly ten minutes before the waitress appeared with his beer. She set the glass before him. "Your friend ain't back yet?" Not waiting for an answer she whirled away again.

What was taking him so long? Johnson took a sip of his beer, scowled at the empty chair, then decided to check on his charge. He rose and headed for the men's washroom. When he pushed the door open, all he saw was a small, slightly dingy washroom with two empty urinals and toilet stalls.

The marshal's mouth dropped in disbelief. He hurriedly checked each stall again but there was no mistake: no Lincoln. He rushed back to the restaurant to frantically check if he was at the bar. No Lincoln in the restaurant. He couldn't disguise his worry and fear. He ran back to the washroom then noticed a second door near its entrance. The door was not closed properly, and when he banged it open, he saw that it led into a back alley.

"Shit," he muttered, scanning the empty alley. "Shit! Shit! Shit!" He darted down the alley, which led to Johnston Street, and began his frantic search for his escaped prisoner. His lunch was forgotten.

O'MALLEY'S BAR, HELL'S KITCHEN,
NEW YORK CITY
6:20 P.M., MONDAY, JANUARY 17, 1916

The Count was not pleased when he saw the latest newspaper headline. "Another German-American plot to blow up a power house at Niagara Falls was exposed," it screamed. When he read the accompanying article, he was even less happy. The conspirators were planning to destroy the powerhouse and the international bridge on the Canadian side of the border, but they had been under surveillance by the Secret Service from the moment they left New York until their arrival at the American side of the Falls. They had not yet crossed over to the Canadian side when they realized they were being followed. They tried to destroy the evidence by tossing the explosives into a nearby river. Unfortunately, it was shallow and the authorities were able to recover the explosives.

Idiots! thought Count Jaggi. *I'm surrounded by idiots.* The Count intended to make his displeasure known to Müller. First, he wasn't aware that there had been a plan to blow up the powerhouse and bridge at Niagara Falls. Second, they were nearly caught. Third, according to the article, the men were allowed to escape and were still under surveillance. He would have to cut them loose, because he couldn't take the chance they would compromise other operations or lead the authorities to him.

The Count sighed wearily. He wanted to be continually informed and updated on his operatives' activities, but his communications needed to be improved and secure. He needed to minimize in-person meetings as much as possible. What he really wanted was to set up a series of dead letter boxes where his agents could leave and pick up messages. But finding the time to do it was a quandary. Meanwhile, what was he going to do with these idiots? The Count was getting tired of trying to stay clear of their blunders.

It was extremely frustrating that at every turn his plans were being reported in the newspaper. *Gott in Himmel, we are supposed to be doing our work in secret — not on the front page of the daily papers!*

"How was your trip to Canada?" a voice with a thick Irish accent asked him, interrupting his train of thought.

The Count turned from the paper to the man who now stood beside him at the battered oak bar in O'Malley's. It was a seedy Irish bar in Hell's Kitchen, the meeting place Kevin O'Brien had insisted upon. The Count didn't think it was wise to meet here, but O'Brien demanded a face-to-face at O'Malley's because he felt secure there. The Count didn't have much choice; he was dependent on the Irish. They could get into places his people could not.

"It went well," replied the Count as he folded the paper and put it on the oak bar. O'Brien was a burly man in his early thirties with broad shoulders and thick arms from working as a stevedore on the New York docks. The Count didn't particularly like the man. He was crude and uncultured, but he did possess a natural cunning, which he had needed to survive in Ireland as a member of Sinn Féin. He was forced to escape to New York, one step ahead of the Irish Constabulary.

"How did you know?" The Count frowned. He was not pleased that the man was aware of his movements.

"Müller mentioned it," O'Brien said with a grin.

It was unlikely Müller had told the man of his trip. Had he made a slip or was O'Brien letting him know he was keeping tabs on him? The Count was worried about how far Captain Gaunt had penetrated the Clan na Gael. Did the infiltration reach the leadership, and did the British already have his name in their files? The Count resisted the urge to search the crowded bar for surveillance.

The Count turned glacial. "You called this meeting. And I'm here."

Kevin rubbed his cheek as he picked up the mug of dark beer which the bar passed off as Guinness. The Count tried one swallow and grimaced in distaste. It was barely palatable.

"We need more cigars," Kevin stated.

The Count blinked in surprise. "The last shipment is gone already?"

"Yes," replied O'Brien.

The Count studied O'Brien for a moment then asked, "What really happened to the shipment? Did the bomb squad get them?"

O'Brien returned the Count's gaze, which pleased him; he wanted O'Brien to know that he wasn't a fool. "Last Sunday. That bastard Tunney raided one of our flats. We were only storing them there temporarily before moving them to a safe location."

"Did he get the entire shipment?"

"Yes. All of them."

"*Scheisse*," exclaimed the Count. They had sent over a dozen or so pipe bombs to the Irish for placement in British cargo ships. The British didn't allow German longshoremen to be anywhere near their ships. "How did Tunney find out?"

"I'm asking you," O'Brien demanded with a thin smile.

The Count didn't miss the implication. His lips thinned in barely controlled anger when he retorted, "What makes you think that I would have anything to do with it?"

"They raided a day after your people had them delivered to the flat," answered O'Brien.

"So. It could have been one of your own people," the Count snapped.

O'Brien glowered. "It's not my people. I've known them for years, and they are from the old country. I trust them completely." He reached over, tapped the newspaper, and said sardonically, "With your people, it is a different story."

The Count was furious, but he couldn't deny the truth of what O'Brien had said. "So what do you want then?"

O'Brien lips turned into a crooked grin. "We are allied against the British, are we not?"

"Yes. Germany will support Irish independence."

"Only if Germany wins."

"And your point?" demanded the Count.

"Boyo. You need to tighten your security. The English are right bastards, and they play by their own rules."

"Is that why you called me to this meeting. To tell me that?" the Count said brusquely.

"Partly. But also I lost two good men in the raid. I need to get them good lawyers, and I need to care for their families," declared O'Brien, leaning closer.

"It's money then."

"Among other things. About $5,000 will do for now. We also need replacements for pipe bombs and we need about a thousand rifles by next week. Preferably Lee-Enfields."

"The pipe bombs I can do. As for Lee-Enfields, they are hard to get. We may be able to get Mausers or even Springfields. For next week, that could be a problem. Our current supply has been committed elsewhere," explained the Count.

"Mexico?" asked O'Brien. When the Count didn't answer he continued, "Your affair. Now, about the money —"

"That I have to discuss with my superiors. It's a sizeable sum and they will need to approve it." Not exactly true, but the Count didn't plan to hand over money to the Irish without some strings, which he would blame on his superiors.

O'Brien wasn't pleased. "How much can you give us next week?"

"I can get you a thousand next week. When I've talked with the embassy I'll try to get more."

"Well … all right," O'Brien reluctantly agreed. "It will have to do for now. But don't take too long — I'm not a patient man. You pay for the drinks."

The Count tossed a quarter on the bar for the two beers and a five-cent tip for the bartender, then walked out.

A man sitting in the corner watched the Count leave the bar. He mentally noted the man's description so that he could include it in his report to Tunney. His orders were to keep surveillance on O'Brien and report on anyone he talked to. O'Brien was a wily, slippery character, and it was just luck that he had learned the man would be here this evening. He wanted to follow the other man who'd just left, but if he did, he wouldn't find O'Brien again for days.

MACNUTT RESIDENCE, LAURIER AVENUE WEST, OTTAWA
11:35 P.M., TUESDAY, JANUARY 18, 1916

Katherine was putting a kettle on the cast-iron stove to make some tea when she heard the front door open. She couldn't stop herself from glancing down the hall through the open kitchen door as her husband hung his coat on the coat tree. He appeared exhausted. *Damn, damn*, she thought. It still hurt to see her husband so tired and beaten. She hated that she couldn't make up her mind about Andrew. One moment she loved the man, the next she despised him. Andrew entered the kitchen with a touch of wariness, which Katherine also hated. She could feel his eyes searching for signs of her mood. She turned toward him and indicated the table with her head. He took the seat nearest the door.

He broke the silence first, a small victory for Katherine. "You're up late. You couldn't sleep?"

"I was listening to the Victrola, and I lost track of time," Katherine replied.

"I thought you went out with Nicole this evening?" he hinted.

"Nicole was invited to the dinner party that General Hughes and Lady Hughes were having this evening."

"I'm sure that she is having a good time," remarked Andrew.

"She likes Lady Borden," answered Katherine. "So how was your day?"

"I've had better. Are you making some tea? I could use some," he said as he ran his hand tiredly through his hair.

266

"If you'd like some." Katherine went to the cupboard and took out a cup and saucer. As she placed them in front of MacNutt, her hand touched his. His hand lingered near hers until she moved it away. Her hand tingled from his touch. "Rough day at work?"

"Yes, it was. The easiest part of my day was seeing the Duke off."

"Oh," murmured Katherine as she picked up the kettle that was beginning to steam. "I didn't realize they were going on a trip."

"It's just a day trip to Montreal. Their aides and ladies in waiting were going with them in the private train car the Grand Trunk had ready. They should be back tomorrow evening. I had to check if I needed to send one of my men with them. I had let the Montreal police know they were coming. They'll take care of them."

Katherine poured tea into Andrew's cup and then her own.

"I just thought that Bourassa was causing trouble again," she asserted. "Some people think it would solve a lot of problems if you arrested him and tossed him in jail."

Andrew didn't meet her eyes. He already knew her feelings. Ever since Jamie died, Katherine's attitude had hardened. She was particularly critical of those who did not support the war effort wholeheartedly. "That's unlikely to happen," he replied quietly. "I have enough trouble without adding more. Things are bad enough in this town with Regulation 17."

"I heard that the mayor of Hull was thinking of getting involved," Katherine mentioned.

"Great! That will go over well," replied Andrew sarcastically, standing up from the table. "Would you like some milk?" He went to the icebox and took out a bottle of milk. It was a new bottle, with the cream in the neck. He poured the cream carefully into his cup and offered the bottle to Katherine. She put up a hand.

"So what have you been doing today?"

"Nothing much. Still organizing the Belgian Relief show in two weeks," replied Katherine.

"In two weeks?" said Andrew, startled. "January is flying by fast."

"Yes, it is. There are only two weeks left to get things ready, and there are a ton of details that still need to be ironed out." Her eyebrows dipped in concern.

"When is the Count coming back to Ottawa?" Andrew asked casually.

Katherine wasn't fooled. What worried her was his reason for asking.

The image of him stepping into the elevator at the Russell flashed into her mind. "The last I spoke with him, he said that he should arrive a day or two before his lecture. He wants to make sure that everything is properly prepared," she replied warily, shooting a quick concerned glance at Andrew.

"You met him in New York?"

"I had afternoon tea at the Plaza with him," she said truthfully.

"What did Nicole think of the Count?" He studied her over the lip of the teacup.

"Nicole wasn't there. She was shopping when I met him for tea," she said. She didn't like the tone or the direction Andrew was taking. "Andrew, are you questioning me?"

"No. I was just curious, that's all."

"I certainly hope not. You have more important things to do. Like arresting that German spy," she declared.

MacNutt jerked up. "What! Where did you hear about that?"

A strange expression crossed Katherine's face. "That German spy who escaped from New York."

"Oh. Him. I wouldn't worry about him," he said, visibly relieved. "The borders are being watched. We'll catch him if he tries to cross the border."

She took a sip of tea then was struck by a thought. She frowned. "Hold on. Who did you think I was talking about?"

"Why, Ignatius Trebitsch-Lincoln — the spy who escaped in New York."

Katherine shook her head. "I know you, Andrew. I know you quite well. When I said a German spy, you thought it was someone else. Are you searching for another German spy?"

"I can't talk about it."

"What do you mean, you can't talk about it?" Katherine demanded. "I'm your wife, for God's sake."

"There are certain things I really can't discuss," Andrew said stubbornly.

"Right!"

"Don't be that way, Kath." Andrew tried to keep the pleading out of his voice. He knew that when Katherine was in this mood, arguing with her would be futile. From her expression, she wanted to continue the argument, but he didn't. He simply didn't have the energy. He pushed his teacup toward the centre of the table. He rose listlessly. "I'm calling it a night."

Katherine was not happy to leave things as they were, but she let him go. She heard his heavy footsteps on the stairs leading to their bedroom on the second floor. She sat in the chair fuming for a few minutes in the silent kitchen, a kitchen full of memories. Some were now painful. Unbidden, she drifted into one.

She remembered frying eggs on her stove. The table was set with her everyday stoneware for three. As she was shaking her cast-iron pan so the eggs wouldn't stick, Andrew quietly entered the room. When Katherine turned from the pan to get a plate from the table, she found him grinning at her. "What?" she demanded.

"Nothing," he replied. But he had a look on his face that she knew well.

"You wicked man, you," she said with a hint of a smile.

Andrew's grin grew wider. Katherine wagged a finger at him. She knew what he wanted. "Not now. Jamie will be here any minute."

"I certainly hope not," he said with mock horror.

Suddenly, they heard the sound of a door slamming shut. A moment later, Jamie, a gangly seventeen-year-old, his sandy hair freshly cropped, entered the kitchen. Her irritation at his bad timing turned to fear when she saw that he was wearing a brand-new khaki uniform. She glanced at Andrew. He was beaming with pride until he saw her dismay.

"Do you like it?" Jamie asked. He ran a hand over his chest to smooth a wrinkle.

Katherine couldn't put any joy into her voice. "Yes, it's fine. A bit too large for you, though."

"It's fine, son," answered MacNutt.

"Thanks, Dad. I've got to go and show Emily my uniform."

"You want to have a bite to eat first?"

Jamie shook his head. "No thanks, Mom. I'm too excited to eat. Bye. I just wanted you and Dad to see me first in my uniform," he said as he started to leave the kitchen.

"Be on time for supper," Katherine ordered.

"I'll be eating at Emily's," he replied.

Katherine said firmly, "I want you here for supper."

Jamie turned to his father for support. "Aw, Dad."

Andrew knew from Katherine's glower that she wouldn't brook any arguments. "Get the snow out of your ears, lad. Do what your mother says."

Jamie made a sour face, but he nodded. He turned and left the kitchen, and in a moment they heard the front door bang close. Once he'd gone, Katherine sat down at the table, her head in her hands, tears beginning a slow roll down her cheeks. Andrew stood behind her and put his hands on her shoulders.

"Andy, he's just a boy!"

"He's a man now. He's got his duty and a job to do. He'll be all right. He'll be home by Christmas," he said softly.

Jamie never came back that Christmas and would never come back for any of the many Christmases ahead of her. Katherine dried her tears with the back of her hand. She picked up her cooling cup of tea from the table and put it into the sink. She would wash the cups in the morning. She left the kitchen and made her way to the spare bedroom on the second floor.

CHAPTER 25

The Count was standing on Bow Bridge and looking across the lake at the New York skyline. It was a crisp, sunny January day, and New Yorkers were enjoying Central Park. There was a steady stream of people, the young and the old and families, all strolling along the lake. He spotted Müller easily as he walked down the path, recognizable by the forest green overcoat and black homburg he always wore.

"*Guten tag*," the Count said. Müller wore a worried expression. He was scanning the strolling people, searching for something. "Rough night?" asked the Count.

"Yes," he growled. "It's been bad ever since Trebitsch-Lincoln escaped."

"The Americans have been busy," agreed the Count.

Müller nostrils flared in disgust. He lifted his homburg, ran his hand through his hair, then reset his hat firmly on his scalp. "You don't understand. They have been arresting a fair number of our people."

"How badly have we been hurt?"

"They've picked up about ten of our men that I know of."

"On what charges?"

"Does it really matter? Until Trebitsch-Lincoln has been caught they will make life extremely difficult for us," replied Müller hotly. His tone caught the attention of a couple who were walking past, arm in arm. He glared at them and they scurried off.

"Keep your voice down," the Count ordered. "You don't want to draw notice to us."

"That's easy for you to say. You're always up in Canada," retorted Müller.

"I said, *keep your voice down*," the Count said sharply. "Now, what about the bomb factory?"

"I've shut it down till things cool off."

The Count frowned. "For how long?"

"I have no idea. A week, maybe two. In the meantime I have to find a new place to stay. I can't go home. The police may be waiting for me."

"Damn! I had promised the Irish we would replace the cigars that the police confiscated last week."

"Why did you do that?" demanded Müller.

"We don't have much of a choice, as you know."

"I might be able to replace them, but I'll need at least a couple of days. It'll be Friday, Thursday at the earliest."

"The Irish are not going to like it," the Count pointed out.

"That's too bad," said Müller scornfully.

"What about Boy-Ed? Does he have any that he could give us?"

"You can always ask," said Müller, though his tone said they could pin no hopes on the captain.

"When could he meet with me?" the Count persisted.

"I have no idea. All I can do is pass on the message. Why do you want to meet with him?"

"While I was in Canada I found some information on British subs that he might like to know about."

"I'll send him a gram."

"That will have to be good enough."

"What are we going to do about Lincoln?"

"Do you know where he is hiding out?"

Müller shook his head. "No, I wish I did. But we are not going to help him out, are we?"

The Count grimaced, telling Müller he was crazy to even ask the question. "Major Nicolai might have helped him out of Hungary. But now he is a liability, and a traitor as well. Wasn't he helping the Americans break our codes?"

"Thank God he didn't gain access to them. So what do you want to do?"

The Count shrugged. "Put the word out that no one is to help him. If someone knows where he is, let the police take care of him."

"I don't have a problem with that."

"Good, I'm glad to hear it."

"When do you want to meet again?" asked Müller.

"When you get the supplies we need, we'll set up a meeting," replied the Count.

"As you wish."

"Do we have more to discuss?"

As Count Jaggi watched Müller walk away towards the Central Park exit, he knew that soon he would be in the same situation as Müller, searching for a new place to stay. He removed a letter from his jacket pocket and scowled. It had been delivered to his hotel yesterday, and he was trying to decide what to do about it. The letter was from the Rockefeller Foundation, inviting him to a meeting to discuss how the Foundation might help with his Belgian Relief efforts. If he had known that King had such a close relation with John Rockefeller, he would not have spent so much time on the train with the man. He read the letter a second time and decided that he had a week or so before he must reply. Maybe it was time to switch identities. He had new papers that would transform him into a Swiss businessman. Most Americans wouldn't know the difference between Swiss and Hanover German, he thought as he headed for his hotel.

BOMB SQUAD, NYPD POLICE HEADQUARTERS,
CENTRE STREET, BROOKLYN, NEW YORK CITY
3:15 P.M., WEDNESDAY, JANUARY 19, 1916

Captain Tunney was in his office reading with disgust the articles in the *World News* about von Papen's expenses. He slapped the papers on his desk and cursed the British. It would have been invaluable if the bomb squad had received copies before they were leaked. It would have allowed his men to pick up and interview the people that von Papen had listed. The bulk of the expenses, he suspected, were legitimate payments for services rendered such as catering and laundry. It was the others that interested him. He suspected that the Germans would have buried themselves deeper, making his job more difficult. It would have been satisfying rolling up another of von Papen's network. Yes, German activities were temporarily disrupted, but eventually they would reorganize and be back at it again.

Detective Sergeant Barnitz entered his office with two cups. "Coffee, Captain," he said, placing a steaming cup beside the *World News*. "Reading the *News* again," he remarked, balancing his coffee as he lowered himself into an office chair across from the captain's desk.

Tunney picked up the cup Barnitz had brought and leaned back in his chair. "No point in crying over spilled milk. So what do we have?"

"We found another bomb attached to a ship's keel yesterday," Barnitz informed him.

"I've read the report. A good job of defusing it. How many does that make this month?"

"About three of the large ones. This one had one hundred pounds of TNT."

"That would have blown the keel off a battleship, let alone a cargo ship. You got a good view of the mine after you defused it?"

Barnitz answered, "The bomb was constructed to be attached underwater to the rudder-post as the ship lay at the pier. It had rubber gaskets to prevent water from getting in and damaging the clockwork. The clock was set to ignite two rifle cartridges into the explosive chamber. It was just plain luck that someone noticed it when they were inspecting the rudder. Whoever made that one made the other six acid-tube pipe bombs that we confiscated from the Irish last week."

"Damn," said Tunney. "We have a bomb factory. Is it the Irish?"

Barnitz made a fluttering motion with his hand. "Unlikely. The ship bomb and the pipes bombs were just too well made. They are too sophisticated for the Irish."

"Well, we have to find the factory," Tunney snarled in frustration.

"We might have a lead. One of my snitches said that O'Brien met with a German the other night."

"Is the man reliable?" asked a skeptical Tunney. His experience was that informers frequently weren't.

"As trusty as any informer can be. He saw O'Brien and the German talk for about half an hour or so a couple of days ago. It seems O'Brien was asking the German to replace the ones we have in the evidence locker by the end of the week."

"Now, *that* is interesting," remarked Tunney. "Did your informer know the German?"

"He had never seen him before. From his description it's not someone I'd recognize either."

"Did he get his name?"

"Afraid not. But if he is going to deliver new bombs, we'll get him."

"Good. I really want him," said Tunney impatiently. "Has anyone heard anything about Trebitsch-Lincoln yet?"

"Not so far. We've been picking up a bunch of Germans on various charges, but none of them seem to know a thing or at least won't admit to anything. The U.S. marshals are keeping an eye on the women who were visiting in jail, but so far Trebitsch-Lincoln hasn't made contact." Barnitz scowled. "I heard that young man Johnson was suspended today."

"Did you expect anything else?" said Tunney. While he sympathized with the young man's predicament — he had been new to the job without much experience — he should have certainly reported the loss of his prisoner immediately rather than waited for two days after his escape.

274

Barnitz sighed. "Well, I believe that Trebitsch-Lincoln's still in New York. If you can believe it, he dropped a letter off at the paper saying that Johnson shouldn't be punished."

"Well, that's real decent of him," replied Tunney sarcastically.

"You never know — he could walk in on his own."

"That'll be the day," Tunney said with a snort of derision.

"I guess. By the way, did you hear that the Germans were booking hotel rooms next to Captain Gaunt?" Barnitz chortled. "They were bringing in Dictaphones and trying to record his conversations."

"Can't say I'm surprised. They do love playing games, don't they?"

"True, but wouldn't you love to hear those recordings?"

Tunney laughed. "Would I. But best get back to work. We have a busy day." He made a shooing motion.

Once Barnitz was gone, Tunney turned his chair to view the New York skyline through the window behind his desk. It was *his* city, and the Germans and the British were fighting their war in it. Sometimes he felt as if he were a referee between two teams. There was even talk of renaming his squad; he was unenthusiastic about the idea. He turned back to his desk and regarded the manila folder in the in-tray. It contained papers he and his men had confiscated from Koenig's office in December. What interested him most was the pocket-size black memo book at the top of the stack. For all his faults, the ex-chief detective of the Hamburg-American line was meticulous in maintaining records. There was ample evidence to convict Koenig on the charges that had been laid.

The memo book was a loose-leaf affair with two holes punched at the top of the neatly typed pages. Koenig updated the book regularly, with the last entry written just a few days before his arrest. From the notes, Tunney could piece together a very good picture of Koenig's activities. When Koenig was hired by the passenger line, he quickly rented an office at 45 Broadway and had a private phone installed. His main duties were to deal with the various criminal activities that afflicted a passenger line, problems such as stowaways, vandalism by disgruntled employees, passenger ticket fraud, theft from passengers and the cargo holds, and smuggling.

On August 22, he had been approached by the German embassy to help wage war on British interests in New York. Koenig had expanded his organization of two divisions to include a third division, the Secret Service, which did most of the dirty work. The first division, the Pier Division, provided wharf protection for the Hamburg-American line's ships and facilities, while the second, the Detail Division, provided protection for German embassy personnel and residences, which included Count von Bernstorff's residence in Upper New York.

Koenig had been a busy man. So busy that he had to keep track of all the aliases he had been using when he met with his operatives, neatly recorded in his memo book. At last count Koenig had twenty-six aliases. He had code names for his various meeting places too. What was also interesting was that he kept notes on his dealings with von Papen. Tunney ran across a notation that Koenig had sent two men to spy on the Canadian Army's primary assembly and training camp at Valcartier. Tunney wrote a reminder on his blotter to pass the information on to the Canadians for investigation. One of the items that caught his notice was a lodging house at South and Whitehall Streets. He decided to send one of his men to check on the lodgers at the rooming house. As he continued to read the memo book, he jotted down more notes for his men to follow up on.

HENDERSON TAILORS, SUSSEX STREET,
BYWARD MARKET, OTTAWA
5:15 P.M., WEDNESDAY, JANUARY 19, 1916

The door chimes tinkled above MacNutt's head when he entered the shop. The boarded-up window gave the shop a dark, gloomy air. The electric lamp didn't seem to lighten the permanent shadow that covered Denon's face.

"So, Inspector, back to inspect the damage?" Denon grumbled.

MacNutt took in the depressing shop carefully. "Business is slow, I see."

Denon lifted his shoulders in a gesture of resignation. "You know why."

MacNutt did indeed know why. He also knew that the glass should have been replaced by now, but local merchants were not too keen to sell to a German. Also, if business was slow, could Denon afford to replace the window in the first place? "I've ordered my men to keep an eye on your shop."

Denon became even glummer. "Don't do me any favours. Now everyone believes that I am a spy."

MacNutt nodded sympathetically. He decided to get straight to the point. "I need some information."

"Information?" Denon said disparagingly.

MacNutt had planned carefully what to say. He knew Denon well enough to know that this wasn't the best time to ask for the man's help. If he had the time, he would have backed off. But the way things were going, he doubted he would ever find Denon in a good mood.

It took the U.S. marshals a day or so before they informed anyone that Trebitsch-Lincoln had escaped. In a way, MacNutt didn't blame them, because it *was* rather embarrassing. He suspect they were hoping to get their hands on him before they had to notify anyone. But when they realized they needed help, they contacted the U.S. Secret Service and the New York police. Canadian Customs had been notified.

When he found out he had sent a telegram to the Montreal police to put an alert out for him. Trebitsch-Lincoln had lived there for four years from 1900 to 1904. He was ordained a minister in the Presbyterian Church in Montreal. He had spent most of his time travelling across the Canada trying to convert Jews to Christianity, until he left for England and politics. So he was quite familiar with Montreal, and he may still have friends who could give him a place to lie low.

"Yes, information," he reiterated.

Denon studied him warily. "What kind of information?"

MacNutt tried to make his request low-key. "Nothing terribly important. I was just curious if you have heard of anyone new in Ottawa or Montreal?"

"I don't know. I haven't been to the station in quite some time," said Denon with a sly smile.

MacNutt made a face. "You know what I mean."

"Yes, I do. What would you give me if I did have news?"

MacNutt concealed the sudden flare of interest he felt. "You know I can't do that."

Denon shrugged. "You don't even know what I want yet."

"What *do* you want?"

"Ah, that is a difficult question," he answered, rubbing his chin thoughtfully.

"If it is something I can do, then I need to know. Just tell me what you what."

Denon turned his attention from MacNutt to stare at the boarded window. "I would like my friends in Kingston to get some mail and to have family visit them. Some of them have not seen their wives for months."

MacNutt hesitated before answering. He was relatively certain there wouldn't be a problem in granting the man's demand. But he needed to think out the office politics. He finally gave Denon a politician's answer. "I'll see what I can do."

Denon sniffed. He wasn't that easily mollified. "That is not good enough."

"I'll see what I can do!" restated MacNutt. He never made promises that he couldn't keep.

Denon nodded.

"So, do you know anything?"

"Nothing."

It took a moment for the word to sink in, then it took all of his willpower to control his temper. "What do you mean, nothing?" he barked.

A smile began to creep in the corners of Denon's mouth, which MacNutt didn't particularly like. He knew that Denon was trying to play him, and he was not happy about it. "I wouldn't suggest trying my patience. I can't blame you after all that you've been through. But it would be wise if you uncover information of interest to let me know. Meanwhile, I'll do what I can be done for your friends in Kingston."

"I'll consider it," Denon replied. MacNutt nodded, and the chimes tinkled when he closed the shop's door behind him.

Denon came around from behind the counter to the door to watch MacNutt as he strolled up George Street. As he scanned the street traffic, someone caught his eye. A tall, thin man, dressed in a trench coat too light for the weather, emerged to watch MacNutt disappear down the street. The man then turned his gaze towards Denon's shop. Denon had noticed him hanging around for the last few weeks. At first he thought he was one of MacNutt's men, but the clothes the man wore were too expensive for a constable's salary. Denon couldn't put a finger on it exactly, but the man's mannerisms suggested that he was not from Ottawa. It was a real puzzle as to what he should do, since he didn't know what the man was after. Denon was certain, however, that the man was not looking after Denon's best interests.

CHAPTER 26

The sunlight streaming in through the open window lighted the Count's face. He put up a hand to shade it then shifted over to the empty right side of the double bed. It was empty, since the blonde he had met on the Ottawa train had left to meet her fiancé. She had been an enjoyable romp. He had seen her off then crawled back into bed and closed his eyes to doze for another half hour or so. He was just starting to think about getting up when there was a knock on the hotel room door.

"Yes," he yelled.

"Room service," said the male voice.

"Give me a moment, please," he shouted. He reached for his dressing gown and answered the door.

"Good morning, sir," said the waiter as he wheeled in the service cart. He glanced at the bed then at the closed bathroom door. "Breakfast as you ordered."

"Thank you," said the Count. He lifted one of the plate covers, revealing two eggs, sunny side up, four strips of crisp bacon, and hash browns. He had ordered for two, not realizing that the woman would not be staying. Beside the plate was a side dish with several slices of thick white toast, a pot of steaming coffee, and various jams and jellies. There was also a morning paper on the dolly. He replaced the cover to keep the food warm till he was ready to eat.

"Is everything satisfactory?" asked the waiter expectantly as he handed the Count the room service chit.

"Yes," answered the Count as he signed it. He fished some coins from the pocket of his trousers draped on the chair near the bed and gave the waiter a nickel tip. As soon as the man was gone, he poured the coffee and walked over to the window. The street below appeared relatively quiet. It was Sunday, and it seemed that most people were attending church.

After the first cup of coffee, his mind finally started working. He had a busy day planned. The most pressing item of business was deciding what to do about the men on trial from the Labour's National Peace Council. The lawyers had informed Müller that the grand jury had found a witness. They needed to locate the witness and convince him, one way or another, not to testify. The second item was that Müller had sent word that a meeting was arranged with Boy-Ed so that the Count could give him a briefing on what he had discovered in Ottawa. He sighed when he thought of his next trip up north. The long train trips were becoming tiring. Müller indicated that Boy-Ed wanted to meet at the Pabst Club, which he refused, because it was a well-known German haunt. Müller was arranging another location. The other item was his interview of a man Müller had found for some sabotage work they were planning. He was hoping that the man would be reliable. Then he had to check out the Mexican situation. It appeared the initial reports that Pancho Villa was dead were premature. He really needed to meet with Felix Sommerfeld, but the timing could be a problem.

The Count turned away from the window and walked over to the breakfast tray. *Too much to do and not enough time*, he thought as he lifted the cover off the tray and sat down to eat.

OTTAWA CANAL, LANSDOWNE PARK, OTTAWA
11:15 A.M., SUNDAY, JANUARY 23, 1916

MacNutt tightened the laces on his battered black leather skates that had seen better days. He remembered the times when he and Jamie came out to the canal so he could teach his son how to skate and play hockey. Today it was cold, but the ice seemed to be in good shape. He took a few first slow steps then began to get into a glide. It had been nearly a year since he had his blades on, and he knew that tomorrow he would be sore.

He needed this skate to unwind after his chance meeting with the very trying Mrs. Ramsey. He had turned on his street, taking care not to step into any of the slushy puddles that lined it. He was coming from Sunday mass. Katherine had gone with him to church but after the mass had told him she was going to visit Nicole for early afternoon tea before coming home. Which was fine with him, because things were still tense between them. When he saw who was coming towards him, he swore silently. He easily identified Mrs. Ramsey's gait as she strolled down the street. His heart sank because there was only one reason why she would be walking down his street. The urge to turn around and walk in the other direction had been strong. It would have been the height of bad manners, but he could have lived with it.

Unfortunately, Mrs. Ramsey had spotted him and made her way around a snow bank to cross over to his side of the street. She waved with a gloved hand. "Good morning, Inspector," she called. There was nothing for it; he had to stop.

"Good morning, Mrs. Ramsey," he said, his hand politely touching the brim of his hat.

"So, Inspector, did you arrest him yet?" she asked bluntly.

MacNutt blinked in surprise. "Madame?"

"That German spy, Denon. You went to arrest him yesterday afternoon, didn't you?" she repeated.

MacNutt glared at her coldly. "No, madame, I did not. Furthermore, it is a confidential matter which is none of your affair." Rude or not, he was determined to walk away from her, but Mrs. Ramsey refused to budge. She gave him a small smile that raised the hair on the back of his neck.

"How is Katherine?" she inquired, making it sound like an innocent question, but her sly smile indicated something else.

"She's fine." *Why is she asking?*

"I'm so glad to hear that. She hasn't been in the office for the last few days. She said she was coming down with the sniffles."

"She seems to be coping," was all that he could say. He had been so busy for the last few days that he didn't even notice she was getting a cold, but he'd be damned if he would let Mrs. Ramsey know that.

"Good. I'm glad that she is spending so much time resting at home. She has been working a great deal with the Count of late. In my day, if women and men spent so much time together people would talk." She eyed him expectantly.

MacNutt returned her glance. *Is she going to ever get to the point?* "Yes, I'm well aware of how people can talk. I'm afraid I must be going now." He turned and strode to his front door, leaving Mrs. Ramsey standing on the sidewalk seething.

It took MacNutt about ten minutes to skate from Echo Street down the canal to Lansdowne Park before he decided to turn back. A loud cheer from the sports stadium caught his attention, but he couldn't see what had caused the excitement, since the ice surface was about several feet below the canal walls. He wouldn't be surprised if the 77th battalion were playing a pick-up game of football.

The thirty-acre Lansdowne Park was the primary sports facility and exhibition centre for the City of Ottawa. MacNutt remembered vividly the game that the Silver Seven played in the Aberdeen pavilion to defeat

the Montreal Victorias to win the Stanley Cup in 1903. He and Jamie
were among the three thousand fans that had flocked to watch the game.

Now the park was a military barracks and recruitment centre. Jamie
had done his basic training there, with the Princess Patricia's Canadian
Light Infantry, before they shipped out to France. After the Pats had left,
the 2nd, 21st, 38th, and currently the 77th Battalion did their recruiting and their basic training at Lansdowne before heading to England
for advanced training. Once the 77th had left, the next unit — the last
MacNutt had heard it would be the 207th — would take its place.

As he skated back towards the railway station, he began to wonder
where the men would come from for the new units, which took his
mind off Mrs. Ramsey. He knew that the battalion's authorized strength
could be as high as 1,400 to 1,500 men. This meant they had already
recruited approximately 9,000 men from Ottawa and the surrounding
area. That didn't include the recruitment of various support units. The
well would soon be running dry unless some solutions could be found.
As he considered various possibilities, his skates found an unconscious,
comfortable rhythm of their own.

MACNUTT RESIDENCE, LAURIER AVENUE WEST, OTTAWA
11:30 A.M., SUNDAY, JANUARY 23, 1916

Katherine was walking up the slushy snow-covered street to Nicole's
place for afternoon tea. Her chin was buried in the wool scarf around
her neck. She was so lost in thought that it took a few minutes before
she registered the shouts and screams of the children playing in the yard
a few houses down. She watched as the young boys played king of the
castle over a large mound of snow. She brightened in amusement, but
she darkened when she remembered Jamie at their age. She had been
standing on the front porch without a coat, shivering slightly and calling
out, "Jamie, it's time for you to come in now!"

Her son, with his dark blond hair sticking out from under his dark
woollen cap, stopped playing long enough to give her a disbelieving
stare. "Aw, c'mon, Ma, I'm still playing!"

"Jamie, it's getting late and it's cold."

"Ma!"

She noted his rosy cheeks and the snowy fort he'd been working
on all afternoon. "I guess you could have five more minutes, young
man — but that's it!"

"Thanks, Ma." His lips split into a huge grin and she couldn't help the warm feeling of joy that spread through her at seeing his happy face.

He then ran back to join the other boys. Just then she saw that Andrew was strolling up the street towards the house. Jamie spotted him too and whispered with the other boys. The boys scurried off and quickly made snowballs, and then they lay in ambush behind the wall of Jamie's fort. When Andrew got into range, they fired.

"What the...!" exclaimed a startled MacNutt. When he spotted the offenders, he quickly grabbed some snow and fired back. Through the hail of snowballs, he advanced and then grabbed Jamie. "Gotcha." Jamie squealed in delight as MacNutt lifted his son above his head, put him on his shoulders, and headed to the house.

As Katherine wiped the tears away from her cheek, Noah, an eight-year-old boy with a mop of brown hair, spotted her and motioned to the other children to be quiet. They all knew that she didn't like them playing when she was around.

"Noah. Have I not told you before that you should not be playing here?" she chastised sternly.

All Noah could do was lower his toque in pretended disgrace. He had learned early that this was the best way to deal with mean old Mrs. MacNutt. "Yes, Mrs. MacNutt. But we were just having some fun."

Katherine wagged a finger at him. "If you don't behave, I will tell your mother. Do you want that?"

"Oh no, Mrs. MacNutt," he replied quickly. His mother had admonished him several times that he should be nice to Mrs. MacNutt.

"Good. Let's not have it happen again."

"Yes, ma'am."

Katherine turned around and walked away towards Nicole's place. When the children were quite certain that she was out of earshot, they picked up their game where they had left off.

CHAPTER 27

It was nearly three o'clock when MacNutt entered his office. As usual, Lacelle was at his desk banging at the typewriter. Looking up he asked, "How was question period?"

MacNutt snorted. Every day, when Parliament was in session, the opposition parties seeking information or bringing the government to account could pose questions to the prime minister or to a cabinet minister. Question period was held at 2:15 for about forty-five minutes to an hour, except on Fridays, when it was held at 11:45, to allow the members to break early for the weekend. "The usual," he replied.

Lacelle wasn't surprised. Question period was, for political junkies, a spectator sport where they could cheer or jeer as MPs drew blood from their opponents. On occasion, the sport would turn physical and a brawl would break out, requiring the sergeant-at-arms to intervene. Not that surprising, considering that the members regularly resorted to catcalls and jeering at the one posing the question and at the minister who was attempting to answer it.

"Except when Carvel asked a question," answered MacNutt with a humourless grin. He normally did not attend question periods, since he was too busy with his duties, but when he had heard rumours that Carvel wanted to pose a question, he made a point of dropping in. Especially after William Pugsley, the Liberal member for the City of St. John, New Brunswick, had criticised the Shell Committee the week before and asked for a special investigation.

"He did?" Lacelle grimaced in anticipation.

"He did."

"I'm glad that I wasn't there." Lacelle knew Mr. Carvel's reputation. It was substantially different than Pugsley's. He was known as *Sweet William* to his friends but *Slippery Bill* to his enemies due to his reasonableness and mild manner. If Carvel, the member for Carleton, New Brunswick, was posing a question, it would not be good news for the government. Carvel had a sharp and aggressive style. The year before he was instrumental in the resignation of two MPs, and he also managed to drive the premier of New Brunswick out of office. You didn't want to be in his sights.

284

"What question did he ask?"

"What do you think? About the Shell Committee, what else? You know he hates Hughes," MacNutt answered. "The galleries were packed, especially the Press gallery. He started off complaining about the decommissioning of the battleship *Niobe* in Halifax. He said that if they hadn't dismantled the ship to honour pre-election pledges to Bourassa and Lavergne, she would have captured more German ships off the coast, and the ship would have paid for itself." MacNutt had doubts about Carvel's assertions, because he had asked Commander Stephens about it during one of their meetings. Stephens' response was that the ship was obsolete ten years ago and was expensive to maintain. The ship's seven hundred officers and sailors could be used more effectively on other ships. The ships conducting anti-submarine patrols in the Bay of St. Lawrence needed experienced men.

"Then he laid into the government, and he didn't hold back an inch," said MacNutt with a half-admiring shake of his head. "One of the Conservative MPs said it was a fine way to maintain a truce. Carvel put him in his place by pointing out that while men are suffering at the front, private political profiteers are huckstering and peddling shell contracts."

"Did he say who they were?" asked Lacelle.

MacNutt smiled unhappily. "He did. Whether he would say the names outside the House of Commons was a different manner." Members were protected from libel and slander suits if the accusation was made in the House. Outside the House of Commons chamber, it was not the case. "All the details will be in Hansard or tomorrow's paper."

"*D'accord.* Will we be involved?"

"Difficult to say right now. I'll need to talk with the commissioner about it," replied MacNutt. "By the way, how are things going?"

Lacelle knew the real question he was asking. "Gillan and Briggs are still at it, but they haven't found anything yet."

"I guess that it was too much to expect," MacNutt grunted. Ken, the ink expert, had arrived at his office the previous morning, beaming with excitement. The first thing he exclaimed was, "I did it, Inspector, I did it."

"Really?" MacNutt said in surprise. He had not expected the young man to succeed.

"Yes, Inspector, it took a couple of days and a number of tries, but I managed to get the developer right. I tried heat first, and then I tried chemical baths, and the chemical bath worked — you see..."

MacNutt had put up a hand to stop him. "I don't really need the details. I believe you, but can I read them?" Ken had placed the letters and the postcards into the inspector's hands. MacNutt opened one of the letters and examined the handwriting. Between the lines of text, which had nearly been washed out because of the developing solution, there were a series of numbers in five-number blocks. "Damn," MacNutt said. "It's in code."

"Sorry, Inspector. I tried to decipher the text but I was unable to."

"Nothing to apologize for. You did an excellent job. This," MacNutt pointed to the letters, "is proof that we do have a Hun agent in our midst."

When the inspector ushered Ken out, he reminded him about confidentiality and assured him that he'd be in touch if there was more he could do.

"So Gillan and Briggs haven't found anything?" repeated MacNutt.

"You'd be surprised how many people are visiting Ottawa at this time of year," Lacelle pointed out. "We've been trying to compare the letter's handwriting with the handwriting in the ledgers, but it's not easy." The letters had been copied by laying onionskin paper over top of the letters and tracing the script.

"Why not?" demanded MacNutt.

"About a third of the names and addresses have been written by the desk clerks," answered Lacelle. Seeing MacNutt's frown, he added, "Some of the visitors can't read or write, so the clerks fill in the registers for them. Others are regular customers, so as a courtesy they sign them in."

MacNutt groaned. "Great!" The task was monumental, especially with his limited staff. He needed more information to go on.

"We know the name on the letter is a false one, but matching the handwriting is a nightmare. Some of the handwriting is nothing but a scrawl."

MacNutt paused to think for a moment then made up his mind. "Okay, give it a few more days. If we don't find a sign soon, we may have to give it a rest. It's looking for a needle in a haystack."

"Yes, sir," replied Lacelle.

"Right." MacNutt glanced at the clock. "Well, I'm off to another meeting with Simms. If something urgent comes up… " Lacelle knew the rest.

When the Count got off the elevator at the meeting place, he was impressed despite himself. Usually, when clandestine meetings were arranged, they were in seedy bars or flophouses, which made sense since most of the men he had to deal with were not exactly well-heeled. This meeting with Captain Boy-Ed had been arranged in an apartment building loft just off Fifth Avenue. Much more than a loft, the apartment appeared to occupy the entire floor. The few pieces of furniture he saw in the entrance hallway were expensive.

When he knocked on the white-painted door, a stocky middle-aged woman with streaked black and grey hair, pulled back into a bun, opened the door. He flashed a charming smile at her, but her eyes were hard with suspicion. "Good afternoon, sir," she said flatly.

"Good afternoon. I'm Karl Krutz. Mrs. Kemper is expecting me," he answered. Her expression didn't change much, but the Count got the impression that she didn't approve of him.

"May I have your coat," she muttered. She hung it in the closet then instructed, "Please follow me. The madame is in the salon." As they made their way through the apartment, the owner's wealth was more and more apparent. When they arrived at the salon, it had a single occupant, another middle-aged woman, this one with peroxide-blonde hair. Her dress was expensive, as was her jewellery, but the dress didn't quite fit her figure. It seemed as if she had bought it on the simple basis of how much it cost rather than how it would enhance her looks.

"Do you need anything, madame?" the first woman inquired.

"No, I will be fine. The captain will be along any moment. When he arrives please show him in," she ordered. The wealthy woman's voice had a squeaky quality that grated on the Count.

"As you wish, madame," the maid replied unhappily before she left the room.

"Mrs. Kemper," said the Count, taking the hand she offered and kissing it gallantly.

"My dear Karl, it is indeed a pleasure," she giggled. "So you think you can help poor Ignaz?"

The Count grinned. "I think we might be able to. But we don't know where he is at the moment. Do you?"

She shook her head sadly. "He hasn't contacted me at all. I don't understand why. I was his favourite. The poor man, I pray that he is all right. At least he is out of that horrid prison."

"Yes, it must have been quite trying," he said, trying to keep the sarcasm from his voice. They were interrupted by the maid, who now led Captain Boy-Ed into the salon. He was dressed in a worsted civilian suit.

"Captain, it's good of you to come." She beamed with relief.

"The pleasure is all mine," said the captain with a bow that pleased the woman.

"Please let me introduce you. Karl Krutz, this is Captain Boy-Ed, the German naval attaché."

"Captain."

"Herr Krutz." The captain acknowledged him with brisk nod. He appeared amused by the charade.

"I'm so glad that you came. A mutual friend said that you may be able to help my poor Ignaz," cried Mrs. Kemper. The Count knew the mutual friend was Müller, but how he found her, Jaggi couldn't hazard a guess. It was obvious that she was a German sympathizer, or she wouldn't have invited Captain Boy-Ed to her apartment. "Please take a seat." She indicated the tea green settee across from her. Both men complied.

"As you know, Trebitsch is wanted by the police. It would be best if he gave himself up," suggested the Count.

"I agree with Herr Krutz," said the captain.

She vigorously disagreed. "There must be another way. There must! Can't you get him out of the country? To Canada or Mexico?"

The Count and the captain glanced at each other. The Count cleared his throat. "That may be possible."

"Yes?" said Mrs. Kemper hopefully.

"Frau Kemper, this is a quite delicate matter, and it would be best if the captain and I could speak privately for a moment," said the Count.

"But I want to help," she whined.

"But you are helping, Frau Kemper. If the police come calling, it would be best if you can tell them truthfully that you don't know a thing," the captain interjected. She was not a particularly good liar.

"I understand, captain," she replied, dejected. "I'll see to the refreshments." She left the room in a bit of a sulk.

When she closed the door behind her the captain turned to the Count and demanded, "How did you manage to arrange this?"

The Count laughed. "The woman is enamoured with Trebitsch. She'll do anything to ensure that he is safe."

"*Mein Gott.* You're going to help him?" exclaimed Boy-Ed.

"Of course not," retorted the Count. "He's caused us enough problems. Besides, we don't want Frau Kemper to know that if we send him back to Germany he will be shot."

The captain gestured in agreement. "We'll just tell her we have a plan, and we can't provide her with the details. And that the fewer details she knows the safer he will be." The captain then said, "You've called the meeting. What do you want to discuss? Time is short."

"I found some information in Ottawa that might interest you."

"Really?" asked the captain.

The Count nodded with a slight grin. "At the opening of their Parliament I had an interesting discussion about submarines."

"You did, did you?" replied the captain. He gazed at the Count with interest.

"*Ja.* It seems that the British and the Americans have taken over a shipyard in Montreal and are building submarines."

"I suspected as much, but it's good that we have confirmation," answered the captain.

"You knew already?" said the Count in surprise.

The captain snorted derisively. "I do have my sources. It seems that somehow the Electric Boat Company and the British government made an arrangement to evade the American neutrality laws. What they did was prefabricate the sub parts, then ship them to Montreal for final assembly. Once the subs were assembled, they sailed them down the St. Lawrence to Halifax and then on to England," the captain explained.

"How many have they built?"

"Based on train shipments, I'd say about ten or so, but I don't know for certain. The subs are a General Electric design. The 602. It's mid-size, about four hundred tons displacement, and it's just entered service with the U.S. Navy. It's armed with four eighteen-inch torpedo tubes in the bow, and they carry eight torpedoes. It has a range of 1,100 nautical miles with a top speed of 13 knots on the surface and 11 knots submerged. Normally, they have a twenty-two crew complement."

"Supposedly two of their new subs are having problems. They were holding hearings about them."

"They can't be the General Electric Boats," suggested the captain with a frown, "because those are quite reliable. They must be the ones on the West Coast."

"Is there any way of sinking the subs when they are still in Canadian waters?"

"A modern destroyer or cruiser would do the trick, but it is unlikely we can get one into Canadian waters. Not that the Canadian Navy could do anything about it if we did. They only have two old out-of-date cruisers. They recently decommissioned one of them and converted her to a depot ship. She's in the Halifax Harbour. The rest of their fleet is comprised of various converted civilian vessels and yachts. The largest may displace perhaps 1,000 tons. They are mostly armed with 7.62-cm or 4-cm guns. Some with 36-cm torpedo tubes."

"So what are they using them for exactly?" asked the Count.

"Their Admiral Kingsmill has them doing anti-submarine and mine-sweeping patrols. There was a rumour circulating that four U-boats were planning to attack Halifax."

The Count laughed. "Obviously they believed the rumours."

"The rumours were not that farfetched. Our new class of U-boats has the range to operate off the Canadian and U.S. coasts. We can attack their ships when they leave the harbour."

"If that happened, the Royal Navy would deploy ships to this side of the Atlantic, wouldn't they?"

"That is likely, but I don't think they'd really want to divert any more ships from their blockade of the Fatherland and the North Sea. Also, they have been sending their ships across in convoys, which makes attacking them more difficult."

"Hmm. What of this Admiral Kingsmill?" asked the Count.

The captain stroked his chin. "Rear-Admiral Kingsmill is a Canadian. He was actually born in Canada. He joined the Royal Navy in 1870. He did quite well for a colonial. He was a decent enough destroyer captain. However, when he was promoted to rear-admiral he was sent to Canada to command the Canadian Department of Marine and Fisheries." The captain said the last statement with some disdain. To go from commanding destroyers to commanding a fleet of coast guard ships that were the equivalent of fishing vessels was not an exactly a career path to being Lord Admiral. Also, it was unlikely, no matter how skilled, that a colonial would ever command the British Home Fleet.

The captain continued. "That is when the admiral got lucky. In 1911 the Canadian government decided to create its own navy. He was appointed naval director. I must admit that I'm somewhat envious of the man."

"Why?"

"To have the opportunity to create a navy from scratch, to develop and mould it as one sees fit. What naval officer wouldn't like that opportunity?" replied the captain with a wry smile.

The Count understood him quite well.

"Are you going back to Canada?" demanded the captain.

"Next week. Is there something I can help you with?"

"What I really would like is any information you can get on their radio-telegraph network. It's a vital part of their naval intelligence system. I'd be grateful for any information you can find."

"I'll see what I can do, though I can't promise anything," answered the Count. "The other thing I found out is that there seems to be some corruption in the British Shell contracts."

"I'm not surprised. There's a lot of money in the munitions contracts these days," the captain said.

"Berlin wanted us to tie up the American munitions plants as much as possible. Since I have been here, I finally understand how naive that idea was."

"Berlin, naive?" the captain said with a touch of sarcasm.

The Count chuckled. "But there might be some opportunity to take advantage of some of the corruption."

"À la Bridgeport?" suggested the captain. He was referring to the von Papen Bridgeport Projectile Company scheme. Von Papen had developed a strategy of buying American war supplies and of tying up the production of manufacturing companies. Under von Papen's behind-the-scenes manipulation, Bridgeport had ordered as much as two million dollars' worth of gunpowder to keep it from reaching the Allies. The company also took money for weapon orders but never delivered the guns.

"*Ja.*"

"I have no objection," answered the captain.

"*Das ist gut.* Now, I think that our hostess must be anxious and we had better invite her in."

"I agree," said the captain. He rose from his chair and opened the door. In the hallway, he found the maid waiting.

The Count wondered if she had been listening at the door. Even so, he doubted that she could have heard much of the conversation, since he and the captain had kept their voices low.

"Could you tell your mistress that we are ready," requested the captain.

The Count watched her eyes carefully when she acknowledged. He saw a flash of frustration in them before she headed dutifully down the corridor to summon her mistress. That flash told him what he'd suspected: she'd been listening, but now she would not have the chance to tell her mistress what she'd heard.

CHAPTER 28

The dawn sky was slowly shading from slate to cobalt as the sun began its ascent above New York harbour. The harbour was already teeming with activity. There were fishing boats heading for the Manhattan docks, the day's catch already aboard. Some of the boats had to change course to make way for a passenger liner being pulled up the Hudson by a tugboat. The liner was painted battleship grey to avoid detection by U-boats. More than likely it would dock at the Chelsea piers, the main passenger terminal on the lower west side of Manhattan. A U.S. Navy destroyer was heading in the opposite direction for the open sea.

On Count Jaggi's left, the Statue of Liberty grow larger as the lighter he was sailing on headed back to Manhattan from Staten Island. The ship was indistinguishable from other cargo lighters, flat-bottomed boats that were used to transfer cargo from the freighters that couldn't or wouldn't dock at one of the New York slips. The boat was sixty-five feet long and nearly twenty feet wide at the beam. It had eight feet of draft at the stern and four feet at the bow. The boat was powered by steam, and the Count could hear a seaman shovelling coal into one of the boilers. *Sally-Ann* was painted on the bow.

The Count glanced at the crates that had been lashed to the lighter's main deck, just below a derrick capable of lifting a ton of cargo in a single load, as he walked over and climbed to the ship's bridge. On the bridge the ship's captain manned the tiller. Müller, bundled up and slightly pale from motion sickness, stood beside the ship's captain.

"The harbour seems quite busy," commented the Count.

The captain grunted. "The war has been good for business." He turned the tiller slightly to adjust his course.

The captain was in his sixties and dressed in clothing that had seen better days. His hair was black but his beard was streaked with grey, and in need of a trim by the Count's reckoning. His skin was weathered from a lifetime at sea. He was not a particularly talkative man. The Count really didn't expect the man to be, considering the task at hand. Although he was German — and a fair number of lighter captains in the harbour were — he spoke bad German.

Though Müller had picked the man and his ship, both he and the

293

Count knew that they'd have to keep them under close supervision; they couldn't be fully trusted. The Count and Müller were armed, Müller with a .38 in his waistband, Jaggi with a .32 in his pocket. The main reason Müller had picked the captain was he had leverage on the man. With the increase in the harbour shipping, the owners of the lighters, tugboats, and barges were making good profits. Where there was a way to make a lot of money with little or no risk, scams abounded. One of the more popular ones was the sugar scam.

The war made the scam very simple and quite profitable. The lighter captains would load a cargo of sugar from one of the several refineries that dotted the harbour, such as the Domino and Brooklyn Sugar refineries and the Warner Sugar Refinery in Jersey. Midway between the refinery and the waiting freighter, some of the sugar would be offloaded and sold to a waiting harbour pirate for one-sixth of the local market price. The pirate would resell the sugar to local merchants at a handsome profit. The scheme depended on paying off the freighter's cargo checkers to stamp the bill of loading as received in full. The lighter captains' attitude was that the scheme was relatively risk-free, since a U-boat would likely send the freighter to the bottom of the ocean anyway. Still, not all the freighters were sunk. A word in the wrong ear could make the captain very unhappy.

The Count stared out through the dirty window of the pilothouse at the activity along the pier on his left. A couple of freighters, several lighters, and some barges were tied up at the pier, which stretched a mile. Derricks were busy loading cargo on and off ships. A plume of moving smoke indicated that there were train tracks hidden behind the warehouses that lined the pier.

"What's that?" asked the Count.

The captain glanced over and saw what the Count was studying. "Black Tom Island," he muttered with some sourness.

"What's a Black Tom Island?"

"It's the major munitions depot for the northeast."

"Is it?" The Count gave Müller a sharp glance. Müller had not told him about Black Tom Island. He wondered why.

The captain caught the glance that the Count threw Müller and decided to elaborate. He didn't like Müller. "It's owned by the Lehigh Valley Railroad. They have a work yard for the trains. It's not really an island any more. They keep using landfill to expand. The warehouses belong to the National Dock and Storage Company."

"I see." The Count understood now why the captain was sour. The business would have been lucrative, but because the captain was German, he would never be considered. "Security must be tight?"

"I've only seen a couple of guards," the captain said.

They were interrupted by a seaman who entered the pilothouse with white mugs and a dinged black coffee pot. "Coffee?"

"Why not," replied the Count. He took a mug and the seaman filled it halfway so that the coffee didn't spill when the harbour's waves rocked the ship.

The Count didn't mind the distraction. The captain didn't ask any questions about the cargo he was carrying. He was being paid so he wouldn't. He might not be too pleased that the crates in his holds were carrying 200 pounds of dynamite, 350 pounds of chloride of potash, 200 percussion caps, and about 200 metal casings of various sizes from pencil bombs to those large enough to be attached to the keel of a ship. As he sipped the coffee, the Count glanced back at Black Tom Island with a speculative expression.

MACNUTT RESIDENCE, LAURIER AVENUE WEST, OTTAWA
9:30 A.M., THURSDAY, JANUARY 27, 1916

It was just five days before the Belgian Relief fundraiser, and Katherine had a crisis on her hands. Late yesterday afternoon she had received a phone call from the manager of the hall they were renting for the event. He informed her they were being bumped to make way for a patriotic fundraiser. Katherine was so shocked at the news that she was rendered speechless. When she became coherent, the manager had already hung up. She tried to call him back, but no one answered the phone. This morning she rose early and visited the manager in person. He was apologetic but would not budge. When she got home, she quickly got on the phone and called the other ladies on the committee.

When they arrived at her home for an emergency meeting, they arranged themselves in the salon, with Mrs. Ramsey, naturally, taking the wing chair so that she could dominate the meeting. Nicole, Helen, and Claire sat on the sofa while Katherine sat in the Queen Anne chair opposite Mrs. Ramsey. On the coffee table was a tray with teacups, cream and sugar, and a pot of steaming tea. Katherine reluctantly repeated her conversation with the hall's manager.

Mrs. Ramsey sniffed. "So you couldn't persuade him then." Her attitude indicated that had she been there, they would not be in this mess. Nicole, seeing Katherine's flash of anger, spoke up quickly in an attempt to avert a confrontation. "What are we going to do now? We've placed ads in the *Citizen* and the *Journal*, and we have put up posters all over Ottawa with the time, date, and location."

"All that money wasted," moaned Claire, Belgian Relief's book-keeper.

"Not if I can help it," said Katherine firmly.

"I agree with Katherine," said Nicole. "All we need is another hall."

Mrs. Ramsey snorted derisively. "At this late date? It can't be done."

"We don't know until we try," pleaded Claire, rallying from her initial dismay to support Katherine.

A smile briefly appeared at the corner of Katherine's mouth. "We don't have much time. The Count told me that he would arrive on the Monday train when I had dinner with him in New York." The moment the words slipped out, she realized she had made a mistake because of the sudden gleam in Mrs. Ramsey's eyes. Well, the damage was done. "If we can't get a hall by tomorrow afternoon, I'll have to send him a telegram. I don't want to waste the Count's time."

"Sounds good," agreed Claire, nodding vigorously. "But we still have the problem with the adverts and the posters."

"I'm sure that the *Citizen* and the *Journal* would be glad to print corrections. As for the posters, we can have some kids paste the new hall's address on them," Nicole pointed out.

"It's a plan," said Katherine. "I'll make some enquiries and try to find out if a hall's available."

"It sounds as if everything is in hand," remarked Mrs. Ramsey, disgruntled that they had coped without her contribution. Still, the meeting had not been a complete waste; she'd acquired some interesting information. "I'd best be on my way."

Katherine rose swiftly and saw her to the door. She re-entered the salon and said cheerfully, "Ladies, I'd say that went very well. Let's adjourn."

DOMINION POLICE OFFICES, EAST BLOCK,
PARLIAMENT HILL, OTTAWA
11:30 A.M., THURSDAY, JANUARY 27, 1916

Denon walked gingerly up the snow-crusted sidewalk towards the East Block. The wind swirled fiercely around the building, whipping at his face until his eyes watered. He reached the building's entrance with mixed feelings. On the one hand, he was eager for warmth; on the other hand, he felt trepidation about what he was about to do. When he opened the door, he found two Dominion Police constables in the small foyer standing behind an oak security desk barring his path.

"Good afternoon," Denon said politely.

The taller of the two gave him a suspicious look then demanded, "What can we do for you, sir?"

Denon paused. He was at a loss, because somehow he had assumed it would be a simple matter to find MacNutt's office. He hadn't considered the building's security.

"I'm here to speak with Inspector MacNutt," he stated.

"Are you now? Is he expecting you?" asked the tall one, opening a binder that contained a daily listing of the authorized visitors to the East Block.

Denon shook his head.

The irritated constable ordered, "Please wait here a moment. I will check if he's willing to meet with you. Your name?"

"Denon."

The Constable arched an eyebrow in surprise; he recognized the name. He spoke to the other constable. "Keep him here while I check with the inspector."

"Will do," answered the other constable, turning his gaze on Denon.

The constable walked briskly down the corridor then disappeared into an office. As Denon waited, he stomped his frozen feet to warn them up. He held his coat tight against him to protect himself from the cold air blasts as the front door opened and closed with the comings and goings of the Block's staff. Denon focused his attention on the various wall carvings and moldings decorating the foyer. A few moments later, the constable jumped to attention. When Denon turned to find out why, he came face to face with General Hughes. Startled, Denon couldn't help but stare at the visage he had seen frequently in the newspapers.

The general paused to thrust his hands into gloves. Even Denon could tell that he was not in a good mood, and Denon had a fair idea why. He had been following the Shell Committee controversy in the papers with interest and glee. He was rather pleased that the general might be getting his comeuppance. The revelations concerning the Shell Committee were not good news. It appeared that a fair number of the contracts were going to Hughes' friends and supporters. Denon also knew, being a cynical man, that the general would probably come out of the controversy unscathed, no matter how bad the revelations were.

When the general noticed Denon, he gave him a curt nod, then headed out the door towards a waiting car. Denon noted the admiring way the constable viewed the general as he stepped into the waiting Hudson. The tall constable reappeared just as the car was put into gear. His eyes flickered between the standing constable and Denon. The constable went over and whispered in the man's ear. The tall constable glanced at Denon and then nodded.

"Come," he ordered as he led Denon down the corridor to Inspector MacNutt's office. Sergeant Lacelle was at an open filing cabinet when the constable let Denon in. The officer went over to Lacelle and whispered in his ear.

"*Merci*, Constable, I'll take care of him," Lacelle said as he closed the cabinet. The constable turned on his heel and left.

"Just take a seat, Mr. Denon. The inspector will be available in a few minutes." Lacelle sat at his desk doing paperwork while watching Denon out of the corner of his eye. It was about five minutes before MacNutt poked his head around the door of his inner office.

"Come on in," he said. He caught a look from Lacelle. He took a step out and Lacelle whispered in his ear.

"Interesting," commented MacNutt. He ushered Denon into his office.

"Good afternoon, Inspector."

"Have a seat," said MacNutt, indicating a chair in front of his desk. The desk was neatly organized. All the papers had been slipped into manila folders and were stacked on the corner of the desk. "How are you feeling today?"

"I'm getting old, aches and pains." Denon took off his hat and then his overcoat. He put them on his lap after he sat down.

MacNutt smiled. "Aren't we all?" He took a moment to read Denon's expression.

Denon snorted. He hesitated as if he didn't know where to start. MacNutt kept quiet as Denon gathered his thoughts. "I may have some information for you."

"What kind of information?"

"Before I give it to you, here is the list of some of my friends in the internment camps that I want to send some letters and personal items to."

Denon drew a sheet of paper from his overcoat pocket. The inspector took it from him and unfolded it. "There is nothing here that would pose a problem," he remarked when he had finished reading it. Denon gave MacNutt a hopeful smile. "And the other matter?" continued MacNutt.

Denon's smile faded, and his eyes dropped from the inspector's scrutiny. MacNutt sighed and dropped the sheet on his desk. He placed his hand on the sheet and tapped the paper gently with his index finger.

"I know very little," Denon said reluctantly.

"Come, come, Denon. You are not here today just to tell me that," MacNutt said impatiently.

Denon took a deep breath and plunged ahead. "A number of friends have been coming to me for the last couple of weeks. They have been rather concerned."

"What is concerning them?"

"A man has been approaching them, asking for information," Denon said slowly.

"Information! What kind of information?" MacNutt sat up in his chair with interest.

"He's been asking about railway train schedules and how many troops there are in Ottawa. He even asked if there was an aerodrome near the city."

"What have your friends been telling this man?" barked MacNutt.

"Nothing. Absolutely nothing," Denon insisted. "They were afraid to."

"Why haven't they reported this man to the authorities?"

"And end up in an internment camp!"

MacNutt sighed regretfully. He understood the fear. He pulled a sheet of paper out from a drawer and a pen from the case in front of him. "What's the man's name?"

"I don't know."

Irritated, MacNutt persisted. "Can you provide me with your friends' names so I can chat with them?"

"*Mein Gott, nein, nein!*" exclaimed Denon. "They asked me to speak on their behalf. They will deny everything if you speak with them."

"A night in the Nicholas Street jail might loosen their tongues," retorted the inspector. He saw Denon's stubbornness. "Is there anything you can give me about the man. A description? His nationality? Is he a local or from out of town?"

Denon tried to remember. "What I have been able to gather is the man is not a local. He is from out of town. One of my friends said he let slip that he was from New York. He has been in Ottawa a number of times."

"Do you have a description at least?" the inspector asked in desperation.

"Regrettably, no. However, what I have been told is that the last time was during the opening of Parliament," explained Denon. "Oh, someone said he might have stayed at the Château Laurier. He saw someone who resembled him leave one day when he was driving by. Is that of any help?"

Yes, it was. It gave him a date and a location. It was a simple matter of going through the Château's guest books. He wouldn't tell Denon that. Instead he coaxed, "So, you can't provide me with any description at all?"

"Not really. He is a tall man and balding. What was left of his hair is brownish. His clothes are not cheap. They are well tailored."

MacNutt grimaced. "Nothing much to go on." Denon appeared crestfallen. "But still I'll look into it. If it pans out, I'll honour your request."

"That is all that I can ask," replied Denon in a resigned tone.

"I do appreciate that you came to me this afternoon. It must have been difficult," said the inspector, rising from his desk. Denon rose and paused for MacNutt to open the door. In the other office MacNutt ordered Lacelle, "Sergeant, please escort Mr. Denon out of the building."

"Yes, Inspector," replied Lacelle.

When the East Block door closed behind him, Denon lifted his coat collar and pulled down his hat. He began to grin as he walked away from the building. He hoped that MacNutt would find the information he provided interesting. It was a small payback for the humiliation he had to endure.

CHAPTER 29

Inspector MacNutt and Sergeant Lacelle walked quietly down the dimly lit corridor to the door numbered 17. The inspector glanced at Lacelle then took a deep breath before rapping on the door. There was no response.

MacNutt watched as Lacelle upholstered his .45 from his belt. The hotel clerk had assured them the room's guest was in. The mid-priced hotel had been a favourite drinking spot of Sr. John A. It was comfortable without being expensive. The clerk had confirmed what Denon said. The man had been a regular guest who stayed at the hotel on several occasions for several months. He paid regularly, was quiet, and kept to himself. The clerk assured the inspector that the man was English, upper-crust English judging from his accent, probably a second or third son who came out to Canada to make his fortune. Either the man didn't hear the knocking, or he had a surprise in store for them. The inspector unholstered his gun as well. In his years with the force, he had never had to use it, and he hoped that he would not have to today.

He knocked louder. After a moment, the doorknob rattled and the door opened to reveal a thin man with a crown of blond hair. He was dressed in a pair of grey trousers and a shirt with the top button unfastened. From the fresh nicks on his face it appeared he had just finished shaving.

"Yes?"

"I'm Inspector MacNutt of the Dominion Police. I would like to have a word with you."

The man, puzzled, said, "Certainly. Please…" He motioned for the men to step in. MacNutt shook his head. "I would prefer to talk with you in my office."

"Why? I have not done anything wrong, have I?" the man exclaimed with a touch of concern.

MacNutt stared at the man steadily. "Mr. Evert, we would like to have a word with you concerning seditious activity." Evert goggled at MacNutt in stunned surprise.

INSPECTOR MACNUTT'S OFFICE, EAST BLOCK,
PARLIAMENT HILL, OTTAWA
1:30 P.M., FRIDAY, JANUARY 28, 1916

MacNutt was sitting at his desk, and he was furious. With every glance at Evert, he became even angrier. Evert was wise enough to stay silent as he sat uncomfortably on the chair in MacNutt's office. Both men turned their heads towards the door when they heard it open. The arrogant Major Simms entered the office without even bothering to knock. The arrogance was knocked down a peg when he spotted Evert. He tried to cover his reaction quickly, but it was enough to confirm what MacNutt already knew.

"Good afternoon, Major Simms," MacNutt said coolly. His anger now was on a slow burn. "We've been expecting you." MacNutt knew that he would take the major down several more pegs, and he was going to enjoy it. He was going to enjoy it very much.

"Inspector, what was the meaning of that impudent communiqué?" Simms demanded in an outraged tone. "And to have the gall and temerity of threatening me with arrest if I didn't come immediately?"

"I believe you know Mr. Evert," MacNutt said, disregarding the major's outburst. He knew the major was trying to buy time to figure a way out of the mess he had created.

"I have not had the pleasure," the major said, matching MacNutt's coolness.

"Come, Major, are you sure? He seems to know you quite well."

The major, for all of his arrogance, was no fool. He knew that he was in a difficult position. Simms couldn't help giving Evert a glare before answering, "If I do, it's no concern of yours."

"But it is, it is," MacNutt said persuasively, leaning forward in his chair. "I arrested Mr. Evert this morning for espionage." Simms' mouth dropped open. *He is actually speechless*, thought MacNutt. It lasted only a minute, but he found it very enjoyable.

"That's outrageous," Simms sputtered, his coolness quite gone. "Mr. Evert works for MI5."

"I know. But my question is what is Mr. Evert doing here? As far as I know, I did not request any assistance from M15. So, I'm just curious." When Simms didn't reply, MacNutt repeated, "What is he doing here?"

Simms glared at MacNutt. He replied in a condescending tone.

"It was obvious to everyone that this colony was being overrun with German spies. Your police force was not taking stern measures."

"So if I understand correctly," MacNutt said, slowly and clearly, "on your own initiative, you decided to involve MI5 in Canadian internal affairs."

Simms waggled his finger brusquely at MacNutt. "I called MI5 in to ensure the safety of His Royal Highness."

"The governor general's safety is a Canadian responsibility. If we had required imperial assistance, we would have asked for it," MacNutt retorted.

Simms sneered, "Your Secret Service does not inspire confidence."

"Really, how did you come by that conclusion?"

Simms turned to Evert and said, "Tell the good inspector what you told me." Evert, startled by the turn of events, stared uncomfortably at the floor.

"Yes, please do tell me," the inspector demanded.

After he coughed to clear his throat, Evert explained. "Based on information that the major had supplied me, I have been keeping Henderson's Tailor Shop owned by Mr. Denon under scrutiny. I believe that you are familiar with the man."

"Yes, I have heard of the name."

"Well, inspector, I have been keeping an eye on him for some time now. I have seen him meeting with quite a number of people of German descent and various other prominent people. I have a list, if you would like to read it."

MacNutt waved the statement away dismissively. "Major Simms, we have had Denon under surveillance since the beginning of the war. We have been reading all the letters and telegraphs that he sends and receives. We are well aware of all his activities."

Simms stared at MacNutt in disbelief. "I was unaware of this. Why was I not informed?" he demanded angrily.

MacNutt simply shrugged. "If you had a need to know, you would have been informed."

"The information I was given indicated that Denon was a dangerous sort. That he was consorting with German reservists in the United States and that he was helping them in their invasion of Canada," continued Evert, trying to support Major Simms.

"Really?" MacNutt raised an eyebrow, his interest piqued. He leaned forward in his chair. "Who supplied you with this information?"

Simms retorted. "It was given to me in the strictest confidence."

A hard edge entered the inspector's voice. "When it comes to the security of this country and the governor general, there are no strict confidences." MacNutt pointed to Evert. "Mr. Evert has already cost us valuable time and resources. Who gave you the information?"

Simms refused to budge. The phrasing that Simms used caused a light to go off in the inspector's mind. He chuckled when he realized who it was. Both Evert and the major stared at the inspector as if he had gone mad. MacNutt reached into his desk drawer and drew out a file folder with a red top-secret stripe on it. He tossed it to Simms.

"Read this! It may be of interest to you." The major opened the file. He jerked up at MacNutt when he read the first line. "Oh, yes," proclaimed MacNutt. "You might be interested in my conclusions on the last page."

"But Mrs. Ramsey is a lady of substance," sputtered Major Simms.

"Really?" MacNutt said again. "Let me reiterate my conclusions. None of these allegations have been confirmed by any other agency. Her suspicions are based on hearsay and rumours and are not supported by factual evidence."

Simms replied lamely, "She is a lady of quality."

MacNutt's expression said plainly that Simms was an amateur and a fool. "Leave the intelligence work to the professionals. We know what we are doing. In the future, stay out of Canadian affairs." He turned to Evert. "Mr. Evert, I'm afraid that the services of MI5 are not required. I wish you a safe and speedy journey back to England."

Simms interjected, "Inspector, he could still be of assistance. After all, there is a real German spy in Canada."

MacNutt's smile was stern. He was not about to back down now that he had the major on the ropes. "It is my opinion that Mr. Evert is not familiar enough with Canada and the States to be of much use to us in the investigation. Besides, Mr. Evert did not do me the courtesy of informing me of his presence here. I have wasted valuable time and manpower that could have been used more effectively."

"I'll have a word with the prime minister about this," Simms growled.

MacNutt simply shrugged. "By all means, if you think it would be wise. Borden might agree with you, but I wouldn't count on it. You do recall that little misunderstanding with the governor general at the beginning of the war?" Major Simms reddened with rage. MacNutt was alluding to the dispute as to who was actually in charge of the Canadian war effort. "No, Major Simms. I want Mr. Evert on the first available ship back to England."

Simms, seeing that MacNutt was holding all the cards, ordered, "Come, Evert." Evert rose from his chair and followed Simms out of the office.

"It went well," Lacelle said, standing in the doorway after they left.

MacNutt chuckled. "I did enjoy that. You'd better ensure that Evert leaves." Lacelle chortled as he grabbed his coat and hat and left the office.

CHAPTER 30

MacNutt estimated that the large crowd, which overflowed from Queen Street onto Sapper's Bridge, numbered about three thousand. Despite himself, he was impressed by the turnout. Three thousand Franco-Ontarian students carried placards and chanted "*Français, Français*" in front of City Hall. They were noisily protesting City Council's decision to withhold over $87,000 it had promised to the French Separate School Board. Whether Mayor Porter would accede to their noisy demands was doubtful. Curiosity got the better of MacNutt and he decided to get a better view. He walked down Sparks Street and turned left onto O'Connor Street. The crowd had spilled onto O'Connor, blocking the entrances to the YMCA and the Carnegie Library.

He recognized one of the Ottawa police officers monitoring the crowd. "Good morning, Sergeant Cain. Quite a crowd."

"I know. I knew that there was going to be a protest, but I didn't expect so many to come," the sergeant replied with concern.

"They seem peaceful so far," said MacNutt, scanning the crowd of mostly young students dressed in their Sunday best.

"So far," agreed the sergeant. Memories of the Guigues School rally were still fresh. "I just sent a message to the chief that we may need more men."

"Where is he going to get them?" asked MacNutt. The Ottawa police didn't have enough men if things got out of hand, and both men knew it wouldn't take much.

"I suggested that the 77th Battalion be placed on alert," the sergeant answered. MacNutt knew the 77th drilled regularly at Cartier Square a few blocks south of Queen Street near the canal. They would be able to arrive in a few minutes, if required.

"Good morning, Sergeant," said a voice behind them. MacNutt and Cain turned towards the voice and saw that it belonged to Fire Chief Graham. He studied the crowd with some concern. "Inspector," he observed curtly, "quite a crowd." He gestured at his main station, which was situated on Queen Street, near City Hall. "I hope that we don't get a call." The street and the main entrances to the station were blocked by the crowd.

"We'll clear a path if we need to," said the sergeant.

"It might not be fast enough, Sergeant. Every minute counts in a fire." Chief Graham came from a family of firefighters that included his father and three uncles. His father had been the first Ottawa firefighter to die in the line of duty, in 1877. His son was quite progressive, though he was reluctant to have the old fire bell removed from his station. He was currently pressing the city council to have phones installed in his firemen's homes to increase response times. Since he became chief in 1910, he was slowly but surely transforming the department into a modern motorized firefighting service.

MacNutt knew that the chief and Inspector Giroux, who was mainly responsible for fire protection on the Hill, generally got along, with just the occasional bit of friction. The chief made safety inspections and recommendations for the Hill, which Giroux then supported and instituted, such as having the May-Oatway alarm system installed on the Hill with a direct connection to the fire department. However, the chief's suggestion to have firemen instead of policemen patrolling federal government buildings did not sit well with Commissioner Sherwood, nor with the deputy ministers of Justice and Public Works. The general feeling was that the chief was trying to increase the strength of the City of Ottawa's fire department but was trying to upload the costs of the firemen to the federal government to make it palatable for City Council. It was unlikely his proposal would ever get federal government approval.

"Well, keep me apprised of the situation. You know where you can reach me," said Chief Graham.

"Yes, Chief," replied Sergeant Cain as the chief made his way through the crowd to his fire station.

MacNutt gave the crowd a final perusal then said as he turned towards the Hill, "I better be going, I have a ton of work to do. If your chief needs anything let me know."

"Right, Inspector," answered the sergeant. He had turned his attention back to the crowd, so he didn't see the inspector pause when he reached Spark Street. Something to his right had caught his attention, so he headed down Sparks towards the Russell Hotel.

RUSSELL HOTEL, ELGIN AND SPARKS STREETS, OTTAWA
3:30 P.M., MONDAY, JANUARY 31, 1916

"The Russell Hotel welcomes you and hopes that you have a pleasant stay," the clerk said as he handed the Count his room key.

"Thank you," answered the Count after signing the guest book. He and the clerk exchanged the pen for the room key. "I had a difficult time gaining entrance to the hotel. There is a large crowd outside. Some kind of protest?"

The clerk curled his lip. "It's the French Canadian students who are protesting. The city council decided to keep money from their school board."

"I don't understand," replied the Count, perplexed.

"Neither does anyone else," declared the clerk. Realizing he was on dangerous ground, he tried to change subjects. "If you have a need, don't hesitate to contact the front desk." The clerk then shifted his attention to someone behind the Count. "Inspector! Can I be of assistance?"

The Count turned and saw Inspector MacNutt approaching. A strange expression crossed the inspector's face, which puzzled the Count. For a fleeting moment he thought the inspector had discovered who he was and had come to arrest him, but the inspector was alone and he didn't appear to be armed. He may have found out about his wife's dalliance, but Jaggi knew the look of a jealous husband all too well, and he didn't see signs of it on MacNutt.

"Harold," the inspector said, nodding to the clerk, then, "Count."

"Inspector MacNutt, it's a pleasure meeting you again," said the Count, offering the inspector his hand with a smile.

"How was the trip from New York?" inquired MacNutt.

"Fatiguing. I can't wait to get to my room for a brief nap," replied the Count. "How is Mrs. MacNutt? I have a meeting with your wife tomorrow morning to discuss details for tomorrow night's lecture."

"She is well. She mentioned your meeting to me this morning," returned the inspector coolly.

It was obvious MacNutt did not care for him. Had whispers reached his ears? One more worry. "Well, I'd better be off to my room," stated the Count with a quick grin. "It's a pleasure seeing you again."

"Till then, Count Jaggi," said the inspector. The Count could feel MacNutt's eyes boring into his back as he walked to the elevator. When he entered and turned to face the doors, he saw the clerk hand the inspector the guest book he had just signed.

GANDAR'S ROOMING HOUSE, SOUTH AND WHITEHALL STREETS,
BROOKLYN, NEW YORK CITY
5:07 A.M., TUESDAY, FEBRUARY 1, 1916

Barnitz was standing outside the rooming house on the corner of South and Whitehall Streets, near the Battery District. He glanced at his watch, which in the early morning light read 5:07. Most of the occupants would be asleep and would give his men few problems, he hoped. He spoke to the man standing beside him. "It's time."

Corporal Roma acknowledged by saying, "I think that they should be in position by now."

"They better be," Barnitz said curtly. "The captain would not be happy if anyone got away."

"I know," answered Roma.

Barnitz turned his attention to the rooming house across the street, which was their target. For some time, the Bomb Squad had been investigating a series of mysterious fires and explosions on a number of ships. Barnitz had reviewed the files so often that he had the list memorized: on Jan 3, 1915, the steamship *Otton* suffered an explosion; in early February, a bomb was discovered in the cargo hold of the *Bennington Court*; in late February, the steamship *Carleton* caught fire; in April, the *Cressington Court* caught fire while at sea; in May, two bombs were found in the cargo hold of the *Lord Erne*; and a week later, a bomb was found in the hold of the *Devon City*.

After months of investigations, they had very few leads. They finally got a break when four bombs in sugar bags were discovered in the hold of the steamship *Kerkoswald*, out of New York, that had docked in Marseilles. They had requested that one of the bomb casings be returned to the New York Bomb Squad for analysis. Further investigations revealed that nearly all the ships that had had fires or explosions had also had sugar cargoes. Since sugar was highly flammable, it made fighting the ship fires very difficult.

They began to investigate the sugar trade, trying to find leads to the bomb makers. Initially, they tried to follow the sugar bags but quickly ran into problems. All sugar bags that went aboard were either hand or machine-stitched. The machine-stitched bags were the hardest to tamper with, because any attempt left easily identifiable traces. The only time that the bags could be tampered with was en route from the refinery to the cargo vessel. Once the bags were loaded on the lighters, the lighters were next to impossible to follow. Most sailed at night, which meant the captains were cautious of any approaching ship for fear of collision. The Bomb Squad patrol boat's loud motor, which could be heard for nearly half a mile, didn't help. When they did cut the motor and drifted, they lost the ship they were tracking. Other times they got the ship's lights confused and ended up following the wrong ship. They tried putting undercover men on the lighters, but that didn't work either, since they stood out as police officers.

The Bomb Squad went back and reviewed the shipping records and identified the lighters. They matched the lighters with the ships that had suffered fires or had bombs found aboard. Once the captains were identified, they were followed, on the theory that they would lead to the bomb makers. They soon discovered that their theory was wrong. Instead, the men were simply involved in pilfering sugar and selling it for a black-market profit.

They were still following the captains, because the fires and explosions continued. One of the lighters they were following was the *Sally Ann*. Barnitz had two men on the docks the previous night when the lighter unloaded her cargo. One of his men followed the cargo to a warehouse, while the other man followed the members of the crew to the boarding house across the street. Both the warehouse and the rooming house were being raided this morning.

"Let's go," said Barnitz. He and Roma crossed the street.

* * *

Müller was asleep in a room on the third floor of the boarding house when voices woke him. It took a moment to clear his mind. Then he heard someone shouting "Police." He froze in fear. When he could finally get his arms and legs to move, he hurriedly tugged on his trousers and coat and pulled on his shoes. He rushed to fling open the window, but it took a couple of tugs before frame would budge. He opened it just wide enough to get his chest through. When he had stuck his head out, a voice called, "Going somewhere?"

When he saw the policeman on the fire escape, Müller jerked his back in and made for the rooming house door, but it burst open before he could reach it, and two police offices rushed in, billy clubs at the ready.

"*Nein, nein!*" he shouted. He knew it was stupid, but fear made him charge the men in a desperate hope that he could break free.

One of the police officers swore then swung his billy club at the charging Müller, catching him in the chest. With the wind knocked out of him, Müller was forced to his knees, gasping for breath. The other officer roughly pulled his arms behind his back so that he fell face first onto the dirty wooden floor. Handcuffs bit painfully into his wrists. Then the groggy Müller was hauled up to his feet and roughly led, half stumbling, out of the room.

CHAPTER 31

The egg slipped out of Katherine's hand and fell on the kitchen floor. "Damn," she yelled as she stared at the broken egg. This was the second item she had dropped this morning. She hoped it wasn't a sign of how her day was going to go. She wished that it were Saturday, the day that her maid, Isabelle, came in to clean. She picked up a dish rag from a drawer, wetted it, and bent down to wipe the mess. She rose from the floor, rinsed the cloth in the sink, and turned to start breakfast for Andrew, who would be down soon.

"Good morning," he said behind her.

"Good morning. I didn't hear you come down."

Andrew was concerned when he saw the shadows under her eyes. "You look tired. Didn't you sleep last night?"

"I'm fine," replied Katherine, turning to crack a new egg into the frying pan of eggs already started on the stove. In fact, she had only managed to drift off near dawn.

She shook the frying pan gently so that the eggs wouldn't stick to the pan. Behind her, she heard Andrew pull a chair out from the table, then the creak as he sat down on it. She slid two eggs onto a plate beside two slices of bread and several rashers of crisp bacon, then placed the plate before Andrew. She placed another plate for herself on the table. She picked up the coffee pot from the stove and poured out cups. Then she sat down opposite him.

They ate in silence for a few minutes until Andrew finally spoke. "I saw the Count yesterday."

"You did?" Katherine glanced at her husband as she lifted her fork to her mouth. "Where?"

"At the Russell when he was checking in."

Katherine didn't like the way he was watching her. "I didn't realize that he was staying at the Russell," she replied.

"Where did you think he was staying? The lecture is at the Russell, isn't it?"

"I thought he might be staying at the Château," replied Katherine. She was surprised at the hint of jealousy that flickered in his eyes. The flicker didn't disappear when she continued, "That's where he stayed the last time he was in Ottawa."

"When are you meeting him today?" asked Andrew as he pierced one of the bacon strips with his fork.

"This afternoon. Why do you ask?"

"Just curious as to your plans," he said, giving her a brief smile.

"The Belgian Relief committee will meet this afternoon to go over some final details. Then we plan to have supper with the Count before the lecture," she explained, her voice beginning to rise. His expression irritated her.

Andrew put up his hands in surrender. "I was just asking, dear."

"Sorry, I felt you were interrogating me for some reason," replied a tight-lipped Katherine.

"Occupational hazard with my job. You know that," he said with an exaggerated sigh. "So you will be home late this evening." He stood up to get the coffee pot from the stove then drained the last of the coffee.

"You will have to make your own supper," answered Katherine, still annoyed.

"I'll manage. It's not the first time," replied Andrew with a hint of a scowl. "I better go or I'll be late for work."

"Please be careful, Andrew," said Katherine out of habit.

"Always," said Andrew. He pushed back his chair and headed to the front hall without another word.

RUSSELL HOTEL, ELGIN AND SPARKS STREETS, OTTAWA
8:00 P.M., TUESDAY, FEBRUARY 1, 1916

"I don't know," said Katherine to Nicole when they entered the Russell from the Elgin Street entrance.

"Well, if the Manitoba government gave women the right to vote, I don't understand why the Ontario government won't do the same thing," argued Nicole.

Katherine snorted. "If President Wilson didn't think that women should have the vote, what makes you think that an Orange Ontario government is going to do any different?"

"Tell me about it," said Nicole. She was an ardent suffragette and a great admirer of Nellie McClung. She had gotten a hoot out of the mock parliament where McClung pointed out the ludicrousness of the men denying women the right to vote. "Well, one day they will recognize our right to vote."

"Do you think it will make a difference?"

Nicole shrugged. "It can't be any worse." Katherine laughed. Nicole asked, "Where are we meeting the Count again?"

"We are supposed to meet him in the lobby, then we will go to the restaurant straightaway for supper," answered Katherine. "After the lecture, we have a reservation for coffee and dessert."

"Sounds good. There he is." Nicole pointed out the Count, who was conversing with Mrs. Ramsey and Claire, Belgian Relief's accountant.

"Oh, great," muttered Katherine under her breath. Nicole overheard her and grinned. Katherine put on a smile then said cheerfully, "Count, it's so good to see you again."

Mrs. Ramsey glowered at the interruption.

"Mrs. MacNutt, it's my pleasure," replied the Count, causing Mrs. Ramsey to give him one of her infamous sharp looks. He irritated her more when he smiled brightly at Katherine.

Katherine cocked her head. "Mrs. Ramsey."

"Mrs. MacNutt," Mrs. Ramsay said frostily. Her eyes jumped from Katherine to the Count and back. "I understand that the opening of the Sir Fleming home went well. From what I heard the governor general was pleased by what he saw," she commented, trying to steer the conversation.

"Yes, it did," replied Katherine. "Were you able to make it? I didn't see you there."

"Unfortunately, I had other commitments," she said cryptically.

"Convalescent home?" inquired the Count.

"The Women's Canadian Club is sponsoring two wards at the Sir Sandford Fleming convalescent home for the recuperating wounded soldiers. It was officially opened yesterday," explained Katherine. "It's heart-breaking seeing the wounded soldiers." The pain in her voice was evident.

Mrs. Ramsey broke the silence. "Are we ready for dinner?"

"Of course," answered the Count. "Shall we?" He bowed gallantly, which brought shy grins from the ladies. Katherine made a point of standing beside the Count, forcing Mrs. Ramsey to walk behind them.

"Are you ready for the lecture?" asked Katherine.

"Of course," said the Count, tapping his coat pocket. Then horror appeared on his face.

314

"The speech?" he muttered.

"What about the speech?"

"I don't have it."

"Did you leave it in your room?"

"No, I'm sure I put it in my pocket before I came down."

"You lost the speech!" Katherine exclaimed in disbelief as she stopped in her tracks. When a teasing smile crept over the Count's face, Katherine's hair shook in exasperation. "Don't do that! You gave me such a fright. It's not right to tease us like that, is it, Mrs. Ramsey?" Katherine glanced at Mrs. Ramsey, who reluctantly nodded.

"I'm sorry. Please, do you forgive me, *Mesdames*?"

"Of course we will, Count, but we will make you sing for your supper," Katherine said gaily as they entered the restaurant.

* * *

When the Count entered his hotel room a few hours later, he took off his jacket and dropped it onto the back of a chair. As he loosened his tie, he took a bottle of good-quality brandy he had brought back with him from New York and poured out a glass. He dropped with a tired thud into the chair, picked up the tumbler, and tossed back the contents. It had been a long day but a satisfying one. The lecture had gone better than he expected. About two to three hundred people were in attendance, and they managed to raise about $475.00, a tidy sum.

He was disappointed with Katherine. While she did not speak directly on the topic, she had made it abundantly clear to him that what had happened between them in New York was a one-time fling. Unfortunate, since he had enjoyed himself immensely with her and would have been glad to have another go. Several ladies at the gathering had subtly signalled their interest, but for once he wasn't in the mood. Best not to burn any bridges if he didn't have to. He pulled a sheet of paper and a pen from the room's desk drawer so that he could write Katherine a thank-you note for all that she had done.

CHAPTER 32

Katherine was lying in bed with her eyes closed, trying to identify what had awakened her. It took a few moments to realize that it was Andrew quietly trying to get dressed. The sounds of a bureau drawer being pulled open and the creaking of the closet door were sufficient to wake her.

"What are you trying to find, Andrew?" she demanded groggily as she opened her eyes. She was facing the window, and there was a small tinge of grey in the night sky.

"Sorry, Katherine. I didn't mean to wake you." He had slept in the spare room and had been trying, rather ineptly, to get a change of clothes without waking her.

"What time is it?" she asked as she rolled over to face him. She pulled the comforter up to her neck to keep the chill from penetrating the warm bed. When he turned on the light, she squinted until she adjusted to the brightness.

"Six thirty," he replied.

"God, that early," she exclaimed.

"I'm afraid so."

"You want me to get up and make breakfast?" she asked. She really didn't feel like it, since she was still feeling exhausted from the previous night. She had started to pull the comforter down when Andrew stopped her by shaking his head.

"You went to bed late last night. I was hoping to be off to the office without waking you." He came over and tucked the comforter back in around her.

"Why are you going in so early?"

"Just some business at the office that I need to deal with," he answered. "How did it go last night?"

"It went very well. We raised nearly $475.00."

"Impressive."

"Well, we had nearly three hundred people there to listen to the Count's lecture."

"That's good to hear," replied Andrew. "You were kind of tense and worried about it."

Katherine nodded. "Don't remind me. Mrs. Ramsey was no help."

Andrew snorted. "Tell me about it. I need to chat with her today."

"Oh really? Lucky you," said Katherine with a lack of sympathy. "Work-related?"

"Unfortunately, yes. It appears that she's meddling in affairs she really shouldn't be involved in." He was not looking forward to the conversation, but it had to be done.

Katherine's ears perked up. "What did she do now?"

Andrew sighed. "Unfortunately, I can't talk about it."

"I don't know why not. I'll probably find out in the end," Katherine pointed out.

"Well, not from me you won't," muttered Andrew. After a moment's pause, he continued. "So the Count gave a good lecture?"

Katherine knew that he was trying to deflect her questions concerning Mrs. Ramsey, but she needed to be cautious in what she said about the Count. "He did. He spoke for two hours and practically no one left the room."

"What did you do after the lecture?"

"The girls and the Count and I went to celebrate in the Russell Hotel restaurant," she said. She wasn't so sleepy, she didn't recognize that he was probing. *Does he know?*

Andrew smiled then said, "So what are your plans for the day? Will you be seeing the Count?"

Katherine returned Andrew's gaze and said truthfully, "No. I was planning to go to Sir Fleming's this afternoon and visit some of the soldiers."

"I see," said Andrew as he put on his socks.

"Will you be home for supper?"

Andrew stood up. "I think so. But I'll call if I'm going to be late." He paused at the door. "Do you want the lights off?"

"Yes, please. Bye, Andrew. Say hi to Lacelle for me."

"I will." He switched off the lights as he left the bedroom.

INSPECTOR MACNUTT'S OFFICE, EAST BLOCK,
PARLIAMENT HILL, OTTAWA
7:00 P.M., WEDNESDAY, FEBRUARY 2, 1916

MacNutt entered his office around seven that evening to find Sergeant Lacelle still at his desk. A number of ledgers and registers in various shades of black, brown, and red covered the desk. The sergeant was diligently going through them again. They might have missed something during their initial examination.

"Still here?" remarked the inspector.

The bleary-eyed sergeant looked up from the battered ledger he was thumbing through. "*Oui.* I've gone through about a third of them again. I've found a couple of new names that I've added to the list. I'll send a constable to check them out tomorrow."

"Anything solid to go on?"

Lacelle replied dully, "Dead ends, more likely."

"Damn. We know that he's been in town. I really would like to get a solid lead on the man," said an exasperated MacNutt.

"The time we spent with Simms' agent set us back," Lacelle pointed out.

"Don't remind me."

"How did the interview go with Mrs. Ramsey?" asked Lacelle wearily.

"A vile woman," hissed the inspector.

The sergeant winced. "That well?"

"I had to take a walk to cool off," MacNutt growled. He then changed the subject. "Have you gone through the Château's books yet?"

"No, why?"

"The manager over at the Château wanted to know when we would be returning them. It seems that they are expecting one of the GTR inspectors sometime this week," MacNutt explained.

Lacelle acknowledged with a slow nod. "Their inspectors are tough. I could start on them tonight."

"No," commanded the inspector. "It's been a long day. I want you to go home to Marie and the little ones. I need you fresh tomorrow morning. I'll take the registers and go through them myself."

"Are you sure?"

"Yes, Sergeant, I'm sure," MacNutt replied. He glanced at the clock and grimaced. "I better be off myself. Katherine will not be happy that I'll be late for supper."

"Yes, sir," said Lacelle. "We have to keep our wives happy on occasion." MacNutt broke into a grin.

Lacelle rummaged through the various date books and ledgers until he found the black leather registers with "Château Laurier" embossed in gold letters and handed them to the inspector.

"Do you need a copy of the intercepts?"

MacNutt shook his head as he took the volumes. "I still have my copy. It should be in my office unless I have taken them home."

"*Bien. Bon soir. À demain*," Lacelle said.

"Until tomorrow," said the inspector as he headed into his inner office.

CHAPTER 33

Katherine knew that Andrew was not yet home when she walked up the path to the dark house. She shivered slightly as a gust of cold wind whipped her coat around her legs. The lights from the neighbouring houses lit the path to her front porch. She checked the white-painted wooden mailbox beside the door for mail and pulled out a small bundle of letters. When she entered the hallway she deposited the letters temporarily in the brass bowl sitting on the entrance table. She then found the switch and turned on the lights. She took off her gloves, hat, and fur coat and hung them on the coat tree. She placed her boots on the wooden rack above the floor registers so they could dry.

She was a bit surprised at how chilly the house felt. She thought sufficient coal had been shovelled into the furnace to keep the house warm for most of the day. She would have to go down in the basement to check. When her eyes fell on Jamie's silver-framed picture on the living room mantel, she walked over and caressed it. She felt the weight of her tiredness and melancholy. She sighed and returned to retrieve the mail she had left in the entrance then took it into Andrew's office.

Most of the letters were bills, but she stopped when she found a small envelope addressed to her. She recognized the Russell Hotel's stationery and the now-familiar handwriting. She absent-mindedly placed the bills on top of a manila folder that her husband had left on the corner of his desk. She broke the seal and pulled out the small folded note. She smiled fondly when she read Count Jaggi's message.

When she turned to leave Andrew's office, her hip hit the corner of the manila folder that overhung the corner, knocking it and the envelopes off the desk. As the folder fell, it spilled several sheets of paper. She was so tired that it didn't particularly upset her, since it just was the continuation of her day. Resigned, she bent down to pick up the folder and the papers. As she was arranging the papers back into the folder, one of them caused her to freeze.

She picked up the paper in surprise. What was Andrew doing with one of the Count's letters? It took her a moment to notice the cyphers between the lines, then her eyes were drawn to the signature at the bottom. She stared at it in disbelief. It wasn't the Count's name signed there.

When her mind started working, she sorted out the papers and began to read her husband's file. She had to reread the file a second time before the truth finally sank in. She muttered, "What am I to do?" She rubbed the tears away, telling herself that the man was not worth them. The Count was a spy. He was a dirty, stinking Hun spy. "The fucking bastard!" she yelled out loudly to the empty room, her anger igniting.

She knew then what she had to do. She just knew. She went over to the gun cabinet and pulled the Colt .45 from its case. She knew Andrew kept the gun unloaded in the house, but there was a box of cartridges on the gun cabinet's shelf that was in easy reach. She opened the box and slid five cartridges into the revolver's six chambers. She left the chamber under the hammer empty as she had been taught to do. Her father had insisted that everyone should know how to handle a firearm safely. In the entrance, she put on her winter clothes. She stuffed the gun in her fur muff and left the house.

She didn't turn off the lights when she left. She also left the Count's note on Andrew's desk on top of the manila folder.

* * *

When Andrew walked up the path to his front door, he was worried about Katherine's mood. He was late for supper. When he closed the door, he put his briefcase on the table and took off his winter gear. He fully expected Katherine to check on him or at least shout out, "Is that you, Andrew?" It took him a moment to register that he hadn't heard a sound from her. He sighed. He would likely be sleeping in the spare bedroom again tonight.

He felt the chill in the house. He took the stairs to the basement, opened the coal furnace door, and stoked the embers in case he needed to light it. Satisfied that it was still lit, he picked up the shovel and tossed in enough coal to heat the house till morning. When he came upstairs, he glanced at the closed kitchen door. The lack of sound or smell of food cooking seemed strange, but he assumed she didn't want to be disturbed. He picked up the briefcase he had left on the hallway table and took it into his office.

Still feeling the chill, he went over to the fireplace and tossed a couple of logs on the hearth. He put some kindling and newspapers under the logs and lighted them with a long wooden match. When he was satisfied that the logs had ignited, he went to the liquor cabinet, took out a bottle of ten-year-old rye, and poured himself a glass. He tossed back the rye then poured himself another. He walked over to the desk and sat in the chair carefully so he wouldn't spill any of the drink. He finally noticed the mail bundle that Katherine had placed on the desk. He flipped through the letters, and seeing that they were bills, he placed them back where he had found them. He then noticed the Russell Hotel stationery sitting on top of the red-striped manila folder. Curiously, he picked up it and read it. He grimaced when he finished reading the Count's note. The note had a tone of familiarity that irritated him, especially in light of Mrs. Ramsey's not-so-subtle insinuations that she'd repeated earlier in the afternoon. The real question was, did he believe that there was something going on between the Count and his wife? He really didn't want to think about that. He considered what he should do and decided it was best to do nothing, since the Count would be gone before long.

He tossed the note onto the desk and then opened the manila folder. He didn't think much of the fact that the intercepted letter was the first page of the file. Although he knew the contents by heart, he picked it up to reread it. He had barely read the first word when he stopped and stared at the letter. His eyes flickered to the note he had just tossed aside then back to the letter he was holding.

He carefully laid the letter and note side by side on the leather blotter so he could compare the two. No, his eyes had not deceived him. He leaned back in his chair and began to laugh grimly. All this time the German agent had been under his nose. The Hun spy that he had been hunting for weeks was the Count. Then the ramifications hit him, and he groaned. It was bad enough that they had discovered an escaped internee working at an ammunition plant, especially one scheduled for a tour by the governor general. But to uncover a Hun spy who had close contact with the prime minister and members of his cabinet would cause much embarrassment and consternation. He could already hear Mrs. Ramsey's cackle.

Unfortunately, he didn't have much choice. He had to call Lacelle and tell him they needed to pick up the Count. He rose quickly from his chair to go to the phone, which sat on a table beside the gun cabinet. When he reached for the receiver he stopped when he noticed that there was an empty space where his new Colt .45 normally rested. When he saw the open box of cartridges, he snapped back to the note, the intercept letter, and the bundle of mail. His eyes widen suddenly when he realized how the mail had made its way onto his desk. "Katherine," he shouted. "Katherine!" No answer! Growing frantic, he rushed to check the kitchen, then ran upstairs calling all the while. No sign of her.

When he came back to his office he hurriedly pulled a .38 Smith & Wesson revolver out of the gun cabinet and jammed six rounds into the cylinder. He put the gun and some loose cartridges into his coat pocket. He rushed into the hallway, thrust on his winter overcoat, and dashed out of the house. He had found the elusive spy, and now he was desperately searching for his wife. He hoped that he would find her in time.

CHAPTER 34

When Count Jaggi walked out of the Russell Hotel, he stuffed his hands into fleece-lined leather gloves, and then pulled down his hat firmly as the wind was threatening to remove it.

He paused as he eyed the scattered patches of ice on the sidewalk as they reflected the lights that lit Sparks Street. He debated whether he should keep the appointment he had on Parliament Hill. He was to meet Senator Mead, a member of the Senate's railway committee, which made him a potential source of information on the vulnerabilities of the Canadian railway system.

He sighed. Spending his last night in Ottawa alone didn't appeal to him. A ticket for the morning train to New York sat on his hotel room desk. Ever since he gave his speech, he had been feeling somewhat restless. He finally admitted to himself that spending most of his time from now on in New York was what bothered him. That would make Müller happy, he knew, since he would finally be concentrating on developing schemes that could hurt the Allies. However, it made the prospects of seeing Katherine again rather slim.

She should have received my thank you note by now, he thought. *Maybe an extra trip or two wouldn't hurt.* He might be able to use the excuse that he had to visit Ottawa periodically to maintain the contacts he had developed here, such as the senator. But he needed to keep the trips infrequent, since he didn't want to raise questions about why he was visiting Ottawa so often.

He frowned when he realized he hadn't heard anything from Müller. He wasn't sure if that was a good or bad thing. With the many disasters they had suffered so far, the von Papen papers incident still irked him; Müller could be reluctant to inform him of more bad news.

Maybe I should stay in Canada, he thought. He did have a second set of papers, hidden in the lining of one of his suitcases, so he could easily disappear. Then he laughed ruefully as he shook off his pessimism. Sooner or later things would turn his way. *Duty,* he thought as he headed to the Hill. He just had to face what he had to face in New York when he got there.

LOBBY, RUSSELL HOTEL, ELGIN AND SPARKS STREETS, OTTAWA
8:30 P.M., THURSDAY, FEBRUARY 3,1916

Inspector MacNutt entered the nearly empty lobby of the Russell Hotel at a running walk. He was breathing hard, and he needed a few moments to bring his breathing back to normal as he walked briskly across the lobby. Donald, the desk clerk, looked up as MacNutt was halfway to the elevators. He pursed his lips when he saw the inspector's agitated state. He had seen that particular face on other men before. He called out a greeting, a smile on his lips. "Aye, good evening, Inspector! Is there anything I can help you with?"

"Good evening, Donald," MacNutt replied distractedly, staring at the dial above the elevator. The car was still on its way down. He focused his attention on Donald. "Is Count Jaggi in this evening?" MacNutt shot him a piercing gaze.

Donald raised his eyebrows in surprise. The Count was much in demand this evening. "Is there a problem?"

MacNutt wanted to say yes, but he shook his head. "I was to have a meeting with the Count," he said. Donald was still smiling. MacNutt knew that for some reason Donald didn't believe him. Right now he didn't care.

"Did he say where he would be this evening?" asked the inspector.

Donald's mouth twitched slightly. He was trying to prevent a smirk. "I'll tell you the same as I told Mrs. MacNutt earlier this evening."

"My wife was here this evening?" the inspector demanded. Donald was taken aback by the ferocity of the inspector's glare.

"Yes. Five minutes ago. She was asking for the Count too."

"What did you tell her?"

"That the last I heard, he was meeting an MP on the Hill."

Without another word MacNutt sprinted to the exit. Donald, slightly ruffled, returned to his duties, muttering under his breath. He really wished that married couples would keep their private squabbles at home where they belonged, and out of his hotel.

GOVERNMENT BENCHES, HOUSE OF COMMONS,
CENTRE BLOCK, PARLIAMENT BUILDING, OTTAWA
8:45 P.M., THURSDAY, FEBRUARY 3, 1916

Borden was sitting at his usual seat in the House of Commons, in the middle of the front row on the speaker's right, listening unhappily to one of the opposition members making a speech. When the diatribe ended, Dr. John Reid, the minister of customs, got up from his front bench seat and approached Borden. He leaned forward and whispered, "Prime Minister, it's nearly twenty to nine. Why don't you call it a day? I doubt very much anything important will happen in the debates. At least not tonight."

Borden frowned as he glanced across the House at Sir Wilfrid Laurier's empty seat in the Opposition's front benches. Laurier had left earlier, which signalled that he too expected a quiet evening. The black silk-robed clerks of the House of Commons, who sat at one of two long oak tables set end to end in front of him, had the weary air of men who had been cooped up for a long, boring day with little prospect of excitement. They were required to remain in their seats at the table closest to the Speaker's chair, in case they were needed to provide help and procedural advice to the speaker or House members. They also recorded any decisions made in the House, though it was unlikely there would be decisions this evening with only one-quarter of the 221 members in attendance. There were still a respectable number of murmuring spectators in the galleries above the House at this late hour. The Hansard reporters, who sat at the second table, the one farthest away from the speaker, were writing furiously, trying to record every word of the speech that one of the members was starting to make.

Borden's eyes fell on to Hughes' empty seat, and he grimaced. The prime minister was grateful that the general was attending a meeting at the Château this evening. If he had been in his seat, the House would have been full and the Opposition would now be viciously attacking his minister of militia and defence about the activities of the Shell Committee.

"You're right, John," he murmured. "I have some correspondence that I need to clear up. I'd rather be doing that. If something comes up that needs my attention, send a page to my office. I'll be there for another hour or so."

"Yes, Prime Minister," replied Dr. Reid, who returned to his seat.

Borden grunted as he rose from his seat. He bowed respectfully to Rhodes, the deputy speaker who occupied the speaker's chair this evening instead of Sévigny, who had handed over the chair to his deputy when he had to leave for some pressing business. When Borden took the exit behind the speaker's chair, he turned briskly right and strolled to his Centre Block office in the northwest corner of the new wing. Two offices were maintained for the prime minister, one in the Centre Block and the other in the East Block. Borden used his Centre Block office when the House was sitting, to be close to action, so to speak. When questions arose that required consultation with the prime minister or a quick tactical decision, having Borden a few minutes away was reassuring.

Where the New Wing and the Centre Block joined, he ran into Senator Mead, who was giving a guest a tour of the building. It took Borden a couple of seconds to associate a name with the guest's face, which he recognized. He was tempted to stop and chat with Count Jaggi about the success of his Belgian Relief speech, but he reluctantly decided not to. He was beginning to feel tired, and he had some paperwork to do before he called it a day. He gave the men a nod as he continued to his office. The last he saw of them was Mead leading the Count down the speaker's corridor to the reading room.

When he entered his office he was greeted by his secretary, Boyce, who was sitting at his desk signing a document. "Good evening, Prime Minister."

"Have you gone through my correspondence?" Borden asked pleasantly.

"Yes, Prime Minister. It's on your desk." Boyce indicated with his chin. Boyce, familiar with his likes and dislikes, had removed any letters dealing with patronage requests. When Borden first took office, there had been enormous pressure from his party to replace outside Liberal civil service appointments — outside meaning those not based in Ottawa — with Conservative ones, as was the normal custom. Borden had resisted. He felt it was below the dignity of the prime minister's office to be involved in the political appointment of a dog-catcher in Halifax. Dealing with these appointments also consumed most of his Saturday morning Privy Council meetings, time that could be better spent on other, more important issues. He had received heavy criticism from his party because they thought it was political suicide. "Will you be staying late tonight?"

"A couple of hours. I don't want to stay too late, or Mrs. Borden will get worried," answered Borden.

"Yes, Prime Minister. If you need anything, please let me know."

"Thank you, Boyce. Good work," Borden said.

He sat down slowly in his leather chair. He pinched the bridge between his eyes tiredly and began studying the letters that his secretary had screened, sorted, and prioritized.

VICTORIA TOWER ENTRANCE, CENTRE BLOCK,
PARLIAMENT HILL, OTTAWA
8:45 P.M., THURSDAY, FEBRUARY 3, 1916

Constable Edwards yawned as he adjusted the leather strap on his right shoulder that was attached to his guard tour clock to a more comfortable position. He wasn't tired. He was simply bored. Not to the extent that he was falling asleep, but bored. He had started at four and had more than seven hours to go on his twelve-hour shift. Just then the clock tower began to bong. As he listened, it told him that it was nearly 8:45. He sighed. It had been a quiet evening so far, and it looked as though it would be even duller. After nine, the Centre Block essentially shut down as most of the visitors and guests were escorted out of the building. The remaining MPs, senators, and essential staff might remain for a few more hours to complete their duties. The prospect of the night security rounds didn't enliven his mood. When he joined the force he was hoping for some excitement, but all he did was wander the Parliament Buildings at night and use the keys, found in strategic locations, to set the time on the water canteen-style timepiece he carried slung over his right shoulder, resting at his left hip. The intervals recorded would be verified by the duty sergeant the next morning to make sure that he had actually made his sweep.

He straightened his back when the opening of the entrance's huge oak doors caught his attention. He didn't want the night duty sergeant, Sergeant Carroll, put him on report for slouching. He was somewhat surprised to discover that it was Mrs. MacNutt.

"Good evening, Mrs. MacNutt," he said nervously as he rose from his stool. He gave Katherine a skittish salute.

"Good evening, Constable Edwards," said Katherine. She gave him a quick glance then her gaze darted about the deserted lobby.

"How can I help you this evening?" asked Edwards as she approached him. Mrs. MacNutt appeared pale and somewhat distracted.

"I'm looking for a friend of mine. Did you by any chance see him this evening?" she demanded.

"If I may, who is your friend?" inquired Edwards.

"Count Jaggi," she blurted.

"Ah," the constable said carefully. He had heard some of the whispers concerning Mrs. MacNutt and the Count. He hadn't thought them at all credible, until now. He knew the rumour's source and it would not have been the first time the woman used innuendo to destroy someone's reputation. "Yes, he did pass through earlier this evening. He was meeting Senator Mead in the reading room."

"The reading room?"

"Yes, ma'am," the constable said quietly. He didn't like Katherine's agitation, but he wasn't about to interfere with the inspector's wife.

"Thank you," she shouted as she marched rapidly in the direction of the reading room.

Constable Edwards watched her disappear up the short flight of stairs that led towards the Senate. He frowned sourly, disappointed that there might be some truth to the rumours. He had always liked Mrs. MacNutt.

READING ROOM, CENTRE BLOCK, PARLIAMENT HILL, OTTAWA
8:50 P.M., THURSDAY, FEBRUARY 3, 1916

"Ah, Count, the things I could reveal," the Senator remarked to the Count as a curl of smoke escaped from his lips. Senator Mead was an elderly, overweight man with a large, bushy moustache.

The Count grinned and puffed on the cigar that the Senator had given him. "Reveal them, please." He then gave the senator his best innocent face. "Who would I tell?'

The senator guffawed and gave him a shrewd appraisal. "I'm a bagman, Count. I haven't survived so long by having a loose tongue."

The men were standing in the reading room at one of the tables nearest the House of Commons. It was ironic that there was a "No Smoking" card prominently displayed on the table near the newspapers that hung on the racks along the wall. The senator had ignored the dirty glare from one of the reading room's staff members when he lit his cigar. He knew there was little they could do but complain to the speaker.

With their backs turned away from the Senate entrance, Katherine quietly entered the room. When she saw the Count, her expression hardened, but she didn't slow her quiet approach toward the two men.

Her motion caught the Senator's attention. He turned then gave a start when he recognized Katherine. He had heard the whispers about the Count and Inspector MacNutt's spouse. The Count turned too. The grin died on his lips when he saw her paleness. *She knows.* How she knew, he didn't know or care. Only that that she knew.

"Senator," intoned Katherine coldly, her angry eyes fixed on the Count. The senator glanced at the grim-faced Count then back to Katherine. Rumours were his stock in trade, and it seemed to him now that he was caught in the middle of a lovers' spat. It would be prudent to disentangle himself as smoothly as he could and leave them to it.

He glanced at his wristwatch and saw that it was nearly nine o'clock. "It's been a long day — best that I be on my way. Count, if you are still in Ottawa tomorrow, stop by my office. We'll have lunch," he suggested with a very thin smile, heaving himself to his feet. "It's been a pleasure, Mrs. MacNutt," he said. Without a fuss he withdrew from the room. The last thing they saw of him was a puff of cigar smoke as the glass-panelled doors swung closed behind him.

Katherine's angry gaze had not wavered from the Count. He returned her glare as he managed to draw calmly on his cigar, causing the tip to glow brightly. His calm demeanour enraged Katherine.

"I know what you are," she hissed. Those were the same words she had said when they first met, just outside the post office. Again, she pulled her hand from her fur muff, this time clenched around a large revolver. She pointed it at him. "For you."

The Count's hesitation was very brief. Guns had been pointed at him before by men who could put a bullet into him and not lose any sleep over it. Katherine could still shoot him, but he knew her well enough to be sure that she would need a great deal of provocation.

"What am I?" he asked, stalling.

"You are a Hun spy!" she spat.

"Whatever gave you that idea?" He took a step towards her with a disarming smile. "Please, Katherine, give me the gun before someone gets hurt."

"Stay back," Katherine ordered. The gun did not waver in her hands. "I know you are a Hun spy. I found your letters in one of my husband's files."

"You what?" exclaimed the Count with a start.

"Yes. Don't lie to me. Andrew has your letters. He has been searching for a Hun spy for the last month, and it was you all this time."

The Count reeled. If Katherine knew, her husband couldn't be far behind. He needed to get out of Ottawa now! He looked her in the face then tossed his cigar at her head. Her eyes widened in fear and she ducked, as he knew she would. The moment's distraction allowed him to grab the hand holding the gun with his left hand and twist her wrist hard to the right. Unnoticed, the cigar landed on top of several newspapers that had fallen on to the floor from the racks above.

Katherine yelped as intense pain radiated up her wrist. Her sight dimmed to a grey haze. She tried to squeeze the trigger, but her finger refused to function. As the Count kept twisting her wrist to right, increasing the pressure, Katherine's shoulder groaned as he forced it to lean in that direction. The paralysis from the agony made it easy for the Count to take the gun out of her hand.

"Take your filthy hands off her!"

The Count jerked when he recognized the voice. He held his breath when he twisted his gaze towards the inspector. This man, he knew, wouldn't hesitate. He hurriedly tried to bring the Colt up into a firing position, but the precious seconds that he needed to change his grip on the revolver allowed the inspector to rush him.

The inspector hit the Count hard with a bone-crunching body check. The Count slammed into the heavy oak table, moving it a couple of inches. Off balance, he couldn't react fast enough to block completely the inspector's uppercut. The punch sent the Count sprawling to the floor. The inspector fell on the Count with his knee. The Count saw it coming but knew he couldn't get out of the way. He shifted slightly so the knee would graze his stomach, but the inspector's weight landed on him. His breath whooshed out of his lungs.

The Count, gasping, grabbed at the inspector's throat and squeezed hard. The inspector's hands instinctively went to his throat, trying to loosen the fingers. The Count's hold was too strong, and MacNutt was running out of time. His vision was beginning to fade to black. He stopped trying to loosen the fingers. Instead he slid his hands under the Count's elbows and cupped them. With the full force of his cupped hands, he slammed forward towards the Count's face. MacNutt dimly heard the Count scream in pain and felt the man's fingers loosen slightly, but not enough. He slammed the Count again until he lost his grip completely.

MacNutt gulped a couple of times, trying to catch his breath. Although his sight hadn't cleared yet, Count's scalp was dimly visible.

He grabbed it with both hands and slammed it hard against the floor. Then he held the Count down with his left hand as he hammered the German's chin with his right. Blood splattered as he broke the Count's nose on the first blow. MacNutt grunted in pain when his second blow broke, then scraped against the Count's front teeth.

"Andrew! Andrew! Stop! Please stop!" Katherine pleaded. It took a few moments for her voice to penetrate the inspector's haze of rage. At last he stopped punching the Count, who was by now unconscious. He hung over the bleeding Count for a moment, still struggling to catch his breath. He finally pulled himself together and struggled to his feet. The fight had totally exhausted him.

"Are you all right, Katherine?" he croaked.

"I'm fine," she said, sobbing as she hugged her husband fiercely. As he gently rubbed her back, she looked up at him and cried, "Andrew, are you hurt?"

The doors to the reading room were pushed open. Samuel Francis Glass had stopped by to read the London, Ontario, papers. Glass was the MP for Middlesex East and wanted to keep abreast of the news in his constituency. He recognized the MacNutts, familiar figures on the Hill, but before he could register their dishevellment and their curious embrace in a public place, the smouldering newspapers near them burst into flame.

"What the devil is going on?" he shouted. "Oh my God! Fire! Get an extinguisher!" He frantically scanned the reading room but couldn't find a single one.

"There's one on the Senate side — I'll get it — tell the officer on duty to sound the alarm!" ordered MacNutt.

Glass turned and ran from the room. He hadn't noticed the body, obscured by the table, lying on the floor.

"Come, Katherine," Andrew said urgently, pulling her by the hand as he headed for the Senate exit.

"What about the Count?" she demanded as she glanced over her shoulder at the smoking flames that were rapidly climbing up the hanging newspapers.

"Leave him. Once we put out the fire we'll take care of him," he commanded as he dragged her out of the room. Katherine was shocked by Andrew's tone, but he didn't give her time to protest. In the corridor, he continued to pull her along as he hurried to the red extinguisher. As he tore it off the wall, the fire alarm began to sound and Constable

Moore, the officer who had been guarding the Commons side door of the reading room, appeared. The Senate side extinguisher was the nearest available.

"Here, Constable," yelled the inspector, thrusting the red cylinder at him. "Use the extinguisher to get it under control. I'll get the hose and be right behind you."

Constable Moore ran back to the reading room.

MacNutt sprinted to the fire hose reel that was further down the corridor, Katherine at his heels. "When I get to the reading room turn the water on," he ordered. She nodded sharply.

The unreeling hose clattered behind him as MacNutt rushed back down the corridor then through the open door. He was shocked at how quickly it had grown and how much smoke was filling the room. He barely could see Moore frantically waving the extinguisher's hose at the flames that were climbing up the varnished pine walls behind the rack of newspapers. The spray of liquid, about a thumb's thickness, was grossly inadequate for the job. The extinguisher's pressure scattered fragments of burning papers around the room. As they twisted and turned in the air, some of them landed on the other papers and books lying on the tables and racks, inviting them to join in. With almost destructive glee, they accepted. The blistering heat and noxious fumes forced Moore to slowly retreat toward the Senate exit.

"Now!" MacNutt, fighting a cough in the smoke, yelled down the corridor. Katherine turned the tap frantically.

The flat canvas hose snapped into a hard cylinder. When the water hit the nozzle, the force nearly caused MacNutt to lose control. Fortunately, Moore had just dropped his empty extinguisher and been grabbing at the hose to give the inspector a hand when it happened. As they had been trained, they quickly gained control of the writhing canvas and aimed the spray hard at the base of the flames. The water hissed angrily as it turned into steam. However, MacNutt couldn't help noticing, to his horror, that the blaze was moving towards the House of Commons side of the building.

* * *

Having alerted Constable Moore to the fire, Glass scrambled back to the reading room just in time to see the flames crawling up the newspapers and magazines hanging on the racks. Each time the room's doors flapped open, the fire would glow brighter, gathering strength, the hungry flames gobbling up the fresh influx of oxygen and then spitting out more black smoke. Glass could do nothing but watch as Constable Moore tried to contain it. The extinguisher Moore was using was having little effect. The toxic air was beginning to attack his lungs, making it hard to breathe. The smoke tore at his eyes, causing him to squint so hard to clear the tears that he didn't see Inspector MacNutt storm in with a hose. Glass decided to retreat to the Commons to seek more help. When he slammed open the door out into the corridor, the flames gave a roar and licked higher up the pine-veneered walls. Thick smoke billowed into the corridor and chased him as he ran towards the House of Commons. He burst into the Chamber, instantly grabbing the attention of the members. He instinctively gave a hurried bow to the speaker before he loudly, in a smoke-hoarse voice, interrupted the MP who currently held the floor. "Fire! Fire in the reading room! Everyone get out! *Get out now!*"

PARLIAMENTARY LIBRARY, CENTRE BLOCK,
PARLIAMENT HILL, OTTAWA
9:00 P.M., THURSDAY, FEBRUARY 3, 1916

Michael MacCormac was in the west-side alcoves of the Parliamentary Library, running his fingers over the spines of the books on the third shelf. He was doing some research for two members of the House. As a Parliamentary Library clerk, one of his duties was to conduct research for MPs and Senators. After locating the title, he consulted the volume, reshelved it then left the alcove. As he crossed the library to the east side, he recognized the two gentlemen standing beside the white marble statute of Queen Victoria. One was William Nickle, the Conservative MP for Kingston, and the other was Charles Thornton, Conservative member for Durham County.

"Good evening, gentlemen. May I be of service?" he asked cordially.

"Yes, Michael," said Nickle. "I would like a copy of *War Lord* by Gardiner."

"Of course, sir. It will take me but a moment."

"Hey, look at the smoke," remarked one of the junior clerks whose desk was near the door that connected the library to the House of Commons. At that moment, a House of Commons messenger rushed into the library, screaming, "The reading room is on fire! The reading room's on fire!"

MacCormac stopped the hysterical messenger then ordered, "Close the door quick and lock it."

The messenger gaped at him. "Sir."

With more 100,000 volumes, newspapers, magazines, and other documents to protect, a librarian's greatest fear was fire. A single spark could easily start a blaze that could consume the entire library. When the Parliament Building was proposed, the Chief Librarian Alpheus Todd had insisted that the library and registrar's records rooms be built of fireproof materials. Todd had also insisted that the library be made as separate as possible. It was attached to the Centre Block by a corridor that could be sealed off by heavy iron doors. At the first sign of trouble, the librarians had orders to close the doors to isolate the building and protect the collections.

"Do it!" commanded MacCormac, thrusting his arm at the door.

FIRE STATION NO. 3, QUEEN STREET, OTTAWA
9:00 P.M., THURSDAY, FEBRUARY 3, 1916

The duty officer at Fire Station No. 3 picked up the phone on the first ring. "Fire Station 3," he said. "Yes, the chief's here. Fire on the Hill, you don't say. I'll tell him." He hung up the phone and went to find the chief, who was on the second floor. He spotted the chief's driver, who was entering the station's main garage with a cup of coffee.

"Trouble?" the driver asked amiably.

"There's an alarm on the Hill. You better warm up the car."

"Okay." The driver frowned. He took a long gulp of coffee before sauntering over to the chief's motorcar.

It took less than a minute for the duty officer to return with Chief Graham. The chief jumped into the back of the car and demanded, "Head for the Hill. We've got a call. Probably another false alarm."

"Yes, sir." The driver put the Franklin into gear. He knew there had been a number of false alarms from the Hill of late, and the chief wasn't very happy about the situation. If it were another false alarm tonight, there would be hell to pay, he thought as he exited the garage. The driver turned the Franklin onto Laurier then turned left onto Elgin Street.

When the Hill came into view, they saw black smoke rising from the back of the Centre Block. The driver turned to the chief. "It's the real thing this time."

"So it would appear," replied the chief, grimacing. The amount of smoke was not a good sign. "Drive to the back of the new wing of the Centre Block. I want to assess the situation from there," he ordered.

"Yes, Chief," replied the driver as he pressed his foot on the gas. When he glanced in his rear mirror, he saw that Fire Engine No. 8 was now on their heels and keeping pace.

SPEAKER'S OFFICE, CENTRE BLOCK, PARLIAMENT HILL, OTTAWA
9:00 P.M., THURSDAY, FEBRUARY 3, 1916

"What's that?" Speaker Sévigny asked his secretary, irked. The sound of shouting outside his office interrupted his dictation.

His secretary turned towards the clamour then replied, bewildered, "I don't know, Mr. Speaker. Would you like me to find out?" He started to rise.

The speaker waved him down. "I'll take a look myself." He rose from his desk. As the speaker he was responsible for the administration and smooth running of the House. When he opened the door he was surprised by Médéric Martin, the Liberal MP for St. Mary, Quebec, and the Mayor of Montreal, who were sprinting down the corridor.

"What is going on?" asked Sévigny with a worried frown.

"There is a fire in the reading room," shouted Médéric as he slid to a stop.

Sévigny immediately turned his attention towards the reading room. He was astonished when he saw the black smoke crawling along the hallway ceiling towards his office. Flames were flicking between the reading room's glass-panelled doors. Sergeant Carroll of the Dominion Police was heading his way. A fire hose reel was located beside his office.

"*Tabernac,*" he yelled. His first thought had been the safety of the House. Then he realized to his horror that his children's bedroom was directly above the reading room.

"The little ones!" Sévigny exclaimed.

"Go find your children. I'll call Montreal and get some men sent up, and I'll inform the House," Médéric informed him as he turned and darted down the hall. Médéric was referring to the Montreal fire department. By rail, firemen could arrive in Ottawa in two hours with their equipment. They had done it before, in 1900, when a huge blaze swept through Lower Town. However, the Montreal firemen had been hampered by incompatible equipment. The threads for the Montreal fire hose couplings were of a different size than Ottawa's, so they couldn't connect them to the hydrants and pump trucks.

"*Merci,*" shouted a grateful Sévigny. He turned and headed for the stairs that led up to his apartment on the second floor.

When Sévigny burst into the parlour, his wife frowned at him, displeased that he had interrupted a visit with two friends. "Where are the kids?" he demanded.

"In their rooms. What's wrong?"

"There's a fire. Get out now," he ordered. "I'll get the kids."

The ladies jumped to their feet in alarm. He pounded down the hall to the nursery. Jeanne, his wife, ignoring his order, was hard behind him. When they entered the nursery, they found Nurse Tremblay in a chair, knitting as she babysat the two children. She stood up in alarm when Sévigny rushed in, tore the blanket off his oldest daughter, and scooped her into his arms. The sleepy girl cried out, suddenly frightened, "Papa, what's happening?"

Drawn by the commotion, the girls' other nanny, Nurse Belanger, poked her head into the room. "Take her," he demanded, handing his daughter to the bewildered nurse.

"It's freezing outside. She needs get dressed," protested Nurse Belanger.

"No time. We need to hurry!"

Nurse Tremblay, flustered by Sévigny's abrupt command, simply obeyed. She rushed over and picked up the baby. They were barely out of the nursery when greyish white smoke began filling the room. They fled down the corridor to the stairs that led to the ground-floor kitchen. On the stairs, they nearly collided with the speaker's steward, who was coming up to make sure everyone got out. Nurse Tremblay stopped him by handing him the baby. He grabbed the child in his arms and carried her down the stairs into the kitchen. Nurse Belanger was at his heels with the older child.

At the top of the stairs, Jeanne broke her headlong rush when she glanced behind her and saw that her friends had stopped. "Follow me," she urged as she indicated the stairwell that was beginning to fill with smoke.

"Wait. We need to get our coats," yelled Madame Morin, with Madame Bray nodding in agreement as they turned to go back.

"No! No! Come with me," Jeanne yelled as she pulled at their skirts, but the two ladies ignored her pleas. Worried about her two children, she could only watch hopelessly as her two friends went back for their furs. She turned around and hurried down the stairs, coughing, her tears streaming, to find her children and her husband.

PRIME MINISTER'S OFFICE, NEW WING, CENTRE BLOCK,
PARLIAMENT HILL, OTTAWA
9:05 P.M., THURSDAY, FEBRUARY 3, 1916

Borden jerked in his seat, startled, when his office door banged open, and Phil, one of the House of Commons messengers, burst in. "Prime Minister! There's a fire in the reading room! You have to leave NOW!"

"What!" exclaimed Borden, springing up from his chair. He followed Phil out into the corridor to confirm the messenger's statement. A great volume of smoke rose to the ceiling from the tongues of flame licking at the reading room's glass-panelled doors. He started at the sudden sharp and short sounds of explosions. "What was that!" Borden gasped, startled.

"Could be one of the gas mains," suggested Phil hurriedly.

Borden viewed the corridor leading past the Press Room and saw that the floor was wet from the water spilling from the fire hoses. The hoses were being manned by Dominion Police officers and volunteers, none of them firemen. The ersatz firefighters were cursing as the visibility in the corridor was rapidly being obliterated by smoke.

When Borden attempted to go back into his office, Phil, the messenger, stopped him by grabbing his arm. "Prime Minister!"

"My coat!"

"Prime Minister, no! We don't have time. We have to go now!" the messenger insisted, tugging on Borden's arm. He glanced pleadingly at Boyce.

Boyce, just as insistent, agreed. "We have to go!"

Phil and Boyce led the way with Borden close behind. When Sergeant Carroll, one of the Dominion Police officers unreeling a hose, noticed that the prime minister was going the wrong way, he yelled, "Prime Minister, the fire's serious, you have to leave now! Don't go down this corridor! The smoke is pretty bad! Go the other way. Take the messengers' stairway down to the basement."

"Follow me sir. I know the way," Phil grimly said, obeying the sergeant's order. He led Borden and Boyce into the messengers' room in the basement, following the route he knew by heart, though he could barely make out the features of the hallways' twists and turns. They stumbled through the smoke-filled messengers' locker room to a stairway that led up to the Centre Block's main lobby. The lobby was filled with a milling, confused crowd of MPs, senators, employees, and guests. Fire hoses ran down the corridors, but there didn't appear to be any firemen attending them. Black fog continued to pour out from the House's post office corridor. When some of the members in the crowd saw Borden, they called out in relief that the prime minister was alive and well.

"Does anyone know how it started?" Borden asked Robert Rogers, the minister of public works, when he spotted him in the lobby. Robert shook his head. At one of the entrances a commotion caught everyone's attention. Borden saw Constable Edwards and another man trying to help someone who was groaning in agony. His face, severely burned, was bleeding from red and white blisters. The constable pulled back slightly with a confused grimace whenever the man groaned. Borden gasped when he recognized Martin Burrell, minister of agriculture and the member for Yale-Cariboo.

"Is he all right?" whispered Boyce.

"Someone get him a doctor. He needs a doctor," demanded a voice in the crowd.

Suddenly, someone emerged from the post office corridor, bellowing at the top of his lungs. It was Dr. Michael Clark, the member for Red Deer, shouting, "There are still MPs in the Chamber! Nesbit, Douglas, Loggie, and Eliott! They are still there! There's others as well! We've got to get them out now! Who's with me?"

When he turned to go back into the corridor for a rescue attempt, several men lunged forward to join him. But the smoke was too thick and deadly. It struck at the men's lungs, forcing them to a scrambling, coughing retreat.

Sergeant Carroll rushed into the lobby from the Senate side, where the smoke was not as heavy. He skidded to a stop when he saw the milling crowd. He was alarmed that the prime minister was still in the building. He knew the battle with the blaze was not going well. "You have to leave the building now! It's not safe here! Move out! Move out!" he roared at the top of his lungs.

When he spotted Constable Edwards, he pointed at the entrance and demanded, "Edwards! Get these people out of here now!"

Shaken out his daze, the constable nodded. "Let's go," he shrieked, waving people towards the Centre Block's main doors.

"Prime Minister, we have to go," urged Boyce. Borden hesitated until the concussion of a sharp explosion rattled the stained-glass windows. Some in the crowd screamed in fright. The crowd finally started moving towards the exit. Constable Edwards helped the suffering Burrell struggle to his feet and supported him as he hobbled out of the building.

"Prime Minister?" pleaded Phil.

Borden reluctantly acquiesced. "Let's go."

EXTERIOR, NEW WING, CENTRE BLOCK,
PARLIAMENT HILL, OTTAWA
9:08 P.M., THURSDAY, FEBRUARY 3, 1916

Chief Graham was breathing hard when he jogged around the northwest corner of the new wing. He was frustrated that he couldn't run as fast as he would have liked. He couldn't risk a fall on the icy surface. He already had seen a soldier helping one of his men hook a hose to a hydrant slip and fall. The soldier had fallen so hard that it took him several minutes to get his wind and back up on his feet. Chief Graham had gone to the Victoria Tower's alarm box to send a second alarm. It was quite apparent when he saw the smoke that the blaze had gotten out of control and reinforcements were needed. His department's protocol was that on a second alarm everything was sent except for Fire Engine No. 11, which was kept in reserve in case of a second blaze in the city.

His men struggled with the escaping crowd as they tried to run hoses through the speaker's entrance. Also, people were fleeing down the iron fire escape that ran up the side of the building. Once safely on the ground, they joined the crowd forming to watch the inferno. They were too close to the building, and he wanted to move the throng back, because they were getting in the way of his men. If one of the walls collapsed, spectators would be hurt or killed.

He heard someone shouting, "Hold on! Don't jump! The firemen will save you!" He peered up at the smoking building's fourth floor and saw people he assumed were the Parliamentary Restaurant's staff jammed at the windows. Two firemen were running into position with a life-saving net, and they were joined by two men from the crowd who offered to help. The firemen told them to grab a position on the circular net and hold on tightly.

"Okay!" screamed one of the firemen up at the people in the window. "Jump! We'll catch you." A terrified woman released her grip. Her skirts billowed around her, muffling her shrieks until she hit the net. The men grunted at the impact when she landed in the net, then they gently set her on the ground. They quickly got the net back into position for the next catch. Some of the women from the crowd came over to the woman to comfort her when she started crying hysterically.

Graham was caught off guard when two women emerged from the speaker's entrance, each carrying a crying child in her arms. He automatically headed for them to make sure that the youngsters were unharmed. Several women on the lawns reached the children before he did.

"Oh, you poor things," cooed one of the ladies.

"They must be freezing," announced the other. "Here, take this." She handed Nurse Tremblay her jacket. Tremblay took it and carefully wrapped it around the crying baby. One of the women handed a blanket to Nurse Belanger, who was holding the five-year-old girl. The nurse thanked the woman as she wrapped the blanket around the child.

"Are you the mothers?" asked Chief Graham.

Before they could answer, Madame Sévigny pushed past the chief. "*Mes petites!*" The children's distress began to ease when they recognized their mother.

"What do you want us to do, madame?" asked Nurse Tremblay.

"I really don't know," replied a distraught Madame Sévigny. When she saw her husband emerging from the building, she yelled to get his attention. "Albert! *Viens ici!*"

"Thank God. I was worried," he blurted as he hugged his wife. "The little ones?"

"They are fine," she answered, gesturing to the girls cradled in their nurses' arms. He gave each of the girls a quick check to make sure they were not hurt. "What are we going to do, Albert?"

Albert, still examining his children, ordered, "Take the children to the Château for now. We will decide in the morning."

"Yes, Mr. Speaker," replied the nurses.

Nurse Tremblay asked, "Where are Madames Bray and Morin?"

"They didn't get out?" exclaimed the speaker, whipping around to look for them.

Madame Sévigny shook in despair. "They were behind me, but they went back for their fur coats." She scanned the crowd then put her hand up to her mouth. "I don't see them."

The chief interjected, "Are they still in the building?"

When Madame Sévigny turned to face the chief, movement over his shoulder caught her attention. "*Mon dieu, les voilà!*" Madame

Sévigny shrieked as she pointed at the building. Chief Graham followed her finger. It took him a moment, because nearly all the windows were obscured by swirling smoke, to spot the two women. They were pounding frantically on a third-floor window located beside the iron fire escape.

"Why don't they open the window and get out?" wept Madame Sévigny, nearly beside herself.

"I don't know," said the chief. They would discover later that the window had been painted shut. "McCarthy and Shiner!" he shouted. Two firemen turned their heads toward the chief who was pointing up at the building. "Third floor. Two women are trapped up there."

The two men scanned up the windows until they saw the two women. "Right, Chief. We'll get them." Each man grabbed a ladder from the fire engine and raced to the wall. They planted them firmly and then extended the ladders on either side of the fire escape so they could climb to the third-floor windows.

READING ROOM, CENTRE BLOCK, PARLIAMENT HILL, OTTAWA
9:15 P.M., THURSDAY, FEBRUARY 3, 1916

MacNutt realized that they were fighting a losing battle. The flames were slowly driving them back along the corridor towards the Senate lobby. It ignored the water spray by advancing determinedly along the walls and the ceiling's pine panels. The inferno used the heat and the smoke to hamper their efforts.

He heard shouting behind him. When he turned, he recognized the head of the Senate's messengers and several of his staff. "Hurry, get them down and take them outside," he ordered, pointing at the portraits of the former speakers of the Senate that lined the corridor. His staff, as they coughed and struggled for breath, complied with his orders. They took the paintings down and hauled them towards the exit so they could be preserved.

"Katherine! I want you out of here now!" he yelled.

"No, I'm not leaving!"

Moore, on the hose with him, interrupted hoarsely. "Where the hell are the firemen?"

"I have no idea," grunted MacNutt as he adjusted his grip on the hose. It would be discovered later that when the Senate messengers heard the alarm, they had locked all the Senate entrance doors except one, so that the firemen could not get in. At the moment, as the flames drove him back a step, he was more concerned about his wife.

"Get her out of here," he commanded the nearest messenger. The messenger grabbed Katherine's arm and began to pull her toward the exit. When Katherine began to resist, Andrew ordered, "Go! Now!"

He thanked God when Katherine finally obeyed him.

EXTERIOR, NEW WING, CENTRE BLOCK,
PARLIAMENT BUILDINGS, OTTAWA
9:15 P.M., THURSDAY, FEBRUARY 3, 1916

When McCarthy and Shiner put ladders up on both sides of the black metal fire escape, they didn't realize that all three windows opened into the same room. McCarthy broke the window with his axe then had to pull back slightly on the ladder when the smoke tried to engulf his helmet. He then ran the axe along the window frame to remove any sharp glass shards. He took some deep breaths of relatively clean air before he clambered into the room.

"Is there anyone in here?" he bellowed as he entered the speaker's apartment. The room appeared to be the Sévigny's bedroom, although most of the furniture was obscured by thick black smoke. Before he could repeat his shout, Shiner called out as well.

"I'm over here," McCarthy shouted back.

"Do you see them?" Shiner yelled. Time was running out for Madames Bray and Morin.

"No."

"Where the hell are they?" demanded Shiner. "They were at the window a few minutes ago!"

"How the hell do I know?" retorted McCarthy as surveyed the room in the vain hope they might be on the floor. "They must be in another room."

"Well, the smoke is pretty bad. Let's go down. There might be another way in," suggested Shiner.

"Right," replied McCarthy.

At the foot of the ladder, Chief Graham was waiting for them. McCarthy yelled, "We can't find them, Chief. They must be in another room."

"How bad is it up there?" barked the chief.

"Pretty bad," shouted Shiner.

"Smoke and fire?"

"Just smoke for now."

"Okay," grunted the Chief. "I'll get the smoke helmet from my car, and we'll have another go." He turned to Madame Sévigny and said, "If you can provide a layout of the apartment to my men, it would be a great help." Madame Sévigny nodded.

It took the chief less then a minute to return with the smoke helmet, which resembled a diving helmet. The helmet was made of brass with a glass front plate. In his other arm, he carried a length of rubber hose. He put the helmet on McCarthy. He then attached the hose to the air port at the back of the helmet. The theory was that the hose would be dragged on the floor, where the air would be cleaner.

"Are you set?"

"Set," replied McCarthy. His voice was slightly muffled by the helmet.

"Let's get you up the ladder," ordered the chief.

McCarthy carefully mounted the ladder with Shiner following. When McCarthy got into the room, the smoke was even thicker. He felt claustrophobic in the helmet because his peripheral vision and his hearing were impaired. He had only taken four or five steps into the room before smoke began seeping into his helmet, making it difficult to breathe. Realizing that he was in trouble, he turned back towards the window. He clawed at the helmet, trying to remove it before he passed out, but it was too late.

* * *

Fireman Omar Doust was panting as he dragged a hose up the fire escape. His job was douse any flames that McCarthy and Shiner might encounter in their rescue attempt. He was setting up when he saw McCarthy claw at his helmet and then collapse. "Fuck!" He swiftly kicked in the fire escape window and scrambled through the shattered glass to help his comrade. Shiner had already reached McCarthy and was trying to drag him to the window by his shoulders.

"Omar, get his feet and we'll get him to the window," ordered Shiner.

"I've got them," yelled Doust. When they reached the window, he said, "Get on the ladder and I'll pass him through."

"Right," Shiner replied as he passed support of McCarthy's shoulders to Doust. "You got him?"

When Doust acknowledged, Shiner stepped through the window onto the ladder then steadied himself. Doust lifted the limp McCarthy and passed the unconscious firefighter through. Shiner grunted when McCarthy's full weight settled on his shoulders.

"You got him?"

"Yep," replied Shiner. For a moment, he nearly panicked as he swung back and forth on the ladder, feeling as if he and McCarthy would tumble off. He sighed when he regained his balance by slightly shifting McCarthy's weight. As he climbed down, he held the ladder's rungs with one hand and kept McCarthy steady with the other.

Coughing, Doust retrieved his hose and entered the parlour. Flames trying to climb the staircase into the apartment caught his attention. He immediately headed for them, tugging hard on the hose. He tried to be careful when he manoeuvred around the unfamiliar room. He cursed when he banged his shin against a smoke-obscured end table. His cursing increased when he nearly tripped over an object jutting out from a settee. He leaned down to examine it. It was a woman's leg. He looked up and saw two women sprawled unconscious on the settee.

"Shiner. I found the women!" he shouted. "I found them!"

"Right, I got them," replied Shiner. He had come back to help Doust after seeing McCarthy safely to the ground.

"How's McCarthy?"

"The medics are taking care of him. He's going to make it," answered Shiner.

"Right," replied Doust. "Here," he said as he lifted one of the unconscious women up and handed her to Shiner, who bent slightly as Doust positioned her on his shoulders in the fireman's carry. "I'll grab the other one."

"No," ordered Shiner. "I'll come back for her. You just get some water on those flames."

Doust found the hose he had dropped moments earlier, placed himself in position between the inferno and the remaining woman, then pulled on the nozzle's lever. He was pleased that he was getting good pressure. The flames retreated somewhat but stubbornly refused to surrender. A few moments later he heard Shiner grunt as he lifted the second woman from the coach.

"Omar!" Shiner yelled.

"Yeah," replied Doust, turning his helmet to Shiner.

"The chief ordered us to pull back. A wall collapsed. Some people have been hurt." To punctuate his statement, an explosion shook the building. The rattling of the parlour's broken windows caused shards to fall and shatter on the floor.

"Shit!" shouted Doust. "I'm right behind you." Shiner acknowledged him then turned away, carrying the unconscious woman into the bedroom. Doust continued to douse the parlour with water as he slowly retreated towards the fire escape.

When he made it back to the ground, he saw McCarthy sitting on the running board of the chief's car, leaning forward between his legs and panting, trying to get his breath back. It appeared he would make it.

He noticed a military ambulance parked near the chief's car. Two military doctors knelt beside it. They were trying frantically, using pulmonary devices, to revive the women Shiner had brought out of the burning building. They were lying on woollen blankets on the snow-covered ground. After a few moments, one of the doctors looked up at his chief and at two women Doust did not know, then shook his head. Doust turned away, his shoulders slumped, when he heard the women's cries of grief.

WEST BLOCK GATE, WELLINGTON STREET,
PARLIAMENT HILL, OTTAWA
9:15 P.M., THURSDAY, FEBRUARY 3, 1916

The growing crowd lining up on Wellington Street to watch the conflagration parted quickly when Provost-Sergeant Mortimer led the first squad of soldiers onto Parliament Hill. It wasn't because of his uniform or the badges of the 77th Battalion on his lapels. Nor was it because of the squad of eager eighteen- and nineteen-year-old local boys marching behind him. It was the veteran's bulk and size that intimidated the crowd. He was six-foot-four with a fifty-inch chest that tapered to a forty-two-inch waist. He weighed in at nearly 250 pounds of hard muscle toned by nearly seven months of strenuous exercise and forced training marches.

It hadn't taken long for the battalion to mobilize once General Hughes was informed of how serious the blaze was. It had taken him only a few minutes to arrive from the Château Laurier, where he was having supper with his wife, and take charge. Two of the battalion's three barracks were on Wellington Street. The Mackenzie and Oliver Buildings were nearly directly across from the Parliament Buildings. The third barrack was the old Ladies College on Albert Street. It would take a few minutes longer for those men to mobilize.

"Sergeant Mortimer," he heard someone shout. "Sergeant Mortimer."

He turned and saw that Lieutenant Ashworth was trying to walk with military dignity on the slippery ice surface.

"Lieutenant?" the sergeant inquired as he saluted the boyish-looking officer. The rest of the squad halted. "Change in orders, sir?"

"I'm afraid so. We are to proceed to the Centre Block and render assistance to the fire department, evacuate personnel from the building, and save any furnishings that we can."

The sergeant glanced with a critical eye over at the Centre Block, where people were already beginning to bring outside some of the building's furnishings. "Yes, sir."

"A squad will be assigned to assist the Dominion Police in protecting the East and West Blocks. General Hughes will parade the men to help with crowd control."

The sergeant raised an eyebrow but didn't say anything. "Yes, sir. Very good, sir."

"Any questions?"

"No, sir," answered Sergeant Mortimer.

"Let's get at it then," ordered the lieutenant. He paused before releasing the men. "The colonel's orders are to keep a watch on the men as well. We don't want anyone to lose a finger or toe to frostbite. He also ordered the deployment of the field kitchens so the men can have some hot coffee. We might be here for a while."

The sergeant smiled; the young man was learning. The men were distracted by a car nosing onto Parliament Hill. "Are they allowed to do that?" demanded the sergeant.

"My God. It's the governor general's car!" exclaimed the surprised lieutenant. The car had attracted the attention of Colonel Street, the commander of the 77th Battalion, and his adjutant. The colonel was familiar with the car, since he had been attached to the Governor General's Foot Guard before being tasked to take command of the 77th Battalion.

"Well, we have a job to do," barked the sergeant. "Come on, men. Let's get it done." He saluted the lieutenant and led his squad of men towards the Centre Block, leaving Colonel Street and his staff to deal with the Duke of Connaught.

ROOF, PARLIAMENTARY LIBRARY, CENTRE BLOCK,
PARLIAMENT HILL, OTTAWA
11:15 P.M., THURSDAY, FEBRUARY 3, 1916

Fire Captain Bradley was on the roof of the Parliamentary Library with seven of his men when a series of explosions caught his attention. They had been pouring water on the library to protect it from any flames that could jump across from the Centre Block.

"My God!" he exclaimed as a ten-foot section of the Centre Block slate roof lifted and twirled nearly twenty feet into the air before landing with a dull thud. Rock shrapnel burst into the air and dislodged tiles slid down and off the roof to the ground. Sounds similar to shattering glass could be heard when they landed.

What scared the captain were the next sounds he heard, a groaning and rumbling followed by a series of sounds similar to artillery shells landing. The House of Commons' glass ceiling had collapsed. He froze when he saw a funnel of black smoke billowing up into the night sky, rising one hundred feet above him. His helmet slowly turned towards the Senate. He knew that if they didn't get the fire under control soon, it was only a matter of time until the supports would weaken, and when that happened, the Senate's glass ceiling would suffer a similar fate.

He prayed that no one was caught in the collapse, because he doubted anyone would have survived it. The one thing the captain was grateful for was that the wind was at his back. The smoke and flames were being pushed away from him and his men towards Wellington Street. Even though he was fairly confident that they could save the library, the staff were not taking any chances. Below him soldiers and the clerks were frantically racing to remove as much furniture, books, and other precious artifacts from the building as they could.

The captain glared at the flames. The streams of water from the attacking fire engines were having little effect. Every few minutes a wall would collapse, spewing more smoke and flames into the air.

EAST BLOCK GATE, WELLINGTON STREET,
PARLIAMENT HILL, OTTAWA
12:21 A.M., FRIDAY, FEBRUARY 4, 1916

Borden was standing near the East Block's gate when the Victoria Tower fell. The tower's clock had ceased ringing shortly after midnight when its hands stopped turning. The firemen, realizing that the tower was about to collapse, had warned the soldiers to clear the area, then pulled back themselves to a safe distance. The crowd along Wellington Street groaned when the tower leaned over and broke. Tons of Nepean and Ohio sandstone crashed to the ground. When the dust began to clear, the firemen surged forward to attack the blaze.

"I was hoping that the Senate could be saved," Borden said soberly. The flames had worked their way to the Senate side of the building. He should have gone directly home after his emergency meeting with his ministers at the Château Laurier, but he wanted a final look at the blaze.

"Doesn't look like much will be left," said Reid sadly.

"At least the library can be saved," said Borden.

The chauffeur turned towards Borden and said reluctantly, "Sorry, Prime Minister, but I heard that the library is burning as well."

"Oh no," replied Borden despairingly. The smoke and flames obscured the library from his view.

"Driver," ordered Reid. "Please take the prime minister to his home now." Borden gave Reid a sharp look. He had spotted Inspector Mac-Nutt conferring with Commissioner Sherwood and wanted to speak with them. He was also going to mention to the inspector that he had seen his wife, Katherine, in the Château's lobby providing first aid. The lobby had been turned into a first aid station and emergency shelter for the blaze's victims. "Prime Minister. There is very little you can do here. Let the firemen, the soldiers, and the police take care of it. You need to be well rested for tomorrow. You're going to have a very long day and many decisions to make. You will need your rest."

Borden stared at the burning Centre Block then reluctantly agreed. He knew, however, that he would not be getting much sleep this evening.

CHAPTER 35

Plumes of smoke rose in the early morning sky from the charred wood and stone remains of the Centre Block. The thousands of gallons of water sprayed onto it had turned into smoky grey ice and coated the stone walls. Most of the walls were still standing except for the collapsed central portion of the roof and the Victoria Tower. Some of the small towers had crumbled and fallen away. The fire engines continued to pour water on the building to prevent flare-ups. There were several firemen carefully searching the ruins in the grim task of recovering bodies.

From Borden's position in front of the East Block's entrance, he could see clearly what remained of the building. He was relieved to find that the Parliamentary Library was not, as he had been informed the previous evening, destroyed. He had been told that if there hadn't been a shift in the wind they would have lost that building too.

"Prime Minister?"

Borden turned as Inspector MacNutt exited the East Block. Borden's bodyguards, two husky constables Commissioner Sherwood had assigned, gave the inspector a glance, then returned their attention to the crowd of spectators.

"Inspector MacNutt. I'm glad that you are unharmed."

"Thank you, Prime Minister," replied MacNutt. He had the same air of fatigue that most of the Hill staff wore, since few had slept yet. Borden didn't dwell on the bruising plainly visible on MacNutt's neck. It was minor compared to the other injuries he had seen last night and this morning. Borden saw MacNutt's expression of guilt, a common one among the Hill staff, when MacNutt examined the Centre Block.

Borden turned away so that MacNutt could save face. He focused on the clusters of furniture scattered around the courtyard. Each had a soldier standing guard. Some were slowly disappearing as soldiers and House of Commons staff moved them into the East and West Blocks. During the evening, Sherwood had given permission for the furniture to be stacked in the hallway until a more suitable location could be found. The hallway outside the Dominion Police office was nearly impassable with the stacked items.

"How many dead?" Borden finally asked.

MacNutt closed his eyes. "Seven. Mesdames Bray and Morin, Madame Sévigny's friends. Mr. Law, the MP for Yarmouth. Mr. Laplante, an Assistant Clerk of the House. Mr. Desjardins, one of the House's plumbers. Alphonse Desjardins, one of my constables, and Mr. Fanning, one of the post office employees. And about ten or so were in the hospital being treated for smoke inhalation and burns."

"I will be visiting them in the hospital shortly," Borden said. "I've just been informed that they have found Count Jaggi's body, and they are recovering it now."

MacNutt was expressionless. "I didn't know, Prime Minister."

"Yes. He was found in one of the offices. He must have gotten lost in the smoke and couldn't get out. A strange emotion Borden couldn't decipher crossed MacNutt's ashen face. "It's a pity. Do you know if he has any family that we can notify?"

"No, Prime Minister," replied MacNutt stiffly.

"Perhaps the Belgian Relief people in London might know," suggested Borden.

"Of course, Prime Minister. I will send them a telegram and inform them of the Count's death."

"Good," Borden stated. "The papers have reports that the Providence, Rhode Island *Journal* informed the U.S. Department of Justice three weeks ago that the German embassy had ordered attacks on Parliament, Rideau Hall, and munitions plants. Did you know anything about that?"

MacNutt gazed was steady when he replied truthfully, "No, Prime Minister. We didn't receive any warnings from the Americans."

Borden shook his head sadly. "I've ordered reports from all the responsible officers as to the cause of the fire."

"So Commissioner Sherwood has informed me. I've just finished my report. It's sitting on his desk for his review," replied MacNutt.

"Excellent. I'm considering calling a Royal Commission to investigate the circumstances. If I do decide, you'll play a key role in the investigation."

The only thing MacNutt could say was, "As you wish, Prime Minister. Is there anything else that you need me to do?"

"Yes. I want you to calm Major Simms. It seems he's extremely put out that you didn't send any additional guards to Rideau Hall last night."

"Prime Minister! They had the Foot Guard at their disposal," protested MacNutt.

Borden simply shrugged. "By the way, Andrew, your wife is here," he said. He indicated Mrs. MacNutt with a gesture. She was trying to make her way through the cordon of soldiers. "I'm off to inspect the Railway Commission's Court Room and then the Victoria Museum. We need to decide by noon if we want to hold the session at three o'clock. I'll be waiting for your report." Borden turned and entered the East Block with his bodyguards behind him. MacNutt remained where he was, staring at the remains.

Katherine was finally allowed through the police lines. She had gone home to get some rest only after Andrew ordered her to do so. He had found her helping with the injured after he got out of the building.

"Are you all right?" she asked with some trepidation. She was watching his reactions closely.

"I'm fine," MacNutt replied, and he looked directly in her eyes.

After a few minutes of awkward silence she asked, "So what are we going to do?"

"Borden has asked me to investigate last night," MacNutt replied. Both knew that was not the question she really was asking.

"I see," she said as her hand slipped into his.

AFTERWORD

The day after the fire, on February 4, 1916, Parliament held its regular three o'clock session in the Victoria Museum. The museum would continue to hold Parliamentary sessions for the next four years.

Construction of the new Centre Block began on July 24, 1916. Parliament would have its first official sitting in the new building on February 26, 1920, although the Centre Block would not be fully completed until two years later.

In 1919, the Prince of Wales, Edward VIII, laid the corner stone of "The Tower of Victory and Peace," which today is known as the Peace Tower. The Peace Tower contains the Memorial Chapel, which commemorates the lives of more than 118,000 Canadians who, since Confederation, have made the ultimate sacrifice while serving Canada in uniform.

The Memorial Chapel contains the following seven books of remembrance for those who gave up their lives in defence of their country:

- The First World War Book of Remembrance, the largest, commemorates the names of 66,000 men and women.

- The Second World War Book of Remembrance commemorates the names of more 44,000 men and women.

- The Newfoundland Book of Remembrance commemorates the names of 2,300 men and women of Newfoundland, before Newfoundland became a province of Canada on April 1, 1949.

- The Korean War Book of Remembrance commemorates the names of 516 men and women.

- The South African War/Nile Expedition Book of Remembrance commemorates 267 Canadians who died during the South African War (1899–1902) and the Nile Expedition (1884–1885).

- The Merchant Navy Book of Remembrance commemorates the 570 men and women of the Merchant Marine who gave their lives while serving Canada at sea during the First World War and the 1,600 who were killed in action during the Second World War.

- The Service of Canada Book of Remembrance commemorates, at the time of dedication, the 1,300 members of the Canadian

Armed Forces who have died while on duty since October 1, 1947, with the exception of those who are commemorated in the Korean War Book of Remembrance.

On a daily basis the Commissioners of the Centre Block turn a page in each volume to display the names of the fallen.

Guided tours of the Centre Block of the Canadian Parliament can be arranged by visiting the Parliament of Canada Visitor Information website at: *http://www.parl.gc.ca/information/visitors/centerblock-e.asp.*

After Sir Percy Sherwood retired as Commissioner of Dominion Police in December 1919, the 152 officers of the Dominion Police were absorbed by the Royal North West Mounted Police. On February 1, 1920, the new force was then renamed the Royal Canadian Mounted Police.

Inspector Thomas Alfred Edward Foster, who is considered to be the "Father of Fingerprinting in Canada," continued to head the Fingerprint Bureau until his retirement from the Royal Canadian Mounted Police in 1932.

CPSIA information can be obtained at www.ICGtesting.com
Printed in the USA
LVOW12s1942181013

357601LV00001B/165/P